WELCOME TO
ZERO CITY
BABY

David Racine is author of the novel *Floating In A Most Peculiar Way*. His short fiction has appeared in *The New Yorker* & various literary journals.

Praise for his previous work:

"The writing is strong and the characters are fleshed out."
—*Library Journal*

"Racine's engaging debut...is a charming mélange of nostalgic idealism and humorous realism."
—*Publishers Weekly*

"Racine has a graceful touch."
—*Booklist*

"[A] witty debut...told with a fresh voice and infused with a likeable spirit."
—*Kirkus Reviews*

WELCOME TO ZERO CITY BABY

David Racine

DUFOUR EDITIONS

First published in the United States of America, 2012
by Dufour Editions Inc., Chester Springs, Pennsylvania 19425

This is a work of fiction. Except for public figures, all
characters in this story are fictional, and any resemblance
to anyone else living or dead is purely coincidental.

ISBN 978-0-8023-1351-5

Cover Image: © Warrengoldswain | Dreamstime.com

Library of Congress Cataloging-in-Publication Data

Racine, David, 1958-
  Welcome to zero city baby / by David Racine.
     p. cm.
  ISBN 978-0-8023-1351-5 (pbk.)
  1. Teenage girls--Fiction. 2. Delta (Miss. : Region)--Fiction. I.
Title.
  PS3568.A264W45 2012
  813'.54--dc23
                                                    2012002502

Printed and bound in the United States of America

For Mike Chamberlin

"Hurry up, wouldya! It's going to be light out"

"Shut up, Kayla. You're going to make me mess up."

"It's not calligraphy, for Christ's sake. Neatness does NOT count."

The other one steps back "There," she exhales. "How's that?"

"Super. Wait, gimme." Taking the can, and giving it a defiant rattle, the first one steps to the wall and slashes an exclamation point. "There. Perfect. Now let's get out of here."

They sprint for the Honda, which is idling just off the road. "This is so cool," the other one says.

SUMMER

"Well I think it's terrible," my mother says, in that voice she uses when she's deciding for everyone. "I mean, isn't this exactly the kind of thing we left Baltimore to get away from?" She lowers the paper and looks my way, like I've got her back on this one.

"I was kidnapped, remember. I liked Baltimore."

"Puh-leez," she says, rolling her eyes dramatically for Kayla's benefit. "This would have been *your* next stunt."

"It's a known fact that teen smoking leads to graffiti," I translate for Kayla. "Studies show."

"They told us heroin," Kayla replies, prompting an overly loud guffaw from my father.

"Thanks for the backup, Ed," my mother barks. "Jump in whenever you're through trashing the kitchen."

"Hey, I didn't get any baking sheets in the settlement, O.K.?" He's wrapping his hand in a dishtowel to pull pumpkin cookies from the oven. "Your mother's right though, Teri, we did come here for you."

"Really? I thought we came so Mom could 'implement and enhance her leadership skills in an administrative capacity within the academic environment.'"

"Yeah, well, that too," Pops says, right as he's burning his hand on the second tray, which he sends skittering onto the stovetop. "Shit."

"For God's sake, Ed, use the mitt." Gail does a quick check around while he douses his fingers. "You probably took it over to your side," she decides. "Serves you right."

It's become my father's habit to use our kitchen whenever he's making anything that requires more than the microwave, which is pretty often since he's started working (or *not* working, as Gail is always quick to correct) on his book. It's kind of a sore spot for her, both the book and his coming over here all the time, though she usually sits in that same spot at the table while he tackles increasingly complex recipes. And just for the record, there is no settlement; they're not even divorced. Hell, they're barely separated. And, also just for the record, the appliances work equally well on his side, as far as we know.

Kayla, who has come to observe, watches in silent amusement. She's been itching to get over here since I let on about our rather curious living arrangements, and gave me a lift home today in return for this access. We live in a duplex, see, which is no embarrassment or anything, except that we're renting both halves for the three of us, which is probably no embarrassment, either, but might as well be. Dad's got the left half as you're looking from the road, with the door on the side and the stoop, and Gail and I share the porch half, like roommates, she says. It's not the worst setup in the world, but I think if Gail says, "just us girls," one more time I'm going to lose it.

"Now what does it say again?" my father asks, dabbing his burnt fingers with a paper towel. He surveys the mess on the counter, then adds the wad to it.

My mother lifts the corner of the front page and adjusts her glasses, then pronounces each word with that same precise diction people use when reading directions translated from Japanese. "WELCOME-TO-ZERO-CITY,-BABY!"

She lets the corner fall back and pushes the whole section dismissively to the center of the table. "Whatever that means."

Pops is loosening cookies onto a plate. "Sounds like someone's not too happy here."

"Imagine that," I marvel.

Gail sighs. "I'm glad to see you're still giving it a chance."

Kayla spins the paper and stares at the grainy photo. "All capitals," she notes clinically. "Rather excessive, I'd say."

"I'd lose the exclamation point," I answer flatly.

We'd been here about six weeks when the words suddenly appeared in their mocking, Krylon redness. Or perhaps it was only a month, as Kayla insists, noting that a month has a way of taking six weeks around here. The paper's been running this same photo every other day, so it's kind of hard to say anymore. The ruckus has been unbelievable, what ever the case, the sole topic everywhere, as inescapable as the humidity. "Gangs?' many whisper, the threat of Armageddon palpable in this single, hushed inquiry. "Just punks," others reassure. "Bad seeds." But still the worst thing to ever happen in Delacroix, all seem to agree, which strikes me as a bit overstated for a town whose main intersection is shaded by a sixty foot live oak still referred to as The Hanging Tree.

Pops moves behind us to examine the picture. "You know, this is exactly what my book's about," he says, for perhaps the tenth time this week. It's going to be one big-ass book, by my reckoning.

"Really?" Gail queries, "I figured it was going to be a cookbook."

"I should interview this guy."

"What makes you so sure it's a guy?" Gail demands automatically.

"All short words?" Kayla suggests.

Pops bends to study the photo, the spatula pressed to his lower lip. "Adolescent male," he pronounces. "The color (which we know to be red). The capitals. The act itself. Brash, arrogant, angry. Classic acting out."

"So, how do you account for the precision," Gail challenges, this, too, more reflex than reproach. "The near perfect lettering. And the fact that it's grammatically correct."

"Could be any number of things. Mild psychosis. Bipolarity. O.C.D." His lips press into a thin line. "Not overly problematic."

Kayla arches her eyebrows.

"They're pros," I remind her.

"Though I rather like it," Pops continues. "The fastidiousness, I mean. It lends a certain complexity."

"I like how it's vaguely insulting," Kayla says.

"That, too," Pops agrees.

Kayla folds the paper with a neat crease. "A tagger," she says, almost hypnotically. "How urban."

"Honestly," Gail says. "You'd think this is the asshole of the universe."

Kayla offers a weak, forgiving smile. "It's lower lumbar, at least."

I suppose I should have seen it coming, but who could anticipate this weirdness? There were rumblings all last year, quirky, over-serious discussions across the table about my parents "not getting along," and "thinking about taking some time off," and a half dozen other euphemisms for the fact that they'd gotten pretty tired of each other, but lacked the resolve to just shut the whole thing down. In their reluctance to slay the tottering beast, they instead poked annoyingly at its flanks. My mother, who was

directing one of the areas of study in the Psych program at
Johns Hopkins–more of an assignment than a title–spoke
of moving into administration, if such a position presented
itself, which did not seem likely there. She spent most of
last fall on the phone, getting word of her availability out
among her massive network of colleagues. Pops, who
taught Sociology all over town, though mainly at Towson
State, where he had a staff position and health insurance,
dusted off his vitae as well, but when Eastern Washington
proposed a campus interview he politely begged off, much
to my mother's chagrin.

Through it all they blathered soberly of "preserving the
family unit," and "achieving a viable situation for all concerned," which sounded like a crock to me, two hens
downplaying bacon and eggs to the pig. I managed to
complete tenth grade amidst all this, dean's list, even,
though I did get tossed off the JV field hockey team for
smoking with Gina, which led to additional over-serious
talks, and threats of counseling. "Go numb," Gina
instructed, which wasn't bad advice from someone whose
life is informed largely by Sylvia Plath, Vantage 100s, and
Rage Against The Machine. It proved especially useful as
winter lurched into spring, and the bickering and phone
tag took on more desperate tones. It had become shrilly
apparent that there would be no easy solution, though the
status quo was no longer mentioned as a viable option.
Still, I held out hope, banking on the glorious inertia of
higher education to keep us all in place through another
cycle, at which time I planned to drag out the "senior
year" argument and throw it up in their faces, or simply
move in with Gina and they could do whatever. My
mother was still insisting on a position commensurate with
her perceived qualifications, though job after job closed

before her, and new openings grew fewer and farther between. Pops was no better, though, as always, he was a good bit easier to be around. One day it was Eastern Washington, the next he was staying put. Or he was bagging academia altogether, to tend bar on the waterfront, or hawk barbeque with Boog at Camden Yards. He had notes for a book stacked with maps of Nepal. It was all whistling in the dark, I see now, but it was unnerving nonetheless. He was a mess, to be truthful about it. Like her.

By June, neither of them was thinking straight, which is the only explanation for us all ending up here. Kayla's mother, an old friend of Gail's from their grad school days at Yale, had worked her way up to Vice-President of Academic Affairs at a place called Mississippi Delta College, a school of no consequence not to be found on the short list for my impending matriculation. The plum she was offering my mother, Associate Dean of the College of Education, probably amounted to less of a challenge than the job Gail would be giving up, but by this point my mother had convinced herself that it was solely her lack of a previous administrative post that was costing her all the good jobs, and she'd decided to latch onto whatever opportunity availed itself, come hell, high water, or Mississippi. She could do a year or two anywhere, she declared bravely, convinced that the doors back East would then swing open. She scored a year of administrative leave from Johns Hopkins ("just in case"), and we were on the way. Feet first off the high dive.

"We" meant she and I. Pops would be staying in Baltimore, it was agreed. Or going to Nepal, or whatever. Though not privy to the discussion, I'm sure they must have argued through it at some point. I'd be going with her; that much was set in stone, and no amount of begging, screaming, or threat of self-mutilation was about to change that. The rest of it—the state of the marriage, the house, visitations; the balance of our lives, in other words—went unresolved into July. Who lives like this, I wondered?

Things really got interesting over the Fourth of July, when Kayla's mom called again, this time to offer my father an adjunct slot teaching 2 and 1 while he worked on his book. ("Well how the hell was I supposed to know you were dumping him?" she had demanded amid the immediate excoriations of her new dean. "You might have said something.") I missed any discussion of this development also, recalling only my mother's fury as Pops cashed in the semester sabbatical he was due, then dialed Kayla's mom to say that he'd be coming as well. "Taking one for the team," he told me with a wink while he waited for her to pick up.

"You're out of your mind," I'd felt compelled to inform him.

The whole duplex thing got decided on the road. My parents lead in the Volvo, hammering out this sorry truce while I followed in the Honda, my newly minted driver's license piled with a stack of CDs and a pack of Kools on the seat beside me. I was debriefed at a Denny's outside Gadsden, Alabama, the myriad advantages afforded me by this bizarre arrangement outlined tinnily over sandwiches too cumbersome to lift from the plate. I was incredulous, to say the least. "Six college degrees and that's the best you can do? Seven hundred miles of dialog and that's it?!"

"It's best for you," my mother stated summarily.

My father seemed hurt. "I thought you'd be cool with it, Teri."

"You guys are too weird."

"*Hot on the trail,*" the dark haired one observes from the table they've staked out near the side door. She checks her watch. "*What is that, three-and-a-half days late?*"

The other one, still new to town, looks on in mild disbelief as three of Delacroix's finest stride briskly into Decatur. Even allowing for the somnolent local pace she finds so maddening, and any wish on the part of the sheriff's department to avoid the chaos of a new school year, this is a stretch. "*Do they really think they're going to find anything at this point?*"

"*I doubt thinking enters into it,*" the first one says. "*Give me a cig.*"

The cops set up in one of the guidance offices behind the gym and begin grilling the usual suspects; Ronnie Foster straight off, the alpha male of the new senior class, who they pull unceremoniously from the new girl's Chem lab, despite the fact that the Cutlass had blown a rod weeks previous, and he'd only gotten his wheels back yesterday, and not even Deputy Stanko believes he perpetrated this offense on foot. Then Eddie and Vic, an inseparable pair of sophomore delinquents who'd first appeared on the radar this past June, when they got nabbed up on the water tower one sultry 3 a.m., hammered on malt liquor and pissing like Roman fountains. And the girls' classmate, Delon, of course, because anyone with that many black tee shirts has to be up to something. The interrogations stretch right through the afternoon announcements, at which time the cops close up shop and head off with the rest, as if the final bell has granted their release as well.

They're back on Monday, circulating among the general population this time, on a room by room inspection of hands and fingernails—looking for incriminating traces of red paint, evidently—which, aside from being a full week *after the fact, and therefore moronic, makes for a rather uncharitable commentary on the presumptive hygiene of the student body. It's all for naught, of course, despite several false positives which spice things up early on; nail polish, mostly—though the cops don't really suspect a girl, and then an outbreak of pizza burger residue after lunch that leads to some raccoonish grooming in certain quarters. The day's highlight occurs when the sixth period art class disperses literally red-handed, each Matisse-in-training having coated his or her mitts in "Crimson Sunset," a surprising and laudable display of performance art that nonetheless leaves the uniforms unimpressed. Mr. Tomaselli is nearly hauled downtown for obstructing a police investigation, though everyone knows his real crimes are teaching art and being from New Orleans.*

The principal, Margaret "Peg" Lawson, is everywhere at once: confidently directing her staff; calming her students with a welcoming smile, a brief word, perhaps a touch on the arm, or even a hug; placating the truculent sheriff. The phone on her hip chirps incessantly, and it is only through the accrued wisdom and patience of her lengthy tenure, and an Oprah-like knack for connecting with the broadest spectrum of humanity, that order is maintained. Her authority is unquestioned, even by those wearing badges and side arms, which they've unloaded, unbeknownst to the students, at her peremptory insistence. She is a rare bird in the Delacroix hierarchy: local (Decatur, Class of '71), female (no man, though, it is often noted. Odd, that.), educated (Ol' Miss, '75; Ed.D—whatever that is, Texas A&M, '81). Escape is the usual track for the ambitious, what few there are, so it seems only blessed providence that Peg, for reasons known only to her, is still around. To the students, though, she is simply, "The Law," doing what she must, while they do the same.

And hers is no easy task, even in the best of times. The student body at Decatur is an odd one for the rural South, as is the faculty. While the majority of Peg's charges are local, many with roots in this dark patch of earth going back generations, the proximity of the college changes everything, with its regular infusion of new blood, and all its inherent untidiness. But Peg has chosen to celebrate this diversity, through an upbeat protocol of (occasionally forced) inclusion and harmony. Still, it is an anomalous mix trodding these halls, the progeny of dirt farmers, local merchants and county functionaries rubbing shoulders with the scions of foreign elites, and the displaced children of the overly-educated, fresh from the great and far-flung universities of the world. So the chunky, burr-cut son of the farm implements dealer eyes the dusky, silent girl in the stiff Old Navy jeans. They share his fries; he explains catsup, then asks, "Dhaka, where the hell is that?" She dips, chews slowly, then whispers, "Bangladesh," land of tigers and monsoon. Her father has accepted a two year appointment to study flood control measures along the mighty Mississippi; then, perhaps, they will go back. Her feelings regarding all this are indeterminate, at least to her crew cut benefactor. "I got my license," he says, and the girl lowers her gaze at the implication. These scenes fill Peg to bursting. An adolescent U.N., she has suggested, blended and deep fried.

Amidst the police presence, the students play it cool, feigning disinterest while the cops comb the halls, as if this is an everyday occurrence at Decatur. They are all MTV trained; they know the drill. But beneath the veneer of ennui roils an undercurrent of speculation and innuendo. A spattering of paint could not have caused more excitement had it suddenly shadowed the Mona Lisa's too thin upper lip.

Pollock himself could not have generated this buzz in Delacroix. Eyes trail the usual suspects down the halls, prompting whispered suspicions and furrowed brows, and not a little envy. Theories rise and fall with each class change, the morning's hot rumor relegated to the scrap heap by lunch. Ronnie Foster has settled comfortably into the spotlight, quickly mastering the cryptic non-denial, the conspiratorial wink. Others say nothing, their very silence screaming complicity. A false confession appears imminent. Suspensions loom.

I should mention, in the interest of full disclosure, that I am an inveterate diarist, have been since third or fourth grade at least. I've got a couple dozen volumes of varying thickness and design lining the closet shelf, though why I am amassing this chronicle, and for whom, remains unclear. Gail says it's pure indulgence, which is just like her. She complains I've been narrating my life in real time since I first learned to talk, and not without a hint of regret that I picked up either habit. You'd think she'd be pleased; there's a long and accomplished history of journaling amongst writers/scholars/artists, after all, and she fits into two of those at least. But no, or not when it comes to me, anyway. Pops, on the other hand, is complicit. There's not a birthday or Christmas that goes by that he doesn't present me with yet another bound volume of empty, cream-colored pages, the cover varying from the generic–flowers, plaid–to some reflection of what he thinks I'm into at that particular moment: kittens(?), soccer, Van Gogh, boy bands(?!). Just after we got here he gave me an especially pretty volume, vellum-like, with a magnolia in full bloom on the cover. "State flower," he informed me, which almost ruined it.

So maybe this is how I picked up the habit of organiz-
ing my thoughts a little more linear than is always necessary—overthinking my life, as Gail would have it. And
yeah, sometimes when I sit there staring at the same line
for half an hour, waiting on just the right word, I even
annoy myself . The vocabulary, too, is a constant source of
ridicule from the likes of Gina, who, brilliant though she
may be in some respects, would never use two syllables
when one would suffice. But I come by this honestly, too.
My parents, and most all of their friends, are academics, so
I've been subjected to their elevated language my whole
life. My parents' conversations are duels, and everything—
and I mean *everything*—has a sub-text. I've been deciphering these monologues and diatribes forever, and I guess
I've picked up their high-falutin' habits, kind of like you'd
take up smoking. The simplest comments lead to lengthy
discourse, and I've been accused of this as well. I try to
tone it down, especially around my peers, but it's impossible to be vigilant *all* the time. I can't say that I'm proud of
it, but there it is. And I do kick ass in English class.

Here's what I remember from that first week: sweating.
Like, buckets. I had to change five times a day, and I
wasn't even doing anything. Our stuff hadn't arrived yet,
so we were staying at this cheesy motel with no pool and a
clanky window air conditioner that was totally useless. I
kept forgetting it was O.K. to leave the windows down in
the car; you could never get away with that in Baltimore—
ever—so it was like sliding into Hell every time we went
someplace. After a day or two of that, I badgered Pops into
having the utilities and phone turned on, and moved my
computer, which I'd brought with me in the car, to our
otherwise empty duplex. For the next few days I was
sprawled on the floor, scribbling incessantly, and firing off

desperate e-mails to Gina lamenting my broiling, woeful existence, and alternately demanding news and rescue. Gina said I should just take the Honda, it wasn't like Gail and Ed would press charges, but it would almost certainly lead to one of them flying out to retrieve the car, and probably me, too. Then she convinced me the Greyhound was doable, and even a bit daring, but without being overly dangerous. The greatest threat would be when Gail found out, but the plan was to wait til late afternoon to call, by which time I'd be somewhere in Georgia. I'd be famous, Gina promised, a legend, even. She said I could live with her; we'd share her room, and her mom wasn't likely to notice til Christmas. But before I could gather sufficient nerve to actually do it, the movers arrived, and I got caught up in the unpacking, and playing referee in our house divided, and then, somehow, it was too late.

I figure there's a lesson in there, somewhere.

Pops and I spent several steamy days shifting boxes back and forth, then moving them all again when Gail returned. She'd gone straight to work, this despite the fact that we'd arrived over a month before her appointment (and paychecks) officially began. She's been in this huge hurry since we got here, like she has to cram all those missed administrative years into the next nine months. It fell to me, then, to set up our half, an odd and intimate task I hadn't anticipated, which nonetheless kept me out of the bus station, and cut into the loneliness cloaking me like the heat. Gail frowned at the photos I put out, and the way I'd set up the cabinets to mimic our kitchen in Baltimore, but she had the good sense to keep quiet about it, since she hadn't helped at all. Instead, she blathered of new beginnings, and the blessings of a fresh start and unfettered opportunity, as if we'd embarked on a tall ship for the New

World, rather than skulked off to Mississippi so she could facilitate what was at best a lateral career move. But we were out of the motel, at least, and once again had central air, which was good enough for me.

I felt like a missionary, it was so foreign to where we'd been, where I'd *always* been. Gina and I had watched *The African Queen* the night before I left, and I kept imagining myself as Katharine Hepburn, but without the wrinkles. When Pops snagged a pith helmet at this bait shop outside Jackson, the casting was complete.

He'd adopted this back-to-basics, Thoreau sort of rap, which I was buying into until he dropped four hundred bucks on a futon. "All you need now is a lava lamp," Gail had sniffed, watching him spread it out on the floor beside a shelving unit of plywood and cinder blocks. But Pops was undaunted, spewing this goofy optimism all the while, like the Brits in World War II movies. And whether he believed it or not, he seemed more enthusiastic than her about us all being in one place, even if that place is here.

It was several weeks before I finally met Kayla. Until then, I'd stayed mostly at home, or cruised the curious, flat countryside with Pops, munching boiled peanuts, or pork rinds, or some other local abomination purchased along the roadside, while he threw out chapter topics for the book he'd decided to write, *The New Incivility*. When I questioned the rather broad scope of the project, even suggesting that *Life In America*, might do as well as a title, he replied simply, "It's an overview."

I'd been to the campus a time or two, but there was even less for me to do there than Gail, who'd only dragged me along to get me out of the enemy camp. "Your father needs some peace and quiet," she'd insist archly to the both of us, "to write."

It was in the hallway outside my mother's office that I met Annie, the person I still hold most culpable in all this. "Just like I pictured," she said, swallowing my hand in both of hers and pulling me into a bear hug. "We need to get you together with my Kayla; I just know you'll hit it off." And before I could even attempt to beg off she'd set it up, a little get acquainted soiree at their place, "Just us girls."

Kayla appeared no more hopeful than I when she pulled open the door the following evening. "Your mother's daughter all over," Gail gushed, scrunching them together like she wanted to snap a Kodak moment, which is totally unlike her. "You must be pretty proud of your old lady, eh?" Gail asked confidentially, her grin so obviously forced it made *my* face hurt.

Kayla smiled weakly and stepped away from her mother, who jumped back herself and made busy pouring lemonade. "Yeah, I guess," she said, rubbing her arms like she's suddenly, improbably, caught a chill. She took two glasses from Annie and handed them over. "It sort of reminds me of this movie I saw once, about a coin-op laundry mogul." She took another glass from her mother and swirled the ice. "You know?"

"Why don't you show Teri your room," Annie prompted, in a tone suggesting it wasn't really a question.

"Through there," Kayla directed, waving vaguely toward an open door at the end of a short hallway. She took my glass and added, "Just be a sec."

When she entered from the kitchen a minute later, she was minus the lemonade, but carrying a balled up bath towel, from which she produced two sweating Bud Lights after kicking the door closed.

"There's no movie about a coin-op laundry mogul," I said. "So?"

"Just checking."

She popped open both bottles and handed one over. "Welcome, or something." She lifted her arm in a semi-toast, then knocked off half the bottle.

I took a sip. "Thanks. Or something." We stood there sizing each other up. "How long have you guys lived here?"

"Ten years," she said. "No, wait. Two." They'd come from Chicago, she explained, in much the same fashion that we had, to further Annie's career. "I was hoping to be out of here by now, but...." She let the thought trail off and killed her beer. "I guess my only hope now is the Army."

"Really?"

Kayla frowned and pulled another bottle from the towel. "God, are you always this gullible?"

"I'm not thinking straight yet."

She nodded, then spent the next twenty minutes detailing my misgivings exactly, and with all the appropriate resentments. "Sound about right?"

"Very impressive, Doctor."

"I recognize the look from the mirror."

"What would you suggest?"

"Do something outrageous."

"Yeah?" I thought back on the Greyhound plot, which already seemed remote.

"Worked for me." She burrowed once more into the towel and handed over the last bottle, then draped the towel across the back of the chair. "And drinking faster probably wouldn't hurt."

I tried to stay busy til school started, which was easier now that I was hanging with Kayla. If I could drag myself out of bed in time, I could usually badger Gail into letting me drop her off at the college, and then I'd have the Honda til it was time to go get her again in the afternoon. I'm sure she only allowed this to curry my favor, but I didn't care; it beat hanging around the house all day, and driving the Volvo.

Which is not to imply that there was anywhere to go, or much of anything to do, either, but at least it didn't feel like time had stopped anymore. We seemed to spend most of the day just bumming around, inhaling junk food and Diet Cokes while Kayla filled me in on what to expect at Decatur, and introduced me if we happened to run into anyone, so I didn't feel quite so much like a Martian. It was still slow motion, don't get me wrong; the whole place has this lazy, almost underwater feel to it, and I still can't imagine anything of consequence ever happening here, which is kind of depressing.

If I stayed home I was usually e-mailing Gina, or goof-ing off with Pops, who came over a lot during the day when Gail was gone. He'd decided not to run his air con-ditioner, so it was like an oven on his side after about ten o'clock. He'd gotten it in his head that this was better, somehow, that it was more natural, maybe, and that he'd develop a better sense of his new environment by walking around with a persistent coating of sweat from the time he finished his morning coffee til sundown. To Gail's mortifi-cation, he spent the whole day barefoot and shirtless, mincing languidly from task to task in just a pair of cut-off Levis, while a couple of fans (ceiling/oscillating) moved the fiery air around his place, to no discernible effect.

You could always tell when Gail returned. She'd blow through the front door like a freak storm, and immediately start slamming windows. I ran the AC on low when I was there alone, to knock the edge off, and with the ceiling fan going it was easily tolerable. Usually I cracked a window or two at the same time, and left the front door open for the breeze, which had a sweet, kind of ripe aroma I liked. But Mom was having none of the perfumed air, and she thought the open door too great a temptation for Pops; mostly though, she's long believed that a room is uninhabitable above sixty-six degrees, and so she sealed us in straight away. "How can you stand it?" she'd screech above the sudden roar from the vents. "It's like a sauna in here!" Or a blast furnace. Or a sweat box, whatever that is.

"Dad says you just have to move slower," I'd tell her.

But she was having none of that, either; slow is not her way. "If your father moved any slower, he'd be going backwards." She swore he kept it hot on his side just to keep her out, which was fine with her, she was always quick to add, there was nothing she wanted over there, anyway. And if she did wonder what he did all day, or why he'd developed this sudden affinity for sweating, she wasn't saying.

Sometimes he'd be on our side when she got home, usually with stuff spread all over the counters and a cookbook open, and Gail would be furious that he was steaming up our place, too. "Why is he even here?" she'd demand of me when he'd gone, though I was never sure if she meant generally, or right then. She'd always be close by, though, at the table nursing an iced coffee and carping at him for making a mess, or booting up her laptop and pretending to ignore him, but never actually telling him to go.

He might have been coming over just to annoy her, but I think he genuinely likes the feel of all three of us together; if it bugs her, too, well, that's just a bonus. They're definitely less hesitant about fighting in front of me, I've noticed, but their confrontations are more bark than bite since we've arrived, like they're already tired of it. What's funny is when they forget, and start having a civilized conversation; they're both really smart, and there's a lot of overlap in what they do, so it isn't unreasonable they have things to talk about. And there's me, of course, the main overlap, so sometimes it sounds just like the old days. But then Gail remembers she despises him, and reverts to her sniping. I was spending a lot of time in my room back then, and at first I'd sit with the door cracked, listening, and I swear it sounded like a fucking stage play. A really bad one.

Some nights Gail and I would go to Kayla and Annie's, or meet them at some salad bar or fast food joint, but we never invited them back to our place, which got awkward after the second or third time. Gail was paranoid that Pops would come over and embarrass her, that he'd start yammering about his book, or his latest culinary discovery, or some weird local anomaly he'd taken note of, but I think secretly she worried that his goofiness might actually charm them, which would be infinitely worse.

At some point school started and my sweltering indolence came to an end. Then, two days later, the police arrived en masse, roaming the halls for a week, most of them looking as lost as me. You wouldn't think a little graffiti could cause such a commotion; back in Baltimore you pretty much needed a body before the cops would even put down their doughnuts. But, like they say, nature abhors a vacuum.

Decatur is pretty wide open, I noticed right off. I mean, it's not all locked down like where I went in Baltimore, with permanent armed security at the front entrance, and the entire block fenced in. The campus is this lush rolling lawn, with a lot of stone tables and benches scattered around, and the upperclassmen are allowed outside for lunch and study hall, so it's pretty easy to come and go as you please. Most of the tables and benches got nabbed early, appropriated through some silent lottery or pecking order I didn't pick up on. Kayla staked out a table near the side door first day, and it's pretty much ours now. After a few initial disputes the first week, most claims are pretty much honored all around. Kayla had scoped out this one way last spring; its prior occupants were all seniors, so there was no existing title to it, and, more importantly, it afforded perfect sight lines to both the front door and the student lot, thus providing Kayla's trained eye the perfect vantage from which to observe the comings and goings of our classmates, as well as a central location to hold court, and grab a smoke. And it is mainly from here that my education has resumed.

Ronnie Foster would not have considered himself a bad person, were he given to introspection of that sort. Certainly not criminal, though even Ronnie had to acknowledge the frequency with which he managed to find himself at odds with authority of every type; the local sheriff's department, certainly—those run-ins were legendary by now, the humorless faculty at Decatur, for sure, and every coach he'd ever played for, not to mention his long suffering parents, and even his older brother, Ray, whom Ronnie both idolized and, nominally, worked for.

It was in this capacity, in fact, as chief roadie for Ray's band, Stereo Hogs, that Ronnie again found himself butting heads with the local constabulary. He'd just stepped back from the utility pole to admire his handiwork, and was about to turn and ask Jolene Thompson, who was sitting in the front seat of his Cutlass, thumbing the latest Teen People, *if the flier he'd just posted needed to be raised or not, when the patrol car rounded the curve.*

"Son of a bitch," Ronnie mouthed, tossing the remaining tacks well into the brush as the cruiser crossed the center line and nearly kissed the grill of the idling Oldsmobile.

Deputy Stanko eyed the pole and the boy in the fading gloam, then flipped on his spotlight and unfolded himself from the front seat. *"Thought that piece of shit looked familiar,"* he drawled, pausing to hitch up his pants before stepping across the ditch. *"You couldn't hold it til you got home, Mr. Foster?"*

"Just reading this sign, Sheriff."

"Uh huh," the deputy grunted, checking the ground anyway before stepping closer to examine the flier. *"Final performance,"* he read. *"Well, thank God for that."*

"Final area performance," Ronnie clarified. *"They're leaving for California straight from the stage. L.A."*

"There ain't enough bad music out there already, they got to import it now?" He turned toward Ronnie. *"And dare I hope they'll be dragging your sorry ass along?"*

"I wish."

"Lot of folks do, son."

"Next June," Ronnie promised. *"I'm gone."*

"Tell me another one," the sheriff replied tiredly. *"Like how it ain't you sticking this trash up all over town."*

"What?"

"And that paint job on the overpass, that Zero City shit; I reckon you still don't know nothing about that, either."

"What?"

"Right," the deputy said, ripping the sign from the post. He studied it for a long minute, then folded the paper into his back pocket and nodded toward the Olds. *"Who's the crease?"*

"Handles my body work," Ronnie answered. *"Figured I'd go ahead and bring her along, since every time I'm out*

now I end up with a busted taillight or something." He stepped across the ditch.

"Strange, that," the cop acknowledged, idly stroking his nightstick. He followed Ronnie back to the road. "But there's still the small matter of blocking a public thoroughfare." He pulled a thick pad from his breast pocket and flipped it open. "This vehicle's half in the road," he noted forlornly, as if it pained him just to bear witness. "Person could get killed."

"Shit," Ronnie groaned, slumping against the passenger door and resting his forehead along the roof's edge. "Get me the reg out of the glove box, Joley," he sighed. "Please."

"Don't bother," the cop said. "I got it here somewhere." He thumbed back through the pad, and continued scribbling without looking up. "Seems you're one of our preferred customers, Mr. Foster." He handed over the pad. "By the X, please."

"Seems like," Ronnie agreed, signing with a flourish and yanking loose the second copy.

"Pleasure doing business with you," the deputy said, stowing the pad and re-buttoning his pocket. "Now, how 'bout you get the hell out of here."

Ronnie climbed into the Olds and sat with his hands on the wheel, taking deep breaths. "See," he told Joley. "And if you weren't along, that mirror'd be laying in the ditch."

"So, he just does that to be an asshole?" she asked, louder than she probably meant to, but maybe not. Joley can be a feisty little thing, Lord knows.

The sheriff leaned into Ronnie's window. "Explain it to her on the way, Mr. Foster."

Ronnie shifted the Cutlass into gear and eased around the cruiser. "She pretty much nailed it."

"What do you mean, dead?!" When I sit up my hang-over kicks in full force, knocking me back onto the pillow like I've smacked a five foot doorway.

"It's not an ambiguous term," Kayla says.

I try sitting up again, slower this time, in segments. "We just saw him." I squint at the clock, four fuzzy ones, straight up. "Like, ten hours ago."

"Yeah well, he creamed a telephone pole about nine hours ago, according to Joley." She pauses, then adds, "She's a mess."

"Joley was in the car?"

"We dropped her off, Ter, remember? I meant, you know, emotionally."

"Oh, yeah, right." I twist to rearrange the pillows behind me, which almost makes me puke.

"She had to remind me, too," Kayla confesses, which pretty much sums up the entire night. There's another long pause, and she says, "We should probably do something."

"Yeah," I agree, though I can't for the life of me think what that might be, and my head is throbbing way too much to even try. I can't even remember if I know any dead people, like, for reference.

"I'll be over. Um.... Whenever."

I let the phone fall onto the bed. I feel totally like shit, but I'm doing a hell of a lot better than Ronnie Foster, evidently.

Gail isn't around when I go into the kitchen for water and aspirin, and from the silence next door, I conclude she isn't over there, either. Which is a small, good thing, because she'd want to know all about it if she was here, and I could not deal. And she'd probably never let me out again.

We ended up at this place called "The Trees" a couple miles out of town, which pretty much describes it, too.

There's a small clearing, and this old cabin that no one lives in, that doesn't even have a door, anymore, or any glass left in the windows, but for some reason is still hooked up to the power grid, so that anyone who knew how—Ronnie Foster, for instance—could tap into the place and crank a bunch of amps and floodlights. The clearing is about half a mile off the closest paved road, down a crooked dirt path you'd have to know was there before-hand to even notice, and you still might miss it. And hum-ble though it is, "The Trees" has the luxury of being pri-vate property, and so is more or less ignored by the sher-iff, and therefore makes for a popular gathering spot for the Decatur crowd, even when the Hogs aren't playing. Joley was saying last night that the cops don't even know about it, which I find really hard to believe, considering you could probably hear the band all the way back at the turn-off last night. Kayla says they know, they're just too lazy to drive back there, even to bust people doing it in their cars.

Now back where I'm from, bands play in clubs, or auditoriums, or school gyms, not in the middle of a swamp that was probably a Klan meeting place for everyone's grandfather. But that's all part of the weirdness, Kayla says. As are the Hogs. I had them figured for this thumping Southern rock band, but they're actually pretty good. They've got a twang to them, no doubt, and they did play "Free Bird," though Kayla insists that's mandatory here, but otherwise they did a bunch of their own stuff, which, though it wasn't great, wasn't awful, either. They'll get lost in the mix if they ever do make it to L.A., but still.

The original name of the band, just for the record, was "Astereognosis," which I pass along only because I like it a lot better than Stereo Hogs, even if no one else does. It's a

medical term that the bass player happened to know
because his dad's a doctor, but which no one else could
seem to pronounce right twice in a row, including the rest
of the band, and in the odd way things happen around
here, it got bastardized to Stereo Hogs when some really
drunk friend of theirs mangled it during an introduction.

Ray's digging playing rock star it looks like, or his version of it. And he's pretty much got the look: spiked black
hair with purple highlights, goatee, one well-pierced ear—
four hoops/two studs, and a lot of orphan clothes that
don't really go together, yet somehow do. But he seemed
nice when he stopped to say hello to Kayla and Joley last
night, even as he was practicing his sneer.

"He is, like, sooo hot!" Joley gushed when Ray saun-
tered off toward the stage. She shot me this wicked leer,
then went off looking for Ronnie.

I yanked loose a beer from the six pack Kayla had dangling from her belt. "Nice buns, anyway. And he seems to
like you."

"I don't know if 'like' is quite the word," she said, firing
up a Kool from the pack on the table. She exhaled luxuriously. "See, back when I first moved here, Ray and I did it
a few times, and I think it makes him feel, um, what's the
word I'm looking for? Magnanimous. You know, that he's
not just blowing me off now."

"You slept with him?"

She nodded and took another long drag.

"God, Kayla, how old were you?"

"Fourteen." She sort of shrugged. "Remember that
night I said you should do something outrageous to snap
out of it? You know, back when you first got here."

I nod.

"Well, that's what I did."

"Really?"

"Ask anyone." She exhaled a long plume, like Garbo.

"He told?"

"They all told." She turned to look at me, her lips pressed tight. "There were a couple right together."

"At the same time?"

"No! Jesus, Ter." She mashed out her cigarette on the table, tracing ash along the letters KOTW carved into the surface. Then she laughed. "At the same time...."

"Why?"

She shrugged. "No spray paint, maybe."

"Come on, Kayla."

"I don't know. I was really pissed off."

"And that seemed like the thing to do?"

"What it seemed like was that it was happening to someone else." She turned to face me. "I *do* realize this sounds ridiculous."

"I'm not disagreeing with you," I assured her. "Then what?"

"Well, I've noticed that it tends to follow you around, for one thing."

"Like, good or bad?" The way she said it, it was impossible to tell. "I mean, you're pretty popular."

"Well, I've got a certain access," she admitted. "Let's just leave it at that."

I had no intention of leaving it at that, but Ronnie Foster walked up right then with a microphone cord looped over one shoulder, and a mason jar half-filled with a clear, pungent liquid that he plunked down on the table between us, an invitation, more or less. Kayla shut her eyes and took a generous slug, then passed the jar to me. Moonshine, for Christ's sake; I mean, what fucking planet is this? I held my breath and gulped, feeling the heat immediately and completely, all the way down to my feet. Ronnie paused briefly from chatting up Kayla–he'd been yammering a steady stream since he'd walked up–to stick out his hand and say his name. I couldn't get any words out right then, so I just shook his hand and motioned at my throat. Ronnie nodded smugly.

"It's Teri," Kayla said for me. "She's in your Chem class. She sits right in front of you, in fact."

Ronnie ran his finger around the rim of the jar and licked it. "Right, right. Um, I haven't been there much, yet."

"I noticed that," I said, the words coming out in a gravelly whisper I liked the sound of. I think he's shown up maybe three times in the month since school started.

Ronnie nodded again, like being noticed was his due. He was wearing a purple Stereo Hogs tee shirt I'd seen on a couple other guys, except Ronnie's had some letters across the front pocket, the same four Kayla had been tracing on the table. "Rumor has it the tagger might strike again," Ronnie said, his voice oozing some inner knowledge.

"Oh, really," Kayla prompted.

He grinned wickedly. "So I've heard, anyway." He sipped from the jar and sent it around once more, then lifted it in a toast as he walked off. "Get high on the Hogs, ladies."

"Did you hear that?" I demanded. "He's like, so full of shit."

Kayla lit another cigarette. "Yeah, but he shares."

"You think he really will? I mean, go out there?"

"Who knows what he'll do."

"Shit," I said. "And what's this, anyway?" I tapped the letters where she was again flicking her ashes. "It was on his shirt, too."

"King Of The Weedheads."

"Translation, please."

"That's what the Hogs call him," she said. "I think Ray came up with it. They call the roadies 'The Weedheads,' and Ronnie's in charge, I guess. Not that they're ever on the road."

"And he's cool with that?"

"I think Ray could call him 'King Of The Shitheads,' and Ronnie would tattoo it over his eyebrows."

"And that's why he dogs you like that? 'Cause you and Ray...."

She nodded slowly and exhaled a huge cloud of smoke. "I could take that boy out and ruin him for life."

My father is in the yard when I go out to wait for Kayla, standing there in an 'Ole Miss tee shirt with a cup of coffee, looking up the road at God knows what. I think about walking out to join him, but the sun would probably knock me over, so I settle onto the steps to wait in the shade. A shower, more aspirin, and a couple of Diet Cokes have finally made being upright tolerable, but barely. Getting something in my stomach would probably be a good idea, but I don't see that happening any time soon. I'm still tasting moonshine at the back of my mouth, and right now, I'll consider it a victory if I don't puke in Kayla's car.

Pops lifts his cup when he sees me and bellows a way too hearty, "Good afternoon." He looks into the cup, then tosses the rest on the lawn and walks over. "Late one, last night."

"Yeah," I say, which comes out more of a grunt. I give him the PG version of my evening, omitting the beers and the shine and a few other things, which doesn't leave much to tell. "Guess it was pretty late by the time I dropped everyone off."

"A little after two," he says, which I'll have to take his word for.

"Mom said it was O.K."

"It wasn't an accusation." He sets his cup on the banister and sits down beside me.

"Some guy in my class got killed."

"I heard," he says, and when I turn, surprised, he adds, "There was something on the radio." I forgot that Pops is the only guy in the world who still listens to AM.

"I'm sorry if I kept you up. I didn't mean for you to worry."

"That's O.K.," he says, giving my shoulder a squeeze. "I should probably get used to it. I forget sometimes how old you're getting."

I nod. "What were you looking at out there?" It occurs to me that nothing I've said so far follows. And that I seem to be taking a lot of deep breaths.

"Nothing, really. I was thinking about how relieved I was last night when I heard the car, and I remembered feeling kind of silly after for worrying like that. And now I hear about this kid–"

"Ronnie Foster," I blurt, for no reason at all.

"Yeah, dead as Julius Caesar, just like that." He snaps his fingers. He heard that in a movie once, and he's pretty much adopted it as his standard for deadness. "So I was deciding never to feel silly for worrying again."

I'm all clammy, and I swear I can smell moonshine coming off me. Plus, I'm sure Pops knows the deal, that's what this last bit was all about. It could have been my drunk ass plowing into that pole, is what he's really getting at; and now I feel like even more of a lowlife for being all hung over, and him sitting there all cheery and clean and promising to worry. "Kayla's coming over," I say.

And just like that, she pulls up, leaving Annie's Camry in the street and crossing the yard with a Big Gulp balanced in each hand. She says hi to Pops with a lot more enthusiasm than I could muster, and hands me one of the tubs. "Dr. Pepper," she says, "Full strength." I accept it gratefully; the sugar is like heaven, but I'd drink gasoline right now if it was cold enough.

I zone out while she talks with Pops, though I hear Ronnie's name a few times. It's a generous assessment of him from what I know, but perhaps not overly, considering he's dead. "So, the question is, what do we do now?" she concludes. "I mean...." She finishes with a shrug when nothing else comes.

"Well, coming together is a good start," Pops answers, which sounds kind of new-agey, but O.K.

"Maybe we should go to Joley's," I suggest. I can't imagine that being too pleasant, but she's been really sweet to me so far, so we probably ought to. When Kayla says there's no answer at her house, my relief makes me feel like scum again.

"I'd go out to the crash site," Pops says.

"Why?" I ask. It's an empty stretch of road, if it's where I'm thinking, and Kayla already said they took away what was left of the Cutlass. "There's nothing out there."

"I'd still give it a shot," Pops says. He goes off on this riff about ritualized grief, mentioning Princess Di, and big piles of flowers, and candlelight vigils, and school shootings. It all kind of flows, but I think he must have worked a lot of it out before, because he rattles it all off without stopping, which appears to impress the hell out of Kayla.

"I think he's right," she says. "Let's head out there." I go in to get my purse and smokes while Pops walks Kayla to the car. When I get out to the curb he's holding her empty cup and declining an invitation to join us. I give him a hug and we take off.

"I can't believe you asked him to come," I say as we're pulling away.

Kayla lights up, then exhales out the window. "How come your mom rags him so much?"

"Mostly because he's not enough like her."

Kayla nods. "People like him better, huh?"

I mull this over as we pass through town. "Yeah, I guess." I've never really thought about it, but she's right, and it probably does annoy my mom. "Gail's O.K., though. Just kind of high strung. And she's worse around your mom. Half of that is for show."

"I didn't mean it bad about your mom."

"No problem." I've said far worse myself. "But you still shouldn't have asked him to come along. Jesus!"

"He wasn't going to come."

I put down the window and dump my ice. "Still."

Kayla frowns at the empty cup. "Why didn't you just leave that if you didn't want the ice?"

"Might need it."

The headline Monday will read: Youth Dies In Auto Mishap, *though beyond this one bare and undeniable fact there will be precious little by way of useful information. The deceased, a senior at Stephen Decatur High School, was last seen alive at the Waffle House on Route 44, eating a farewell plate of ham and eggs with his brother, Raymond Foster, and other members of the musical group Stereo Hogs, after which the band piled into a sagging Ford van and an equally decrepit Toyota Corona and turned west, while the deceased, following hugs and high fives all around, climbed into his prized Olds Cutlass and got rubber for a hundred yards heading east back toward town. From this point, things get sketchy.*

The cops are gloating, the kids say. And lying. And covering up. How can they be sure it was Ronnie who added "Hogs Rule 2004" to the defacement out at the viaduct, unless they saw him, in which case he'd have been arrested on the spot, right, (which he wasn't, and so still be alive, right, which he most definitely isn't); or, more likely, chased down the dark back roads, (which hasn't been stated or implied, either, quite the opposite, in fact); chased at a very high rate of speed, most likely, so that, perhaps, he'd misjudge the curve near Buford Jackson's place and spin across the gravel, jumping the ditch, and perhaps getting airborne a foot or two before shearing off the utility pole just past the bend at that exact height. Which explains everything, the kids insist, except the Sheriff's repeated denial.

Hooliganism, the Sheriff answers. Plain and simple. We're sorry this young man is dead, any loss of young life is tragic, and our thoughts and prayers go out to his family, but this department will not shoulder the blame. On the contrary, the actions of Deputy Stanko, who happened onto the scene almost immediately, were admirable, even heroic.

By mid-afternoon on Saturday the stump of the pole is buried beneath a small mountain of flowers, photos, banners, and bootleg Stereo Hogs CDs. The kids mill about, several dozen, at least, sitting or standing in groups along the roadside, pointing to the torn patch of earth where the Cutlass came to rest, upside-down, the kids say, with the roof squashed flat, though the vehicle was removed long before any of them arrived.

The kids know what happened. They know it was Ronnie's handiwork at the overpass. He all but autographed it

this time–KOTW. And everyone knows how that deputy–
Skanko, the kids call him–had it in for Ronnie, harassing
him every time he got caught out, busting out his lights
with that nightstick he's always stroking, and writing him
bogus tickets, until Ronnie started dragging Joley along
everywhere just to have a witness. Now sure, Ronnie put
the pedal to the metal, no one's denying that, but he knew
every curve in that road. No, that deputy was on his tail,
you can bet it, dogged him right into that pole, and then
tried to make like a hero to cover his own sorry ass.

So things tense up fast when the Sheriff arrives. The
kids shout questions–accusations, really–across the ditch,
refuse to disperse, disrespect the uniform. The Sheriff sizes
them up, looking for the leaders–Ronnie, perhaps, til he
remembers–but they're all defiant, lined up shoulder to
shoulder along the ditch, eyes blazing. So he radios for
backup: we have a situation, he tells the dispatcher. Which
is the only thing all are agreed on. You sure got that shit
right, the kids concur. One honest to God situation,
indeed, and one very dead body to account for. But the
Sheriff has forgotten, until it is much too late, just who his
backup will be. And when Deputy Stanko roars up, lights
flashing and siren screaming, all hell breaks loose. The
kids pelt the new arrival with rocks, dirt clumps, soda cans,
sheared chunks of the utility pole, and dislodged pieces of
Ronnie's car, pinning the deputy inside. They scream,
curse, point; there are tiny girls and scarecrow punks who
don't even shave flipping off the law! The deputy ducks
out and takes cover behind the front wheel of his unit, gun
drawn. He looks to his boss, his eyes begging permission.
But all the sheriff sees is tomorrow's headline, and a fleet
of network vans parked outside his door. 60 Minutes, *for*
God's sake, or worse, Geraldo. *Oh no, he decides, not on*

my watch. Not my pension. He signals the deputy to fol-
low and speeds off, stopping a quarter mile down the road,
where his minion joins him.

"Ain't right," the deputy says, staring back at the rab-
ble. "I say—"

"Shut up." The sheriff watches patiently, his glasses
glinting in the sun. When several cars pass undisturbed he
knows the danger is over. This crowd won't make trouble;
they just haven't got anyplace else to be. Time and bore-
dom are his allies. Tonight's kickoff is at eight; he'll run by
after that and chase off what's left, though he doubts
there'll be any need. "Let's go," he tells the deputy, his
tone leaving no room for debate.

Back in the crowd, the new girl watches them drive off.
When a cheer erupts from the throng, she winces, con-
founded as to just what has been won. Someone fires up a
joint. The Hogs blast from the trunk of an open car.
Where the hell am I, the new girl wonders silently.

"I can't believe I'm doing this."

"He was your classmate," my father says, tucking a
stray lock of hair back behind my ear. "I'm sure his family
will appreciate it."

I'm wearing the only dark dress I own, navy blue and
way too hot for this weather. I turn my back to the mirror
and tug. "I barely knew him."

"Stop fussing. You look fine."

"What do I say to them?"

"Just say, 'I'm sorry for your loss.' If you stay out of the
way, you might not have to say anything. The important
thing is that you're there."

I grab the keys to the Volvo and step into the withering
heat. "God, why me?"

Kayla is waiting in the shade of the porch when I pull up, looking blessedly cool somehow. "Linen," she explains as she settles in. "Jesus, it's a hurricane in here."

I cut the AC a notch. "Which way?"

She directs me through town to a white clapboard church on the same road where Ronnie crashed. We get the last two seats in the back pew. Fans are cranking in all four corners and the slightest hint of breeze brushes my cheek. "I'm melting," I whisper.

Kayla frowns. "It's bad form to complain at someone else's funeral," she says, like I'll have that option at my own.

"Whatever." I'm new to this. There was a kid back in second or third grade, a sledding accident as I vaguely recall, but he was a year ahead, so none of us had to go. "I've never been to a funeral."

Kayla's jaw drops. "Ever?!" I shake my head just as the preacher appears and everybody stands. "You are an alien," she says. "I swear."

The church is packed, and what looks like half the school is crowded into the vestibule—apparently any excuse to ditch class will do. It's not a big church, maybe twenty rows, and I can hear some crying in front. Joley's up there with the family, filling in for Ray, maybe, who doesn't even know about any of this yet, since he hasn't seen fit to phone home from the road, or L.A., or wherever the hell he is. Which seems tragic, almost, but fitting, too, in a rock and roll sort of way, and I have to resist the impulse to suggest that Ronnie would have wanted it like this. Joley is sitting quietly next to Ronnie's mom, which surprises me a little. They'd only been seeing each other since July, and it was already going south. She'd spent most of their last evening with Kayla and me, while

Ronnie more or less ignored her setting up the instruments, and then standing at the soundboard nudging
switches back and forth, to no discernible improvement.
Which happened every time, Kayla informed me. The
neglect, it turns out, probably saved her life, since it pissed
her off enough to give Ronnie a final reaming during the
encore, and then catch a ride home with us. I remember
her hinting that they might break up, though she seems to
have forgotten all that now.

The service is much shorter than I expect. When it's
over we file out, the Decatur crowd milling in front, oddly
well appointed, strangely subdued. Most of the girls are
dewy-eyed, dabbing delicately with balled up Kleenex;
the guys kick up dust with their good shoes, faces grim,
hands buried in their pockets. I still don't know most of
them, so, except for a discreet wave or two, I hang off to
the side with Kayla til we're all directed toward the small
cemetery behind the church. When I see the hole I shiver,
despite the heat, and my gasp is probably audible. How
macabre, is all I can think. I can't believe anyone even
gets buried anymore.

And then this, too, is over; the fistfuls of dirt tossed, the
"ashes to ashes" uttered, and I'm daring to hope I'm home
free. Kayla and I stop to hug Joley, who has drifted out to the
fringe. We promise to stop by later, but when I turn toward
the car I step smack into Ronnie's disconsolate grandmother.
I reach to catch her and she envelopes me in a ferocious
hug, which I resist at first, but then return. She's barely
there, a figment, almost. "I'm so sorry," I hear myself say,
meaning, I think, for almost knocking her over. She feels
like kindling in my grasp, and smells faintly of wool and
hairspray. We start to separate, but then she clasps my
arms; her grip is vise-like, and I feel a sudden tightness in

my throat. "For your loss," I blurt, blinking down into her rheumy gaze.

"So much life." Her voice is ethereal, though I have no idea what she means.

"Ronnie was full of it," I tell her, immediately wanting to disappear when I hear what I've just said.

But she seems not to have noticed, seems placated, even. With a final squeeze of her bony fingers she releases me. "Thank you, dear."

Kayla takes my arm and we're out of there, kicking up dust across the sun-baked lot without a word. "Thanks," I say when we're safely inside the car.

"Well, I figured I better get you out of there before you called Ronnie a dickhead or something."

"O.K., I panicked," I admit. "I told you I never did this before. And I didn't see you doling out a whole lot of comfort."

"Relax," she says, giving my arm a reassuring pat. "I'm just giving you a hard time." Sometimes it's like she's a lifetime older than me.

"My dad told me to say that."

"That Ronnie was full of it?"

"The rest of it." I let out a· long, pent-up breath and start the car. "Man, I hope I don't have to do that again any time soon."

"You did fine," she says. "Ed would be proud. Now drive."

We spend the afternoon cruising around, eating the worst forms of junk food from the Circle K, and feeling vaguely like there's someplace else we ought to be. Joley is hollow-eyed on the couch when we finally get over there mid-afternoon. Her mother abandons the TV room to the three of us—not without some relief, it seems—and we sit in the curtained dimness, swirling ice, while Joley flicks through the channels, talking in spurts. She doesn't know what to feel, she says, and her confusion has brought anger; Ronnie's gone, and she's left, and *she's* the one that has to deal with it. She doesn't even know if it's sunk in yet; she keeps expecting the phone to ring and it will be him, saying he's on his way over, or that she'll hear the gravel crunch in the driveway and the summons of his horn. She's sorry for all their harsh words, and for being mad at him now, again, still, whatever. "Fuck him," she says into the pillow she's been hugging since we got here, her eyes brimming with tears. She spikes the remote and the channel morphs to MTV, an ancient episode of *The Real World* I remember seeing in Baltimore. Joley stares at the set, her mouth bobbing gently into the pillow clutched to her chest. Within moments her comments turn to the show: the trampy chick is actually O.K., but kind of fat; the guy with the bleached hair is an asshole; and, like, do they absolutely have to have a fag every time? Is it a rule or something? When that one ends, and another comes on right behind it, we get up to leave. Joley hugs us, but doesn't see us out. We stop in the kitchen where Kayla has a brief exchange with Joley's mom. When I look back into the TV room, Joley is again slumped on the couch, strangling the pillow, rocking slowly.

My father is standing in our kitchen talking on the phone when I walk in, one leg propped on a chair, studying the back of a bottle of barbeque sauce. I wonder, in passing, if he's been over here all day. "I wouldn't necessarily assume that," I hear him say, setting the bottle on the table next to a bulb of garlic. "It's entirely possible that he was looking to get caught this time." He gives me a wink, and adds, "Ex-act-ly," as I cut past him to get out of this dress. I still can't get over the heat, the way it just hangs on and on and on, and no one ever mentions it. It's almost October, for Christ's sake; there ought to be frost. I detach the hair stuck to the back of my neck and listen to my father. He's got the rap flowing, that's for sure, and even with all the psycho-babble it sounds pretty impressive. When I walk back out he's giving the number on his side. He hangs up and turns to me. "So, how was it?"

"O.K. Weird, but O.K." I drape my limp dress across the back of a chair, not entirely certain why I've even carried it out here. I tell him about it; the stifling church and the oddly exuberant spirituals, the crush of scrubbed classmates, my awkward encounter with Ronnie's grandma. I remember something else, then, something I'd meant to ask Kayla about, but totally spaced in my haste to get out of there–the barefoot guy in the cemetery with the perfectly tanned feet. I almost mention it now, but I can't even be sure I didn't imagine the whole thing. Sometimes I'm not sure any of this is happening, and that I'm not going to wake up in my little bed back in Baltimore, late for school again. I open and close the fridge. "Who was that?"

"Newspaper. They wanted the psychological angle for a follow-up piece on your friend. Called for your mother, actually." He says this like it's odd that they'd call Mom's number to talk to Mom.

"He wasn't my friend," I remind him again, though it hardly matters now. I start to ask why he even picked up, but he pretty much treats our side as his, too, not in a rude way, like it's territorial or anything, more like he just forgets, or like it's all just temporary anyway, so what's the harm. "Where's Mom?"

"On the way," he says, picking up the garlic and the barbeque sauce. "So I better hit it." I slip his keys into his shirt pocket and follow him out, and we stand on the porch in the heat, looking up the road. "You going to be O.K.?" he asks.

"Yeah." I flap the bottom of my shirt, which helps not at all. "I mean, I barely knew him. It's more, I don't know, just creepy." I turn to face him. "Is that mean?"

"Not really," he says. "And I didn't mean so much about, um, Ronnie, is it?" I nod. "This is your first brush with any of this, right? So I'm sure it's a bit unsettling. Particularly with all the other adjustments you're having to make. I can't help but think that it couldn't have come at a worse time, though I suppose there's never a good time for something like this, is there?" He puts an arm across my shoulder and squeezes me to him.

"I'll be fine." I hug him back, hard.

"O.K.," he says. "But if you need to talk, I'm here." He steps away and motions lazily with one arm toward his place. "Well, I'm there, actually." He goes down the steps, tossing the bulb of garlic in one hand. "Come over later for something to eat. I'll bet you're starved."

There's a clump from the Circle K talking to me, this congealed mass pushing against my ribs, with the digestive half-life of uranium. "I don't think I can eat yet." I'm hoping for a little time to myself before Gail gets home, actually. Then later, when she starts driving me nuts, I can head over there. Like most nights. And wonder if my stuff is in the wrong half. Like most nights.

When I log on I've got four unread e-mails from Gina, and I'm thinking there's major news until I notice they're all different days, and not one urgent clump like she sometimes does. It's the longest I've gone without checking, and weird that I hadn't noticed til now.

The first, from last Friday—Ronnie was still alive, I marvel —is pretty standard for Gina:

Wassup?? I am sooo ready for this weekend! School totally sucks. I'm flunking Calc, but so is everyone, so I don't even care! Purvis is such a dick that no one knows what's going on. Oh well, Goodbye Princeton. Randy got suspended three days for coming to play practice drunk. Half the people there were, but only he got caught. Man, I'd take three days off right now! Oh, listen to this: Matthew broke his elbow skateboarding the other day, and Dawn goes over to see him, right, and he tells her he needs some space til it gets healed. Huh??? She's like, whatever, and starts calling this guy from Dunbar. Now he's all pissed. Stay tuned. Suzan knows about some party tonight so we might do that. Mama Jane is out with some new dork from work, so the gin is too!!

Bottoms up! Hey to Kayla!

G

Then, from Sunday night:

Yo, girl! How's it going? Must be good if you don't have time to write. That party sucked! There was, like, one cute guy there, and his girlfriend ends up shoving Suz into a fence for talking to him, and they almost get into this huge fight, and the guy whose house it is makes us leave. Suz is like, fine, fuck you, asshole! Real nice, huh? Then she pukes on the curb when they're dropping me off, and I get grounded?! Jane is such a bitch!!! She marked the gin! Can you fucking believe it?

Slept all day today.

Talk to me!

G

Monday (with URGENT flag):

Are you pissed at me, or what? Did Miss. secede
from AOL? I mean, what's the deal? Climb off that
redneck and let me know what's going on!
          G

And then, today (also URGENT):

WHATEVER, BITCH!

Like I need her all pissed off right now. I kind of don't
even want to answer, but she doesn't know about any of
this, and she's been real cool about keeping up with my bar-
rage the last couple months. So I quick hit REPLY and start
pounding. I tell her about Ronnie hitting the pole, and the
crowd, and the pile of stuff out there the next day, and
going to the viewing, and then the funeral, and how I fucked
up talking to his grandma, which I know she'll think is hilar-
ious. I hammer through it really fast, and hit SEND without
even reading it. Then I realize I hardly said anything about
us being loaded that night, or Stereo Hogs, or Joley, or even
much of anything about Ronnie Foster except that he's
dead. So I send her another one with all that stuff, even
though my brain hurts from thinking about it, and then a
third one about Pops and Gail and the latest from our
weirdo house because I forgot to mention that in the first
two, and then one last one so we'll be even that just says:

SO THERE, BITCH!

Which totally drains me. I buzz around the *Baltimore
Sun* web page real quick, then slide onto the floor directly

under the ceiling fan. I figure I'll give it a few minutes to see if Gina's there and still talking to me. The breeze from the fan is luxurious as I'm picturing events back there: Suz being belligerent, Randy half-bagged at rehearsal, Matthew in a cast; all are easily conjured, but hard to hold. My mind keeps drifting back to the church; the hushed solemnity, and the sonorous tone of the preacher as he sends Ronnie along to meet his maker. I don't think I even believe any of that stuff, but it's strangely comforting to recall it now. Even all that in the cemetery, the creepy ashes-to-ashes nonsense, is weirdly calming. But what's the deal with the barefoot guy?

I wake up twenty minutes later to the sound of Gail slamming windows. My skin is already chilled from the arctic blast pouring out the vent, so I switch off the fan on my way back to the desk.

> WHOA!! (begins Gina's response)
> That is sooo amazing of a story! It's totally like a movie! Or like a real life tragedy or something. I can't believe you already knew that guy. I mean, you just got there and he's dead already. What are the odds?
> Are you really, really sad?
> Suz is here and says she can't believe it, either. She says nothing like that ever happens to us (she means here, I think). And she wants to know if you got on the news??
> Gotta go. Hope you're O.K.!
> G

Got on the news? Suz is so weird.

Gail raps on the door and enters without waiting. "Just seeing if you were here." She does a quick check around the room, then holds out my dress. "What's this doing in the kitchen?"

"I think it needs to be dry cleaned. I wore it to the funeral."

She holds it out by the shoulders. "You must have cooked," she says, folding the dress over her arm and turning toward the door.

"It was pretty unpleasant all around," I say. "Thanks for asking."

She stops abruptly and turns around. "It was a funeral," she says. "They're all unpleasant. What's there to ask about?"

"I don't know. Like, maybe if I'm O.K.? If I need to talk?"

"Didn't your father ask all that?"

"God, Mom! I can't believe you sometimes."

She sighs. "So, did he?"

"Yeah, he did."

"And did it help?"

I shrug.

"Well, it couldn't have helped much from the look on your face."

"At least he cares!"

"Spare me," she says. "Why would I ask if you're O.K.? You're *not* O.K. One of your friends just died. The funeral was awkward and uncomfortable and probably hot as hell. You're sad and confused and scared, and right now you're probably feeling very vulnerable. There's a lot of stuff racing through your head that you can't get a grip on." She pauses, and her face softens. "Which means you're paying attention. The fact of the matter is that death is a sad, hard thing, Teri. You don't need that explained to you. You feel bad because you *do* understand it. But that's part of the deal, and, unfortunately, it's something you have to work through for yourself. My telling you it's O.K. won't make it so, and I refuse to talk down to you."

"Sometimes talking helps."

"I suppose so; but most times it's just talk. Look, darling, I do know what you're going through, and I do know it's difficult, and I don't like seeing you suffer. Believe me, if there were something useful I could offer you now, I would. But making you the focus isn't going to help. Talking is mostly self-indulgence, and you'll have to go next door for that."

"Jesus, Mom!" She was starting to sound almost human. "Would it kill you to make someone feel better?"

"Maybe that's what you should be doing. There are people suffering from this a lot more than you. Maybe think about them. If you hurt, cry. That's what I do. Then move on."

"You don't cry."

"It doesn't require an audience," she says. "Contrary to prevailing notions. And don't be so mean."

"Me?!"

"We're all dealing with a lot right now, Teri. Try to keep in mind that it's not the best of times for any of us." She starts to go, then turns back. "And I am here for you," she adds. "You know that." For a second I can't reply, totally flummoxed as to how she's managed to steal the moral high ground right out from under me. She waits another moment, then moves into the hall.

"Do you really cry?" I call after her.

She turns back and stares at me, her face unbelievably sad, then walks away without answering.

And once again, I feel like shit.

FALL

The heat broke amid a crashing thunderstorm the first Saturday of October, ending the seasonal inferno roughly on schedule with a twenty minute deluge of Biblical proportion. When it was over, and his father had gone back inside to finish his nap, Nother Martin tucked his pant legs into a pair of duck boots and, slipping his day pack over his shoulder, stepped from beneath the decrepit carport into a misty drizzle trailing the storm eastward. He crossed the backyard through ankle deep grass, splashing past several out buildings and the remnants of numerous automobiles in various stages of decay. When he reached the tree line he turned and stared back at the house, a ramshackle conflation of the original three cinderblock rooms, and again that many add-ons, each addition sticking out at an odd and slightly misaligned angle, so that no geometric description accurately defined it. The section jutting into the backyard nearest where he stood was pine, coated in a light hospital green. Through an open window a recording of his father's throaty blues floated across the thickened air. On the far side a section covered in tarpaper sagged against the original homestead, so that the roofline gave the impression that the whole portion might be melting. The carport was cobbled of wrought iron and tin, and opened at the back onto a slab of cement, now submerged, that passed for a patio, upon which sat a red brick and split drum barbeque. Several detached buildings in equal disrepair dotted the yard; the abandoned privy at the back corner, an unpainted shed not much larger than the outhouse, and a small barn that perhaps at one time had served a blacksmith. It was not a place you could invite just anyone, Nother had long understood, nor did he want to. The rooms inside were equally singular. It was home, though, and his gaze now was fond and unembarrassed. In another few years, he strongly suspected, the professors would show up, from Oxford or Hattiesburg, or perhaps out of state, and declare the whole mess folk art of the highest order, much as they'd done with his father. And he'd be right there to witness it, he knew, as unlikely to depart this patch of earth as anything now in his view. He sighed softly and stepped into the woods.

The thick loam of the forest floor yielded beneath his footfall, and he paused, as he did each time, wishing to chuck the boots back into the yard and proceed barefoot, before dismissing the notion as both foolish and potentially lethal, as he also did each time. He had raised himself in these woods, and his knowledge of all that surrounded him was intimate and encyclopedic. He'd experienced firsthand the myriad dangers of snakes, spiders, and other small critters, as well as the mundane inconveniences of mosquitoes, thorns, poison oak, and rusted fishhooks. He'd spent many nights beneath this canopy, most planned, though a few of necessity, and he felt as much at home under these branches as within the walls of the mongrel structure he'd just departed.

He tramped east along a narrow path that paralleled the county road, making for the series of curves in Lazy Ass Creek that gave the water its name. From there he *would turn right and plunge into the deepest recesses of the woods, slowly tacking his way through the trees and thickening underbrush, leaving behind the road, and, indeed, most any evidence of the present day. He was headed for a small clearing that touched the creek, far past where he'd ever suspected the creek even went, to a flat, open patch of earth the size of a church lot well off any of the known trails, at a spot where the sunlight seldom reached the forest floor. He'd found the place quite by accident one mid-summer afternoon, led there by an enormous shadow he'd been stalking single-mindedly through the branches overhead, until the shadow's source lighted briefly in the clearing, and then was gone, leaving him instantly unsure that he'd even seen what he knew he'd seen. He'd made weekly treks back, amazed each time at his ability to find the spot again, its remoteness having rendered the site almost prehistoric in his mind. He'd lately constructed a deer blind there, though how he would manage to pack out his quarry from this distant place was still only a vague notion. The platform had weathered the storm, he was certain, the trees above it so thick that the stand might, in fact, be dry. He had in mind to sit there now, and the rest of the day, perhaps, perched above the swollen creek. But it was not deer that preoccupied him this day. His focus now, evidenced by the well-thumbed field guide in his pack, was purely ornithological. It was his fervent hope that the deluge might flush out what he could not.*

As he mounted a small rise near the curves he heard voices from the bridge, and instinctively ducked into a copse of Dutch elm to reconnoiter the scene. Three quick steps elevated him to a pair of woven branches about shoulder height, which afforded an unobstructed view of the bridge and river, while lifting him within the cover of the leaves. He had originally thought to construct his deer stand here, the low, open expanse of the curves providing a clear path for his arrows, the water itself bait for his prey. But it was much too near the road, he'd quickly realized; young boys and old men fished this spot regularly, their voices alone enough to spook a deer, while the roar of the eighteen wheelers screaming past could send a bull elk fleeing.

By positioning himself just so, he could observe the activity on the bridge through a nearly rectangular opening in the latticework of branches, so that the three girls were framed as if part of a painting. He watched unobserved, silently mouthing the words, "Les Jeunes Filles au Pont," as if so titling the scene. The three were engaged in an animated discussion, though he could not make out their words, save the occasional shriek or expletive, and once, he was sure, his own name. He watched the middle one produce a collection of objects from a cloth sack at her feet, which she then released, in ascending order by size, from the railing into a shallow pool that had formed adjacent to the swollen creek. The one to her left, the new girl, studied a watch cupped in her palm and called out numbers when cued by the third, who was stretched over the railing staring intently after each object as it disappeared beneath the surface. The exercise proceeded methodically until, finally, the middle one was steadying a maroon-colored bowling ball on the railing, and all three were leaning forward in anticipation of its descent.

Nother slid silently back to the ground and proceeded, unobserved, into a swath of shoulder-high grass. The water rose to above his ankles for a brief stretch; the curves in the creek had been obliterated by the runoff, so that the low expanse nearest the road was now a shallow lake. It *would be a sloppy hike in, but well worth it should the cloudburst have flushed his elusive, and, unless he missed his guess, supposedly extinct, quarry. From behind him came a splash considerably louder than the ones preceding it, followed by the loud cadence of the new girl marking time, and then the third one shouting, "Goddamn, I think he's right!"*

"Indeed," he whispered, ducking past a low branch into the trees.

"I have never seen rain like this in my whole life. I mean, ever." We're on Kayla's front porch, and I'm half-shouting just to be heard over the clatter from the roof and gutters. You can't even see the road, that's how hard it's coming down. Sandy's car is parked at the curb, but you'd never know it from here. "How do people drive in this?"

"They don't," Sandy says. She's sitting on the railing and keeps sticking one leg out in it. "Pretty much you have to pull over and wait it out, preferably under a bridge or something. And good luck hearing the stereo."

Kayla is sprawled across the glider, smoking silently, and for the remainder of the downpour we sit without talking, while the rain pounds the shingles and sidewalk. The sky is this huge, angry bruise, of a shade I've never seen on clouds before, and all I can think is that this is what it's going to be like at the end of the world. The shrub beds on either side of the porch steps are a moat, and puddles are already forming in the front yard, which, at this rate, will be a lake within minutes. A stiff breeze has kicked up with the rain to cool things off, so at least when I sit down again the wicker doesn't grab the backs of my legs.

And then, as suddenly as it comes on, it's over. The rain slackens to a thin drizzle and the wind dies, so that all that's left is a thick calmness, and this ripe smell like the whole history of the world, or maybe just worms. Kayla rolls over and drops her cigarette butt into an empty Coke can. "You know, your mom was right."

"Whose mom?" Sandy demands, in a tone implying it couldn't possibly be hers, and that, indeed, the whole notion is preposterous.

"What about?" I want to know.

"Gail," Kayla clarifies. She sits up and pulls her feet onto the cushions, so her chin is resting on her knees. "All this talking about Ronnie is self-indulgent. This 'supposed' talking about him, I mean. People are talking about themselves."

Much as I hate to agree, she's got a point. For the last two weeks it's been possible to turn any class into a healing session, or group hug, just by mentioning Ronnie's name. And so, of course, someone does. Lawson brought in this army of grief counselors the first week, so you didn't even have to sit through class then; if you could manage to look forlorn enough, you could just bail. Now, they're trying to get things back to normal, but they've spoiled us, and so the same crap gets rehashed each period, and we take turns dragging it out until the bell. On the plus side, I haven't had homework since the funeral.

"You'd rather have class?" Sandy asks, as if this, too, is preposterous.

"I didn't say that," Kayla answers. "But I'm not sorry that it's tapering off, either. I mean, no one talks about it anywhere else."

"Joley's still pretty devastated," I say.

"I don't mean her! Of course she's still upset. But I'm sure having it dragged up fresh every forty minutes doesn't help."

"You don't think it's important to her that people remember?"

"Come on."

"Hey," Sandy cuts in, "have you guys noticed how all these girls are acting like they had this special bond with Ronnie now that he's dead? Like, the other day, in French class, Cathy what's-her-name, that snotty bitch with the British accent, was going on and on about how her and Ronnie had been so close, and that now she's feeling really untethered—"

"She said 'untethered'?" Kayla asks.

"I swear. And, like, I can't even remember ever seeing them together, and she's making it sound like they just climbed out of bed. And poor Joley's in there. In the class, I mean, and fucking Duvalier is up front, like, totally oblivious, saying what a wonderful giving spirit Ronnie had—for hitting on the Brit bitch I guess—and looking at Joley all significant and shit, and she's about to lose it."

"That's exactly what I'm saying," Kayla replies. "This whole thing would probably be a lot nearer to 'closure' by now if they got all the counselors the hell out of there and quit asking everyone how they felt every five seconds."

"On the other hand, what else is there to talk about? And at least the cops are gone. It's like, oh good, the tagger's dead. We can all go back to the Krispy Kreme."

Kayla and I exchange looks. It's pretty much gone into lore already that Ronnie was the sole tagger. The bridge is this weird memorial to him now, like if anyone else went out there with a can of spray paint it would besmirch Ronnie's memory or something. Which, touching though it may be, is still pretty ridiculous. "I still think it's O.K.," I say. "I mean, to talk about it. It's only been, like, three weeks, right?"

"I think two," Kayla corrects.

"Damn," Sandy says. "Poof! Gone without a trace."

"No shit!" I agree, the suddenness of it just hitting me. "You'd think it would have lasted a little longer. I mean, it's not the kind of thing that happens every day."

"Actually, it is," Kayla says. "Which is kind of my point." She rises from the glider and crosses the porch to the door. "I heard a pretty interesting theory about all that the other day," she adds, stepping inside. "Which we should check out now." She's gone for several minutes, then reappears carrying a bulging pillowcase, like she just robbed the place.

"What's all that?" Sandy asks.

"Well, we were talking about Ronnie in one of my classes and someone was saying how, no matter what it is, that people get over it. And how even when, like, someone dies, it gets reconciled pretty much like anything else, even though it seems really intense at the beginning. Kind of like, you break up with someone, then it's over; you get fired, or the dog runs away, it's over; someone dies, it's over."

"Please tell me Joley wasn't in there," I beg.

"No. Anyway, then this guy says it's like if you throw something in a lake, that the ripples tend to die out at pretty much the same time no matter how big the splash is. Like, the water absorbs it at the same rate."

"That's not right," Sandy says. She looks from Kayla to me. "Is it?"

"That's what we're going to find out," Kayla says. She reaches into the pillowcase and begins to pull things out.

"I don't know," I admit. "Doesn't seem like it, but maybe. It might be like when Galileo dropped those balls from the tower, and they hit at the same time, even though one was way heavier. And now it's known that if you have a perfect vacuum, that a feather will fall as fast as, say, a bowling ball. And that doesn't seem right, either."

"Did someone say bowling ball?" Kayla asks, pulling a swirled, scarlet Ebonite from the sack. At her feet are a broken radio, a clay flower pot full of dirt, a sixteen ounce bottled water, a can of pears ("Heavy syrup," Kayla points out), and a grapefruit. She goes down the steps and returns with a brick from under the spigot.

"And the plan is?" Sandy asks.

"Bombs away."

"And where are we going to do this?"

"Lazy Ass Creek," Kayla says, replacing the projectiles into the sack. "You're driving."

"You're going to drop that bowling ball into some creek?" I ask.

"Price of knowledge."

"And you don't think Annie's going to notice?"

"Nobody bowls anymore," Kayla says. She hoists the pillowcase over her shoulder. "Your watch does seconds, right? We need to time it."

"It's got a stopwatch function."

"Perfect. Let's go."

"Wait a minute," Sandy says. "This won't work. There's a current and stuff. And that grapefruit's going to float."

"So will the bottled water," I say. "Not to mention that all that stuff has a different surface area, which *has* to make a difference, or the fact that the surface of the water isn't going to be smooth to begin with, and there's going to be all kinds of stuff floating in it already, which will distort the ripples, so the times won't be accurate, either, or—"

"Hey," Kayla says, "that tower Galileo used was eight degrees off-center or something, and nobody gave a shit."

"That didn't have anything to do with anything," I point out. "I mean, if the bridge wasn't level, it wouldn't matter, either."

"The bridge is fine," Kayla says. "Now, can we just go?"

Sandy has pulled out her key ring and is twirling it enticingly. "And whose brilliant theory did you say this was?" she demands, though I can't see how that matters.

"I didn't. And I don't really care where it came from. If I really wanted to know, I'd look it up. So, how about this: It's Saturday. We're bored. We've got nothing better to do. So unless either of you has a better idea, I don't see anything wrong with dropping a bunch of shit into Lazy Ass Creek." She glares at us, waiting, slightly stooped in her St. Nick pose.

Sandy catches her keys mid-twirl and shrugs my way. "Works for me."

I've had worse days; I mean, I must have. I just can't remember one off the top of my head. The weird thing is, I was having a pretty good week, otherwise, even forgeting at times that I hate it here. Then, this morning, Kayla and I are sitting at our table, just chilling during study hall, digging the cool weather and looking at people, and we start saying how this seems like the first normal week all year, with no cops or counselors around, and stuff actually getting taught in class, and not much distraction or anything, except when Joley's around. And we're both agreeing that it's about time, how sometimes you just want things to be normal, even if that does mean tests and homework. I say how weird I think it is that Sandy, and pretty much everyone else, assumes that Ronnie was the tagger, just because he'd done other stuff in the past, and he never denied doing this. Which indicates a frightful lack of imagination on the part of our peers, I say, along with being sexist.

"Well, I warned you about overestimating this crowd," Kayla says. She takes a long drag on her cigarette. "And it's better than having everyone blame us."

"Why would they blame us?"

"Well, he never thought of doing anything like that before. Til after we did, I mean. So it pretty much stands to reason that if we hadn't gone out there first, he never would have come up with it on his own, and so wouldn't have let Skanko run him into that pole." She grinds her filter into the tabletop. "Right?"

"You're saying it's our fault?!"

"Not our fault," Kayla says evenly. "We didn't send him out there, or tell him to haul ass drunk at two in the morning. But us doing it pretty much instigated him." She stops and stares at me. "This really hasn't occurred to you?"

"No," I say, though it suddenly seems incandescent. The bell goes off but I sit there, with this heat radiating out from my stomach as Kayla gathers up her things.

"Are you O.K.?"

I jolt myself out of it and run my hand through my hair. "Yeah. Um...sure."

"Then let's go."

And so I spend the rest of the day dragging that around, which Kayla notices thanks to my increasingly zombified state at each successive class change. "Look, forget I even brought it up," she says as we pull in at my house. "That's just my weirdness."

I guess I notice the Honda, but it must not register, because I do a double take when I see Gail sitting at the table typing furiously. She normally doesn't blow in til around seven. "Hello," she calls out, still typing away.

"How was your day?" Her eyes never leave the screen.

"I've had better." I set my books and backpack on the counter and turn to face her. "Mom, let me ask you something." I've got this sudden notion to come clean. "Um...what are you doing home now, anyhow?" I get a second sudden notion that I'm a coward.

She pauses to stare at the screen, then punches a button at the top of the keyboard. "I'm going out later and I needed to come home first. So I decided to beat the rush and clear out some e-mails from here."

"Where are you going?"

"I have a date," she says, in this so fake off-hand manner, and immediately starts typing again.

"What?!" I shriek. "What do you mean you have a date? Like, a date, date?" She's still typing, and not even looking at me. "Stop that!"

"Then you stop shouting. For God's sake."

"Wait, is this, like, with Dad? You're making him take you out again. Is that it?"

"Your father teaches tonight," she reminds me. "And that nonsense only happens in movies."

"Who, then?" I demand.

"A colleague," she says. "A gentleman in the Provost's Office." She rests her arms on the table. "Is it so amazing that someone would want to ask your mother out?"

"You're married, Mom." I can't believe I just said that.

"Separated," she corrects. "We're separated."

"He's right over there." I point at the wall. "That's hardly separated. Does he know about this?"

"I don't see how, though I'm sure he will five minutes after he gets home. Look, it was going to happen sooner or later, whether it was me or your father, so you might as well get used to it. It just happens that it's me."

"So some guy you don't even know asks you out, and you just think, 'yeah, why not?'"

"First, we're serving on a committee together, so we've talked quite a lot already. Second, it's only dinner, so just relax. And third, did it even occur to you that maybe I asked him?"

"Jesus, Mom! Did you?" Someone should be taping this.

"No," she says. "But that's still no excuse for your attitude."

"My attitude!" I stare at the ceiling. "Why do I even try to have conversations with you?"

"What, I'm not supposed to have a life except as your mother? Or some appendage of your father? That's all I am to you? Still?"

"You're hardly an appendage, Mom." I let out a long breath and pick up my pack. "It's only dinner," she says again as I start down the hall. "Don't make it into some big deal." She sighs and starts typing again, then stops abruptly. "Weren't you going to ask me about something?"

"It can wait." This day doesn't need any more lunacy. I pause at my door. "So, like, this guy's coming here?"

"Carl," she says. "And yes. At seven."

"I'm not coming out."

I want to call someone and just scream, but Kayla isn't even home yet, and I think I'd be too embarrassed to tell anyone else. I could probably call Joley, but she's got enough to deal with as it is, and kind of a big mouth. Then I start to wonder if Joley even knows that it wasn't Ronnie that first time, if she ever even asked, or just assumed it was like everyone else. Would he have admitted it wasn't him, even to her? I kind of got the impression that his posing didn't stop when they were alone, that he might have been just as full of shit with her as he was with us that last night.

Though it's possible Joley knows; it's exactly the kind of thing Kayla would tell her. She fancies herself a no-bullshit sort of person, the kind my dad calls a straight-shooter, and thinks that gives her the right to say rude and hurtful things for no reason other than they might happen to be true.

I log on to look for Gina. Maybe I'll tell her. She did help a lot last year when they were both weirding out.

Hey! You there??

It's been a while, so maybe there's some news, too.

You're alive! (she answers) What's up?
Gail has a fucking date, man! Can you believe it?
Yeah, I mean, Jane goes out a lot. I thought you said it wasn't like that.
I don't know. Gail seems to want to move on, I guess. That's what she says, anyway. But I thought it was just talk. But he's coming over.
Weird. What's Ed going to do?
He teaches tonight. I'm going over there before this guy gets here. I mean, I don't want to have to talk to him. Jeez!!
No, man, hang around, and then ask Gail for money in front of him, like you need to go get something. Those guys are a gold mine. I swear, I got enough for roller blades once. You just have to wait til she leaves the room.
She'd be so pissed.
Even better.

Leave it to Gina to put a positive spin on a totally bad situation.

Hey, remember I told you about that guy getting killed in the car wreck. Well, like, did you ever think it was sort of our fault? You know, for putting the idea in his head, maybe?

Why, is that what everyone's saying?

No, but Kayla said it, and now I can't quit wondering. I don't know if anyone even knows it was us. They all think it was him both times.

That is the strangest fucking place.

So, is it?

Your fault? No, I don't think. Probably not. I mean, you're just sort of tied into it. It's like when someone commits suicide, and their parents blame it on a CD. That's just dumb, right?

Yeah, that's a good comparison.

You still might catch shit, though, so be prepared. Or, better yet, just don't tell anyone.

It won't be me. Kayla's the one.

Well, good luck. Sorry, but I've g2g. Suz just walked in. Later.

See ya! Thanks!!

It's after six by the time I log off, so I need to get going. I hear Gail in the shower when I go out, and call to her through the crack in the door. "I'm going over to Dad's."

"What?" In the mirror I see her head pop out from around the curtain. "You're not at least going to say hello?"

"No." We're looking at each other by way of the mirror, which has begun to cloud up. "Maybe next time." I see her frown just as her expression fogs over.

"I suppose that's understandable. You're not going to eat?"

"I'll make something over there. Um...have fun, I guess."

"I won't be late."

"Right. It's only dinner."

I let myself in next door and poke around for a few minutes, though I don't expect to find anything shocking, or even very interesting. I make a point of straightening up as I go, so it looks obvious and he won't assume I was snooping. I doubt he could do anything that would really surprise me, which is not always a bad thing, and probably explains why I'm over here so much.

I flip through a thick stack of index cards on his desk, all in his firm scrawl, each bearing a single note, quote, or reference that makes no sense in this context. I open a folder lying across the keyboard and find a sheaf of near-hieroglyphic text, scratched in the same hand, and full of circles, arrows, and cross-outs, with words running in all directions on the page and almost no hint of margins. There are a couple of dozen pages, at least, representing his most significant output in years. Which, despite what I just said, does surprise me. A lot. I can't believe he's really going to do it, actually write the book he keeps talking about. That he *is* doing it. I notice a knee high stack of books next to the desk, checked out for the term from the college, most with half a dozen or more markers in them. Damn! I think; you go, Dad. I can't believe he's going to write the whole draft longhand, though. Who does that anymore?

I take a Coke from the fridge and spread out my stuff. I've got pages of French homework I've been blowing off that needs to get done tonight, but instead I sit for a long time picturing Pops, toiling away across the room, all those books spread open, loose papers and note cards everywhere, like a real scholar. Like Gail, I think, though she's such a pain when she's writing that it almost ruins the image. Then, as soon as I do get going, I hear a car door, followed by footsteps on the porch. *Le Dorque*, I enunciate, then walk to the kitchen to avoid going to the window. I don't even want to know what he drives, let alone what he looks like.

I can hear them talking through the wall, and I can't help but wonder what Pops would feel like if he were here. Like shit, no doubt; I know I would. I do now. Did she even think of that? I start going through his cabinets, just for something to do. His kitchen is stocked, and I get this idea that I'll make something for him, for when he gets home tonight, but he's missing at least one main ingredient for anything I know how to make. I find a roll of cookie dough on the bottom shelf, so it looks like that's going to have to do. I end up eating half of it raw, and the rest I have to slice out into a couple of baking pans, since all the cookie sheets are on our side. The whole process yields only about a dozen cookies, but at least it'll smell good when he gets here. And Gail and what's-his-name are long gone by the time I loosen the last one from the pan, which was the whole point to begin with.

I'm so agitated from sugar and weirdness that it takes me until Pops gets home just to finish my French. I wanted to be gone when he got here, but I've still got two sentences to translate when I hear him pull up.

"Hey, what smells good?" he calls in from the stoop, riffling through his mail before coming inside.

"I made those cookies." I scratch out the last translation and pile up my books. "Hope that was O.K."

"Yeah, great," he says, taking one from the plate. "Take some with you."

"I had a few," I tell him. "The rest are yours."

"Suit yourself. What's wrong with your mother?"

"What?!" It comes out like a yelp. "I mean, why?"

"It's all dark over there," he says. "She not feeling well?"

Her car's sitting out front, I surmise, so he must figure she's next door sleeping. "Oh, um...." I shrug. "I've been here." I pick up my books and give him a kiss on the cheek. "Night, Dad." The evening air is cool on my flushed cheeks, and I'm all the way back in my room before I realize I forgot to ask about the book.

"So, you did lie to him, then," Kayla concludes.

"I did not! That's why I took off, so I wouldn't."

"Same thing."

"No, it isn't." We're at our table, and a lot of people are passing by, so I'm talking kind of low, which amuses her to no end.

"You are tripping me out," she laughs.

"It's not funny."

"You are, though. I mean, weren't you the one saying how you might all be better off without each other? And how lame they are for not just ending it. Like, first you're all embarrassed about the duplex, because they're not split up enough, and now, when one of them busts a move, you freak out about that, too. Make up your mind."

"Don't say 'bust a move' about my mom. Jeez."

She doesn't even try not to laugh. "You are a little prude, I'm starting to think."

"I am not," I insist. "It's just...well, I don't know. It's rude."

"Rude!" This comes out as a hoot.

"Well, I mean, what do you think Ed thought when that guy's car pulled up, and she didn't get out for ten minutes?"

"I don't even want to go there," she says.

"You're not helping."

"Maybe he didn't wait up like you did."

"It was only eleven-fifteen," I tell her. "It was just dinner." Oh God, did I just say that? "So I know he was."

"Well, maybe he didn't time it."

"Kayla!"

"Well, what was she supposed to do, have him drop her off on the corner? I mean, if it's all so innocent like you keep saying, why would he even care? He's probably more wondering why you lied about it."

"Goddamn it, I did not!" I jump up from the bench and grab my books.

"O.K., O.K. I'm sorry. Really, I'll stop." She grabs hold of my arm. "I thought you could take it." She smiles all warm and contrite. "Now sit down."

"Look, it's just really weird for me, O.K." I'm trying to sound firm, but I notice I'm already sitting again. "So—whoa, here comes Joley. So, like, shut up."

Kayla is still grinning when Joley sits down. "Hey kids, what are we talking about?" She's doing a lot better this week.

"Hooking up," Kayla says, flashing me a wicked grin. "What else?"

"You?" Joley asks, meaning me. "Did he ask you?"

"What?"

"Did Dylan ask you to homecoming?"

"Who?" I look from her to Kayla. "No. I mean, what?"

"He said he was," Joley says. "Well, that he might."

"The guy with the streaked hair?" I ask. "That guy?" This is the first I've heard of it. I think we've stood around in the same group a couple times, but we've never actually talked.

"My, my," Kayla says. "How many is that now who 'might' ask you?"

"Who else?" Joley demands. She's already announced

that she plans to attend alone, which is all but unheard of here, according to Kayla, but no one is saying anything. Which leaves Joley totally free to get into everyone else's business, which she is, having become the liaison of choice for every doomed connection on the horizon. Hooking up around here is like making a movie; your people have to get with their people first—to spread the blame around, I guess—and then it's still fifty-fifty that it'll ever happen. But at least it's gotten Joley's mind off Ronnie enough so she's quit crying every ten minutes.

"Ed Farris," Kayla answers for me. "And Bob Carney. Um...."

"He's asking Janice," Joley says. "That's happening tonight, I think." She turns to me. "You want me to see what's up with Ed? He's cute. Or I can say something to Dylan."

"Just let it go." I'm not really up for any of this right now. I don't even know any of these guys, and I don't want to get roped into something that'll take the rest of the year to get out of. "I think I'll just sit this first one out."

"Oh, don't be like that," Joley whines. "It'll get you in the swing of things. You don't want to keep being the new girl, do you?" She looks to Kayla and says, "Talk to her."

"Sure," Kayla says.

"Oh, there's Caitlin. I need to get with her about Steve."

"Broussard?" Kayla asks.

"Yeah. Is he slumming, or what?" She stands up and turns again to me. "Or it doesn't have to be either of them. Who do you want to go with?"

"What were you yakking with Bethany about?" Kayla asks, taking one for the team. She couldn't care less.

"Oh, they still need chaperones. So she was asking if

I'd ask my folks, since, you know, I'd be there alone. But I was like, no fucking way. She is such a geek."

"Student Council will do that to you," Kayla explains.

"Totally." She takes off, calling over her shoulder, "You're going, Teri. Let me know."

Kayla and I exchange looks. "Joley seems to be transitioning nicely," I suggest when she's out of earshot.

"Ronnie who?"

"Ouch!" The bell rings and we start to gather up our stuff. "There! That guy," I say, motioning past her shoulder. "With the black shirt hanging out."

"Should I get Joley back here?" she asks, turning to look.

"I swear I saw him at Ronnie's funeral barefoot."

"Yeah, you did," she confirms. "Nother Martin."

"Nother?"

She shrugs. "He's the last of nine."

"I'm calling bullshit."

"Well, he answers to it."

"Why was he barefoot?"

"Well, it was too hot for boots, and it's doubtful he even owns a pair of dress shoes. So, he probably figured barefoot was more respectful than tennis shoes."

I stare at her hard. "And that makes sense to you?"

We're still standing at the table, and she motions that we should get moving. We join the trail of kids heading inside. "The whole family is pretty much out there." She purses her lips and nods without elaborating. "But Joley would never approve. Which is fine, because he'd never go, anyway. Which makes you compatible right there." She frowns slightly. "Too bad, though. If you could talk Gail and her man into chaperoning, you guys could double."

"Not funny."

"Yes, it is. And he could help you with your French."

"*He* speaks French?"

"Fluently, though infrequently."

"How do you know all this? And who said anything about hooking up anyway?"

"Relax," she says as we enter the building. "It was just a suggestion."

"What would I do without you guys?"

"Probably nothing," Kayla says. "Like now."

I look again across the sea of bodies on the staircase, but Nother is long gone. "He's kind of cute."

"I'm not saying he wouldn't take some getting used to," Kayla says. "But it probably wouldn't do you any harm." She flashes a sly, loaded grin and starts up the stairs.

At least now I know I didn't make him up.

There is a type of shorthand that people of long acquaintance sometimes avail themselves; an unspoken, shared history, quite often, or perhaps some other similarity of circumstance which allows for much to pass between them beyond the sum of their words, at times rendering the words themselves redundant. Which is not to imply that all such communication is illuminated, or even, necessarily, clear. When she steps next door to mention the opening she's seen listed in the Chronicle of Higher Education, for instance, it is as direct an inquiry into the status of their moribund union as has been made by either in months. This overture, however, takes form under the pretense of soliciting his input as to her suitability for the posting–a mid-level administrative position at Tufts, outlined so nebulously as to leave nearly anyone likely to read it both entirely unsuited and grossly overqualified–and it is left to him to divine the true question being put forth: So, what's the deal?

He is taken aback to find her at his door, let alone seeking his counsel. She has not made this short walk in months, and when he had first called out, "It's open," without looking up from his desk, he had assumed it would be his daughter, who visited nightly, usually with a pile of homework.

What follows is an almost coded discussion; they speak obliquely, and at length, of various things, but really only one. He questions the wisdom of another move so soon; they are barely settled, after all, her new duties hardly begun, and she cannot possibly expect any hiring committee to validate so brief a tenure. But what he means is: Haven't we just been through all this? Are you being intentionally disruptive, or just selfish? She contemplates his words, surely able to note their veracity, then counters that there is hardly anything to be gained by staying, least of all any academic cachet. Which might as well translate: Well, I certainly can't be expected to commit career suicide and tolerate this charade.

He looks up from the desk, where he has been scribbling marginalia on a scattered manuscript. "There's Teri, too," he reminds her casually, implying by his tone that this is an oversight she might well be expected to make. "She seems to be settling in here," he adds, flipping one of the pages and continuing to write.

"She'd leave in a minute," she says decisively, suggesting that for all the time father and daughter spend together, they might well be speaking different languages. "I know my daughter."

"I wouldn't be too sure," he replies without looking up, leaving it unclear whether he is referring to her first statement, or the second.

"Look at me when you're talking," she demands. "What is that mess, anyway?"

"My book," he informs her, pointedly keeping his head down. *"It's beginning to come together, I think."*

"Your what?!" She strides across the room, stepping over several open volumes she had failed to notice on the floor, and surveys the evidence on the desktop. Dozens of marked up manuscript pages, xeroxed journal articles, hilighters in various hues, post-its. Smoking guns all around, a veritable armory, so that when she asks, *"How much have you got?"* she sounds like the perp when Columbo shows up.

He shrugs, motions vaguely over the desktop. *"A chunk."*

Her mouth tightens in consternation. He's writing! On top of everything else—the hours spent with their daughter, whose laughter she hears nightly through the thin wall; the ease with which he's settled into this fetid backwater; his department-wide popularity, which she's gotten wind of two buildings over; even his culinary skills, a joke when they'd first arrived, are rounding into shape, if the samples Teri smuggles back are any indication—he's actually doing it. She unleashes a string of pointed questions, as if he were one of her grad students at Johns Hopkins, which he deflects in roughly the same manner, until she is able to dismiss the whole exercise as pap. Still, she is dumbfounded, and then annoyed, as if he has stolen her thunder. This migration was precipitated by her ambitions, not his. Who even knew he had ambitions anymore? The pages before her now match his output from the entire previous decade, perhaps longer. And what's worse, she's getting nothing done. She's performed well enough—the bar is set rather low at the college—but what of it? Committee work mostly, meetings, reports, hours lost learning the vagaries of Excel and PowerPoint. What did that amount

to beyond the title? And did she even want it? She'd ceded
her academic pursuits upon coming here—who had time
for both—and was suffering the resultant guilt. And now,
here he was, the all-time slacker of Sociology, pounding
out a book like he was, well, her! And thriving otherwise,
when he shouldn't even be here. Talk about salt in the
wound, even if it was destined to be lightweight pop-Soc.
Who wouldn't be annoyed? Who wouldn't strike where
she struck next?

"Well," she says, without enthusiasm, "persevere, I
guess."

"I'll drop some off when I have a section ready."

"Fine." She steps back near the table and picks up one
of her daughter's sweaters, which is draped across the back
of a chair. "Look, I'm going out tonight, so maybe check
in on Teri if you think of it."

"Sure." He scratches a name in the margin, a reference
to be checked later, and looks up. "She'll probably be over
anyway."

"Right." She pauses, then says, "I'll have my cell off,
though. I'm going to a play."

"I'm sure we'll be fine." He finds it odd, this sharing of
information, as she's been quite particular about her
restored autonomy up til now. "What are you seeing?"

"It's a student production. Night Of The Iguana. I've
been thinking I should be more visible about those things
now, with my position and all. So, when the invitation
came...." She shrugs.

He nods, glances down at the desk, taps his pen. "With
Annie, then?"

"No," she says quickly. "Someone in the Provost's
Office, actually. I imagine Teri's mentioned him?"

He sets down the pen and swivels the chair to face her.

"Not that I recall."

"Oh. Well, his name is Carl Huffman. We've been doing a lot of budget work lately. He's a big fan of Tennessee Williams, so we decided to get away from the numbers for a few hours."

"No need to explain."

"I wasn't. I was just saying." She smoothes the sweater over her arm. "Do you know him?" she asks. "I mean, you seem to know everyone else."

"Haven't had the pleasure," he answers. "You say Teri's met him, though?"

"No, I've just mentioned him."

"So then, are you dating? I mean, just so I know what the deal is."

"There's no deal. We had dinner once, that's all. I wouldn't call it anything, really. But I thought I should mention it."

"Right," he says. "Well, thanks, I guess."

"I can't believe Teri didn't mention it. She freaked out when we had dinner. She's a little drama queen, sometimes."

"Never said a word. Probably decided to let you do your own dirty work."

"Dirty work? Is that what this is?"

"Figure of speech," he says. "I mean, think about it, her coming over here to tell me that. Would you, if you were her?"

She purses her lips and considers this. "I see your point. And she doesn't say what goes on over here, either, now that I think about it. This book," she continues, waving at the desk, "who knew?"

"Speaking of," he says.

"Yes, I need to get ready, too."

"She leaves that here for when it cools off," he says.

She replaces the sweater on the back of the chair. "Right," she says, taking her leave with a slight wave. When she's gone he sits motionless, and suddenly hollow, parsing over all that was said and unsaid, while the room fades to darkness.

Which is not to imply that all such shorthand need be so weighted with import, as in this second instance. It is entirely serendipitous, in fact, that the two old friends find themselves together for this significant milestone. The visitor, and certainly more widely acclaimed of the two, has no idea that his host is marking the passing of another year this crisp fall Saturday, though he would be the first to agree that, at their respective ages, any birthday that includes the regular and unassisted intake of breath qualifies as significant.

Thaddeus "Crosscut" Martin watches from the back end of his driveway as the barge-like Lincoln negotiates the cratered path. The car eases to a stop, and after several minutes the passenger door opens slowly, and a bent figure emerges in stages. "Damn, Bud! Thought that was you," the first one says. They eye each other across the clutter of the carport. "Get on back here now."

The other one begins picking his way through the mess; tools, mostly, car parts, broken furniture, building supplies. He'd seemed about to pass some negative judgment on the pitted driveway, given the position of his hand on his lower back as he exited the car, but when, finally, he speaks, it is the chaos at his feet that engages him. "'Nough shit here to start a store," he mumbles from the shadow, "Fella could get hisself kilt." He emerges onto the back patio, which is ringed in colored lights for the occasion, and the two exchange a creaking embrace.

"*Thaddeus Martin," the visitor says, then says again, his voice nearly as gravelly as that of his host.*

"*Lord word, Bud," Crosscut says, turning him gently by the elbow. "Get on over here and have a sit." They take up kitchen chairs near the barbeque, itself draped in twinkling lights set into plastic chili peppers. Crosscut settles himself and follows Buddy's gaze. "Stevie Ray give me those once," he says, meaning the chilis.*

"*Stevie Ray. Um um. There was a sound."*

Crosscut nods with sufficient solemnity. "Lights is good for remembering."

Buddy sighs. "Him gone and us still here. Figure that." They pass a moment, figuring, then Buddy says, "He tol' me you stole them lights." He gives Crosscut a squeeze on the knee, to say he's just kidding, or it doesn't matter, or both. "Heh, heh, heh."

Crosscut shrugs. "He'd of forgot, else."

The screen door opens and a girl pushes through backside first, with a mounded tray of buns and a heaping bowl of slaw, both of which she sets on the side of the barbeque, where several large briskets are just finishing. She notes the new arrival with a shy smile and disappears back inside, returning almost instantly with a large glass of tea to cool the traveler's throat, and a small, empty one for sipping, into which Crosscut pours an inch from the bottle beside his chair.

"*Wife or daughter?" Buddy asks. "I can't keep 'em straight."*

"*Second from the youngest," Crosscut says. "Ruth."*

"*Live close?"*

"*Live here, and her husband."*

They toast and sip while the young woman makes several more trips, her arms loaded with beans, rice, pickles,

and, finally, a Texas size pan of cornbread, all of it covered in plastic wrap.

"Pretty as a song."

Crosscut nods contentedly for this blessing. "He O.K., too."

Buddy eyes the banquet. "That's a whole ass of food,
there. Who all gonna eat it?"

"Family coming," Crosscut answers. "Some of 'em
here, now." He waves his hand indeterminately, taking in
the house, the wide fields, and the woods. He looks at
Buddy. "My birthday, see."

"How many?"

"Sixty-seven."

"Sixty-seven," Buddy echoes. "I'll be."

And, in fact, most of them are already there; daughters
and wives in the kitchen, mixing, slicing, talking; the sons
possibly down to the barn, where a calving is imminent, or
more likely in front of the TV watching the Rebels do battle with LSU; the grandkids–a dozen or more–underfoot
somewhere, though blessedly not the patio, where they'd
only interrupt, or worse, kick over the bourbon. And then,
too, the seeker, out from the Plantation House B&B by the
big river to have her fortune told in the dim, incense-
choked room his wife uses to ply her talents, at roughly
$65 per hour. So it is a houseful, then, and a minor miracle
in and of itself that the two old bluesmen have the chance
to pass some time alone, a luxury not lost on either as they
sip and sigh and take in the cool evening.

Into this calm, presently, comes the sound of a lone
guitar. The two glance toward the open window and listen.
"You?" Buddy asks, thinking it may be a recording.

"The boy," Crosscut answers, his head cocked to catch
each chord. They listen to the notes tumble and break,
the progressions assured, patient, seductive.

"*Him, too?*" Buddy asks, meaning, *is he also afflicted?*

"*He says no.*"

"*Lord.*"

When the window falls silent, Crosscut calls in. "*Nother, step out here. There's company.*"

A moment later the boy appears. "*Hey,*" he says with a shy nod. He stoops to offer his hand, so Buddy won't have to get up. "*I didn't know you were coming.*"

"*Wasn't,*" Buddy says, taking the boy's hand. "*Then did.*" He looks Nother up and down. "*That was nice.*"

The boy smiles. "*Just learned it.*"

"*Can't conjure the name, though.*"

"'*Love In Vain,*'" Nother says.

"*That's it.*"

The back door opens again and one of Seth's boys rushes out, flushed and breathless. "*Poppa,*" he huffs, skidding to a stop in front of Crosscut. "*You got to come! Esme needs help.*"

"*Which one are you, now?*"

"*Jacob.*"

"*Well now Jacob, take a breath and tell me what's the matter.*"

"*Esme's hurting,*" the child reports between gulps of air. "*Daniel says the calf is twisted.*"

"*Uh huh,*" Crosscut says. "*Who else down there?*"

"*Just us kids.*"

"*I'll go,*" Nother says.

"*She's early,*" Crosscut calculates, rubbing his nose. "*You done that before?*"

The boy nods.

"*All right then. Keep Daniel and send them rest back up here.*"

Nother nods. "*Good seeing you, Mr. Guy.*"

"*Pleasure's mine, son.*"

The patio is again quiet but for the sound of Crosscut reloading the small glasses. "*What you doing here, anyway?*"

"*Come to share your good fortune,*" Buddy says.

"*Heh, heh. We'll see how that all works out.*" He sips and smacks his lips. "*How'd you find us?*"

"*Come out that curvy road from Jackson til I seen the comic book house. How hard is that?*"

Crosscut nods. "*Onliest way from there, I guess.*"

"*Road is a sum' bitch, though. All tight and twisted.*"

"*Like us,*" Crosscut says. "*Young fella just got killed. Hit a tree or something. Went to school with the boy.*"

"*That them flowers I saw piled up?*"

"*Probably.*"

"*Lord.*"

"*Turns out that boy's daddy helped build that road way back. Now think on that for a minute. Fella lays out a road and then his own son rides it right into oblivion.*"

"*Somebody ought to write a song,*" Buddy says, and in the brief silence that follows, it is entirely possible that someone does. "*That gentleman pay you yet?*" Buddy asks presently, watching a pair of headlights bounce up the driveway.

"*Says when it comes out,*" Crosscut tells him. He is speaking of his collected catalogue, or more accurately, that scant portion of it that has been salvaged from dusty tapes and demo pressings, or re-recorded from memory over the past several months in a Nashville studio. No one kept track before, wasn't any need. Swing a cat and you could clobber a bluesman down here, and there wasn't enough vinyl in the whole South to get it all down, let alone from a white man with a voice like a rusty saw.

Then, a few years back, this white kid from Illinois or somewhere starts nosing around, back seat all full of scratchy cassettes and old play lists and whatnot, pulling up driveways asking after people most folks forgot they even knew, most of whom turned up dead, or gone without a trace. Kid saying he's making it his life's work to preserve the art form, that's what he calls it, or heritage, not knowing at all how much of it was gone before he was ever born, which might make him call the whole thing off. Finally, last winter, he'd showed up here, directed out that same tortuous road by a Hattiesburg professor he'd seen quoted in the Chicago Sun Times, then nearly drove off again after finding that the voice he'd come to preserve belonged to a white man, which took some of the sanctity out of it, evidently, despite the obvious poverty and woe and requisite amalgam of bad habits. And it was only after Crosscut's bona fides had been confirmed—by a handful of roadhouse rogues, scalawags, and scholars—that any mention of money arose, which Crosscut had the temerity and good sense to promptly reject, thus giving him the permanent upper hand with the suddenly resolute impresario. As in all forms of desire, the more obstinate Crosscut behaved, the more determined his suitor became. Negotiations dragged through the spring, the offer seeming to rise as deliberately as the temperature, until finally, in mid-May, Crosscut agreed to release forty-one of his songs on a three CD set, roughly a tenth of the play list he'd been performing the last forty years on a sweeping arc from San Antonio to Jacksonville, and extending up to St. Louis and Chicago.

"You's black, you'd have that money by now," Buddy says. "Heh, heh, heh."

"Do tell."

They watch a second set of headlights jounce up and pull off next to the car Buddy arrived in. "And when you get that money, do everyone a favor and pave that drive."

The back door bangs open and a pile of kids burst upon them, followed by Ruth, lugging two pitchers of tea and flashing a "sorry 'bout all this" smile, and another daughter, Esther, equally pretty, equally ill-named, carrying a serving plate and a long carving knife. "We're about ready, Dad," she says above the din. She smiles at Buddy, who lifts his glass.

"Best tell your driver to come eat," Crosscut says, as another wave barrels through the door.

But the swirl of activity renders this overly complicated, Buddy decides. "He'll figure it out."

Crosscut knocks back the last of his drink and reaches for the bottle. "Buckle up, then."

"Dad, you're being ridiculous. I mean, this is going to be over, like, so fast. Mom's just...what's that term you guys all use now? Acting out. Yeah." We're taking this roundabout way home from Vicksburg, meandering back roads through the gloaming in the general direction of Delacroix, and Pops has let on that he knows about Mom and Carl. Not that there's anything to know, but he does, and it's messing him up.

"I don't know," he says, leaning forward over the steering wheel to navigate some whopping roadkill. "Maybe we should have made a clean break back there, and it'd be over with by now."

"Except neither of you wants it over," I point out, just to cut off any discussion in that direction. I mean, he's here, she's here, and all their stuff's here, and I really can't see Carl being the catalyst for getting half of it moved again.

They've only been out twice, for God's sake, that one time for dinner, and then to a play. I'd hardly call that a hot romance, and I can't for the life of me decide why she even told him in the first place. He sounds so sad, and I know I'm going to end up in this huge fight with her about it. I'm wondering if he's been thinking about it all day, and putting on this brave front while feeling like dirt. We spent the afternoon looking at Civil War shit, which is a hobby of his, and one I've shared since I was old enough to keep up. You stack up three cannonballs and we're there. I've followed him across the fields at Gettysburg and Antietam, and down that twisted road to Chancellorsville, and through more perfectly aligned cemeteries than any little kid should ever have call to be in. And since Gail's never been big on walking or sweating, or doing anything my father knew more about than she did, it's always been just us two. I've never gotten the bug like him, but I always seem to tag along.

"Well, I'm glad you're so confident," he says, settling back and easing his grip on the wheel. Which I'm not, of course, but it seems to be my turn. He looks at me and adds, "You know, I never would have thought three months ago we'd be having this conversation." He shakes his head like it's the damnedest thing.

"Yeah, well, there's been a lot of stuff I never would have figured on," I tell him. "So just add it to the list."

We pass a battered red and gold sign advertising a fortune teller and Pops slows to take the next right. "I think this gets us back."

"Yep," I agree, wondering what it means that I can confirm this. "And just so you know, I never would have come here with just her, no matter what she thinks."

Pops laughs. "That would have been interesting."

"And I'll tell you what else, if you had any room over there, I'd be living on your side by now."

"Really?" He glances over, his face equal parts surprise and delight. "You'd rather live with me?"

"Sure."

"You would?"

"Well, all things being equal, I'd rather have a triplex. But, yeah."

Pops nods. "I'll take that."

We drive in silence down the deserted road, the sun bleeding crimson behind us and casting long, ominous shadows across the asphalt. As we crest a small rise the Volvo starts to sputter, and then the engine cuts out completely, and we coast quietly as the car decelerates from sixty. Pops eases off the road, finally, and fully onto the edge of someone's ill-kempt yard, braking just before yet another sign proclaiming the powers of the omniscient Madame Marie, who is, apparently, in residence just to our right. Pops grimaces and taps his fingernail on the balky gas gauge, the same one he warns me about every time I take the car out, then kills the headlights and shoots me this overly-serious frown. "See."

"I never doubted you," I tell him, "You didn't need to prove it." But neither of us is upset. It's too in keeping with everything else to be pissed about. And we're only a few miles from home, anyway, at least I think, so getting a lift should be easy enough, if Madame Marie will let us use the phone. We step out into the cool air and stand behind the car, watching the gruesome shadows of the live oaks lining the driveway, as the last bits of color get snuffed from the sky.

The house is well back from the road, strangely lit as if
to catch every odd angle and corner, and looking more
like the false front of a theme park ride, or a movie set,
than an actual place where anyone might live. There are a
dozen cars parked in no discernible pattern in the yard–
apparently Madame Marie is the real deal–and the definite thrum of activity coming from somewhere, though I
can't see anyone for sure in the near-darkness.

"Well," I say after we've surveyed the place for several
minutes, "we probably ought to tell her we're here, and
see if we can use the phone."

Pops slings an arm over my shoulder and we start for
the house. "Shouldn't she know?" he asks.

We walk along the edge of the driveway til it ends,
then cut beneath the carport which opens onto the backyard, where a party is in progress. A couple dozen people
are sitting at picnic tables, or standing in pairs or small
groups with plates of food, and there are two old men at
the center of it all with their heads tilted toward each
other, seemingly oblivious to the commotion around
them. There are strings of cheesy colored lights all
around, so that the whole scene looks like the courtyard
of a Mexican restaurant in Syracuse. No one seems to
notice us as we stand at the fringes, observing. Two small
children start dodging about the furniture and people in a
breakneck game of tag, until the younger of the two,
maybe five years old, I'd guess, barrels our way before
skidding to an abrupt halt when he spots us in the
shadow, at which point his pursuer plows into him and
they both go down at our feet.

"Hello there," Pops says, in that aggressively cheerful
tone adults use on little kids they don't know.

"Mom," the younger one calls out, his eyes never leaving us.

A girl of about twenty or so sets down a pitcher and walks over. "Get up," she says, reaching down to lift them, one in each hand. "Go finish your supper." She turns them loose and gives us this "what are you going to do?" smile and says, "Sorry."

"No, no," Pops says, "we're sorry for intruding."

"Are you here for a reading?" she asks.

"Reading?"

"With Madame Marie."

"Oh, um, no," Pops says. He's been staring at the two old guys the whole time, and still is. "I mean, well, actually, we ran out of gas in front, and we were hoping to use the phone." He glances quickly at the girl, then back to the old guys. "If that's all right."

"Of course," she says, and begins leading us across the patio. A few of them glance up, then go back to their food.

"Excuse me," Pops says, bringing us to a halt. "That old gentleman, I swear I've seen him somewhere before."

"Most likely," she says. "That's Buddy Guy."

"It sure is," Pops says. He looks quizzically at the girl, who smiles back without elaborating, then begins walking again. "And the other?" Pops asks.

"Crosscut Martin."

"Damn," Pops breathes, though this name means nothing to me.

We stop behind the two men, who leave off talking to check us out. "Well now, daughter," the one she called Crosscut says, "who's this here?"

"Haven't said yet," Daughter replies, prompting my father to start rattling a mile a minute introducing himself, and apologizing and fawning and gee whizzing like a madman and shaking hands like he's running for something, even with Ruth, which is Daughter's name, it turns out. And through it all he never does get around to saying why we're here, interrupting Crosscut's birthday barbeque, which falls to me when Pops finally remembers I'm there, too.

"Well now," Crosscut says, seeing as how Pops has finally shut up, "we got a big old tank of gas down the barn. Why don't we just get you a couple gallons of that and you be on your way? No call to be made dragging someone way out here on a Saturday night." He turns to Ruth. "Nother down there still?"

"Nother Martin?" I blurt, which makes them all look at me, even Pops.

"Not likely there's two," Buddy says.

"You know Nother?" Ruth asks.

"Yeah. Well, actually no. I mean, we're in the same class." I can feel my cheeks getting all red, and I'm worried I'm babbling too. "I'm new this year, so we haven't really met. I just know who he is."

"Well, now's your chance," Crosscut says. "Just follow the driveway across the road and there it is."

"I'll show her!" It's the younger one from the game of tag, who has suddenly reappeared at Ruth's side.

"You stay up here," Crosscut tells him. "And find our new guest here a chair, why don't you. We about to pick a few."

The way Pops' face lights up—the first really happy look I've seen all day—I know he just wants to kick it here, so I have no choice but to refuse his half-hearted offer to come along.

"This way," Ruth says, and we retrace our steps back toward the driveway.

"Lord word, daughter," Crosscut says. "Girl looks like she can find a barn by herself. How 'bout you fetch us another glass instead."

Ruth rolls her eyes and directs me across the road, where the driveway continues, sort of, through a semi-fenced lot and up to a large barn door, which I can see from here is open, as there is a dim wedge of light bleeding out. "Stick to the driveway," she suggests, "you're less likely to step on something."

"Thanks, I think."

Ruth laughs. "You'll be fine," she assures me. "And Nother will take it from there. He'll be just inside the door and over to the right, with Daniel and Esme."

The driveway is so cratered I deem it safer to walk along the edge in the grass, critters or no. It's dark as a cave out here now, and the live oaks along the far side of the drive rustle ominously in the breeze, their branches waving like cartoon trees that have suddenly come to life. I spot a pair of eyes once, I think, blinking just below a branch when a car passes along the road, so I drop my gaze to the ground and pick up the pace. If there are things out there watching I don't want to know. Across the road–which itself is pitch black this far from town–is mostly open pasture land, and I cross the short distance to the barn feeling a bit safer. I pause in front of the door; it seems like I should knock, or somehow announce myself before I just walk in, but that seems kind of dumb, too. It is a barn, after all, and I wouldn't know if they heard me or not, anyway, or how long to wait. While I'm debating this, a large gray cat moves into the square of light near the door, its jaws filled with something furry that I'm guessing was alive until quite recently. When it goes in, I follow.

The barn is dimly lit, bare bulbs protruding from sporadically placed sockets lining the crossbeams, and a brighter fluorescent light set over a large pair of slop sinks against the far wall to my right. Between the sinks and where I've come in stands a boy of about twelve–Daniel, I assume–loosely holding a rifle and staring intently into one of several wooden stalls at that end of the barn. I begin to cross the distance between us slowly, scraping my feet and making enough noise so I won't spook him and get one between the eyes. But he takes no notice, his gaze locked on the stall, so that I wonder if it's Nother and Esme he's watching so intently, and if so, why, and what's with the gun? As I get closer a low, calm voice becomes audible from within the stall, along with snuffling, labored breathing, and the rustle of movement. Oh God, I think, what's this now? But I'm too close to turn back, so I opt for the direct approach, clearing my throat loudly and more or less demanding, "Excuse me."

The boy glances over, his expression more consternation than surprise, and I wonder if he's been aware of my presence all along. He motions me forward and lifts a finger to his lips. "Shhh."

When I get close I hazard a glimpse into the stall, expecting I don't know what, but certainly not this. What I see is Nother, his back to us, leaning over the flanks of a spotted Holstein, like a quarterback getting ready to take a snap from center. His cheek is pressed against the side of the swollen animal, and he is coaxing the beast to relax in a soothing, monotone that seems to be working, and which I assume would be even more effective if he'd step up to where the skittish animal could see him. Which is precisely when I notice where, exactly, Nother's hands are–well up past his forearms, I might add, which accounts for the peculiar way he's standing, but does not begin to explain the why of it, and conjures in my head every nasty farm boy joke I've ever heard, which I thought were entirely made up until just this second.

"What the hell are you doing?" I hear myself bellow, which makes Nother look back, and the cow lurch forward a foot or two, dragging him along.

"Re-positioning," Daniel says clinically. "Now shush if you're going to stay."

"Don't spook her," Nother whispers over his shoulder in the same composed tone.

"Me?!"

"Easy, girl," Nother coos, and I'm about to get really pissed because I think for a second he's talking to me. "Easy now, almost there." He shifts slightly and the cow does this series of half-hops, so that part of a shiny forearm appears as Nother shuffles beside her. "Good girl. Easy now. Daniel, calm her down."

The boy looks at me appraisingly, then back into the stall. "Which one?"

"Esme," Nother says. "She's about ready."

The younger one steps tentatively into the stall and begins stroking the animal's neck with the back of his hand, murmuring in the same soothing timbre Nother is employing at the other end, though with somewhat less conviction. "We're with you, girl. It's all good."

"Annnnddd...there," Nother says, like he just got the vault door to swing open. Without interrupting his litany of sweet talk, he makes a final movement, and slowly sinks back on his heels behind Esme, his arms retracting as he sits, until his glistening hands are resting on his thighs, and he lets out a long and overdue exhalation. Only then does he look back at me, entirely unruffled, it would appear, to find this total stranger, unannounced, observing this insane behavior.

My eyes dart around the stall, from Nother up to Daniel, who has stepped back, yet continues stroking the cow's flank, to the poor animal herself, who still appears to be agitated from her ordeal. A thousand impulses occur to me at once; knock both of them away from her and soothe the beast myself, pounce on Nother in sisterly retribution, turn and flee and never speak of it again, or, childishly, stamp my feet and yell, "I'm telling!" because if there was ever justification for tattling, I'm thinking this is it. But what comes out, finally, seems painfully obvious, even trite. "You guys are *sick!*" We stare at each other, me fuming, Nother with an expression of patient amusement, so that my urge to pummel him rears up again.

"There's the head," Daniel shouts just then. "You did it!"

Nother swivels to look, and when I step forward to peer over his shoulder I see, in graphic progress, the miracle of birth. "We did it," Nother corrects, rising to stand beside me, his arms out and turned up like a surgeon. We watch in silence as the head appears, Esme jostling slightly, but otherwise doing fine, all things considered. "Good girl," Nother urges, lightly stroking her other flank, "Easy does it." He reaches out to support the calf's head, easing the way for the lower shoulder to slip out.

"I don't want to watch anymore," Daniel says. "Can I go since she's here?"

"Yeah, go on," Nother says, rotating the exposed shoulder slightly to release the other. "Tell them everything looks O.K. now. Leave the gun." While Daniel races off, Nother steps out of the stall, rubbing his arms with a doo rag he's pulled from the back pocket of his jeans. "I think she can take it from here." Which she does, magnificently, while we watch. It is now that he explains what I've walked in on, the manual re-positioning of the fetus to avert a breech birth, which could have resulted in the loss of both cow and calf. His voice is even and unhurried, as if to calm me as well, as the birthing unfolds. And in what seems like only moments, the newborn has made the short drop to the floor, which Nother explains will start the breathing, and is curled on the straw, bleating and flinching while Esme licks it clean.

I exhale loudly the breath I had not even realized I was holding. "That is, like, the most amazing thing I have ever seen," I tell him when I can speak again, my voice an awed whisper. "I mean–" And as I raise my arm to point into the stall, I find his hand is clasped in mine, warm and slightly sticky, which I release immediately with a muttered apology, whatever point I was about to make lost. He directs me to the sinks and we scrub off using a soft bristle brush and this liquid soap that smells strongly medicinal, and amazingly hot water from the tap. Nother scrubs all the way past his elbows, and beneath his fingernails with the brush, just like on all the medical shows. There's no towel, we discover too late, so he wipes his hands dry on his shirt front, then does the same with mine, which, like everything else he's done so far, seems incredibly intimate without being intrusive. "How did you know how to do that?" I ask as he works the warm inside of his shirt over each finger.

"Seen it done a few times." We move back to the stall and Nother puts out water and some clean straw, and fills a shallow pan of grain for the new mom. "Kind of a practical thing, actually. Just someone has to do it."

I've boosted myself onto this shelf in the stall and I'm looking down at him. "Well, better you than me." Nother squats next to Esme, who is now resting beside the calf, talking softly and rubbing her neck, telling her she did fine, and that we're proud of her and we'll let them be in just a minute, and to think up a pretty name for her young 'un.

Which makes me almost cry it's so sweet to watch, but still so un-sappy and not fake either, and I'm shaking my head thinking, how can this guy be in my same grade?

Nother stands up and moves in front of me, a hand resting on either side. "What's your name?"

"Teri."

"Well, Teri," he says, taking a half step back and placing his hands on my hips, "we can probably head back to the house. Not much else to do here."

I put my hands on his shoulders and he lifts me to the ground. "What do I call you?"

"Nother."

"That can't be your real name, though."

"Could be."

"Well, Nother, I'm not going to insist, since I just now remembered those terrible things I said before. But I didn't know, I mean, what you guys were doing."

"It probably did look kind of odd," he allows.

"Well, I'm sorry and I take it all back."

"It's forgotten," he says.

"What was he doing with the rifle?"

"Nothing," Nother says. "Just holding it."

"Like, in case the cow flipped out or something?"

"No, it's only a pellet gun, anyway." He goes to the next stall and brings it back. "We keep it here to run off possum and such when they get in."

"So he was, like, guarding you?"

"Hardly. Boys his age just like guns," he explains. "And since he didn't much want to be here in the first place, I figured it might take his mind off things." He snaps the piece open. "Not even loaded."

"Seemed to work," I decide, amazed that he'd think of this with all the rest of it going on.

"Yeah, he did good. Took off first chance, but still." He lifts the rifle onto a high shelf and puts out the light over the sink. "Ready?"

We leave one bulb burning over Esme's stall and I rub my arms in the cool night air as Nother latches the door. "Aren't you cold?"

"It was warmer when I came down." Which doesn't really answer the question, I notice, which, I'm also noticing, is kind of a pattern with him. "You sit with that other new girl a lot," he says as we start across the damp ground. "I've seen you out there."

"Who?"

"Wears that chain bracelet all the time."

"Kayla? She's been here a couple years I thought."

"Yeah."

O.K., I think. "So then, I take it you've always lived here?"

He nods. "Every single day."

"I'm from Baltimore."

"Maryland," he answers, then says, "Warm," as we step onto the asphalt road.

"That's the one." I glance back at his footprints. "So, like, do you ever wear shoes?"

"Why's that?"

"I've seen you before, too," I inform him as we cross into the yard and start up the right edge of the driveway. "You were at Ronnie Foster's funeral and you were barefoot then, too."

"Just at the cemetery. I missed the service." He says this like he's explained something. "I knew him a long time. Not good, but, um, long." I'm starting to think he's messing with me.

"They were all in back before," I say when we get near the house; from the sounds of it, they still are. "This is some setup," I add, in regards to the house. I mean, it's all over the place; walls sticking out every which way, an open porch sagging off the other side, and that carport tacked on out back covering God knows what, and each part made of something different. The wall nearest us is medium blue, like the inside of a pool, almost, except a little darker than that, even, and stucco as best I can tell, since the only lighting is this string of tiny yellow bulbs drooping from the edge of the roof. Plus all these cars out here at odd angles, like everyone just jumped out wherever they happened to stop. "Is this for your grandpa's birthday?" I ask. "Or is it always like this?"

"Father," he says. He does a quick check around as we duck beneath the carport, then adds, "Usually less cars."

My father has joined the two old men, I observe from the shadow, seated more or less in the middle of the patio with a short glass in his hand and a used paper plate setting beside his chair. He's facing kind of sideways from me, his gaze locked on the other two, who are both seated forward in their chairs, extracting the most amazing sounds out of the guitars propped in their ample laps. There's a lot of background noise, what with all the others milling about, but most everyone is listening, and every little while someone lets out an appreciative whoop. "All you now," I hear Buddy say, and Crosscut nods and shuts his eyes, plucking out sounds like a lie-detector would make if you could hook it up to his amp.

"Damn," I whisper, glancing over at Nother. "Sorry." Which I say for calling Crosscut his grandpa.

"He's old," Nother absolves, his head rising and falling in perfect time to the sounds his father is unleashing.

Buddy squints into the shadow and shoots a half-grimace, half-smile our way, just as Crosscut says,

"Now you," and so slides his one hand right down to the base of the guitar's neck and cuts loose this string of notes with the other that about lifts me off the ground.

Pops doesn't even notice us clapping when the song's over, and keeps rocking his whole upper body in his chair long after the sound fades. Nother leads me along the edge of the patio to this car seat that's been lifted from somewhere—one of the wrecks littering the back yard, perhaps—and propped on this low wall past the barbeque. He's plucked two cans of beer from an open cooler and hands one to me when we're sitting. "You drink beer?" he asks, though he must have decided, since it's open. "I don't figure your dad will notice."

"Thanks." I knock off almost half of it, in case he does come over, but I doubt he even knows we're back here. "How'd you know that was my dad?"

"He's got a Maryland sweatshirt, for one thing," Nother points out. "And everyone else is us."

Ruth comes over a couple minutes later with a plate for each of us, but when I try to protest Nother ends up taking both of them from her, and then setting one beside me when she leaves. "She'd have stood there all night."

"That's your sister?"

"Yeah, next closest. That's her husband in the green hat over there." He motions toward a large, friendly looking hulk in overalls, with a goatee and earring. "They live here, too."

"And the rest of them?"

"They live around." He identifies most of the rest, the adults, anyhow, who all seem to be siblings and in-laws, then sets his plate in his lap and lifts his sandwich carefully to his mouth. "You should at least try the meat," he says, taking a small bite. "Cooked all day."

Buddy and Crosscut are at it again, and they more or less take turns when they're not playing together, so that it's a long time before the music stops again completely, though time is beginning to seem a remote notion. I have no idea how long all that in the barn took, or even how long we've been back here, but I notice that my plate got cleaned somewhere in there, and another beer opened, and he was right about the meat. And it takes even longer to remember I went down there to see about getting some gas in the first place, but completely forgot.

I start telling Nother about our trip to Vicksburg, and then about cruising all over the countryside on the way back, and even, for reasons I cannot fathom entirely, about my folks being split up, but not really, and how we all live in a duplex together, and my mom sort of dating, and how that was pretty much the bulk of the conversation my father and I were engaged in while we were running out of gas in front of his house, which, I conclude, was kind of weird.

Nother listens without interruption, nodding from time to time like he's overly familiar with this sad old verse, which, if the songs we've been hearing are any indication, he may well be. "Look at him now," he says, nodding at my father, who is sitting there like a wrung out dishrag, with this look on his face like every song they've played so far is written on his soul. Nother looks at me like he just answered something, and says, "He gets it."

"He does seem to be coming around," I agree. "Or he's totally ripped."

We cut around the far side of the house, past a section made of wood, and then another that looks to be covered in shingles, then through the front yard and back across the street. We duck inside and I look in on Esme while

Nother goes for the gas can. The new mother is already back on her feet, swaying peacefully while the calf sleeps beneath her. Nother slips up behind me and I assume he's luxuriating in the same beatific scene. "How does that make you feel," I ask him. I realize it's kind of a corny question, but it's giving me this glowing feeling, and all I did was watch, so he must really be feeling it. But when I turn for his answer he's staring into the rafters. Then, in a single motion he raises the gun from his side and fires, and a rat the size of a man's shoe—a big man's shoe—drops to the dirt floor with a mortal thud. I hear myself gasp, then look back at Nother, saucer-eyed and gaping.

"They get into the feed," he says, then replaces the gun and returns with a shovel to remove the rat, which he carries to the door and flings well into the next pasture over. When he's replaced the shovel and found the gas can he returns to the stall. "Tank's outside."

We fill the can and I lead the way back to the Volvo. Nother has me get in and pump the accelerator while he does something under the hood, and it starts up directly. We let it run for a few minutes to clear the gas line or something, standing in silence in the cool evening, then Nother reaches inside and shuts it off. We start up the drive, but I stop at the sign for Madame Marie, something else I'd forgotten about during this strange evening. "Who's this?"

"My mother," he says. "She sees things, they say."

"Does she?"

"They say," he repeats.

"What do you say?"

He shrugs. "I think she does."

We resume walking. "Which one was she?"

"She keeps inside."

Things are starting to break up in back. The guitars have been set aside and my father is slumped in his chair, listening while the other two talk, but not joining in. Past them, Ruth is directing the remaining kids on a cleanup detail, though it seems like a pretty hit or miss proposition from where I'm standing. We make eye contact and I mouth, "Thank you," and she smiles and gives a little wave.

We cross the patio. "Ready?" I ask when my father looks up.

"There you are," he says, like he just remembered I'm even here.

"This is Nother."

They shake hands. "You missed it. Man, you really missed it," he tells us.

"We heard a lot of it," I tell him. I turn to the two older men. "Thank you." They both nod, and when I wish Crosscut a happy birthday he touches his hat brim.

"The car ready?" Pops asks.

"All set."

He stands and bows deeply to his two new friends. "An honor and a pleasure," he states venerably.

"All right," Buddy says, while Crosscut just nods.

I turn to thank Nother, and hopefully make some really clever comment on the strangeness of the evening, but what I hear myself say instead is, "Can we go out?"

"I was getting to that," he says unhurriedly. Buddy nods, which is funny, but kind of weird, too, and then we're all just standing there, waiting sort of. "We can talk at school," Nother says finally, because there are at least twice as many people in this conversation as there need to be.

"We better," I tell him, which causes Buddy to chuckle and say, "Look out."

I put a hand on Pops shoulder to get him moving, because he looks like he's waiting to be dismissed. "How about I drive?"

"I was going to say."

I feel like I should be hung over. But I wouldn't be up at nine on a Sunday morning, then, sitting at the table listening to Gail bitch about how lame the newspaper is. Again. I'm thinking if I sit here long enough she might offer to make breakfast, which is definitely a long shot, but I don't have anything else to do. I'd like to go next door and see how Pops is doing, but I doubt he's up yet, and it seems in poor taste to be checking up to begin with. Not that he was such a mess or anything, but I noticed the bottle Crosscut had was empty when we left, and my father appeared to have had his share. He sounded a little out of sorts on the way home, overwhelmed, maybe, aside from the booze, like a whole bunch of things hit him all at once: haunted Vicksburg; the interloper, Carl; this strange, foreign landscape, and just how the hell he'd come to find himself in it; all marinated in generous draughts of Rebel Yell, and that amazing sound. Which seem to have added up to one of those "life moments" that knock you on your ass from time to time, but which you don't necessarily want someone else watching.

"So, are you going to make breakfast?" I ask.

There's a loud snort from behind the business section. "Good one." She lowers the paper after a moment. "I'll drive somewhere," she offers.

"I don't feel like getting dressed."

"Best I can do." She thumbs the paper and opens another section. "What did you eat last night?"

"Barbeque."

"Yuck."

"It was good."

She lowers the paper again. "Would you like to visit Baltimore after Christmas?"

"Huh?"

"Fly up there for a week, stay with one of your friends?"

"All of us?"

"No, you. I'll be busy here."

"What about Dad?"

She rolls her eyes. "I just thought of it," she says, tapping an ad on the travel page. "The fares here aren't too bad."

"I could probably stay at Gina's."

"Well, she wouldn't be my first choice, but let me know. I'm sure these will fill up fast."

"So then, you won't make me an omelet, but you'll fly me to Baltimore?"

She sighs emphatically. "Just decide," she says as I get up to e-mail Gina.

I've been neglecting the whole East Coast crowd pretty bad lately, so it'll be fun to drop this whole idea about a Christmas visit on Gina now. I give her the unabridged version of last night, even though it takes forever to type. It sounds so trippy that I start to forget I wasn't all wasted, til I notice how vivid the evening still is in my head, and that I'm not dying of thirst. When I finish that I start on a take-home Chemistry quiz that's due tomorrow, which soon has me more confused than when I started, and gives me a hell of a headache on top of it, so even though I'm not hung over, I might as well be.

And then, thankfully, I've got mail:

About time!!! (Gina writes)

What kind of fucking place is that, anyway?? I mean, first it's cops in the halls and car wrecks. Then funerals and floods. Now there's cows getting violated and rats murdered, by the same guy. Who is a FARMER, and who you're dating!! And whose name is Nother!! And whose mother is a fortune teller!!! Hello!!!

I've heard of "meeting cute," but come on! Is it still earth where you are?

Like, this is what we did that same night: drove around, drank warm beer, saw NO cute guys, watched Suz puke (again!). Which is what we do every weekend, and then it's Monday again, so you are totally up to date from here.

I might be jealous.

Oh yeah, Carrie asked about you the other day. She might walk on at BC for soccer if she gets in. Boston might be cool, what do you think? She's still with Doug and wants to know about the guys down there. Wait til she hears this shit!!

Is he at least cute???

G

It occurs to me that I might not be able to take a week of Gina anymore.

It's past noon when Kayla calls, and I concede that this Chem quiz isn't going to get done. Which is fine, there's probably a college for dummies in Boston, too. "How was Vicksburg?" she asks.

"It was O.K. How did you know?"

"Gail was here. I didn't know it stayed open so late."

Which I take as an invitation to run through the evening again, though it still doesn't sound any less absurd. Kayla interrupts periodically to ask a question or clarify something, and I swear she's taking notes. Gail walks in at one point to say she's leaving, and is gone again before I can even pause to ask where. I go out to get a soda, and finish telling it in the living room, which takes, like, an hour. "Probably sorry you asked, huh?"

To which she replies, "Interesting."

"What did you end up doing?"

"Nothing like that," she admits, which comes out a little like an accusation. "Like I said, your mom was over here, but she didn't know where you were, so I went to Joley's and watched movies."

"How was that?"

"It kind of sucked. I mean, it would have been cool with more people there, but no one else was around and Joley, well, she doesn't have much going on these days."

"Yeah, now that the dance is over, she's kind of out of business."

"Exactly. And I'm starting to notice she's one of those chicks that always needs a guy around or she's lost. I mean, she's practically brain dead sometimes."

"Ouch."

"Oh, I'm sorry, was that mean?"

Kayla seems a little edgy today. "Well, so I don't have to call her, how about telling me what you know about Nother."

"Like what?"

"Like anything. I mean, I asked him out, so some background might be nice."

"You probably know as much about him as anyone after last night. I mean, he's not around much, except at school, and he doesn't say a hell of a lot, either."

"Who does he hang out with?"

"No one really."

"Why not? I mean, what's the matter with him?" I'm starting to get a little nervous.

"Nothing that I know of. He just seems to go his own way, and everyone else seems to let him."

"So, people don't like him?"

"I don't think people like him or dislike him. He's just sort of there."

"How can that be, if he's lived here all his life?"

"I think he's got a lot of cousins, you know, that he hangs out with."

"So, what do you think? I mean, if he asks me out?"

"Go," she says. "I mean, if you want to."

"Well, yeah, I do. I think. That's what I'm asking."

"You're asking me if you want to?"

"No, I'm asking if there's any reason I shouldn't?"

"You're starting to sound like Joley. Just go. Hell, you've already met his parents. Around here, that clears you to sleep with him."

"Kayla!"

"Look, go. Have fun. Do whatever."

"You think?"

"Yes. What could it hurt? And you're certainly interested. Maybe offer to drive, though. Any time I've ever seen him, he's in this pickup from the fifties."

"Good to know. Thanks."

"Look, I've got to get going, so unless he said anything about me...."

"Now who sounds like Joley? Later."

This day has totally gotten away from me. I go out on the porch, thinking I might sit outside for a while, but it's too chilly and I end up back inside ten minutes later making tea. I put on some music instead, and lay down on the couch to start reading *The Sun Also Rises,* which I'm supposed to have finished by Friday. Which isn't likely, since it's just a bunch of people drinking and talking funny, without much else to recommend it except for being short, no matter what Mr. Russell said when he assigned it.

My mind keeps drifting back to last night, how I felt so in the moment the whole time, and how cool that was. It was probably just another evening for him, other than me stumbling into it, but I still haven't got it sorted out, even though I've been through it a hundred times. And I hope we do hook up, I decide for sure, so maybe now I can knock off some of this book. But the next thing I know it's after six and Gail is banging through the front door waking me up, back from wherever it is she went. "It'll take a long time to finish that way," she calls out.

I lift the book off my face. "Then just tell me what happens."

She lifts several bags to the table and steps out of her shoes, leaving the front door open, amazingly enough. "Let's see; drinking, fighting, fishing, Jew-baiting, bull fighting, and...impotence."

"That old story."

She frowns down at me. "I brought you a sandwich." I listen to her putting groceries away, then taking down plates, because she won't eat off just the wrapper. "Have you been next door?"

"Nope."

"Oh. Well, how did he seem when you were with him yesterday?"

I take a large bite of my sandwich and chew slowly. "It varied."

"Why do I bother asking you anything?"

"Well, if you mean about Carl, which you do, why don't you ask him yourself?"

"Wow, I never thought of that," she sneers.

I motion toward the wall. "He's right over there."

She picks up her burger and sighs. "It must be so nice to live in your world."

"Yeah, I've been thinking that all day."

His daughter had been largely correct in observing that he had experienced what she called, for lack of a less ridiculous term, a "life moment," though it had far less to do with his being star struck or soused than she suspected, despite his being some of the first, and a good bit of the latter. The "moment" had begun much earlier in the day, actually, back in Vicksburg when the sun was still high, while they tramped the bluffs overlooking the strategic kink in the Mississippi. Their guide, a pleasant, angular woman well suited to the task, though dressed more for bird-watching, it seemed to him, took them through the long siege and ultimate surrender that would mark Grant's first significant victory. The recitation was smooth and practiced, and impeccably timed, though anyone not well versed in the history of the period would be hard pressed to say who'd won the engagement, let alone the war.

But the quirk that had struck him most keenly was how she had lapsed repeatedly into present tense, as if the discord between the states were not yet entirely resolved, a tendency that did not go unnoticed by his daughter, either. "It's like they're still fighting that damn war down here," was how she put it. "I mean, get a life!" She was prone to outbursts of this sort, more so since they'd uprooted her, constantly testing the limits in regard to language and provocation, though he was privately convinced that the majority of her more risqué notions were unleashed as trial balloons rather than firm convictions, vetted primarily to see how they sounded to her own ear. Their dialog had been quite open of late, in fact, which he believed to be largely for the better, though it did add a rather rude edge to her demeanor that was at times unattractive, and occasionally counterproductive. Still, this openness served them well; there was little that she deemed off limits, it appeared, which itself implied a certain degree of trust, and overall their relationship had not been this good in years.

The "moment," such as it was, stretched through the late afternoon, encompassing the meandering trek home over ancient two lane roads, which seemed, somehow, to fit into it as well. What he had been noticing almost since their arrival, but had been unable to configure into any coherent framework until now, was the slow urgency peculiar to life in the rural South, though perhaps this languor would, by definition, preclude any sense of urgency. A relentlessness, then, the inevitable tumbling of events that could no more be separated or hurried than they could be prevented or cut short. Things run their course, he was finding out, which was no radiant discovery, of course. The insight came with the realization that these things, and the course, were largely out of your hands, and rarely was the end of that course obvious. As his daughter had rather harshly noted, these people were still fighting Vicksburg.

So it was this rumination that had occupied him on the quiet, circuitous drive, and it was only when he had come to these meager conclusions that he realized he had been neglecting his daughter, who had generously given up yet another Saturday to join him in revisiting an epoch she otherwise had scant interest in. And it was for this reason that he brought up Carl; he felt he owed her more than the superficial, "Penny for your thoughts" type of inquiry, and in truth, he believed they'd moved well past that in the preceding few months. He was quite sure that Carl was a subject of significant interest to her, though one she had not seen fit to broach to him—a fact he generously attributed to her tact and newfound maturity. Not that he was attempting to pry information now, he wouldn't put her in that position, or that he even believed she'd have much to offer, anyway. She was sixteen; what could she know of such nonsense? It was simply an attempt to engage her in a topic of interest, to let her speak her mind with the reckless certitude she was so enamored of; anything useful would be gravy. And engage her it did, with great animation, so that in the give and take that followed, he simply forgot to allow for the balky gas gauge until it ceased to matter.

He thought at first they'd come to rest in front of a whorehouse, the weathered sign proclaiming the various talents of Madame Marie being some strange code for what was really on the table. It was certainly not out of the question in this isolated landscape, which he was coming to consider a realm unto itself, and the odd configuration and dim, come-hither lighting of the place more than lent itself to such an enterprise. If not that, then surely a roadhouse of sorts, a honky-tonk, perhaps licensed for such pleasures as it afforded, or perhaps not. He hadn't assumed a private residence, in any case, particularly in view of the horde of cars parked about, but when that turned out to be the case, he was not overly surprised, either. And then, in turn, clasping the gnarled hand of Buddy Guy while being passed three thick fingers of bourbon, neat—just more of the same.

What stayed with him when he awoke the next day, fuzzy headed but otherwise no worse for the wear–which he attributed to the mountain of savory meat he'd consumed in defense of the Rebel Yell–was how the music had seemed to mirror his observations. How each note had hung briefly in the air, beautifully alive and fully realized, before tumbling into the next, or sliding, slipping, crashing, drifting. The blues, too, had this deliberate urgency, this same inevitability, while still offering the prospect of improvisation.

He lay beneath a thin cotton blanket chewing ice as morning slipped into afternoon. He thought again of the neglected, crumbling back roads, how they'd twisted, circled back, or dead-ended–simply bled out into gravel, then ruts, then nothing. And yet the two of them had got where they were going, eventually, though they hadn't known at the time where exactly that was. The blues were the same, if you didn't insist on being too exacting, and a picture began to emerge. Misdirection was the constant, perhaps; order the fallacy. And to succumb to this disorder was no weakness. It was, perhaps, simply life. Sloppy, negligent, meandering life. You could not dissect it into its parts to any good purpose, any more than you could appreciate a song one note at a time. Life was not something to be assembled that way; it was cut from whole cloth, and it existed on those terms, and your life was defined by which parts you chose to embrace, and which to merely endure.

He had begun to pick up on this much earlier, in the torrid days of August when they were first restructuring their lives, and largely surrendered to it–"going native," his daughter had called it. He had felt, briefly, the imposter, the foreigner parachuted in, the alien; but this feeling passed quickly and quite naturally. Why fight the heat, the

sapping humidity, the odd customs and foodstuffs, the somnolent pace? Better to strip to your shorts, take small bites,
smile, and relax. Get on with it, in other words.

Which he'd done, he realized now, was still doing, and
it was good. The foreignness was diminished, and though
he would never be mistaken for a product of the local soil,
he no longer felt the imposter, either. Ceding control had
empowered him; with a less firm grasp on the rudder he
had achieved greater focus. The book was evidence of
that; when he'd first begun airing his intention, even he
had scant reason to believe he'd follow through. But he
had, the stacks of typescript on his desk irrefutable proof.
Now granted, he had parts of six chapters in the works
simultaneously, with none completed, but this still repre-
sented his most prolific output since grad school. And who
had determined that his work must progress in order, at
least at this stage? It was in following his ideas where they
might lead, rather than attempting to direct them, that the
manuscript was taking shape. It seemed more organic this
way, and he had vowed not to fight it.

And on the more significant aspect of parenting, it was
working as well, at least from what he could discern. She
had not, to this point, taken advantage of the license he
had granted her, which amounted, mainly, to treating her
as an adult, with all the requisite respect and accountability
that entailed. And what he had noticed, as a result of this
enhanced liberty, was an increased desire and regard for
his opinions on the part of his daughter, who seemed
much more agreeable to being answered than instructed.

Which perhaps explained how he had come to decide, at
some indeterminate point the previous evening, to extend
this same moderate policy toward his wife. He had
assumed, on the dazed drive home, that this benevolence

was the bourbon and the blues talking. But he saw now, in the chill, overly-bright light of day, the obviousness of it; the music had simply confirmed that, the booze letting it seep in. He could no more control his wife's deportment than straighten the river at Vicksburg. So let it go. Their union would play itself out on its own terms, and, if events tumbled right, at least they'd all be here to sort out the pieces.

It pours all day on Monday, so we're stuck in the gym instead of out at our table, which totally messes things up as far as people watching goes, not to mention grabbing a smoke. Kayla suggests I get used to it; it rains a ton all winter, she says, which is mainly how you can tell it's winter. But I've pretty much exhausted my summer wardrobe, anyway, so bring it on. Now it's almost perfect in the evening, or if you're not in the direct sun, and if it's not raining like the end of the world. It shouldn't be eighty degrees in the fall, anyway.

We're up high in the bleachers and I'm looking over the crowd at everyone hanging out, working it, striking the pose. It's weird how fast you can get set in your ways. What I mean is, I know all the people at the tables near us, and the ones who use the corner door, but the people out on the lawn, or the parking lot crowd—they might as well go to a different school. And now that we're all crammed inside, I don't even recognize half these people.

"He's not in here," Kayla says,

"Who?"

"Who? Right. Your man, Nother."

So I guess it's more obvious than I thought. I haven't spotted him either, though I haven't a clue where he'd be in the first place, or who with, if anyone. I even resort to a quick scan at ground level, looking for bare feet, because you just never know. Truth is, I'm not even sure he has study hall this period, or if that one time I saw him was just by chance, or because he came late or something. And it's a stretch to think he'll find me, since he only seems to know me from our table, which is why I opt to go high for visibility. Which didn't work, and now I have to listen to Kayla blow me shit about it and laugh because I have no way at all to get a hold of him, not even a phone number, and he probably doesn't even know my last name. "Do they even have a phone?" Kayla wonders. "Maybe that's why they gave you the gas."

"Of course they have a phone," I snap, though I have no idea whether this is true or not.

"Touchy," Kayla says. She likes to pick, I've been noticing.

"I mean, why wouldn't they? His mom must need one, right?"

"The fortune teller, you mean?"

"Shut up."

He doesn't call that night, though it's not like I expected him to, and I'm kind of annoyed at myself for even noticing, and then for hanging with Gail longer than usual just in case, before walking over to see Dad and cram for a French test. Right off Pops asks if I ran into Nother today—my new friend, he calls him—and I start babbling about school, and study hall inside, and the rain, which I'm sure he figures hasn't got anything to do with anything, least of all Nother, but I can't seem to shut it off, either. And of course Pops picks up on what's happening right away, and pretty soon he's got this dopey grin plastered on his face that finally compels me to shut up, which is when he says, "Oh, my."

"And I'm probably going to flunk this test, too."

"A focus issue, I'm guessing."

You'd think he'd try to keep me on task after that, being my father, and an educator himself, but instead we end up talking most of the evening away, not about Nother, specifically, but not avoiding the topic, either. This gets us talking about his book, somehow, which a lot of things seems to these days, and which he's got spread out all over the desk when I get there, so it might still count as work for him, but it's not doing me much good. The thing is, no matter how deeply he delves into it, or how often—which is often, trust me—I can't get past the notion that his subject is just really...broad. And as glad as I am for him to be working, I wonder if it all isn't too obvious to be worthwhile, and I'm really curious just what's on all those pages he's cranking out, because what's left to say after you've said that people behave rudely because it's easier, and nowadays there are a lot more of them?

I don't get much studying done, needless to say, and since it's still raining when I wake up Tuesday, I tell Gail I'm sick and she calls me in before flying off to campus. It helps that she's always in such a hurry, but it was probably good that I didn't mention the test, either. Which is totally lame, I know, but so what?

When Kayla calls after second period I'm eating toast and watching *The Sun Also Rises,* which I've pretty much convinced myself makes up for cutting school. "Ava Gardner is about as pretty as it gets," I inform Kayla.

"You sick?"

"Nope."

"I'm coming over."

I throw on some clothes at the next commercial; I kind of want to shower, but the movie is already farther along than I am in the book, and I don't want to miss anything in case Russell decides to spring a quiz on us.

Kayla is pulling up when I come out of my room, and she's got some guy from her Psych class tagging along who she introduces as Zed, and who seems nice enough, but also like Psych might be a tad ambitious for him. He's got a joint, though, which explains why he's here to begin with, so at the next clump of commercials we go out back and burn it, after which Kayla decides she has to eat.

"Bodean's," she says, which means fat-ass cheeseburgers and Cajun fries.

"Right on," Zed seconds. He's already spread out on the couch again, and he keeps nodding for a good while about lunch.

"After this," I say. "It's almost over. And I have to shower real quick."

"Go now," Kayla says. "We'll tell you what happens."

Zed points at the TV. "Hey, that dude's from *Green Acres*."

Kayla rolls her eyes. "O.K., *I'll* tell you what happens. Now go."

But when I come back out she's in the kitchen on the phone and the final credits are rolling. Zed lifts his chin from his chest and watches me combing my hair. "Eddie Albert," he says.

"I know who it is," I tell him, a little more rudely than called for. "What happened?"

Zed's face tightens in concentration. "I think she fucked the bullfighter." He nods, then adds, "Definitely."

Kayla hangs up the phone and comes up behind me. "We ready?"

I bitch most of the way to Bodean's (Bodacious Burgers & Barbeque 24 Hours!), because now I'm going to have to read the end of the book, at least. Kayla insists on buying my lunch to make up for it, but mostly so I'll shut up. Once

the food comes I start feeling a lot better. "This is unbelievable," I moan. "I can feel it going right onto my ass."

"Bodacious!" Zed says.

"I thought you were running now," Kayla says.

"I'd have to run to New Orleans to burn this off."

"We should make a run to New Orleans," Zed says,
though not to anyone in particular, and I look at Kayla
like, where did you get this guy? Once I'm full I start feeling guilty for bitching so much and offer to buy dessert,
which prompts Zed to say, "Righteous," even though I
didn't necessarily mean his, too.

"Let's get coffees," Kayla says. "Those caramel
thingees."

"Coffee?" Zed says. "That's not dessert. D.Q. is dessert.
What's up with you new people, anyway."

"New people," I repeat. "He sounds like Nother."

"What's *that* supposed to mean?" he asks, like I
insulted him, which is a mind boggling thought in itself.

"He called us new the other day, which I thought was
funny since Kayla's been here two years. That's all."

"She's dating him," Kayla warns Zed.

Zed gives me the slow once over. "What's that like?"

"Now, what's *that* supposed to mean?" I ask back, since
he made it sound like I live in the woods or something.

Zed shrugs. "So, what do you guys do? I mean, when
you go out?"

"We just hung out one night, actually. At his house." I
shrug. "It was fun. Buddy Guy was there. My dad got loaded."

"You take your dad on dates?"

"It wasn't a date. We just kind of ended up there." I
don't know why I'm backing away from it, especially to
this moron, though he probably doesn't mean any harm.
"It was O.K."

"They delivered a calf," Kayla informs him, which answers his first question, more or less.

"See," Zed replies. On the way to the car I ask him if he's known Nother a long time. "Since we were little," he says, holding his hand out level about waist high. "But mostly just who he is. We never did nothing."

"What's his real name?" Kayla asks.

"He's always been Nother that I know of."

"He's got to have a real name," I insist. "Like, for his permanent record and stuff."

"Why?" Zed questions. "Not like he's going anywhere."

I exhale loudly and slam the car door.

"I didn't mean it bad," he says. "They just stay around is all."

"Whatever."

Which makes him feel bad, I guess, because he says O.K., fine, he'll buy the coffees, which prompts Kayla to inform him that he's not even going. "I need to talk to Teri alone," she says. "Nothing personal." So we're all smoothing things over on the ride back to school—it's not like he's even pissed, actually—with everyone saying "no problem" and "that's cool" about six hundred times each before we dump him in the parking lot to smoke out with the people cutting whatever period it is now.

We have to go all the way over by the college to get coffee, because it's the only place around that makes the fancy ones we like—the ones that don't taste like coffee, in other words. I start imitating Zed just to give Kayla a hard time, asking why she brought that goofball along in the first place, which she would certainly demand of me if it was the other way around, and she says because he had weed, of course, which we could be smoking more of right now, she adds, if I could have mellowed out a little, because it turns out she really didn't need to talk to me alone, she was just ditching him so we'd quit arguing, which I say we weren't even doing that much. "And coffee's way better when you're buzzed," she says, "And mine wore off at lunch."

We turn onto Faulkner and I start counting my money while we wait at the light, to make sure I can cover the coffees. "Man, I need a job," I decide. So far it's been just my allowance, but Pops has been slipping me money too, or making up things for me to do so he can fork it over. "I need some cash flow."

"I hear that," Kayla says, scanning the next block for a parking spot. "Maybe those people are leaving." I look up as we ease through the intersection and there's my mom coming out of The Chickory with some guy. She stops next to one of the tables out front, and when he catches up they exchange words and laugh, their heads almost touching. "Shit," I say, sinking as low as I can get while we cruise by. My mom must be looking over, because Kayla fucking waves, and I can't tell if she's laughing at the look on my mom's face, or that I'm curled up like a shrimp on the floor.

"OH-my-God!" she says between gasps. "Now I really wish I was high." She drives another couple blocks then turns to circle back, howling the whole time. "Now I have seen everything."

"Let's just get out of here."

"We didn't get coffee yet."

"We can't now! What if they're still there?"

"They were leaving," Kayla says. "I saw them turn up toward the Ad Building." She looks down at me. "I think it's safe to come up now."

We're back at the same intersection again. "I'm supposed to be sick. Getting caught over here wouldn't be good."

"Well, this is the last place you're likely to run into her now, right? And I doubt she wants to see you any more than you want to see her." Then she busts up again pulling into an angled slot across from the coffee place. "If you could have seen yourself down there."

And still I pay for her coffee. She tries to get me talking about finding jobs, like maybe we can get some place to hire both of us, but I can't focus. I've got to assume that guy was Carl, and even though it wasn't anything, they did look pretty comfortable together. Enough so I felt embarrassed to be watching. And what if Pops had seen that; I mean, he's just on the next block at the campus, which isn't that big. Before long I'm pretty agitated, and so, naturally, I start trashing Zed again. Like, what is that blockhead doing dissing Nother, who, by his own admission, he doesn't really even know. "I mean, look at *him!* Hat on backwards, that snuff circle on the back pocket. I'll bet he's got a spit cup in his car."

"That's why I drove," Kayla says, which is a joke, I think.

"So then, who's the freak?"

"Am I arguing?" she asks.

"Sorry. It's not even him. He's just the easiest target." I put out my cigarette. "Maybe I should rent that movie tonight so I can see the end of it *and* have a reason not to talk to my mom."

"You need a reason?" She crumples a napkin and sticks it in her cup. "Your French test got pushed back til tomorrow."

"Who said that?"

"Zed. He's got Duvalier last period, and he's assuming theirs is postponed, too."

The concept of Zed speaking French totally freezes my brain. "Is he at all reliable?"

"Well, I'd verify about the test, but I'm pretty sure he's right about the bullfighter."

I finally catch up with Nother on Wednesday. It's a bright, breezy day so our table is dry, though the stone bench on my side is pretty cold, and I have to sit on my French book to keep my butt from freezing. Kayla is telling me how Joley called asking if she thought it was too soon to start dating again. "You know (long dramatic sigh), after Ronnie," she mimics. "I mean, Jesus!"

"Well, it's been six whole weeks," I calculate. "And she's still so young." But my heart's not in it today, so I page through my French notes to see how I made out on some of the conjugations, while Kayla provides commentary on our parading classmates, yet fails to announce Nother's approach. So he just sort of appears, a sudden shadow across my notebook, and I have to squint to tell who it is.

"Hey," he says. He doesn't smile, exactly, just has that same placid look from the other night, and his hair is kind of blown forward, haloing his face.

"Hey, yourself," I answer, lifting a hand to shade my eyes. I scoot down the bench, which turns out to be not the most graceful maneuver as I have to reach down to move my book, too. "Sit down. Do you know Kayla?"

"Hey," Nother says again.

"Hey, yourself," Kayla echoes, deliberately mocking me, though Nother doesn't seem to notice.

He turns to me. "I didn't know where to look but here," he says.

"I figured that." We sit for several minutes without anyone saying anything, which you'd think would be really awkward, but isn't. It happened a couple times the other night, too, but Nother exudes this calmness, like how you get listening to reggae, or with Vicodin.

"Hey, you guys should exchange numbers," Kayla chirps when she can't stand it anymore, like this is some really clever idea she just this second thought of. "That way, if it ever rains again, you could, like, still stay in touch!" She smiles hugely across the table while I tap my middle finger on my notebook.

He gives me his number, dictating in French when he sees my notes, then unslings his backpack to stow the corner on which I've written mine. "I got something," he says, reaching into the main compartment of his pack. He pulls out a CD, the cover of which is a digital photo obviously snapped the other night: three figures seated in silhouette in the faint light, two of them bent over guitars, the third facing them, mesmerized. A spangle of colored lights borders the top, and near the bottom is scrawled the crooked signature of Crosscut Martin—with regards. "For your dad."

"Whoa, he'll freak," I say, turning it over in my hands. The back has a list of songs, the first three of which, it is noted, were recorded the other night. "Thanks," I say, passing it to Kayla, who has her palm out to see. "He's going to lose it when I give it to him."

"You can hear them talking between songs."

"My dad?"

"All of them. It's not the clearest recording, I'll warn you right now, but after I messed with it a little you could understand them."

"So, is that what you were doing when you left me with Ruth?" He disappeared inside for about twenty minutes at one point, which was fine, actually, as it gave me time to devour my food before he got back.

"Yeah. I cleaned it up later, though."

"I wondered where you took off to."

"Well, they're getting up there, those two, so it's a good idea to keep the tape rolling." He says this totally matter-of-fact, absent of any gloom or morbidity, yet sincere as a prayer. Then, perhaps to address any suggestion that he'd abandoned me, he says, "And you didn't look like you would touch your food while I was there." My jaw drops slightly, and I can feel my cheeks flush when I look at him. "Ruthie's like that," he says. Kayla arches her eyebrows and studies Nother across the table. When she hands back the CD she grips it a second too long, and her expression suggests to me that this could all get pretty interesting.

But then Joley breezes up, breaking free from a group heading for the parking lot while blathering conspicuously into her new cell phone. She drops her books onto the table and frowns quizzically at Nother, then glances from Kayla to me as if to determine which of us is to blame for this. She turns suddenly and half sits on the edge of the table, and begins speaking emphatically to whoever is unfortunate enough to be on the other end. Joley has this odd talent for always making it seem like you interrupted her, and I can tell already that this new toy will play right into that.

Nother re-shoulders his pack and shifts so he's straddling the bench facing me. "Can you come out Friday?" he asks.

"Yeah, that'd be great." I'm not sure if "come out" is just his weird way of saying "go out," like on a date, or if he means come out to his house again, but I figure either one is O.K.

"You don't have to leave," Kayla tells him. But it's obvious to anyone within fifty feet that Joley is winding up her call, and then someone will have to deal with her. And Nother, I suspect, is too sharp for that.

He stands up. "I'll call you tomorrow," he says, which comes out almost as a request, so I nod, then thank him again for the CD. He adjusts his pack and then dips his head slightly toward Kayla. "See you."

We watch him move past the babbling Joley, then disappear into the corner door of the building. "Where do you figure he's going?" Kayla wonders. Next period doesn't start for another ten minutes, and you're supposed to stay in or out.

"No idea," I admit. I can hardly picture him sitting in class at all. "Told you he was nice."

"We shall see." She passes me a Vantage and we light up. "I've got to admit I'm a little let down, though." She pauses to unleash a huge plume of smoke at the back of Joley's head. "I mean, I was figuring he'd do a C-section on a goat or something."

"I said all RIGHT!" Joley says into the phone. She pushes off the edge of the table and settles next to Kayla, who rolls her eyes at the performance. "Yes. Yes. Fine. Bye." She takes the phone from her ear and stares at it til the light goes out. It's a recent acquisition, the latest in a series of palliatives offered up by her bamboozled parents–along with a pierced navel and new Doc Martens which she's also sporting today, among others–in the aftermath of Ronnie Foster; Kayla says if she was ten she'd have a pony by now. Joley sighs loudly and snaps the phone shut. "Total access is not the godsend we've been led to believe," she announces, cramming the phone into her purse and pulling out her smokes.

"I told you not to give him that number yet," Kayla says.

"I know, Kayla." She lights up and shakes her head resignedly at me. "Am I a total sleaze to go out this soon?"

she asks. "I mean, like, my mom says just go if I feel like it, and let people think what they want."

"Who listens to their mom?" Kayla asks.

I nod. "It does set a dangerous precedent."

"Shit. You know, we didn't even go out that long is the thing. I know that sounds really bad, but like, if we'd have just broke up that night, and all the rest of that wouldn't have happened, I wouldn't think twice." Which, I calculate, would probably double her running total for thinking. "And that car is soooo bitchin'."

I glance over at Kayla; all I can think of are all those hugs and tears, and us sitting with her in that stuffy TV room listening to her sob for two weeks straight, and her taking a front row seat at the funeral. And now she's ready to bag all that because someone else came along. But she's going to do what she wants, so what's the sense in bringing any of that up? "Well, it doesn't matter what anyone says," I tell her. "Your mom's right about that. So, I guess if it feels O.K. to you, then you should probably go."

"Yeah...but I still don't want everyone trashing me the rest of the year."

"Well, couldn't you keep this new thing low profile for a while. Not like you have to sneak around or anything, just kind of, you know, under the radar. Let people get used to it, and a little more time go by."

"Like Charles and Camilla," Kayla suggests.

Joley glares at her. "That's a good idea," she tells me. "Kind of like we're just hanging out, right, not really dating, *per se.*"

"*Per se,*" Kayla mocks. "You kill me. And need I remind you that this guy's got a TIDE logo across the hood of his Firebird. Somehow, I don't think low profile is going to suit."

"Is she serious?" I ask.

Joley nods. "He races," she explains. "I'm supposed to go watch him in Jackson on Saturday." She puts her hand to her ear like she's on the phone. "That's what that was all about."

"Does he go here?"

"Used to. He's older."

I nod. "What year did he graduate?"

"No one said that," Kayla points out.

"Shut up," Joley says. "Ruckus is a mechanic," she says. "He makes good money, too."

"All of which goes back into that car," Kayla says.

"Not all! He got me these already." She lifts her hair away from her ears and I swear, she's got these little crescent wrenches dangling from her earlobes. "They really open and close, too."

I'm speechless. Half is the earrings, but I'm also dumbstruck at what someone named Ruckus could possibly be like. But then I think, Nother? and figure I'd best let that one slide for now. "Well, Jackson is probably safe," I offer up instead. "I mean, how many people are you likely to run into there?"

"The whole auto shop class, to name twenty," Kayla says. "Maybe you and Nother can check it out, too."

"Oh yeah," Joley says, "what was *he* doing here?"

"Talking to me, why?"

"Because he's a loner freak, I guess."

"Why does everyone think that?"

"Don't they live way out in the boonies, like on a farm or something? And where does he get those clothes?" She says "farm" like you'd say "landfill." Or "Mongolia." "And supposedly," she adds, leaning across the table and lowering her voice, "there's mixed blood. Just so you know." Her phone goes off, and she mouths the word "black" while she digs in her purse. She flips it open to check the faceplate, then says, "Yes, Ruckus," while she gathers up her stuff. And with a wave, she's gone, cigarette in one hand, phone pinched between her ear and shoulder while we stare after her.

"Not bad enough he's farm trash," Kayla laments. "T'aint even *white* farm trash."

"*Per se.*"

The answer to the going out/coming out confusion winds up being both. Nother apologizes for the ambiguity when he calls Thursday night, and confirms that he did mean go out, like to a movie or something. But since then he's learned that his nephew's birthday is being celebrated on Friday, at Esther's house, which he wants to go to at least long enough to drop off a present, and if I'd like to join him, then maybe we could do something after. Which is cool with me; I've met half of them already, and Ruthie will be there, who I already like a lot. I offer to drive out to his place, in view of Kayla's warning about his ancient pickup, and Nother says he was hoping I'd say that, so score one for me.

I ask about the new calf and he tells me both mother and daughter (daughter!) are doing fine, and that they've named her Madeleine, at his mother's behest, which strikes me as pretty elegant for a cow, but I don't say anything. It gets me thinking about his mom, though, and I ask if she'll be at the party, and he says yeah, unless she has a client show up unexpectedly, which happens a lot. When I suggest that this seems like a rather incongruous blind spot for a seer, he doesn't get the joke—he doesn't laugh, anyway—and says he's hopeful she can come. He doesn't seem to have much of a sense of humor, actually, at least that I've noticed so far, but it doesn't make him all gloomy, either, like you might think.

We talk for twenty minutes. I'm expecting it to be awkward since we've just met, and Nother doesn't seem like much of a phone person to begin with. But he holds up his end just fine, and he's actually quite charming, not even getting flustered when I flirt with him a little at the end, though he doesn't flirt back. He has this seamless way of turning the conversation back on you, which most guys never do, so I end up talking a lot–though that's no big surprise. But what is surprising is that he actually responds to what I say, without boomeranging everything back onto himself, like any other guy I know would, but which is actually sort of a downside in Nother's case, because there's way more than just farm boy going on here.

He's not eloquent, exactly, and well-read probably isn't accurate either, but his background seems wide-ranging, to say the least, and certainly eclectic: music, of course; animals wild and domestic, which was vividly apparent that first night; the woods; more art than you'd think; a good bit of history; and an almost grandfatherly insight into people and circumstance that totally belies his (our!) years, and which I guess could only come from being the offspring of an itinerant balladeer and an ethereal reader of cards. In this same twenty minutes he manages to reference (yes, I made a list): Elvis, Sun Records, Charlemagne, cubism, Annie Oakley, Debussy, the Doppler effect, Sitting Bull, First Manassas, Theresa of Avila, William Tell, a play by August Wilson, and Woody Woodpecker. Which is quite the mix no matter who you are, especially in light of the fact that it seems like I'm steering the conversation the whole time, and I know nothing about half this stuff.

All of which has me even more confounded by the time I hang up. I mean, he seems really sweet; I barely know him, I realize, but no one else does, either, so why this massive disparity in assessments? I mean, you'd think he was a serial killer the way people's faces twist up, and how their voices get all curious and questioning when his name comes up. Why is it I see unique and introspective where everyone else sees geek-loner?

"Herd mentality," Pops says. "Someone said it once, and someone else thought it sounded good, and it goes from there. People tend to get weird around things they don't understand, and your new friend here seems to fall into that category."

"Dad, could you do me a huge favor and start calling him Nother, please? Instead of 'my new friend,' or 'my little friend?' It's like you're talking about a vibrator or something."

Pops arches his eyebrows and his lips pinch in distaste. "Point taken."

"Well, you met him, what did you think?"

Pops exhales and takes a minute to answer. Finally he shrugs and says, "He seemed like a nice kid, I guess. I'm sorry if that sounds overly fatherly, but to be honest, I didn't give it too much thought at the time."

I nod. "Yeah, it was getting kind of late by then. I mean, for you guys, anyway."

Pops chuckles at my politesse. "Honey," he confides, "if that bottle had made it around one more time, I'd have thought he was twins."

Which is pretty funny for my dad. I'm not even sure why I ask, actually. It's not like Pops would notice what he was wearing, or his hair or anything. So even if he'd said he thought Nother was totally cool, that would have just been one more thing to worry about. "The important thing is what you think," Pops says.

"I like him," I say, which comes out sounding like I'm trying to convince both of us, so I add, "I think he's hot," which only elicits another pinched frown from him. "It's just kind of weird how everyone else thinks he's a freak. I mean, it feels like there's this giant practical joke going on, and I'm the butt of it."

"And yet," he reminds me, "two months ago you couldn't have cared less what any of these people thought."

"I don't really care *now*. I'm just saying it's just strange, is all."

"Well, it would be worse to miss out on something good because of it. Then it goes from strange to pitiful, maybe even pathetic. So why not go with your instincts and see what happens? And keep in mind he's taking a chance on you, too. No one here knows what you're about, either."

"Very true," I allow. I think back to Baltimore, and the several new kids who invariably appeared each September. I remember thinking how weird that must be for them, to come into a new place with no baggage, while all the rest of us were already tagged and sorted and stuck in our little niches and cliques. I recall being jealous of how they were free to make their choices now, rather than back whenever it was that all the rest of us had cast our lot, and how they were even able to reinvent themselves completely without any of us knowing they had, which would have obliged us to make fun of them, of course, mocking their audacity, as we did the few of our own who dared return transformed at the end of summer. And now I'm one of those people; no one knows what I'm like or who I was before. So if I start hanging out with Nother, they'll all just kind of shrug and think: I guess she's the kind of chick who'd hang out with someone like him, and go back to concentrating on their own measly lives, just like we did in Baltimore.

The thing is, I don't really sense that freedom, that feeling of infinite possibility I was sure all the new kids in Baltimore were savoring. And I have no frame of reference for Nother, either, which you'd think would be of only marginal concern to the new girl, the one with nothing to lose, anyway. Not so, it turns out.

Nother's place looks a lot more like a house this time. A funky house, to be sure, but definitely somewhere people might live. When I pull up right at seven, there's a spotlight bathing the driveway in a harsh white glare, like someone might be working on their car, though no one is, or shooting baskets, except there's no hoop, either. The drooping strings of lights along the roofline and window trim are off today, and there aren't so many cars in the yard, so it doesn't seem quite so much like a roadhouse, or some equally lurid business best tinted in flickering reds and blues. It's still an odd looking place, though, with all its bungled corners and shadows that even the gloam can't mask. Each unfortunate addition seems to have its own door, too, so that when I park and get out (just off the gravel in the yard), I'm not sure at which one to announce myself.

The spotlight, angled downward from the nearest corner of the roof, has obliterated the view under the carport, and it is from this wide, black shadow that Nother emerges. He approaches slowly, crunching (shoes!) across the gravel to the side of the car where I've paused to ponder this wealth of doors.

"Different car," he notes by way of a greeting, giving the Honda the once over.

"My mom's." We stand there a minute, and then I nod toward the house. "Which is the front door? I might have stood here all night."

"Over here," he says, angling back across the driveway. He indicates a side door just before the awning, which might be the one nearest the driveway, I'll grant, but by no stretch could it be considered the front-most. I notice he's holding some sort of tool, which glints under the light when he waves at the door. "That's the one we use most, anyway." He steps half into the shadow and waits til I catch up, then leads the way through the clutter to the backyard. "I was back here, though," he says, which I take to mean he wouldn't have heard me knock, anyway.

The scattering of tables from the other night is gone, save the hulking one near the barbeque that looks to be permanent. A light beside the kitchen door illuminates the patio, though at a much dimmer wattage than the one out front; the chili peppers hang darkly this night. On the lone table sits a radio tuned low to gospel music, along with what appears to be a really wide belt, an open pocket knife, a flat round can of shoe polish (I think), and several rags. It seems I've caught Nother in mid-task. "What's all this?"

"Daniel's present," he says. "Who you met the other night in the barn." He holds up the leather, which I calculate would circle the kid I saw twice, and has the strangest buckle I've ever seen, and which I must be gawking at because he says, "It's a guitar strap."

"I knew that," I reply instantly, meaning, of course, I had no clue. He passes it across the table, and it is only when I have it in my hands that I take note how elaborate it is. The outside is tanned to the deepest brown, barely shy of black, and an intricate pattern of swirls lace up and down the hide. On the inside a wide quilted lining is stitched into the leather, blood red and speckled with stars, like it's been cut straight from some sorcerer's coat. The ornate fastener, what I mistook for a buckle, is polished to a high, silvery shine. I turn it over several times, massaging the pliant leather with the ball of my thumb, at one point pressing the pillowy cloth to my cheek. "Where'd you find something like this around here?" I ask, breathing in the musky odor of the hide before handing it back. "Must have cost a fortune."

"Made it," he says. "Hardly cost anything."

"What do you mean, 'made it?'" I demand, snatching it back from him. I examine it again, letting my fingers run over the etched markings, each perfectly inscribed, then meticulously worked over with some type of oil or emollient to soften the cut edge, so that it has the antique look and conditioned suppleness of something a hundred years old. The sewing, too, is precise, each suture half the distance you'd expect from the last, without a dropped stitch or loose end to be seen. And then, near the bottom and still moist with oil, three initials which I'd failed to notice the first time, Daniel's I assume, aligned, darkened, and softened just above the shiny metal edge. I glance from the leather to the implements scattered on the table, then to Nother, who stares back expressionless. Then, despite myself, and all the evidence spread before me, I allow the question to slip out. "You did this?"

"Yeah." He takes it back and stands up. "I'll show you." I follow him beneath the carport where he yanks a pull chain to snap on a dull yellow light. Beneath the bare bulb is a stout, homemade workbench, atop which is spread a piece of animal hide perhaps three by four feet. Nother sets the finished piece along the edge from which it was cut. "From here, see." I run my hand over the skin, which is smooth and stiff and only slightly darker in color than my fingers, hardly able to believe the two segments had recently been one. Around the edge of the table are several knives and leather punches, a pointed dangerous looking thing I believe is called an awl, and various lighter-fluid type cans of tannin and leather conditioner. "Almost ran out of time," he says, continuing to work the oil into the letters with his thumb. "Didn't think to do the initials til after." He frowns at this, like he can hardly excuse the oversight, then kills the light, chasing us back onto the patio. He takes a rag from the table and works over the spot some more, til any glistening evidence of the last application of oil is gone. "Hope he likes it," he says, laying it carefully on the table.

"I'm sure he'll love it."

"You want something to drink? Some ice tea?"

I stare at the strap until he returns, following the paisley curves with my eyes while my head swims in the music of the Lord. "Thanks," I say when he sets a glass in front of me. "Who's this singing?"

He listens for a moment. "Mahalia Jackson."

"Nice." I sip my tea. "How'd you learn to do that?"

He shrugs. "Just learned, I guess." Then he says, "Ruth helped with the stitching."

"Still."

"My brother made a saddle once." Which might be the answer to where he learned, possibly, though I haven't begun to unlock just how his mind works.

"I'm certain Daniel would rather have this," I kid, which he doesn't get. "He, uh, does play, doesn't he?"

Nother nods. "Getting good, too." He flips the strap over to expose the cloth. "This here, it's from his favorite pajamas when he was little." He half rolls his eyes, like it's too corny to report, let alone think about for too long. "That was Ruth's idea."

"That is totally cool."

"We'll see."

We sit on either side of the table with the guitar strap laid out between us. The music seems to fill the void just right, and I doubt there's much either of us could say that would sound better. Nother periodically leans over the table to scrutinize one part of the leather or another, like he's seeing every miniscule imperfection on the thing, though it's nothing short of gorgeous no matter how close you look, the care and craftsmanship obvious as a lighthouse.

Ruthie comes out from the kitchen and gives me a quick wave as she approaches. "Sorry to interrupt this lively conversation, you guys, but I'm going to head over."

"Mom, too?"

"She's with someone. So just go on."

"You want to come with us?" I ask.

"Thanks, but I've got to take Dad a car," she says. She turns to Nother. "He left the barn lit again. Could you?"

"Yeah, we're going to go look at Madeleine, anyway."

"Madeleine," she echoes, a hint of wonder in her voice. "And I get called Ruth."

"Does seem we do better with animals," Nother agrees. Once Ruth leaves we start down the driveway toward the barn. "You don't mind going over there for a while?" he asks as we cross the road.

"I want to see when you give Daniel his present," I tell him. "How old is he?"

"Thirteen." We pass through the gate and down the tractor path. "In here," he says when we get nearer the barn, indicating the small pasture to our right. We crawl through a split rail fence into ankle deep grass, where Esme and Madeleine are huddled beneath a stunted oak. "Watch for shit," he advises as we start across the field.

Madeleine steps cautiously out to meet us. "She is sooo cute," I say, bending to pet the calf, who begins rubbing her neck against my leg. I put out my other hand and she begins licking my palm with her sandpapery tongue, while Esme goes back to her grazing.

"Looks like you made a friend," Nother says, then goes off to extinguish the lights and close up the barn. When he returns we start back. Madeleine escorts us as far as the fence, and when we turn for a last look after clambering through, she's staring after us quizzically, as if we've stepped through a mirror. When we start up the path she unleashes a short, sharp bleat, then gambols back to her mother.

"It must be nice being around animals everyday," I say. "I mean, I know it's a lot of work, but it must make you feel...centered, maybe?"

He doesn't say anything at first; probably he's never thought of it before, or maybe he's just never heard anyone use "centered" like that. "It does give perspective," he says finally.

I offer to drive to Esther's house, so he goes inside to tell his mom we're leaving. When he comes out a minute later he's got a flannel layered over his tee shirt that gives off the barest hint of sandalwood as he settles into the car. The gift for Daniel is cradled in his hands, folded several times and tied with a red bow.

Except for a few houses set well back from the road, and the occasional gas station/bait shop, the countryside is unlit and empty, but Nother's directions are precise. He gives ample warning for each turn, but without the extraneous details most people throw in, so we're able to talk around it. I say something about it being too bad his mom can't come, and he says it happens a lot. Someone calls all freaked out or depressed, or just shows up from somewhere through word of mouth, and Madame Marie will usually see them. Nother implies that she's amply compensated for her gift, which is partly why they've put up with the steady stream of hollow-eyed strangers for all these years.

"That would be weird, I think."

"She does O.K. with it," he says. "You don't get much choice with something like that, anyway." He points to the flashing signal in the distance. "Left there," he directs. "I mean, it kind of picks you."

"So, when did she first know?" I ask. "That had to be a pretty spooky thing to discover about yourself. Or did she always have it?"

"Since me," Nother says. "She almost died when I was born. They never did figure out why, but she was really close. She claims she did for a while."

"Die?"

"Yeah. She was in a coma for three days. Then she just woke up, and one of the first things she did was predict this barn catching fire."

"You mean, just like that?" I snap my fingers.

"She was home a few days," he clarifies. "Then she got this premonition, but really strong. The thing was, she hardly knew the people whose barn it was, but she saw it just the same in her head. And then there was a lightning storm and *Boom!* There went the barn."

"Wow! Had she warned them?"

He shakes his head. "Didn't see the point. They wouldn't have believed her, and what could they have done, anyway? Then, when it happened, she got really scared. For a long time only my dad knew, but then she decided she had to deal with it, and so she started reading about it, and keeping a log of all her dreams, and making trips to New Orleans where she knew other people like her, so she could get some control over it. Because at first, it was really random. Or at least it seemed that way. But after a while, patterns started to emerge, and she started to figure it."

"And you believe this?" I ask. "I'm not being mean or anything, I'm just asking."

"I think I do."

"Does she do you guys? I mean, does your whole family always know everything ahead of time?"

"It doesn't seem to work so well with us. But sometimes when something happens, you can tell she knew. Mostly, though, it's other people. Like when Ronnie Foster got killed, she knew that."

"She did? Really? How do you know?"

"She described it to me. That same night, I mean, just after midnight. The skid, the pole, the car flipping over; pretty much the whole scene, just like she was there. And she knew somehow that the person driving was a kid, which is why she told me, because she figured I'd know him."

"But it didn't even happen til after two."

"I know. But she still got it all right; it was like she watched the whole thing happen." He turns toward me. "What I think is, I think she saw what that cop saw. Like through his eyes. I think he was there."

"Lot of people have said that."

"I think that's why she asked me to go to the funeral. Not that there was anything she could have done about it, she didn't even know who it was, but sometimes she feels obligated. I think this time she was feeling that cop's guilt.

Not that I know that much about it, psychologically or whatever, but it makes sense that way to me."

"It does," I agree. "It makes perfect sense, in fact. Has she mentioned that to anyone else? Like, official?"

"My mother doesn't talk to anyone official if she can help it. Most of them think she's nuts." He points again. "Right, here."

I start forming this really exotic picture of his mom; this total gypsy woman, all dark and mysterious, with a bandanna and big hoop earrings, and all these layers of skirts and capes and stuff, which I want to dismiss even as I'm doing it, except that everything about these people is some degree of unlikely, so ruling out anything at this point seems premature.

"Would you want to know?" I ask him. "If she knew something about you?"

"There was something about me, once," he says. "But she's never said what." He waves out his window at an aluminum sided ranch house with half a dozen cars out front. "This is it here."

I park on the lawn, since that seems to be how they do it, and we listen to the engine tick and watch people inside move past the picture window. "That would creep me out" I say. The breeze through his window wafts the scent of sandalwood over me, and again I see my image of his mother, though now cast in a more ominous light.

Nother tightens up the bow. "Ready?" he asks, curtailing any further speculation.

"Could we at least wait til they're out of the driveway to start talking about them?" Ruth suggests. She scans the assortment of containers on the counter, then selects one and begins transferring globs of potato salad into it from a

serving bowl. "My Lord."

"Relax, Ruthie," Seth says from the table, where most of the remaining adults, and one dozing child, are arranged. "Nobody means anything by it."

Ruth glances over and frowns. "Then why say it?" She places two cold hamburgers in aluminum foil and runs hot water over the congealed fat on the plate.

"Honda," Ron announces, entering from the front room with Jacob in a headlock. He releases the boy and retakes his place at the table. "Thought that was a Jap car."

"Nother and that girl was holding hands," Jacob reports. "I saw."

"Lots of people drive foreign cars," Ruth says tiredly, crossing the kitchen with several Tupperware bowls and the meat balanced on one arm. She opens the refrigerator and stares, then wedges the container of potato salad, and another of sliced melon, onto a crowded lower shelf. "And it's not nice to spy, Jake."

"I wasn't spying," Jake replies. "We're playing flashlight tag and I was hiding by the cars."

"Your wife's losing it," Seth tells Ron. "Little brother starts getting some and she flips out."

Liza shifts in her father's lap and half-opens her eyes. "Some what?" she asks dreamily.

"Good one, Seth," Esther says. "Nicely done." She gets up from beside him and begins gathering cake plates and coffee cups, which she carries to the space Ruth has just cleared.

"Nothing, baby, go back to sleep," Seth coaxes, stroking the girl's hair.

"I know what that means," Jacob says.

"It means shut up and go find your brother," his father tells him. "We're fixing to leave in a minute."

"Now, how old is that one?" Esther asks as the boy slips

out the patio door. She gathers up the remaining cups and frowns at the large chunk of untouched birthday cake, then carries everything to the counter.

"Nine," someone says from the table.

"Lord," Esther says. She whacks off a chunk of the cake and wraps it on a paper plate. "Take this for your mom," she tells Ruth, who is placing the last of the cups in the dishwasher.

"You want me to start this?"

Esther nods. "Thanks, Hon. Now go sit; I can get the rest."

This gathering of the clan, just now winding down as the hour approaches midnight, is thinner than last week's soiree; it is all but unheard of to see all nine of Crosscut's children together at once, save for his birthday bash at the homestead, just past, and perhaps Christmas Day, though attendance then tends to be serial rather than aggregate. It's not that the siblings don't get along—they do, and remarkably well at that, but with spouses, ex-spouses, and children accounted for, the total approaches thirty, far too unwieldy a number to pull together very often, let alone twice in the same week.

Six of the nine have turned out this night, along with assorted spouses and children, and several unrelated friends of the celebrant, now a lofty teen. The most surprising presence is Crosscut himself; when he is not on the road, Fridays will usually find him headlining at The Sawmill, a blues shack on the road toward Jackson he assumed ownership of a dozen years ago, which is now operated by two of the missing brood, which accounts for their absence. Attendance at the 'Mill, it has been noted, along with the nightly take, tends to swell when Crosscut is in the house, and never has it been suggested that the man can't add.

He had arrived in late afternoon, just as the first round of food and drinks were put out, a token appearance, Esther had assumed, but welcome nonetheless, for Daniel's sake. He'd come to sit a spell and pick with his grandson, he'd announced, who had lately shown both promise and inclination. And with that he handed over one of his several venerable instruments, a well-fingered Gibson several times as old as the boy, who could barely maintain a grip on the thing for his excitement. Daniel was effusive in his gratitude, his thanks a jumbled and seemingly endless torrent, until the old man quelled the nonsense with a flick of his wrist and the instruction, "Zip it and play, boy, night's a coming." And so they did, knee to knee on kitchen chairs while the house filled and the sunlight faded, the old man instructing, cajoling, directing the mostly two man jam with a series of grunts and nods until nearly eleven, at which point Crosscut bid a laconic farewell and was gone–bound for the last set at The Sawmill, all present assumed, thus freeing the rest to take their leave as well.

Nother, who had briefly joined the session at his father's insistence, but then solely to demonstrate to Daniel a rather convoluted chord progression the boy couldn't quite envision, is the first to follow. There ensues an extended leave taking, in which his companion is challenged to circle the table matching names to faces, which she does, more or less, to their great amazement and laughter, culminating in loud applause and high-fives from Seth and Ron, along with instructions to never refer to either of them as "sir" again. Ruth pauses in her clean up to give the girl a hug, then Ron walks them as far as the porch, at which point, precisely, the conversation at the table shifts to the youngest of the siblings and the girl.

"Well, I think she's nice," Rachel concludes, following the requisite crudities from Seth, and Jacob's progress report. She is the oldest, at forty-five, half-sister to Ruth and Nother, nearly the age of their mother. "And putting up with this bunch, too."

"Amen to that," Ruth concurs.

"Nobody said she wasn't nice," Seth points out. "And I think we're all glad the boy's hooking up."

"Dad sure took a shine to her," Elizabeth notes. "Had her sitting over there next to him half the night, talking at her between songs about God knows what. He never does that."

"He was acting pretty nice," Esther agrees.

"Never does that, either."

"Yeah, and he gave Daniel that guitar. All of a sudden he's Mr. Personality."

"And yet, you wouldn't let him take your son over to the 'Mill for a birthday jam," Seth laments.

"That's because I didn't want my son ending his thirteenth birthday underneath some bar slut his grandfather found for him."

Ron looks up. "Really?"

Ruth nods toward Seth, who shrugs. "I think I was fifteen."

"Wait, so like—"

"I'll fill it in on the way home," Ruth says. "Let's just drop it for now."

"Call them kids in here, would you Philip?" Esther asks her husband, who is standing near the back door. Without answering he steps onto the patio and whistles twice, loudly, then yells for the hiders and seekers to round it up. Esther looks up from wiping the table when he steps back inside. "Thanks."

Seconds later the screen door bangs open and the cousins pile in, all talking at once in breathless gasps.

When the last is inside and accounted for, Phil slides both doors shut and latches the interior one, then herds as many as possible down the hall to wash up, but mainly to get them out of the kitchen.

"Can she baby-sit us?" Liza asks, roused from sleep by the commotion.

"I'm going to," Daniel says. "I'm thirteen now." He looks at his uncle and rubs his fingertips over his thumb. "Money."

"Hey, bring that guitar in here one time," Seth says, ignoring the job application. "Crosscut never gave me no guitar."

"I want Nother and Teri," Liza whines. "Daddy."

"We'll see, baby. Now stand up a second so Daddy can see this." He takes the instrument from his nephew and whistles. "Probably older than your aunt, here," he tells Daniel, nodding across the table at Rachel, who immediately begins rubbing her eye prominently with her middle finger.

"Any of your cousins start acting up you can just whack them with that strap," Philip says. The rest, who have begun filtering back in, stop and eye each other warily.

"Don't put ideas in his head," Esther warns.

Seth rests the guitar in his lap and examines the leather acutely, his fingers slowly tracing each stitch and swirl. "Damn," he says finally, stretching out the word with due reverence. "That boy does nice work." He looks around the table. "I'm serious."

"We know," Ruth says.

Seth fingers the leather a minute longer, then hands the instrument back to Daniel. "Hell, if he's that handy with everything, it's no wonder the girl is smiling like that."

Rachel exhales painfully. "Jesus Christ, Seth, there's only, like, ten kids standing right here."

"And you're embarrassing my son," Esther informs him with a nod toward Daniel, who is beet red as he exits the kitchen.

"He's thirteen; nothing he doesn't hear everyday at school."

"I know what that means, too," Jake says. "And I'm only nine."

"And if you want to make it to ten, go get in the car," Seth tells him, "we're leaving."

"Right behind you," Ron says, giving Ruth a nudge. "You ready?"

"Don't forget that cake," Esther reminds her. "And that's your bowl there, I think."

The gathering disperses quickly, as usually happens when the first of them finally recovers from the post-feast stupor and makes for the door. Ordinarily, they'd have all followed Nother's lead an hour ago, but it's likely to be Thanksgiving before the next gathering of any size convenes, so the opportunity to discuss this latest development–courtesy of Nother's timely exit–delays the departure of the others.

"Well, that went O.K.," Ron determines on the ride home, in that way couples assess social events in the immediate aftermath.

"Yeah," Ruth agrees distractedly, drumming her fingers on the side of the bowl in her lap. After another minute she says, "They make a cute couple. I'm happy for Nother."

"They seem pretty, uh...."

"Smitten," She decides for him.

"O.K.," Ron allows, "I'll go with smitten." There is another quiet stretch, then he asks, "So, what was that Seth was saying."

"I was hoping you'd forget," Ruth sighs. "It's kind of embarrassing, actually. See, my father likes to help, um, break in the men in the family." Ron glances over, eye-brows fully arched. "Not himself," she clarifies, backhand-ing him across the arm. "He takes them on the road at some point, and well." She ends the explanation with a shrug. "It's a fucked-up right of passage, I guess. Like, he took Seth with him to New Orleans once, then kind of looked the other way." She shrugs again. "Of course, Seth couldn't keep his mouth shut about it, and we come to find out he did the same thing with Ezra, except it was Kansas City, I think. Maybe St. Louis. And he's probably back working it for Luke since his divorce."

"Damn," Ron says. "Nother, too?"

Ruth nods. "Hell, Crosscut dragged him all across Texas for a month two summers ago. I figure he's been inside every honky-tonk between here and Abilene, and Lord knows what else."

"I'll be."

"Don't go romanticizing it now, Ron. It's fucked-up."

"I didn't say anything. I just said, 'I'll be.'"

"Then you agree it's fucked-up?"

"I don't know. Big Bob never took me out like that. I'd have to think about it."

Ruth rolls her eyes. "Fucking men," she says tiredly.

"Hey, he didn't take me to New Orleans. How is it I'm catching the blame for this?"

"You have a dick, don't you?" This, too, is an accusation, though delivered with more resignation than acrimony.

Now normally, this inquiry might have led to any number of indelicate, and perhaps humorous, responses, but he has already misspoken once, and Ron is some-what less simple than he is inclined to let on. "Well, he doesn't seem any worse off for it," he replies instead. "Nother, I mean."

"*Yeah, but how would you know with him?*" she points out. "*I mean, he wouldn't be announcing it every time, either.*"

"*I've never even see him with any girls. Anyone at all, for that matter. He spends all his time in the woods. Or working on something out back.*"

"*Well, he spends a lot of time at The Sawmill, too. Mostly sitting on the coolers listening to music, according to Sara. But when Crosscut's out there, he likes to drag Nother up to play with him, and then get him all mixed up with the riff-raff, like messing with all the drunks is a good life lesson for a sixteen year old.*"

"*Yeah, but he sure can play,*" Ron says, slowing for the driveway.

"*That's always the excuse.*"

"*They must not have went out,*" Ron says, motioning toward the Honda parked in the yard. As they watch, the passenger door opens and Nother steps out, then leans back inside for a long minute before letting the door close. He squints into the glare of their headlights, then turns and walks into the house. Ron glances over at his wife. "*Must not have went in, either.*"

"*You think they've been sitting there this whole time?*" Ruth asks. The Honda starts up and they watch it execute a delicate star turn on what little grass there is. The girl edges the darkened car past them with a shy, misty wave, then cuts on the headlights as she turns onto the road.

"*Well, I don't think they design them windows to fog up by themselves,*" Ron answers, taking the spot just vacated and killing the lights.

My mother has decided that we should both make a trip back East at Christmas. It'll be fun, she insists, though I don't recall ever committing to going myself, and if I did, I'm quite positive she wasn't part of the package. She's been hovering around all morning, since we got back with the muffins and the coffees and the Sunday paper a few hours ago, flitting between the kitchen table, where she has papers from her briefcase sorted and spread, and the front door, which is open onto a beautiful fall day. I'm in the recliner with my French book, and her movements are making me nervous. Gail is not the fidgety type, and she does not flit as a general rule, so I fear the worst. "Are you expecting someone?" I ask finally. "Is there someone coming over?" If she invited him here—in broad daylight, I can't help but think—without telling me, I will be sooo pissed.

"What?" she says, turning into the room from the door. "No. Like who?"

"Like anyone."

Again she denies it, then proceeds to remark on the gorgeous crisp afternoon. Which is true enough, though it's not the type of thing she'd be likely to notice, much less comment on. But I agree that it has become a more tolerable place of late, particularly in view of the early Arctic blast they're suffering in Baltimore at present. Which offers precisely the segue she needs to bring up the Christmas trip. My mother is one of those "oh, by the way..." types who tend to impart the most vital bits of incredibly pertinent info in the most offhand manner: "Oh, by the way, I've fixed you up with Martha's son; he's grown since you've last seen him." Or, "Oh, did I mention we're moving to Mississippi?" or, "Oh, before it slips my mind, it seems a meteor's going to hit the house." This time it seems she feels a compelling need to touch base with the crowd back East, though it is unclear why, and apparently is not the kind of thing she can just come out and say.

"Well, I can stay at G's house," I tell her. "But I haven't decided yet for sure."

"Yes, we'll have to see," she replies, returning to the table. Which means I'll come home one of these days and there'll be a printout from Priceline or Expedia laying on the table with our confirmation numbers highlighted, and her nowhere in sight. A done deal, in other words. She's a case study in political maneuvering; like how if the President decides to do something, one or two of his aides mentions it first, in passing, then the President says something about it in a speech to some gun club, or in front of a bunch of factory workers, and then the real spinning starts, and the next thing you know it's administration policy, set in stone, and they've got you half-convinced that you asked for it in the first place.

Which is what's going to happen with this trip, I just know it.

Gail's other way of letting me—or anyone—know what's on her mind, or to warn what's about to hit them, is this weird habit she has of "thinking out loud." Like, she'll want to say something, but rather than just come out and say it, she'll start talking about something else entirely, until eventually the conversation steers near enough to what she really means to say that she can just sort of innocently start touching around it, til *Bam*, she's got you square in the middle of it, and you don't even know how. She likes to bring up "talking points" when she's "thinking out loud." These are both terms she actually uses. So it seems all innocent, almost like you're eavesdropping on her thoughts or something. Then, if you do disagree or protest or get mad, she'll just fall back on this Miss Innocent pose, like she didn't even know she was saying it out loud, and how rude you are for trashing her half-formed musings, and you're the one that ends up feeling like shit. But, if you don't call her on it right then, if you just let her talk like that, then it just ends up happening how she wants it, and she'll say, "Don't you remember us talking about it?" or some such shit. So either way you lose.

But this trip doesn't seem to be the end of it, either, because she's still up and down from the table every ten minutes, or switching back and forth from the piles of manuscript pages on the table and the newspaper, which I'm certain have nothing to do with one another. So when she starts knocking around looking for her laptop, and against my better judgment, I ask, "Mom, is something bothering you?"

"Bothering me? Like what?"

Which I knew was coming. "Anything. You seem kind of jumpy."

"Really? Sorry." She carries the laptop from the kitchen counter to the table and opens it. "What about you?" She settles her hands in her lap and turns toward me. "How are you doing?"

"Fine," I say cautiously.

"Everything's good?"

"Not bad," I answer. I tell her that school's getting better, that I don't feel all new and stuff anymore, and that I met this guy I kind of like, which I think she knows anyway. I don't want to get all into it with her, especially about Nother, but telling her is making me feel better, like I actually am doing O.K.

"Well, good," she says. She starts clicking files open, but I think it's a ruse. "Maybe I can meet him sometime." So maybe that's where she's headed. Maybe Pops mentioned Nother and now she's feeling left out because I haven't said anything to her about it. Which probably would annoy her, as much hearing it from him as being left out of the loop by me. But she's so in her own world nowadays that you don't even want to say anything to her, for fear of disrupting the big picture, whatever that might be.

Or maybe she's getting ready to blast me for not meeting Carl yet, but feels she has to behave better first by asking to meet Nother. Which would not be an overly elaborate bit of misdirection for her. "Yeah, sure," I say. "Maybe I'll invite him over this week." And instantly there's this picture in my head, straight off one of the cable channels Pops favors: a baby springbok, pronking blithely on the savannah, a step too far from the herd, and completely ignorant of the fact that this documentary is about the Big Cats.

"Wonderful," she says. "And I'm glad to know you're settling in." She glances over with a brittle smile, and I understand this isn't entirely about me. "It's a relief to know you're doing well."

"What is it, Mom?"

She sighs. "Nothing, really. I guess I just thought I'd be back on track sooner."

"It's all new for you," I remind her.

She says she knows, but still. And that she's sure she'll get the hang of it before long, and that Annie says she's doing great as it is, but Gail's not so sure. And this doubt has her wondering now if maybe her decision to come here had been a bit rash, perhaps, with too many extraneous considerations factored in. Which is what has her thinking about the trip back East, to show her face around the department again, and catch up on all the dirt and office politics.

"So, what then, you're going back?" I ask. Strangely, I feel no emotion, nothing more than the mildest consternation. "Because that's what it sounds like."

"No, no," she answers quickly. She's just keeping her options open. Maybe hash through a few things with a few trusted colleagues at Hopkins, get some other perspectives. She's committed here til June, she states, though this comes out sounding pretty lame as commitments go. The main thing (she tells me!) is to focus on herself for once, just her, and to figure out once and for all where she needs to be.

Which I can't really disagree with, except that the unspoken corollary in all of this is that any movement *vis a vis* "just her" would automatically include me, too. What I really want to ask is: Shouldn't you have thought about all this *last year*, when all our stuff was still in Baltimore, before you dragged me halfway across the country and plopped me down on the edge of a swamp where I didn't know a soul? Maybe?

"Well, look," I tell her, "if you think going back for a visit would do you some good, then you should go. And, if you want me to come along, I will." I try to make this sound all business-like, because usually if she thinks you're being nice, it just pisses her off. "But otherwise, I want to hold off deciding."

"Thank you," she says.

"You talk to Dad about this?"

"Lord, no." She lifts up a thick sheaf of pages, then slaps it back onto the table. "I've been reading him, though."

"That's Dad's book?" I ask, which probably comes out sounding too enthusiastic for her, though mainly it's surprise—that he actually wrote it, and that she has it now.

"Part of it."

I'm at the table instantly, riffling through the stack, which is clipped into chapters with titles like: "A Brief History Of Anger," and "In Yo' Face: Rap And The Ascendance Of Insolence." She has four sections, a total of about eighty pages, which is pretty good for three months. Hell, that would be cranking even for Gail, and she's a machine once she gets going. For Pops, it's almost a miracle, and I've seen sections on his side that aren't even part of what's here. "Damn," I say, straightening them back into one stack. "Who'd have guessed?"

"Even your father is being productive," she groans. "*More* productive, in fact." She looks toward the ceiling and shakes her head. "Talk about insult to injury."

"Do you think that's why he showed it to you? 'In yo' face.'"

"No, and I didn't say that."

"You *are* happy for him, aren't you? I mean, you ought to be. You've been on his case for years. Even I'm sick of all that publish or perish crap."

"Yes, of course I'm happy for him." Which comes out with no conviction whatsoever, followed by a long sigh. "I'm just kind of surprised, I guess. I figured he'd perished long ago."

I should probably point out that Gail has a whole shelf of books with her name down the binding. Two or three all her own—one of them widely used in her area, and half a dozen that she co-authored or contributed to, along with a few more she edited. This, along with fifty or sixty published articles, and God knows how many presentations at conferences, not to mention leadership positions in several national and international organizations, and rotating editorial duties with many of the refereed journals in her discipline.

Pops, on the other hand, has no books to his credit— jointly, editorially, or otherwise. His dissertation is unpublished as well, except for a chapter that appeared in a collection of related pieces assembled long ago by his major professor. His last, in what amounts to only a smattering of published articles, appeared in a second rate popular culture journal in the mid-nineties. His value is at the departmental level, where he is prominent and tireless; advising the new students (who love him), chairing the search committee, escorting visiting scholars, pouring the wine, cubing the cheese. His inclinations run more toward the gregarious and utilitarian than the academic; he's a mixer and a fixer, my father is, much more likely to help arrange a conference or symposium than sit on one of its panels. So, while my mother is the one you might point out across the lobby to a colleague, it is Pops who you'd call out to, who you might even seek out to ascertain where the day's social hour was convening. And it is this distinction that defines the rest of their lives as well, so that while you might be heartened to find yourself in her good graces, you'd be infinitely more at ease finding him to your left at dinner.

"It is pretty amazing," I say. "Why is it that you have it?"

"He asked me to look at it," she says. "He's been talking about it since we got here, but I figured it was just talk, so when he kept saying he was going to have me take a look, I said, sure, fine. Because I figured it wouldn't happen anyway. I mean, how long has it been, ten years? Then *Boom!*" She riffles a corner of the stack, letting it slap back on the table.

"So, um, is it any good?"

She makes this sort of dismissive motion with her hand, like she's flicking a mosquito at her ear. "I don't know. I mean, I don't ever read stuff like this. I don't know what to think." She looks at me and shrugs. "It reads really fast, so I guess that's good. But, then again, there's probably not one thing in here that any twelve year old with half a brain doesn't already know."

"Ouch, Mom."

"I'm not saying that to be mean. But it's all just really...obvious, I think. The whole premise is obvious. I mean, when you start out with something this broad—basically, an overview of bad behavior—how hard is it to fill up pages with examples? Rap music is rude. *Newsflash!*"

"So it's just a big waste?" I'm going to be really bummed if that's the case, not only for all the wasted effort, but for what it might do to Pops.

"I didn't say that. I mean, it flows nicely, too. Your father has a nice touch, a really nice touch, in fact, which I find totally inexplicable, in that he so rarely employs it. And it's organized. And there's a lot that's easy to grab hold of." She glances down at the pile and back up at me. "So, it's either woefully unpublishable, or a potential best seller. And I suppose nowadays it could be both."

"Can you imagine...." my voice trails off.

"What, your father on *Oprah*? That's no stretch. Hell, he's a walking sound bite as it is. Ever since that friend of yours died, the paper calls him every time they need a quote."

"He wasn't my friend."

She waves a hand at the manuscript. "Eighty pages of sound bite, right there. And he'll probably have a hundred more by Christmas."

"Is that good or bad?"

"It is what it is, as they say."

"I hate when they say that."

"Sorry," she replies with a shrug. "I don't have your father's gift."

"So what are you going to tell him?"

"I think just what I told you, and I'll suggest he push on with it. Who knows?"

Joley is demanding the scoop. "So, like, has he spent any money on you at all?"

"What?"

"Well, so far all you guys do is hang out with his family in the sticks. I mean, what's that about?"

"I like his family. They're fun and they're really nice."

"No, no," Kayla interrupts. "What she means is, when is Nother going to give you some aluminum guitar picks to wear in your ears?"

"They're silver!" Joley declares, the miniature wrenches swinging defiantly from her lobes. "Ruckus ain't no cheapskate."

"I don't know," Kayla says, "sitting in the bleachers watching him spin around in the dirt isn't my idea of a big night out."

"I think we all know what your idea of a big night out involves," Joley answers with a pinched smile.

"I'd rather watch Nother deliver a calf, I think."

"Why do you even sit with her?" Joley asks me. "She is so negative. Do you have to ride in that junky truck of his?"

"We took my car."

"He made you drive? Teri, you need to straighten that guy out. Or better yet, dump him before anyone else finds out. I could get you hooked up in no time." She clicks her fingers twice to demonstrate how fast, which makes Kayla's eyes bug out.

"I'm going to see how this goes," I tell her. "But just for the record, I think you guys are totally off about Nother. He's not at all like you think."

Joley has already gathered her books. "Well, someone's totally off, that's for sure. But, whatever." She stands up and tugs her skirt. "The offer stands, though. I could fix you up easy."

"Click, click," Kayla says.

When she's out of earshot I turn to Kayla. "How much did you tell her?"

Kayla shrugs. "All but the part about his mom seeing the wreck, which I didn't think she could handle. And I kind of glossed over the part where you guys mauled each other in the car. Same reason."

"Aren't you thoughtful," I praise. "Why tell her anything?"

"Well, I had to give her something after she copped to boffing Speed Racer out at the Trees on Saturday night."

"She did! That Ruckus guy? She told you that?"

Kayla snaps her fingers twice.

"In the woods?"

"Hey, she's a sucker for those muscle cars," Kayla says. She digs in her purse and tosses me a cigarette. "Remember that Cutlass Ronnie had?"

"She—"

"All summer long."

"Damn."

Kayla nods slowly. "But at least they weren't doing it in his front yard."

I take the lighter from her. "We weren't doing it, either."

She forces a plume of smoke out the side of her mouth and arches her eyebrows. "Yet," she says.

I cave and invite Nother over to study, because if we start hanging out a lot he's going to have to meet Gail sooner or later, so we might as well get it over with. Not that I assume it will automatically be a disaster; my mother can be a real charmer when she wants to be, but the potential is definitely there. So the plan is to have him come here, and then the first chance we get, we bolt for Pops's side, since he'll be at campus and I can tell Gail we need a quiet place to spread out our stuff. None of which will fool her for a second, but I can deal with that later.

I'm on eggshells waiting, though, even as several things are falling into place. Gail's been having a much better week for one thing; she's got some major new project she's all gung ho about, so her confidence is way up, and at least I'm dealing with the devil I know again. She's got two hulking binders splayed open at the table, along with a couple of wide reams of printed data, a legal pad, and an empty latte grande cup from The Chickory. She's still wearing the outfit she left in this morning, and there's been no mention of dinner. She's totally distracted, I realize, which is good. I think she may have even forgotten he's coming over, which is good, too; she won't have prepared any cute repartee. And with all her work laid out, it makes even more sense that we go next door.

I wrap up my debriefing just as Nother pulls up, and extract a promise from my mother not to ask about, or even so much as comment on, his name. "I'll behave, I promise," she assures me, marking out a column of figures on her pad with a firm line. "Please relax." But her face muscles have been twitching the whole time, and her eyes keep darting down to the pages on the table, so I know she hasn't heard a word I've said.

I snatch up the empty cup as a door closes outside. "Can I toss this?"

"What?" She glances up distractedly. "Yes, of course."

As I step outside, Nother is crossing the yard, the beater Chevy pickup I keep hearing about behind him on the street. "Hey," he says, mounting the steps and handing over a plastic sack.

"What's this?" I ask, squeezing his arm as I take the bag.

"Ice cream." He gives me a quick, warm hug back.

We go inside and Gail stands up from the table. She takes a last, furtive look at what she's just written, then crosses the room. "Mom, this is Nother." I glance at him. "My mom."

Nother sets his backpack against the wall and extends his hand. "Pleased to meet you," he says softly, his head dipping ever so slightly, like in *The Godfather*.

"I've heard a lot about you," Gail replies, which isn't exactly true, but O.K. since it doesn't have any of that nudge-nudge insinuation I might have expected.

I almost start to relax until I notice that they're both looking at me, and I realize I should probably be saying something right about now to keep things rolling. "Ice cream," I blurt finally, hoisting the bag up in front of her like a pelt.

"How nice," she replies, giving me an odd look. She lobs me an easy one. "What kind?"

I peer into the bag. "Rum Raisin–"

"My favorite."

"And...Chocolate Chunk."

"Your favorite." She looks at Nother and raises her eyebrows. "Two for two," she tells him. "You should hit one of the riverboats." She nods toward the fridge, helping me out again, then directs Nother into the living room, where they take seats on the couch.

"Would anyone like anything?" I ask from the kitchen. "Coke? Tea?"

"You haven't eaten," my mother remembers suddenly. "Should we get something? A pizza?" Her eyes dart between Nother and me, the question open to the floor. "I'm sorry, I totally zoned out."

"I'm fine," Nother says.

"I had something with Kayla," I lie, taking the chair nearest his side of the couch.

"If you're sure then." She clears her throat, and suddenly I feel like Nother's defense counsel, sitting there angled slightly toward her, ready to fend off whatever might come. "So, you're from this area, I understand," Gail begins. "Your family, I mean."

"Yes, ma'am, on my father's side." He speaks calmly, unhurried; he mentions several parcels of land that Crosscut has acquired piecemeal over many years, which are now overseen by Ron and two of the brothers. It's interesting the way he lays it out, with an almost methodical disinterest, like it could only have happened this way.

"Well, I'll bet he's seen quite a few changes in all that time," Gail suggests when he finishes.

Nother ponders this briefly, then replies, "It's pretty static, actually."

"Well, that can be good, too, I suppose. Does your father work on the land, also?"

"No, ma'am, he's a musician, mainly."

"I told you that," I remind her. I make it sound kind of like a question, though, like maybe I meant to and forgot. I don't want to be rude and show her up, especially when she's behaving herself.

"Yes, I suppose you did." She makes this waving motion with her hand. "Like this?" she asks, meaning the classical music coming from the radio.

"Bartok? No, ma'am. He plays blues."

Gail and I exchange looks. Neither of us would have a clue in hell if he was right or not, but it's an impressive bluff if nothing else, and I can't help but grin slightly. Nother speaks of Crosscut, and the countless other Delta bluesmen spawned on this same small patch of earth.

He mentions the legends from Clarksdale, and others, and even Gail is paying attention because of the way he tells it, though she doesn't give a rat's ass about music in general. She only listens to classical because there are no words to distract her.

"And your mother?" Gail asks presently. "Is she a musician as well?"

"I guess you'd call her a consultant."

"In?"

Nother purses his lips, then answers, "Contingencies."

"Ooh, sounds complicated," my mother says.

"You look busy, too," Nother comments, nodding toward the table.

"Tell me about it," she says.

Which is the opening I've been waiting for. We've been holding this pose plenty long enough, I figure; things can only tube from here. I pause for another minute, then rise. "Well, look, we're going to get out of your way then."

"I thought you were going to study?"

"We are. But we need to spread out, so we'll just go next door." I make that same waving motion she did and wince. "Maybe listen to something else."

She opens and shuts her mouth. It's too sensible to argue, at least in front of him, and the alternative is to shut ourselves in my room, which she can't very well suggest, either. Her eyes narrow, and she shoots me a look acknowledging all this, and perhaps even some grudging admiration for the maneuver. "All right, then," she says. They both stand and she asks, "What are you working on?"

"I've got a history test," Nother says.

"But mostly he's going to help me with my French," I add. "He just doesn't know it yet." I look at her and nod toward Nother. "Fluent."

"Really?" Gail says, appraising him in light of this new information. "I wouldn't have assumed that around here."

"My mother spoke it growing up," he explains. "Still does with us." He licks his lips. "I didn't know it was two languages until I started school."

We grab our packs and the three of us gather by the door. As Nother stares out, she shoots me another look, this one saying, you've got yourself a live one, sister. "Well, at least take the ice cream," she says, striding to the fridge to retrieve the bag. "You can't just study the whole time." Her mouth immediately clamps shut at the various implications.

I leave her hanging for just a second. "How about we take the chocolate, and you work on the rum stuff?"

"Fair enough," she says, lifting one of the cartons out and handing me the bag. "Or do you like this, too?" she asks Nother.

"The chocolate is fine," he tells her as we step onto the porch, then bids good evening with that same little head bow, and we're out of there.

"Well, that went better than I expected," I tell him as I let us in on Pops' side. I flick on the light and cross the kitchen while he sets our packs on the table. "My mother's not always so...agreeable."

"Is that how come you don't trust her?"

"I didn't say that, exactly."

"Just seems." His eyes slowly scan the room. "This is completely separate, then?"

"Yep."

"Isn't that kind of unusual?"

"We may have invented it."

I get us Cokes and show him around a bit; he's impressed by the reams of pages that will hopefully be Pops' book stacked on the desk, like he never realized that actual people turn those things out. "Weird he'd be so impressed by someone playing a guitar."

We settle in and get down to work, or at least he does. I watch him pull a thick notebook from his pack and spread it open in front of him. He leans close over the table above it, his elbows resting on his thighs, eyes trained on what looks from here to be a surprisingly well ordered set of notes; all titled lists, numerated indentations, and under-scoring. In pen, no less, and definitely not the ragtag scrib-ble my notes amount to, so that half of my time gets taken up deciphering.

He reviews each page exhaustively, his gaze sweeping slowly from top to bottom; when he comes to a list his eyes close while he mouths its contents, before opening again to gauge his recall. It's almost a pity to interrupt him, but I do, several times, the first to ask what, exactly, his test covers. Andrew Jackson to the Compromise of 1850, he says, and then they'll spend the rest of the term (til January!) on the War Between The States, those four years to be accorded equal time to the previous four score and change.

We keep at it for an hour or so, Nother diligently reviewing his precise notes, me interrupting. It's not all that different from being here with Pops any other night, except I think Pops is easier to keep distracted. Still, he doesn't seem to mind the interruptions, which mostly have to do with questions about my French homework that he can handle no problem. I was kind of hoping he'd be more help, but I soon realize any insight I was expecting is futile; he doesn't really have to process it, any more than I have to process English, he just knows it. It's not even translation for him—it's reading.

I get the last few sentences worked out just as Nother reaches the end of his notes. While I finish his eyes scan

the room, and he begins quizzing me down in French:
What color is the carpet? How many apples are on the
counter? Where is my father? I do not even get this last
answered when we hear a car door outside, and then Pops
is fidgeting with the screen door in the dark. When he
finally comes in, he appears surprised to find Nother here,
but pleased. He immediately begins to thank Nother for
the CD, telling him he's been listening to nothing else
since I gave it to him, was listening to it just now, in fact, in
the car, and motions out toward the street like we might
want to step outside and confirm it.

Nother gives that little nod to express pleasure that
Pops is enjoying it.

I get out bowls and the ice cream while Pops sheds his
briefcase, which is actually a laptop carrier with a shoulder
strap that he uses to cart his stuff to campus and back.
While he settles in he mentions—to Nother mostly—that
he's been on the internet doing some research into Crosscut's discography, which he is surprised to find is quite
slim, given his lengthy career and recent eminence. They
begin tossing off names I've never heard of, along with a
few I might have, and pretty soon Pops is kind of nodding
like he gets the picture.

I pause, mid-scoop, and lick my finger. "Wait, so like,
Crosscut is on the internet?"

"Oh yeah," Pops says. "I was finding stuff all over the
place." He looks at Nother. "There's this great old picture
of him up at the rock hall of fame in Cleveland. With
Howlin' Wolf?"

Nother nods. "Esther's mom took that," he says. "Used
to be up in our house."

"Hold it," I say. I look from Nother to my dad. "So, you
knew of him before?"

"Yeah," Pops says, which surprises me. "He's one of those names you're always stumbling across. You hear a song and wonder who it is, and it turns out to be him again."

I carry the bowls and spoons to the table. "So, what happened? I mean, that all these other guys got famous and he didn't?"

"That's just the breaks sometimes," Pops says. "And Crosscut never courted it too much from what I know."

Nother nods. "Used to be a bunch of them like that. Played every day, never made a dime. Most of them gone now."

"I saw where someone's putting together a compilation, finally," Pops says.

"Yeah, they finally got around to him."

"That guy salvaged some old names," Pops says. "Whatever his reasons."

"Yeah he did. Threw some nice money at some of them, too. Or their kin, who didn't mind, either."

"Nothing wrong with that," Pops says, sounding suddenly like the great blues aficionado. "Is your father excited?"

"I think he is."

"When does it come out?" I ask. I want to ask if there's going to be a video, too, but I have no idea if that would be totally stupid or not.

"I saw February," Pops says.

"So figure April," Nother translates. "Nothing happens on time with this guy."

I roll my eyes and give her this exasperated look, though I'm actually kind of curious. Kayla fancies herself a pretty keen student of psychology, and she comes by it

honest given Annie's background, so some of her observations are pretty astute. I wouldn't say she's nailed any
major breakthroughs, but she doesn't miss much, either.

"O.K. then," she says, splaying the fingers of both
hands between us on the table, "I think...that...this whole
business with Carl...is your mom's response to your dad
writing that book." We stare at each other for a long
minute, her expression brimming with a smug confiden-
tiality. "Interesting, huh?"

"Oh yeah," I nod, "except for making no sense."

"But it does," she insists. "I mean, first, look at the timing.
When was it Gail first started mentioning Carl? Right after
she found out your dad was working on that book, right?"

"Which makes it sequential, not causative. You've just
committed your classic *post hoc, ergo*...whatever, fallacy."

"*Propter hoc.*"

"Thank you. And quite frankly, Kayla, that's beneath
you. Besides, why wouldn't Gail just start cranking out her
own book if she wanted to even things up? Hers would be
a bigger deal, anyway."

"Ah, why indeed? Because your dad wouldn't care if
she was writing, too. He never cared before when she was
and he wasn't. If the point was to get back at him, that
wouldn't cut it. So what would she do?"

"You tell me."

"Well, what's the best, fastest way? To get right to the
heart of it, so to speak?"

"Carl?"

"Exactly."

I feel my face twist up. Gail is a street fighter when she
needs to be; but I think this is over the top even for her.
"Well, it certainly doesn't paint her in a very good light," I
say. "Especially if she's using Carl like that."

"It's a drastic situation," Kayla says. "I mean, think what she felt like when she saw all those pages, and her in no position to respond in kind. Now consider this: How do we know he didn't start writing that book to get back at her in the first place, for trying to tear the family apart?" She arches her eyebrows; the plot thickens. "Or that she doesn't realize that, too?" She pauses, giving me a stern, knowing look. "It totally fits."

My head is starting to swim, which is pretty common once Kayla gets rolling. Still, I'm having a really hard time thinking any of this about my parents. Either of them. And knowing that Kayla has taken the time to deconstruct it, let alone give it more than passing notice, is annoying. "I think you might be giving them both too much credit," I tell her curtly. "Or not enough."

She arches her eyebrows at my tone, the scientist scorning the believer. "Or I've got enough distance to see it for what it is." She shrugs. "The irony is that this is exactly what he's writing about."

"Just one more example, huh?"

"Makes for a hell of a last chapter," she says.

Madame Marie holds open the door, pressing back against the wall to let the other woman out. A steady rain thrums the tin roof above them, and both stand gazing at the rented Buick parked thirty feet down the driveway. After a moment Madame Marie instructs her patron to wait, then steps back into the house, reappearing after several minutes with a battered, plum-colored umbrella, which she passes to the other one. To get to your car, she explains, nodding at the dripping Buick as if this needs to be specified. She motions with her arm to indicate the driveway, then directs attention to the space beneath the

*awning the woman now occupies. Pull up, Madame Marie
instructs her still shaken inquisitor, and I can take back the
umbrella under here. She pauses. We're both dry then, she
elucidates, hoping that this* pas de deux *might now
become clear to the woman. The seeker looks up–
Madame Marie has remained on the step leading inside–
then vaguely toward the car. She fumbles with the ancient
umbrella, finally succeeding in ratcheting the dome open
and securing the balky latch, then allows a tight, forlorn
smile of gratitude and moves quickly through the rain to
the car.*

*Madame Marie waits on the step, bundled beneath a
redolent shawl against the damp breeze, hands clasped
before her, pressing into the folds of her layered skirts.
The betrayal card, she laments, shaking her head recalling
the poor woman's ashen face. They all looked like that,
like suicides. There was no other way to describe it, the
mixture of shock and agony so familiar from TV and film,
the twisted, panicked contortion just after the shot, the
thrust, the poison, as if they are amazed, ultimately, to discover the truth of their own dripping, gasping mortality,
one final affront in a life crammed full of them.*

*But she had to have known, surely; her very presence
would seem to confirm this. They all know, but the cards
startle nonetheless: Death, Evil, Betrayal. Their worst suspicions confirmed, the knowledge eliciting pinched gasps
before the card is even flush on the felt. A nasty business
at times, but that is what they pay her for–this one, too.
She watches the woman bounce the car forward, then step
behind the vehicle to hand back the umbrella. The driver
is all but catatonic, failing even to realize that she's left the
back half of the Buick exposed, thereby defeating the
whole purpose of the maneuver. She looks a last time at*

Madame Marie, who is blameless but for her knowledge, and delivers the umbrella. Her lips fumble to form words, though none come, and she leaves in silent despair, sloshing down the pitted gravel and back into the gloom.

Madame Marie remains poised on the step until the slanting rain has swallowed up the car, then turns to go inside. She wonders briefly whether the woman will think to turn on her lights, if she still even believes her life worth this modest effort. She pauses, hand raised to the doorknob, and glances toward the rear of the carport, where the back seat from a mid-sixties Chevy Malibu is propped on cinder blocks facing across the yard at the tree line. Two heads are half-visible above the seat back, a whitish curl of smoke from an unseen cigarette drifting toward her through the shadow. Her husband and son, staring silently into the downpour, as she knew they would be, seemingly oblivious to the clatter above them, or the sad scene just concluded at their back. She contemplates stepping over to join them, but doesn't. Rills of rainwater have plaited the pavement, tracing the myriad cracks so that even the covered portion is glutted with puddles, and she is wearing indoor shoes, slippers really, of dark, unsoled felt that would be ruined by a single misstep. Instead she keeps to the stoop, staring across the deepening shadow, wondering if each is truly so enamored of the falling rain, and if not, then who is indulging whom?

She drifts into the house, chased inside by a recurring sense of unease that has lately plagued her. She moves about the room extinguishing candles, snuffing out sticks of incense, adjusting the light from séance level to a degree that allows her to move about without barking her shins on the heavy furniture. Madame Marie picks up the cards and folds the felt covering from the table and places them *in the cabinet, then takes up the overstuffed ottoman upon which her patron had received her unfortunate fate and places it back near the chair. All of it might just as easily stay in place; the room is used for nothing else, it holds no modern amenities save the lamps—no television, no radio, certainly no computer, no guitars. It is exclusively her studio now, set aside for the practice of her curious trade, fortuitously situated to keep contact between her patrons and her family, and all the concomitant distractions of each, to a minimum. And in truth, it is not a room one would care to spend time in, anyway: the aged wallpaper a textured uneasy union of blues and purples; the bulky furniture of similar dark tones, overstuffed and crowding the room unnecessarily; the sconces like gargoyles, ineffectual and, it must be noted, Poe-like. But it serves its purpose, she knows, hinting of the cluttered unknown in its dim, ill-matched antiquity, the cloying aroma of sandalwood and patchouli suggestive, to those already so inclined, of unseen forces at work. It is a room for conjuring, and little else.*

When she finishes she settles into a dusty brocade arm chair angled into the far corner, unable to recall the last time she had spent any appreciable time alone here. Her unease has not dissipated, and it is here she chooses to examine it, as this murky environment seems eminently well suited to the task. It was not the woman just departed, she knows. Madame Marie had been fine seeing her out, though sorry for her misery, naturally. She often experienced a bad moment or two after conveying such news, save the rare instance when the one seated across from her so obviously deserved their sorry lot. No, it was after the woman had gone that she'd become aware of it, triggered, she now supposed, by the thin smoke of her husband's cigarette.

And when she'd turned that way, it had grown, precisely then, in fact, so that she was sure its source was seated in quiet repose on the displaced car seat.

It is a hollow feeling, as if she has lost or misplaced something dear, that has brought with it some strong sense of agitation, so that she rises from the chair almost immediately and begins slowly pacing the room. Upon closer examination, she is able, finally, to distill the feeling further; it is not loss, exactly, that troubles her now, but its forerunner, dread. It has engulfed her on several occasions in the preceding weeks, prompted each time by the voice or proximity of one of the household. In another moment she has narrowed this further: always in the presence of her husband and son, though she cannot discern which of them, precisely, keys her anxiety.

It is Crosscut, of course, who is the obvious suspect. He is old. His habits are dissolute, his diet ruinous. He is a battered advertisement for himself, a weathered billboard for the life of hard luck and bad behavior he so famously sings of. His demise has been expected, even predicted, for years. Many are shocked to discover him still alive. Not those in the know, of course, nor his family, and certainly not Madame Marie. She senses his strength, is amazed at his steely durability. He has told her there is only toughness left, all else has been lived out of him, or left by the side of the road somewheres. And he tells her something else, which she senses to be true: If you are a guitar player, and you are not too pretty, you can live forever.

Which leaves the boy. But he is only sixteen, in the full flower of his youth, and with none of the destructive habits of his peers or his father. Certainly not like that fool classmate of his who had lately demolished a utility pole, and himself in the process. Her son is rational, even-tempered, moderate, exuding the poise and sedate manner of someone several times his age. It is as if, somehow, he has gleaned the collective wisdom of his father's sad ballads, but without accruing the wear, a trick obviously lost on the bluesman.

So she will not speak of it, this premonition; she is helpless to prevent it, in any case, in the strange way in which these things work. To interfere is to tempt fate, to defy the powers, to enter into some mythic drama of hubris and horrible retribution. And to whom would she tell it, anyway? Her husband? The boy? And what, exactly, might she say: "Oh, by the way, one of you is a goner. You, you're old. And you, well...just be careful." No, it would make for an impossible situation, for which they might look to her for answers she did not have. For truth be told, Madame Marie still does not comprehend her gift after all this time, neither its origins nor its investiture in her, for who can fully understand such things? But she has seen, and believes, and so perhaps her comprehension is immaterial. Her husband, too, is a believer; his is the world of the vagabond, of bogus charms, mojos, hoodoos, comprising the marginalized and the bereft, each and all in search of something to latch onto, though vague as to just what. The rest, her children and stepchildren, are believers of the passive sort. Or so she supposes; none has ever challenged her, nor disputed the veracity of divinations attributed to her. But they wouldn't, this bunch; it is a family of tongue-holders, for better or worse, and she must carry her knowledge in silence, too, the price extracted for her prowess. She stops her pacing midstride, a long sigh escaping her lips as she accepts this additional burden. She hears the two in the kitchen, her son's soft words followed by the other's jagged response;

*the rain has surely stopped then, so she cracks the door to
clear the stuffy room.*

Gail is at a conference in New Orleans when grades
come out, so Pops is going to have to sign off on it, which
he does with great enthusiasm before running it through
the printer to make a copy for her. "This is terrific, Teri,"
he gushes as he hands the signed copy over. "Three-six-
seven is pretty solid. Way to go."

I shrug. "My overall was three-eight at Talbot," I
remind him, "and that's a way better school than this."

"I wouldn't be too sure," he says. "And this is quite the
load you've got here: Chemistry, Trig, French...." He
pauses to count the rest of them up. "Six classes, four A's.
Not too shabby."

It could have been worse, I suppose. English was the
only lock; the rest of them could have gone either way,
though I pretty much saw the B coming in French. You're
not going to get the benefit of the doubt when you're new,
especially between an A and a B. Back at Talbot I'd get all
those breaks; I was lumped in with all the smart kids–
Gina's had straight A's since second grade, for instance–
and way too many teachers just go off reputation, which is
a drag for the dumb group, I'd have to assume.

"And another thing to keep in mind," my father says,
"you've been through a lot of changes since Talbot. The
move; the situation with your mother and I; new school;
new friends; new teachers. That's a lot to assimilate all at
once. Frankly, I'm impressed with the way you've handled
it." He nods at the report card in my hand. "And I
wouldn't be surprised to see them up next time, either."

Pops decides we should eat out to celebrate, though
we've never done that before. Normally, I'd bring home

A's and maybe one B, and they'd just nod and say very good, and sign it. I guess it was kind of assumed I'd tear up, so it wasn't anything to be fussed over. Gail might even ask about the B. So, most likely this is just an excuse to eat out. I suggest Bodean's, since Pops is cool with grease, and he goes off to shower. He keeps talking at me from his room, though I can't make out a word of it, then reappears with a towel cinched around his waist.

"I didn't get any of that," I tell him.

"I was just saying you should think back to the first day of class; it might make you appreciate how far you've come in a relatively short time." He nods succinctly and steps into the bathroom. "Just be a sec."

Well, let's see, I think, settling into his only comfortable chair to mull it over. It was hotter than shit back then; I knew one person, total; and I still had pinprick traces of red paint on my wrist. I'd never been to a funeral, or eaten smothered anything, or even so much as heard of a guitar player named Crosscut Martin. So it has been a breathless few months. I hear the shower come on and shake my head at Pops' unwavering buoyancy, how he can always find something positive to grab hold of no matter how desolate things are, or how negative you try to be. Which makes it real easy to be cynical around him, like I'm being now, I suppose. I recall him walking around in just cutoffs and that stupid pith helmet all through August, when I was sure I was going to melt clean away, and how he kept finding things to get excited about, taking these huge gulps of air and telling me to just smell the life all around us, like we'd never drawn a deep breath in Baltimore. Or pointing out every goddamn thing along the side of the road like I was blind, or Mississippi suddenly held title to all the weird shit there was to see.

But I guess our lives are a lot different. I mean, I don't actively notice this duplex nonsense anymore; I still think it's weird that Pops doesn't live with us, especially that he lives so close without living with us, but since I have the run of both sides, it's only a problem when it rains. And if it keeps them from each other's throats, that's a small price to pay. What is kind of surprising, though, is how my whole past life in Baltimore is fading already, which I never would have believed could happen so fast. I remember thinking that this whole move was a sick practical joke, or a bad dream I kept expecting to wake up from and run out to describe to Gina in all its horrific and sweaty detail. Now I go days at a time without even thinking of back there. Gina and I still keep in touch, but sometimes it's weeks, and the e-mails are way shorter than the novellas we were sending at first.

I guess this is finally getting to be normal for me, which I never would have thought could happen, either. Not that it still isn't a really weird place, I'm not saying that. It's still warm out, for instance, not the blast furnace it was when we first got here, but it barely feels like fall yet and it's November. And the way it rains here—I swear, the first three or four times I thought the world was ending. You couldn't even see, it was coming down so hard. I'd just stand there, mesmerized. The thunder still about knocks me over; it's like the weather has a personality down here, and a massive ego to go with it.

I don't feel quite so much like the new girl. I'm used to the rhythm of the day by now, and I know where everything is, and where I'm going most of the time, and who to watch out for and what I can get away with. I've got a home base to work from—our table—and some pretty good analysis from Kayla and Joley. There are others, too;

Sandy hangs with us a lot, and this other girl, Patti, who might hook us up with jobs, and a handful of smokers who all bum cigarettes from each other and nod in the halls. I know lots of faces and half the gossip, and even a few secrets, so how foreign can it still be?

"So by the time we get done eating, he's got me convinced it's a fucking miracle I can even remember my own name, let alone make honor roll."

"You should've asked for a car," Kayla says, frowning at the interior of the Volvo. She's been out a few days and we're getting caught up.

"He's quoting John Lennon and shit."

"What'd *he* ever say about your grades?"

I pull out of Decatur toward her house. "We were talking about being here, and everything being new, and I was saying that even so, it still doesn't seem like much is happening, that we're just sort of, like, doing stuff. How it's just a whole bunch of little things one right after the other, and you don't even notice because you're just waiting for the next big thing. Which is true, kind of. I mean, what are you going to remember about last quarter except for Ronnie Foster?"

"Who?"

Kayla can be so wicked sometimes. "Anyway, my dad said that Lennon said, 'Life is what happens when you're waiting for what's next,' or something like that. Which is cool, but not as cool as he thinks." I slow to turn. "And I finally remembered to ask about his book, and make a big deal out of it, which was fun, since he's not getting it from my mom."

"Getting it," Kayla repeats.

I frown at her. "It was nice seeing him get excited about it, and talking real fast—"

"Like you are now, and every time you mention Nother?" she asks, sounding annoyed all of a sudden. "O.K., it turned into a big love-fest."

I give her this look, like: what's up your ass? "What if it did?"

"Nothing," she says. "That's fine. Just so you had fun." She smiles weakly, totally on purpose.

"Whatever, Kayla."

We ride the rest of the way in silence. "I take it Gail was less impressed, then?" she asks as I pull up at her house, "since you haven't mentioned her reaction."

"She gets back today."

"Oh, that's right, she's out of town." She adjusts her books and pops the door latch. "You know, I think Carl was part of that contingent." She grins mischievously and steps from the car. "See you."

Sometimes she is such a bitch I wonder why I hang out with her at all. Even when she supposedly likes you she can be so fucking hateful. I'm so annoyed I just start driving around talking to myself. I don't want to go home and risk going off on my dad just because I'm pissed at Kayla, or worse, have to deal with Gail in this frame of mind if she happens to be back. So I get a Coke and just cruise, driving north out of town on this perfectly straight, perfectly flat road, with lumpy, plowed-under fields on both sides, and these shacks set way back from the road that I really hope nobody has to live in, but I know they do because there's smoke coming out of all the chimneys, and toys on the porch. I start wondering about all these people who obviously have it way worse than I do; they're poor as shit, for starters, and they probably work way too hard in these same fields, and I'll bet they get pissed off at a lot of the people they know, too. But then I start thinking how most of them are probably more content than I am, and the rest are probably driving these pickup trucks I see parked in front of the bars I'm passing every few miles, and I doubt any of them are crying in their beer for me.

I play with the radio til I get the gospel station tuned in, then watch the fields slide by in the fading light. Pretty soon I start feeling like part of it, this whole pitiless landscape spread out as far as I can see, and these sad, hopeful songs all full of lost souls. I crack the window and the smell of smoke and damp earth fills the car, along with this feeling that what I'm noticing might turn out to be important.

I drive until the shadows stretch long across the fields and the sky has bled to a burnished orange, trying not to think too much and just be in the moment. When the houses go black against the skyline I turn right in hopes of looping back toward town somewhere soon, since I should have been home long ago. I come to a four-lane with a flashing signal and a sign pointing left toward Jackson. The road number looks familiar so I turn right, roughly parallel, I hope, to my route out of town. There are more cars, more signs, more bars, and a big Family Dollar store that seems to be smack in the middle of nowhere, but with the parking lot half-full, and a line of cars backed up at the Wendy's drive thru near the road. This seems like the way, and I'm pretty sure I've even been on this stretch with Pops, so I relax a little and start looking for anything familiar. There's a big old roadhouse out this way, I recall, painted in this gaudy shade that the Maryland basketball fans all refer to as "Carolina" blue, and so would not be caught dead in. And sure enough, a few miles up on the left I see it, sitting like a big patch of sky in the middle of a cratered gravel lot. I'm doing about forty as I come up on it, and this old man leaning on the trunk of a car by the entrance gives me a short wave when I glance over to catch the name of this fine establishment for future reference. At precisely the same instant, I make out the name along the roofline and recognize the old man's hat, and promptly mash down on the brakes and execute a squealing, dust-kicking, and blessedly crater avoiding spin into the lot. I get the car straightened out and ease across the stones, finally pulling in beside Crosscut, who watches calmly with his lips puckered.

"Thought that was you," I say when I've joined him against the trunk of his car.

"Me, all right." He looks me up and down, like he's checking for damage. "Lord word, darlin'."

It is only now that I recall that Crosscut is not the most loquacious sort, and begin to wonder why it was so urgent that I stop. "How'd you know to wave?" I ask. "Or you just wave at everyone?"

He rocks his head and gives that "heh, heh, heh" laugh that's warm as a campfire. "How many yella' cars from Sweden you figure come past here, dear child?"

We watch the dust settle back into the holes, then I turn to inspect The Sawmill. It's a blockish, two-story rectangle with a pitched roof and the door on the left, next to a long horizontal window about shoulder height on me, tinted so I can't see in. Unlike the parking lot, it appears to be in decent repair, with a fresh coat of paint, and the office windows upstairs look like they've recently been replaced. I glance through the open door past a cigarette machine, but other than some shadowy movements and the glow of a few beer lights it's too dim to see anything. I can just make out the faint click of billiard balls, and there's a jukebox playing some bluesy country wail just like you'd expect, and the faint odor of smoke and stale beer.

"Nice place," I say.

"Welcome," he replies.

I lean back against the car and study the lunar surface of the lot, which is full of beater pickups, as anything smaller runs the risk of being swallowed up, I guess. As near as I can tell, mine is the only vehicle not assembled on these shores. "So, how many people have died out here?" I ask, not even knowing I was going to, or where it came from.

"Couple or some," Crosscut says, like he'd half been expecting it. He leans over and nudges me with his shoulder. "And that's without you plowing through like a freight train, neither." He nods for a long time at this, chuckling to himself. "Heh, heh, heh. Damn." He tells me about some guy who lost part of an ear not long after he'd bought the place, and motions over toward a green Chevy Blazer to indicate where. "Over some gal, as I recall. Always is." He strokes his chin, and I hope he's not struggling to pull up details. "Almost got shut down." He mentions that he's only the third owner since the guy who built the place, and rattles off a list of those who've graced its stage: "John Lee Hooker, B.B., Mississippi John Hurt, Tabby Thomas from Baton Rouge, Muddy his own self." The list goes on; Gatemouth Brown, Howlin' Wolf, til the names themselves start sounding like songs. He lets out a breath. "Elvis was here once," he tells me, like it needs to be said. "Carl Perkins with him."

I nod respectfully, though I'm not even sure I know who Carl Perkins is. "And you," I say.

"Me, lots," he confirms.

There are footsteps on the gravel and then Sara is beside us. She's got a cash register tape in one hand, and a leather apron with a bottle opener sticking out of one of the pockets.

"Oh, hey," she says, smiling as her eyes adjust. "I wondered who he was babbling at." She gives the parking lot the once over. "Is Nother here?"

"No, just me," I tell her. "I was just out driving." I shrug, but she nods like this makes perfect sense.

"Well, don't believe a word of it," she says, motioning with a thrust of her head at Crosscut. "He tends to be a little casual with the truth."

"So the Beatles never played here?" I ask.

"Heh, heh, heh. The Beatles, shit."

"Actually, I didn't even know this was it til I got right in front."

"Child, you was half past," Crosscut says.

"Well, she stopped, didn't she?" Sara rebukes. "How many pretty girls talk to you anymore?"

"True," he admits with a somber nod.

"I didn't know it was this far out," I say. "That's quite a haul every day."

"You come from that way it is," Crosscut says, motioning back the way I came. "Only about ten mile thataway."

I nod. "Ahhh."

"You'll come into town by the bank," Sara says.

"O.K., I know now."

"You want a Coke or something?" she asks. "I know he didn't offer."

"No, thanks, I need to get going. I should have been home an hour ago. Didn't want to just drive by, though."

"Come out with Nother sometime," she says. "Hear some music."

"Am I allowed? I mean, is that legal?"

"No, but come anyway."

"Way you drive ain't legal either, but I don't see you handing over the keys," Crosscut says. I climb into the

Volvo and roll down the window. "Tell your daddy," he adds. "And put your lights on."

Sara taps the door as I back out. "Bye, now," she says. "I'll tell Nother."

I'm pulling up at my house when I think of Kayla again, but decide to put the whole episode out of my mind. I don't know if I'm even pissed anymore, but it looks like Gail's home, so one headache at a time. She's on the phone when I walk in, with Annie from the sounds of it. They were great friends a long time ago and they've gotten close again, enough that I can usually tell when it's her just from my mom's end of it. For no reason I can think of I decide to take a shower, and when I come out again toweling my hair, my mother is off the phone and bent over the table sorting receipts.

"How was it?' I ask.

"What? Oh, fine." She glances up. "It was good, actually. Very informative. We brought back a lot of useful ideas."

"Good," I say. "Did you have fun?"

"Fun?" She shrugs. "I suppose."

"Well, I'm glad it was productive, anyway."

"It was." She drums her pen on the table, then reluctantly sets it down. "How are things here?"

"The same." I shrug. "Grades came out. Dad already signed."

"I saw that," she says, lifting a copy of my report card from one of the chairs. She studies it for a long minute, then sets it back on the chair. "And what did he have to say?"

"He was cool with it. I mean, considering everything."

She purses her lips and nods, to indicate she suspected as much. "And you?" she queries, "considering everything?"

"Could have been worse, I guess."

"What a terrific way to look at it," she replies. "It's only the whole rest of your life, right?"

"Aren't you being a tad dramatic?"

"Am I?" she counters. "I'm sorry I'm not as 'cool' with it as you two seem to be." I can't even tell how serious she is; half the time she just wants to fuss.

"Three-six-seven, Mom."

"Darling, you should have been able to ace any one of those classes with your eyes closed."

"Yeah, well, any one of them I probably would have. But there were six, and I still got A's in four. It's honor roll."

"What does that mean here." This is not a question.

"Look, I bombed one test in Chem, and it cost me. My bad totally. Sorry. And if I'd have signed up for French II, like I should have, I wouldn't still be playing catch-up, which is totally what happened there." I'm kind of pissed at her attitude, and that I have to defend a three-six, though I can't say I'm surprised, either. And the thing is, the B in French is almost entirely on her. See, back at Talbot I took Latin freshman year, but then the teacher left, and rather than rehire the position they discontinued it. So last year I started over in honors French, and made A's the whole year. And then when we came here, Gail figured I should just go right into third year French, because, well, that's how she thinks. But even with the accelerated class at Talbot, I was still half a year behind on day one. In light of which, I'd say a B is pretty damn good. And Chemistry, well, Chemistry is just hard.

"Be sure to put that on your college applications," she says. "They love people with excuses for everything."

I'm about to throw something at her. "Look Mom, I don't need to defend an A average, and taking into account all I've been through, I don't want to hear it."

"You poor thing. Like what?"

I start ticking them off. "Moving. New school, new teachers. You guys."

She waits, then asks, "Anything else? Planets not aligned? Poor lighting? Cramps?"

"That's plenty."

"That's your *life*, dear. Deal with it. The world's not going to stop every time you have a little problem, you might as well know that right now. And adversity isn't a virtue in and of itself. So if you're going to be pointing it out, it helps to have overcome it."

"I'd say honor roll is overcoming it, Mom. And I think most parents would be pretty happy with it."

"Like your father, I'll assume?"

"Yep. He even took me out to eat. To celebrate." Unfortunately, this comes out sounding kind of silly.

"I'll feed you," she says. "Get your shoes. But I'm not going to turn cartwheels when I know you can do better. You're right, most parents would be happy. But most parents don't have the daughter I do."

I open and close my mouth. "How do you do that?"

"What?"

"Bitch about a three-six, and still get me to feel bad about it?"

"I know what you're capable of," she says. "You feel bad because you know it, too. And people making excuses for you aren't doing you any favors."

"Dad, you mean."

"Your father's an enabler; I've told you that before. So unless the person interviewing you for that job, or that admission, or that internship, happens to be him, they're not going to give a shit about your little dramas."

"That's a wonderful world you live in, Mom."

"Well, unless there's an option I'm not aware of, you're stuck here, too. So here's a little advice: Take care of business." She reaches to the floor and brings up her laptop. "Let the rest of it take care of itself."

I drape the towel over my head and start for my room. "Yeah, you guys have really made that work."

I note the ping of her computer starting up. "I heard that," she calls after me.

I'm as agitated as I was earlier, so I try calling to mind those empty fields and quiet shacks, and the calmness I felt listening to those gospel tunes. I change into jeans and a sweatshirt and straighten up a bit, tossing clothes onto the floor of my closet and wiping off my desk and computer, which are filthy. There are unread e-mails, I notice, which gets me thinking of Gina, whose voice suddenly echoes in my head: "Stop thinking so much, drink whatever's handed to you, play along as much as you can stand it. Go numb." It occurs to me that Gina may be the reason I didn't have these issues in Baltimore.

As I start to log on there's a knock at the front door and I recognize Nother's soothing timbre through the wall, in marked contrast to Gail's fitful greeting. We've been getting together most nights the last couple of weeks, just the two of us. Joley is convinced the whole clan is trash, so I don't want him to have to be around her at all, and Kayla doesn't like sharing the attention, so her picking can get tiresome. People just don't know what to make of him. Sandy has History with him, for instance, which she didn't even realize til she heard we were going out, and then switched seats so she could watch him in class, and now he's her favorite topic, and I get daily reports. She told me yesterday they were going around the room compiling a list of all the deficiencies that ended up costing the South

during the war, and by the time it got to Nother the list
was pretty much complete, so he said, "Dead Yankees,"
which amused Sandy to no end. "I mean, it wasn't right,
but at the same time it was *exactly* right." She kept bobbing her head when she finished, with her lips pushed
together like she was afraid she might crack up again.
"He's cute, too." Most people are less generous, though, so
it's better that we get together outside of school.

I run my hand through my hair a few times and check
the mirror real quick, then go to rescue him. They're talking about New Orleans, though I can't imagine there's a
lot of overlap of experience. I grab my purse off the couch
and drag him out, and since I haven't eaten we swing
through town to get a slice of pizza, which we eat in the
truck. I like this truck; it's kind of loud, but the cab is huge,
and the seat is wide and way more padded than they are
today, and there's a decent radio. It's kind of like a couch
with wheels. We listen to this oldies station a lot, and
sometimes Nother tells me how his dad knows the singer,
or whoever wrote it, or he was in the studio when it got
recorded. Which is weird because I've never thought of
music like that before, like personally. It was always just
something that came out of the speaker. Nother wants to
show me the studio where Crosscut made his first record,
which is still standing up in Memphis, oddly enough. It's
just a little brick storefront that houses a tiny radio station
now, but the control room in back is pretty much intact,
except that nothing works anymore. "You can't believe the
people that have passed through there," he says, "even
though it looks like they ought to be selling insurance." I'd
like to go up sometime, I think, drive in the dark listening
to old songs and him talking, with the window cracked a
little and some beer, maybe stay up there for the night,

though that idea just this second occurs to me, and I'd
need to patch things up with Kayla to work out an alibi.

But right now we're not listening to tunes or talking
about Memphis. Mostly we're finishing our pizza and he's
listening to me rag on Gail. I can't imagine he wants to
hear it, and eventually I'd like to get around to telling him
I was out at The Sawmill today, but I got started on my
mom on the way to the truck, and now I can't seem to let
it go. "I mean, what did your parents say?"

Nother swallows then takes a hit off the Coke we're
sharing. "I think the expectations are different," he says.
"Your parents have Ph.D.s."

"Why should that have anything to do with it?"

He nods slowly. "That's a good point."

"What *did* your parents say?" I ask again. He got a
three-two, so I'm curious how that played at his house.

"Actually, Ruth signed it," he tells me. He looks over
and shrugs. "She thought it was O.K."

"Why did she sign it?"

"Well, I'd have had to explain what it was to my mom.
She just doesn't operate on that plane anymore, so it seems
kind of silly to even show her. And I don't think Crosscut
knows I'm still in school."

"Really?"

"He's still asleep when I get home. I mean, the whole
idea of expectations just isn't there."

"Must be nice," I say, "because there's nothing you can
do about it. I mean, those are good grades, right?"

"I'd say so."

"What then? I start out way behind in one class–totally
not my fault, and blow one test in another. Other than
that, A's in everything. My dad says 'way to go,' and she
says 'so what.'"

"What do you say?" he asks. He wipes his mouth and looks across the seat. "They are *your* grades."

"Well, I think considering everything, they're pretty good. But I still expect to do better this time since I'm getting caught up, and I know more what to expect."

"That seems like a good way to look at it. Did you say that to your mom, that you expect to do better?"

"No. I was afraid I might kill her if I didn't leave the room."

"Let me ask you this; do you think this is going to hurt your chances getting into college?"

I wipe my hands, then ball up the napkin in my fist. "Probably not. Hell, some places I've already worked myself out of."

"Most though?"

"Not at all. My grades are fine for the places I want to go. It's the places Gail thinks I should apply that are probably long gone."

"No harm, then."

"Exactly. Which is what makes it so exasperating. And I know we're going to get into it again when I start applying. She's going to make it a total pain in the ass, I just know it." I let my head fall back and stare at the top of the cab. "Life's too short for this kind of shit."

"You know, everyone always says that when they're talking about something that bugs them. But if that was the case, then it would be a good thing that life was too short, wouldn't it?"

I roll my head and look at him. "What?"

"Actually, life's too long. Think about it, when someone quits a job they hate, or gets divorced, or whatever, they always say, 'life's too short.' But if life was really too short, they could probably put up with whatever it was til they died. In point of fact, they get out of the situation because life's too long." He pauses and looks over at me. "That's kind of weird."

I arch my eyebrows.

"Think of it this way: let's say you knew you were going to be dead in twenty minutes."

"O.K."

"And then you noticed you were getting a headache. So what, right? You probably wouldn't even take the time to look for aspirin, since you were going to be dead so soon. But let's say instead you knew you were going to live for fifty years. In that case, you'd probably go get something for it, right?"

"Yeah...."

"But it would be the second situation where you'd be more likely to say 'life's too short.'"

"You thought this up yourself?"

"Just sort of came to me."

I slide over and take his arm. "And the point?"

He tosses his napkin onto the dash. "Just an observation."

O.K., here's what I mean about Kayla messing with people, and this is sooo nasty. This morning we're sitting out at our table kind of patching things up from the other day, which isn't overly complicated, in that I'm the one making all the effort, and she's not mad to begin with. She never is. She doesn't care enough about anything to get mad; she just likes to pick. It's an attention thing, and she's got a positive talent for it. If there's a way to get under your skin, she'll find it. But then, if you get pissed off, she acts all surprised, or she didn't mean anything and you're just being a baby, or else she'll just ignore you right back and not even worry about it. She'd never apologize, that's for sure, but if you start coming around again, she's perfectly willing to wipe the slate clean like nothing happened. And somehow she manages to make this work. You'd hope for a little better from a friend, but to be fair, she sets the rules right up front, and you can take it or leave it.

Anyhow, today we were sitting there ragging on our moms like always, and this guy Tony comes over, who's been dogging Kayla for a couple weeks now. She's always got someone sniffing around, but usually it gets taken care of one way or another by this point, though I've pretty much stopped asking for the blow by blow (no pun intended) because I don't always like the story. Anyway, this Tony guy is a senior, and he's pretty cute, I guess, and since he and I have English together next period it's a good excuse for him to hang around. I think they've gone out maybe once, and I don't know what all happened, but she's got him jumping through hoops now. She likes him well enough, from what I can tell. She's usually pretty nice to him, and they flirt raunchy a lot, but then sometimes she'll just really slam him, like, so even I'm embarrassed, and when he asks her out anyway she says no, even though she's not doing anything that night. Which you'd think would get old, and finally seems to be with Tony, though she's a real pro at stringing people along. But he's started missing a day now and then, and he doesn't bug her so much to go out when he's here, so maybe he's wising up. I'd almost feel bad for him, but I can tell he's played the other end of it a few times himself, so he ought to know better.

He's sitting next to her and we're all just talking and Kayla's giving him shit for ignoring her, and we're kind of laughing about it and I can tell she's waiting for him to take the hint and start asking her out again. But he's just kidding her right back and telling me she's just a big tease, and Kayla's going, "Oh yeah, right!" And it starts to get pretty graphic so I say, "Whoa! That's it, I'm out of here," because the bell's about to ring anyway. We're all still laughing while I gather up my stuff and I go ahead and start walking inside, but then I turn to say something and I see they're kind of arm wrestling and bumping each other and laughing and playing that goofy grab-ass kind of stuff you see by the lockers all the time. And then I see her take his hand and just slide his middle finger into her mouth and go up and down on it a few times, and I'm thinking, holy shit, Kayla, it's broad daylight! Then, I swear, she pulls that same hand into her lap—you can't really tell anything for sure because of the table, but she's wearing a really short skirt, and his arm is angled down there too weird to be doing much else, and then there's the fact that his eyes are about to come right out of his head. And then, I swear to Christ, she brings his hand back up so she's kind of holding it in both of hers, and gives him this really tender kiss on the lips, which I wouldn't think to be her style. So she's got his hand right there, and when she pulls back from the kiss she draws his finger just above his upper lip like she's shading in his moustache, and I worry for a second that Tony is going to fucking pass out. I just stand there gaping, thinking, oh-my-fucking-God! Kayla's eyes flash toward me, really quick, and the faintest smirk dances across her lips.

I don't hear a word for the first ten minutes of English, then the door opens and Tony comes slouching in, no pass or explanation, and moving like he's not sure he's even in the right place. And maybe he decides he isn't, because five minutes later he up and walks out, not a word to anyone. By the end of class I've rerun the scene so many times that it starts to play out like a documentary in my head. I can almost hear the voiceover–hushed, slightly British–calling attention to the agitated state of the tumescent male.

"He just got up and left?!" Kayla cackles when I report back to her later. She pounds the steering wheel with the palm of her hand. "That is too funny."

We're parked in front of the Circle K drinking big cinnamon coffees with lots of cream. "You are shameless," I inform her.

She lights up and passes the matches to me. "He should never have called me a tease."

"Somehow I doubt that stunt is going to change his mind," I point out. "And you are stringing him along."

She exhales a long plume of smoke out her window. "True, but I haven't quite decided what to do with him yet."

"And how is that not teasing?"

"It's only teasing if he's got no chance," she explains. "Which is something you need to start thinking about." This comes out almost like a challenge.

"With Nother, you mean?" I shrug, like: no big deal, and sip my coffee. "Maybe we worked it out already."

"You'd have told me."

"You sound pretty sure."

"You'd have to tell someone, and who else is there? Joley? Might as well post it on the internet. And you sure as hell didn't tell Gail."

"God, no!" I cringe just contemplating it. "Besides, I didn't say how it might have gotten worked out."

"You're still together."

"Meaning?"

"Meaning you either have, or you just haven't *yet*."

I drop my cigarette in my cup. "No, that's you," I say as it hisses out.

She arches her eyebrows, impressed, it seems, with my cattiness. "Right. I'm the only one."

"No one said that. But it's not a hundred per cent the other way, either."

"O.K., maybe the evangelicals," she concedes. "But I think even they're lying. Besides, you want to."

I turn and stare at her. "Do I?"

"Yep." She mashes her cigarette in the ashtray and flashes that same smirk from this morning.

"You know, I hate it when you do that. Just say things about me like you know better than I do. It's really annoying."

Kayla nods. "Especially when I'm right, huh?"

"So, are you not seeing Carl anymore?" I ask my mother one evening. I haven't heard his name the last couple of weeks, since before the New Orleans trip, at least. She's been all wrapped up in this new project of hers, some college-wide budget analysis from what I gather, and I haven't seen much of her myself. This might be the first meal we've eaten together in a month.

"Not much," she says. We're eating pasta out of Styrofoam take-out trays, and she's mostly pushing her noodles around the sauce and focusing on her wine. "We weren't 'seeing' each other to begin with, really. I told you that."

"Isn't he part of this big project?" I ask. "He was at that conference in New Orleans, wasn't he?"

"No," she says, giving me a curious look. "I mean, he was, but he's not anymore." I can only assume she means the project, not New Orleans. She sets down her fork and reaches for her wine.

"Oh," I say. "I just hadn't heard you mention him for a while."

She swallows her wine and takes up her fork again. "It wasn't working out, anyway. With the project, I mean. So it's probably just as well."

"Probably," I agree. She spears the tiniest bit of clam, then chews like it's made of rubber. What a weird-ass situation, I think, watching my mom moping over a guy who isn't my dad. I almost feel bad for her. I'd even like to know what happened, but what if it's something bad, like he dumped her, and she started crying. I don't think I could deal, and I probably wouldn't want the details, either, on second thought.

Gail and I have been ships in the night, which isn't necessarily a bad thing. We've gone days without seeing each other, and I'm starting to like fending for myself, not to mention being able to come and go as I please. Her schedule is completely shot. She has to meet with people from all over the university now, so it's often catch-as-catch-can to arrange a time, and then if something comes up, it's Gail who has to make the accommodation. Sometimes she's gone before I wake up, in which case I have to roust Pops from bed for a lift to school. Other mornings she's still in her robe when I absolutely need to leave, pounding on her laptop or blathering into the phone about allocations, fixed costs, retooled parameters, or some such nonsense, and I have to pitch a fit to get her out the door. "Life on the fly," she calls it, making it sound virtuous. Nights are more of the same; a lot of her meetings run well into the evening, so that I'm either over at Pops' by the time she drags in, or out somewhere with Nother. Once I even waited up just to say hello, assuming that a meeting had gone exceptionally off track, only to discover that she'd slipped in while I was gone and was already asleep in her room.

So this dinner is the exception to the rule of late, and we even took pains to set it up yesterday, to assure that we'd both be here. "You seem to be seeing a lot of that boy," she says. "Things are going well, I take it?"

"Nother," I say, hoping she'll eventually stop referring to him as that boy. "Yeah, it's good. He's really sweet."

"Do you really call him that?"

"Everyone does," I tell her. I quarter a meatball with my fork. "I don't even notice anymore."

"Well, I'm happy for you," she says. "He seems quite nice compared to some I've seen around." She sips her wine. "What are his plans?"

"He doesn't really say. His whole family still lives around here, though, and I think he just assumes he will, too."

"He's not going to college then?" she asks, the slightest trace of alarm in her tone.

"I don't think. I mean, it's almost like it's never occurred to him. Which is weird, because he's really smart, and really talented. He does carpentry and all that stuff. Engines. Takes care of all those animals. And he plays three or four instruments."

"Really," Gail says, "I had no idea." She purses her lips. "I'd think his parents would encourage him, then."

"They're not really like that," I tell her. "It's like...well, they're just not."

Gail forks a few strands of linguine into her mouth. "Maybe you should say something," she suggests.

"We've talked a little, mostly about me going, though." I spear a piece of meatball and chew slowly. "I've told him he'd be fine, but I think the whole concept is just too 'out there' for him."

"That's too bad," she says. "What does he think about you going away?"

"He doesn't say. He's kind of known all along, though. And he's not trying to talk me out of it, if that's what you're worried about."

"I was just curious," she says. "I'm not really worried about anything." She twirls noodles on her fork. "I wonder sometimes about the two of you being here unsupervised, though. I'm not sure it's such a good idea."

"Funny, you sound worried to me."

"I was young once, believe it or not."

"Mom, it's not like there aren't a hundred other places to go if we don't stay here. Not that we're doing anything here; I'm just saying."

"I swear I remember making that exact same argument," she replies. "How serious is this, if you don't mind my asking? Or even if you do."

I shrug. "Well, I like him a lot."

"I can tell that."

"I do realize I haven't known him all that long, but I'd still rather hang out with him than with anyone else, including Kayla."

Gail winces. "That girl," she sighs. "I just don't know. She's...prickly."

"Tell me about it. And see, Nother's exactly the opposite. It's really easy to be with him; you're not on edge all the time. It's just...nice."

"Hmmm," she says. "You'd think that would soothe me."

"Well, I think you just need to trust us then, because I want to see him more often than you're here. And besides that, how could we plan anything when you never know whether you'll be here or not?"

"That's true," she concedes. "And it's not likely to change anytime soon, I'm afraid. It'll be after Christmas at least, before this project is done, and—oh wait, I almost forgot."

She walks to the couch and riffles through her briefcase, then returns with a printout. "I booked us tickets for Baltimore. Twenty-sixth through the second."

"Already?" Vague images of Baltimore run through my head as I scan the itinerary.

"Already! It's almost Thanksgiving. We were lucky to get these."

"Oh yeah, I guess it is."

I've totally lost track of time, which I blame mostly on the weather; which is a month or two behind down here. I'm not sure if there's even been a frost yet. I was shocked when it got to be Halloween last month, and now it's happening again with Thanksgiving. I knew she'd end up booking this trip without telling me, though I let it go because it sounds O.K. right now, and this has been the most pleasant conversation I can recall us having in forever, and I don't want it to blow up over this. "Can you forward this to me so I can have a copy?"

"Keep that one," she says. She sits down and pushes what's left of her food off to one side.

"No laptops at the dinner table."

"I thought you were done. You are done."

I push together the last strands of my pasta and twirl meticulously while she rolls her eyes. "We need to figure out Thanksgiving, I say, "since you brought it up."

"How so?" She drums her fingers on the table, waiting for me to swallow.

"I want us to spend it together," I announce. "You. Me. Dad. Whoever else is fine, but us three, at least."

Gail opens and closes her mouth. "Fine," she says eventually. "I can do that."

"Thank you."

"Maybe Annie and Kayla."

"I can do that." As I'm closing the lid on my dinner she reaches for her laptop. "And look at it this way, we can probably get Pops to cook everything."

"Is he still doing that?" she asks, her fingers already racing over the keyboard.

"Well, not like he was, but I'll work on him." I kind of want to plan it out a little, but when I glance over her eyes are locked on the screen, and she's already a million miles away. I toss the Styrofoam and set our glasses in the sink and go off to e-mail Gina.

Nother is amused when I mention having stopped at The Sawmill that time, though he doesn't get why anyone would be driving around out there for no reason. I compare it to him spending entire days tramping around in the woods, which seems equally bizarre to me, and a lot harder. He's a little surprised when I tell him that Sara's invited me out; they've had trouble with underage kids in the past, so Ezra runs a pretty tight ship. The sheriff is a fan, though, so he keeps his boys out of there and lets the family police itself so long as it doesn't get out of hand, which explains how Nother can be in there so much. We make plans to go Friday night, and when I mention later how Kayla's been on my case for blowing her off lately, he says to ask her along.

We smoke out pretty good on Kayla's porch Friday night, and drink some of her mom's beer before we head out. I can tell she's pretty excited about going to a bar–I am, too–though we're both trying to be really *blasé* about it. When Nother mentions about my last trip, Kayla glances over, visibly impressed, though surprised I've failed to inform her of this. Yeah, I tell her, I stopped in a couple weeks ago, which has her nodding approvingly and

Nother shooting me a look. We take the same roundabout way I did, just because Nother is curious, and we're all so high I don't think Kayla even notices.

The lot is half-full when we pull in a little after ten, but Nother drives all the way around the back and parks beside Crosscut's Lincoln. We go in through the back door and enter from behind the bar, where we stop to say hi to Ezra and let him know Kayla is with us, so he doesn't have someone toss her. We stand off to one side til he returns with the stamp and marks the backs of our hands, then take seats along the short edge of the bar, where the waitresses come to fill orders, and which is darker than up near the stage. Kayla pulls out her smokes and her lighter and sets them on the bar, like she's done this a hundred times before.

There are three guys playing, two on guitar plus the drummer, churning out this slow sort of bump and grind that thumps right back off the walls, and has the bar top vibrating like there's a low-level current running through it. There's a fourth guy sitting at the piano facing out, watching the other three and turning a harmonica over in his hands. It's not a big stage, just a low set of risers clamped together and pushed into the corner at the other end of the bar, so that the players are only maybe half a foot higher than everyone else. There's some track lighting shooting down on them, and smoke curling up through the beams, so that I half expect Bogart to emerge from a dark corner any second. It's fairly crowded already, so we don't stand out too much. We've scored the last three seats at the bar, and most of the booths are taken, along with half of the tables, most of the chairs having been rearranged to face the stage. Ezra passes through the opening on the other side of Kayla and leans across the bar to say something to Nother, who nods and gives him a thumbs up. "Rum and Coke O.K.?" he asks.

"Perfect," Kayla says, tapping the filter end of a cigarette on the bar.

"Whatever works," I tell him. Kayla and I shove our purses behind the counter, and when the drinks come we all touch glasses just as the guy with the harmonica starts making it bleed, and as I take my first sip, I understand that I'll forever associate that moaning pitch with this moment, and boozy, smoke-filled rooms. I set down my drink and smile at Nother. "Where's Crosscut?" I have to lean into him to keep from shouting, which is another thing I like.

"He's around. Somewhere in back, maybe, or upstairs on the couch in Sara's office. He comes on about midnight."

"She here now?"

He nods. "Somewhere."

We sit listening to the music while my head does a slow sweep, taking it all in: the intricate ballet behind the bar, three of them dodging each other like electrons in that thin alley as they mix drinks and pop beers, a fourth washing and wiping in a spotted white apron, refilling the beer coolers and ice tubs by instinct; the waitresses calling orders from the slot beside Kayla while unloading glasses and shoving bills into their already swollen pockets; on stage the performers bobbing at half speed, as if required to coax each note separately; the bouncers far across the room checking IDs beneath a bare blue light at the door, while in between are the dim movements in the booths, the clink of ice, the low hum of conversation interspersed with laughter, and the occasional shriek, all of it played out in a hazy neon glow.

"Your friend know them guys?" Ezra asks, pulling me from my reverie.

"What?" I follow his gaze past my shoulder, where I see Kayla posing at a booth, talking to three guys who look to be in their thirties, at least. She tosses her head back and laughs, flashing several inches of very flat stomach, then the one with his back to us slides in and she sits down. "Doubt it," I tell Ezra.

He frowns and takes her empty glass from the bar. "Keep an eye on that one," he tells Nother before walking off.

Nother nods, his gaze never leaving the stage. "I expect that's the idea."

We settle in without her to enjoy the music; over the next hour both guitar players rotate out, replaced serially by two others who slip in seamlessly, and with no drop off. An old man in a pork pie hat sits in briefly on saxophone, sharing a corner of the bench with the piano player, who nonetheless manages to reach every key. I'm unused to this movement, though Nother explains that it's pretty standard in blues and jazz. He says there are bars in New Orleans where the music never stops, noon til four a.m., the rotation of players as orderly as a stoplight. "Everything should be that smooth," I decide, hoisting the fresh drink that Ezra has just set in front of me.

Nother touches his glass to mine. "Nothing is though."

Sara stops by and gives us both a hug, then takes Nother's seat when he heads off toward the bathroom. We watch him cross the tiny dance floor and stop briefly to speak to the piano player, who laughs and continues to nod long after Nother disappears into the can. "Having a good time?" Sara asks.

"Great," I tell her. "Just waiting on Crosscut."

"You and everyone else," she says. The place has filled up, save the postage stamp dance floor in front of the stage, and people are now standing amidst the tables and along the wall, twirling drinks and waiting on the man. Sara scans the crowd and nods agreeably. "Won't be long," she tells me with a quick glance at her watch. "Probably after the boy."

Nother has reappeared and is now standing just off stage, strapping on a black electric guitar and sharing a joke with the band. He plucks a few chords, then adjusts one of the knobs and nods just slightly to the rest and they launch into the only classic blues number I know by name, a Robert Johnson tune called "Love In Vain" that Nother has recently learned, though it's the Stones arrangement they're playing now, which he prefers to the original. Shouts of "Yo," "Yeah," and "Play it, Junior," echo out of the crowd; Nother, it would appear, is a known commodity. The band's pacing is impeccable, the others follow his lead perfectly, heads bobbing in unison. Nother never does climb onto the stage, remaining on the floor only half-facing the audience, as if he really isn't playing to them at all. He rips through a pulsing solo right in the middle, piercing progressions that elicit spontaneous applause from the room, and further shouting, so it begins to sound like a tent show revival. I see Crosscut, finally, standing just outside the glare of the stage lights, rocking slowly with the rest of the crowd. I follow his gaze across the dance floor and see, much to my dismay, Kayla dancing alone, as rhythmically and provocatively as the music demands, though perhaps a half dozen veils short for the movements she's performing. Like Nother, she seems oblivious to the crowd, though I know this to be a lie. Many of them seem unsure where to look, their eyes flitting back and forth between the lip of the stage and this girl, like they're following some lascivious tennis match. I glance behind the bar at Ezra, who is staring intently at my swirling friend, his mouth drawn in a pinched frown.

For nearly ten minutes the seduction continues, until finally Nother brings it to an overdue climax, the crowd exploding before the final chord has even faded, so that I half-expect the entire house to reach for a cigarette. Kayla's undulations slow, too, until she is barely swaying on her heels, arms crossed in front of her in a low hug, fingers splayed on opposite hip, her smoky gaze suggesting the applause is not entirely the band's.

Amidst this tumult, Crosscut moves slowly into the light. He pauses beside Nother and strokes his chin, then motions across the dance floor with a jerk of his head. Nother nods, then shrugs at Crosscut's response. The crowd erupts again when Crosscut steps onto the stage. He slips a silver Fender across his middle and greets the band. When he turns again, Nother slides over and says something that makes Crosscut smile. He nods and steps to the mike. "This called 'Stray Cat Blues.'"

When the song ends Nother rejoins me at the bar, collecting backslaps and shyly returning high fives as he crosses the room. Kayla trails him off the dance floor, to no slight recognition of her own, I notice, then cuts over to the booth. "Nice," I say when he is again beside me, sensing he'd rather I not make a big deal of it. I knew he played, but the only other time I've heard him was that one song at Esther's, when he was showing Daniel, so seeing him in front of a crowd is totally unexpected, and counterintuitive to everything I know of him. Which is not to say I'm surprised, at his skill or his unearthly composure, and I get the distinct impression he prefers to be underestimated, which is kind of refreshing nowadays.

And then Crosscut weighs in. By the end of the second number, the crowd is swaying like saw grass in the breeze, and Ezra has slid over to watch with us from his side of the bar. He crosses his arms proprietarily and winks; it reminds me that he's blood, too, and has seen this a thousand times before, though he seems no less mesmerized than the rest of us. Then Kayla plunks down next to me and leans over to announce that she's taking off. When I pull back in shock she almost tumbles onto the floor, which has her laughing hysterically, and she almost falls again as she attempts to hug me for helping prop her back up the first time. She is totally bagged.

"That's a really bad idea," I tell her when she's more or less balanced on her stool.

"They're cool guys," she says, her head tilting left, then right. "They've been buying me drinks."

"No shit."

"I swear." Her eyes cross, then refocus. "Lots."

"I totally believe you," I assure her. "But you're still not going anywhere with them. Are you out of your mind?" Ezra has moved over and is leaning on the bar listening.

"Too late," she says. "We already decided." She leans heavily on the bar. "Gonna smoke some more and...whatever."

"That's what I'm afraid of. And what am I supposed to tell Annie if something happens? *When* something happens."

Kayla snorts. "I can handle these guys."

"Hey, that guy sitting next to you isn't Tony. He's not going to stand for that shit."

"Oh, so you know better than me now?" she demands, her eyes overly round and unblinking. To my right I hear Nother slide off his stool and head through the crowd.

"Kayla, I can't just sit here and let you leave with three guys you just met."

She gathers up her smokes and lighter. "Can't really stop me either."

The guy from Kayla's side of the booth appears behind us. "Ready?" he asks.

"My friend doesn't want me to go."

The jerk gives me the once over. "Bring her," he says flippantly. He scans me again, like he's making sure. "We'll squeeze her in."

"No thanks," I sneer, which only makes him smile bigger. I don't even like this role, the friend who kills off the wild good times, but this guy must be thirty-five. He starts chatting Kayla up again, working his investment, while she opens another button on his shirt and buries her face in the opening.

I turn and glance at Ezra, who is staring past me. When I check over my other shoulder—to avoid Kayla's act—Nother is stepping away from the booth and sticking something in his shirt pocket, while the other two commence a heated discussion. As he climbs back onto his stool he gives my shoulder a squeeze. "Change of plans, I think."

Thirty seconds later one of the pair is talking into Kayla's buddy's ear in a harsh whisper, then dragging him back to the booth, where the third guy joins in. Kayla's glance flits past me to the bottles glittering behind the bar. She pulls out a cigarette and lights up dramatically, like these things happen to her all the time, and following the action too closely is beneath her. The other three keep glancing back at us, and when Kayla finally turns, the one who came to retrieve her the first time knits his eyebrows and scowls irritably, then follows the other two out.

"You piss off them other two?" I ask.

"What?" she barks, her expression one of twisted disbelief as they stalk out the door. "I didn't...fuck!" She mashes her cigarette and glares at me. "What just happened?"

I shrug and slide what's left of my drink in front of her. "Like I'd know better than you?" Kayla curls her lip and knocks back the last of my drink. By the end of the next number her head is resting woodenly on the bar.

Nother and I get her to the truck the back way; we need to leave anyhow, Ezra suggests, in case that guy is pissed enough to phone up liquor control and report it. We prop Kayla against the passenger door and climb in the other side. I want to go back in and apologize to Ezra, and thank him for the drinks, but Nother says to let it go, assuring me that the quicker we're out of the parking lot, the happier Ezra will be.

"So, what did you say to those guys, anyway?" I ask him when we're on the road. Kayla's brief revival is over, but I put the radio on anyway so we can talk.

"That she was sixteen, and all three of them were looking at a lot of years." He reaches into his shirt pocket and extracts Kayla's ID. "Stick that back in her bag, would you."

Kayla blinks, then resettles against the door.

"We're they pissed?"

He nods. "Very."

"Poor Ezra," I say.

Nother shrugs. "It's a bar. He deals with worse than that every night."

"Still. He let us in like that, gave us drinks. I probably should have warned you about her. Sorry."

"Why are you sorry?" he asks, giving me a curious look. "You can't do anything about other people."

At nine o'clock on Thanksgiving morning I'm curled on the couch in my sweats, watching Pops on TV from the affiliate in Jackson. He's on the local morning show being interviewed by the genial, stiff-haired hostess, Daphne, who's decked out in this red and green tartan outfit, with a Santa Claus brooch that blinks red at the nose pinned to the wide lapel of her jacket. She's actually not too bad compared to most of her ilk–I've seen her a few times when I cut school, but today she seems to be trying to usher in the holiday season single-handed, and the effort is showing. They've got a pack of third-graders posted on the corner in front of the studio warbling carols, which we're forced to endure every time they come back from commercial, then listen to Daph gush about the voices of angels. Inside, the set is encircled by overstuffed paper sacks, a visual reminder of the station's holiday food drive, which, from the looks of it, could supply a small, sub-Saharan nation through the new year, provided its citizens could subsist on a diet of green beans and hominy.

"Dad's on," I call into the kitchen, then drag myself and the afghan onto the floor to better check him out. He's done a few remote spots on this channel before, those kind that only last a minute or so, where some reporter on the scene barks questions into a mike, and they both stare into the camera like they're about to get rained on. This is his first extended gig, though; the camera has panned across the coffee table and settled on Pops, already seated opposite Daphne in a low slung armchair. He's got on his nice dark jacket, with a muted striped shirt open at the collar, and pleated tan slacks that blessedly haven't ridden up his shins. "Looking good," I report, as Gail enters from the kitchen wiping her hands on a dish towel.

There's a holiday theme going on, and the buzzword of the day is "community," which is what Pops is there to talk about–how we can all come together to get the most out of this rich and blessed season, which, as Daphne is quick to point out, is really "all about people." None of which has anything to do with Pops, exactly; he's not chairing the food drive, or ringing any bells, nor does the subject fall within his area of expertise, other than him being agreeable and gregarious by nature. But he cleans up nice, and he has a relaxed, even delivery when he speaks that puts people at ease, and his comments tend to come out in tasty sound bites that may or may not mean anything, though no one will realize it til long after the "on air" sign has dimmed. Which makes him perfect for television. I recall the scorching day they buried Ronnie Foster–the day I first became aware of Nother, I realize anew–how I'd come in to find Pops talking to some local scribe on our phone, a call that by rights and intention should have been Gail's. How he'd casually given the woman what she'd needed; a few lyric phrases to sum up the loss, the requisite dollop of hope and closure, the number on his side. And how, from that chance beginning, he's become the go-to guy for the local media; pleasant, properly credentialed, available; so that now, amidst this holiday set piece, he's beaming out from the quintessential American medium, mouthing the most Emersonian of platitudes. Gail wouldn't have stood for this nonsense, would have dispatched that reporter straight off, way back when. So it's not as if Pops has stolen her moment in the sun, or usurped her fifteen minutes for his own; she'd have willingly abdicated, I'm sure. Television, like my father, is not serious enough for her, neither as principled nor demanding as she requires. It is batting practice, Daphne lobbing grapefruits, while my mother is strictly a gamer.

In my musing, I miss most of the first segment. It is only when the kids are murdering "Good King Wenceslas" that I'm pulled back to the present. I glance over at my mother, surprised that she is not providing a caustic running commentary of the proceedings. When Daphne welcomes everyone back with her hundred watt smile and blinking lapel, then re-identifies Pops as a university sociologist and authority on social behavior, Gail and I exchange amused looks. Even I allow that this might be pushing it. But Pops is on a roll, and he's got Daph looking like Barbara Walters, which she seems to realize, too. She asks him—inanely—for a thumbnail comparison of the two holidays, Thanksgiving and Christmas, and Pops carries her, nodding thoughtfully like he was just then cogitating on that very question, then suggesting how appropriate it is that a season of giving should begin with a holiday of thanks.

At this, Gail can hold it no longer; she has settled onto the arm of the couch and a pained groan issues from deep within her. "Your father may have finally found his calling," she says soberly, though I'm unsure, exactly, how she means for me to take this. It's as if she's suddenly realized she's married to the world tiddley-winks champion, or, as Kayla once said, a coin-op laundry mogul. She glances from the screen down to me, then back. "He spews that nonsense and they just eat it up," she adds in a tone suggesting fatigued incredulity.

"He does seem to be filling a niche," I agree.

Gail sweeps a lock of hair off her forehead and her shoulders slump. "That may be the worst part," she suggests.

Before long it's over. After inquiring as to Pops' Turkey Day plans, Daphne thanks him profusely, repeating her invitation to come back anytime, "so long as it's soon." As they go to break she tempts us to stay tuned for her next guest, a local icon, who has promised to reveal her secret for perfect Hoppin' John. I switch back to the parade, then follow Gail into the kitchen, where she resumes closing the chest cavity of the turkey. Pops made the stuffing earlier and brought it over before he left. He's doing most of the cooking, but there are a few things he left for us to handle til he gets back. "What should I do?" I ask.

My mother glances around, then nods toward a sack of potatoes on the floor. "You can peel some of those if you want. Six or seven big ones, maybe." I slit the netting and dump spuds into the sink while she goes back to her stitching. She pauses again, almost immediately. "No," she says, "you know what the worst part is? The worst part is how pleased Annie, and the Chancellor, and all the rest of them are going to be that someone from the college was on television. They won't even care that it's just local, or that he didn't say anything. All that matters is he was on."

"Well, Mom, that's pretty much par for the course now, so you might as well get used to it. At least he looked nice. And it is a holiday, so it's probably good that he didn't get all heavy. They had him on to make everyone feel all warm and fuzzy, and he did."

"I know," she says. "I don't really even blame him. It's just more of the dumbing down process. He maybe shouldn't be so complicit, though, being an educator himself, but if it wasn't him it would be someone else."

"Good point," I say, digging onto a low shelf for a pan. "And if he behaves, who knows? He might graduate to CNN."

Gail sighs excessively at the prospect. "Am I the only one who doesn't automatically assume that's a good thing?" she asks. "It's the same with this project I'm working on. All we're doing is looking for more noticeable ways to spend the money. We don't even discuss educational value; that never even comes up. It's all website enhancement, summer programs on cruise ships, a virtual library.

Anything different we can drag out in front of the public. It's like a goddamn carnival."

"Most bang for the buck."

"Yes," she hisses. "I hate that phrase." She flattens her palms on the counter. "Do you know that at the moment we have allocated exactly zero dollars for new books and periodicals—what we're now referring to as 'traditional' books and periodicals." She looks at me, her lips drawn tight. "It's a college! Aren't there supposed to be books?"

"That has always been my understanding."

"And this stuff your father's doing, it plays right into that mindset, and ends up getting acknowledged out of all proportion to its value. It's fine for what it is, and today was supposed to be fluff, I realize that, and good for him if that's what he wants to do, but it's just one more example of the tail wagging the dog. And that's when it gets problematic."

"Which, like you said, isn't really his fault," I remind her, just so she doesn't go off on him the minute he walks in.

She snips off the fragment of excess thread, then adjusts the drumsticks so they aren't sticking out of the pan. "Oh, hell, it's probably no worse than what I'm doing. And at least he still gets inside a classroom once in a while." She sighs heavily. "I might as well be working on Wall Street."

"You don't *have* to do that, Mom. If it's making you miserable, maybe you should go back to teaching."

"Miserable might be a bit strong, but it's certainly not what I thought I'd be doing." She throws flour into the cooking bag and I help her slide the bird in. She checks the clock and ties off the bag. "We better get this in."

"Could you teach here?" I ask once the pan is in the oven. "I mean, they'd work that out for you, wouldn't they? Or were you talking about going back to Hopkins?"

"Actually, you're the one talking about it. But I will

admit I have been contemplating it–teaching again. And getting back to my research. At this point it just seems a lot more, um, useful, I guess."

"You didn't answer my question," I point out.

"Well, I don't know," she says. "I suppose Annie could work that out."

"Would you even want to teach here? Because compared to Hopkins–"

"There is no comparison," she declares bluntly. "And since I'm technically still on sabbatical, it is an option."

"Is that the reason for this Christmas trip?"

"Partly," she admits. "There are a few people back there I want to speak with before I make any decisions." She wipes the counter, then washes her hands with dish soap. "What are your thoughts on that?"

"On us visiting, or you going back?"

"Either."

"I'd actually have a say this time?"

"Don't be mean, Teri. We've been doing so well lately."

"I wasn't," I tell her. "Not that you wouldn't deserve it if the whole thing got reversed. But, at the same time, I think you should do what you need to do. I'm not going to be around after next year, anyway, so you should do whatever works best for you."

"You'd stay here, then?" Her tone is more one of mild surprise than disappointment.

"I didn't say that. It would depend on a couple things, I guess. How things are going here–"

"How are things going here?"

"O.K. right now. Also, what Dad does."

"He'll probably be anchoring the news."

"Now who's being mean? Anyway, I don't know. I can't say right now."

She nods. "It is kind of an unfair question to just spring on you like that."

"Well, I'd rather know sooner than later if you decide something."

"Right. It's just something to keep in mind at this point."

I finish peeling the potatoes while she roots through a box marked "Holiday Stuff" for a tablecloth and resumes bagging on her project. I'm surprised to hear she's this ambivalent about it, given all the extra time and effort she's put in. You'd think she was all gung-ho from watching her, but it turns out she thinks it's a big waste of time, and that the ends don't justify the means, that the ends are even compromised by the means. So it's impressive that she's still plowing ahead with it like she is, and that she'll do a good job, which she will. But that's all part of the enigma that is my mother.

I quarter the potatoes and cover them with water, then set the pan on the stove for later. Next I take down the good dishes and load them in the dishwasher while Gail irons the tablecloth and pieces together the candleholders. It's not so different from past years, really, and I'm even kind of enjoying my chores. I've always liked Thanksgiving; it's pretty low stress as holidays go, and back in Baltimore it was always cold enough to justify lying around inside all weekend. I realize to my horror that I'm on the verge of dragging up a lot of sloppy memories, so I immediately excuse myself to go e-mail Gina and clean up before Kayla and Annie get here.

Gina still hasn't gotten back to me from last week. I sent her a long one catching her up on our night at The Sawmill, and how we managed to get Kayla inside and into bed without her mom getting up. (I let myself in with Kayla's key—into their totally pitch black house—and made it to her room without knocking anything over, while Nother walked/carried Kayla to the side window and lifted her through, where I undressed her and dumped her in bed while she kept calling me Randy the whole time. Then I crawled out the window and we beat it.) But she spent the whole next day throwing up, anyway, so it was a totally wasted effort, and now Annie's kind of pissed at me, too, and I have to keep worrying she's going to rat me out to Gail. She doesn't know we were in a bar, just that we were together and Kayla got hammered, which is more than enough to implicate me. I type Gina a quick holiday greeting in hopes of prompting a response, then leave the computer on while I pick up my room. It's a disaster area, so she's got plenty of time, and sure enough, when I get back from the shower, she's delivered:

> Gobble, gobble yourself! I am so glad this is a long weekend. We're going to my aunt's in a little bit, but the rest of the time I'm chilling. I think school should only be three days a week every week, and start at noon. You wouldn't graduate til 25, but so what? And you'd be legal the last four years.
>
> That story about Kayla is too funny! We need to get her with Suzan. It'd be a puke-fest for sure, except Suz prefers the sidewalk, and she usually unloads by midnight. Kath calls her "Old Faithful."
>
> So what's the deal with this guy you keep mentioning? Quit screwing around and give me some details! INTIMATE DETAILS!! And you best bring pictures or don't fucking come.
>
> Matt keeps asking about you. He wants to hook up for New Years. Should I tell him you're doing someone else?? He's looking not too bad these days, by the way.

Have a good one!!
      G

PS: Mikey got into Princeton!! Can you fucking believe it??!!!

I hear movement in the kitchen and leave off replying to go say hi to Pops. I dig through the mountain of clothes now piled on the floor of my closet for my sweatpants, then shuck the towel and throw on a denim shirt, which I'm still buttoning as I enter the kitchen. But when I look up Nother is passing a casserole dish to my mom, who receives it like he's just handed over his beating heart. I can only imagine what I've missed, and it's all I can do to keep from laughing out loud at this awkward exchange. "Oh, hey," I say, tugging at my shirttail and sweeping a lock of wet hair from my eyes. "Um, Happy Thanksgiving."

"You too." He smiles, then looks again at Gail, who is still staring through the glass top of the dish. "And you," he tells her.

"Yes," my mother replies haltingly. "Thank you. And thank you for this." She turns to me and extends the dish. "Rabbit," she says, meaning: "Take this—Right now!"

But before I can relieve her of it the door flies open and Pops breezes in, still dressed and charged up from the show. "Hey everyone, the star's home. Oh!" He crosses the kitchen in two strides, arm extended. "Happy Thanksgiving, Nother. Good to see you."

"You too." He nods slightly.

"Pops was on TV," I remind Nother. "He doesn't usually look like that."

"Ruth watched," Nother says. "She liked it; said it was real nice." He pauses, then adds, "I was outside."

"Shooting this?" I ask, finally taking the dish from Gail, who immediately sinks onto the closest chair.

Nother glances over at her. "Well," he says, and lets it go at that.

"Nother brought rabbit," I inform Pops, holding up the dish.

He lifts the lid and a sort of sweet, gamy aroma fills the kitchen. The dish is crammed with hunks of meat and bones in a thick *roué*. I pick up a hint of garlic, and spot some onion. "Smells great!" Pops says, taking a big whiff. "I haven't eaten rabbit in thirty years, I'll bet."

"You've had it?" I ask.

"Not like this," he answers, taking another whiff. "Cajun?" he guesses, turning to Nother, who confirms this with a nod. "My uncle used to cook rabbit when I'd visit him in Maine," Pops says. "I was a kid."

"This is cooked through?" I ask Nother.

"Yeah, just warm it up."

"Can you stay?" Pops offers.

"Thanks, no. A bunch are coming over, so I need to get back. But I always make a pot for my dad, and I thought you might want to try some."

"Thanks for thinking of us," Pops says. "You cooked this up yourself?"

He nods. "Crosscut's own recipe. It was his favorite growing up."

"All right, then," Pops says. "We'll show them what the men can do."

"I'll walk you out," I say. I'm not trying to rush him, but my dad will have him standing here all day if I don't intervene.

"You can come over later if you want," he says when we get outside. "Might be loud, though."

"Maybe," I say, taking hold of his arm as we cross the yard.

"Kind of depends on how long Kayla and her mom stay. And how those two are getting along." I motion behind me toward the house. "Could get loud here, too."

"Families," he says, pulling open the door. He climbs into the truck and faces out toward me. "Let's go into the woods tomorrow. I'll take you over to that place."

"What's there?" I lean in and kiss him.

"Us," he says.

"Good enough for me."

"There is something I want to show you, though."

I arch my eyebrows. "Really?" We kiss again. "What?"

"Something momentous," he promises into my ear. Then he draws back and swings his legs into the cab with a nod toward the house. "Your mom's watching."

I wave after him, then go back inside. Sure enough, I have a bad moment as soon as I step through the door. Gail and Pops are debating whether to serve the rabbit with the rest of the meal; Pops says yes, he's picked a hunk clean and pronounces it delicious. Gail insists she has never, and will not now, have it on her table. He says she's being ridiculous; she says he's trying to ruin her dinner. They've decided to leave it to me, on the condition (Gail's) that if it's on the table, I have to eat it. I immediately vote to serve it, which prompts a smirk from Gail and the amused challenge, "All right for you, Missy."

There are numerous testy moments throughout the day; I doubt you could bring this group together without a few, but overall, it could have been a lot worse. Our guests arrive promptly at one, and soon the Chardonnay is flowing. Gail and Annie pitch camp at the table, the better to critique Pops' effort while they sip. Even Kayla is in a decent mood, laughing appreciatively at my father's insider tales from the studio. Apparently, the morning show isn't the happy camp it appears. Daphne isn't nearly so pleasant when the camera is off, according to Pops. Not that he had any trouble with her, they got on well, actually, but she's pretty abrasive with the crew, and it seems she possesses an off-screen vocabulary that could take paint off the wall. And those bags ringing the set, Pops hoots—turns out they were stuffed with the balled up coats and jackets of the staff, or in some cases newspapers, so that what was sticking out the top was pretty much it. Which is sad and funny.

I've managed to squirrel away some vodka in anticipation of the festivities, so I pour a couple of OJs and Kayla and I excuse ourselves to my room. I mix them stiff while she goes on about Tony (either her slave for life or gone for good after last night; either is fine), Randy (the old guy from The Sawmill and infamous subject of her drunken musings), and some guy from the other county school whose name she doesn't even know yet (but who is, nonetheless, "dark, dangerous, and maybe even psycho"). Kayla can unleash more frightening scenarios in twenty minutes than Stephen King.

"Oh, and I got the scoop on Carl," she says, twirling ice in her glass. "I think that's over."

"What?"

"I guess he made his move when they were all down in New Orleans at that meeting." She laughs when I wince. "Not bad or anything. More like: 'hey, we're both down here, what do you think?'" She shrugs. "I guess your mom thought 'no.'"

I sit considering this for a long minute, trying to picture it and not picture it at the same time. Were they in a bar? The lobby? Her room?! His room?!! "How do you know this?"

"I heard her talking to Annie and pieced it together," she says. "I didn't get all the details–thank God–but that's basically it."

"Well, she told me after she got back that it wasn't working out."

Kayla snorts. "Not for Carl, anyway."

Suddenly I don't want to be in here with her anymore, so we go out to see how things are progressing in the kitchen. The turkey is out and resting atop the cutting board, tented in foil and steaming the windows. Mom and Annie are still at the table and Pops is by the counter whacking something with a knife and keeping up a steady stream of chatter. All of them look a little flushed, but from the wine or the heat I can't tell. "How about we open the door?" I suggest, then open it without waiting for a reply.

"I told you they were clever," Annie says, as a blast of cool air pours in. All three of them crack up at this, and Kayla and I exchange looks.

"Watch out," she warns, which sets them off again.

Pretty soon they're back talking about the TV show, which I'd hoped they'd have exhausted by now. As Gail predicted, Annie starts in on how good it is for the college. "You can't put a price on things like that," she says, "It pays off in so many ways. There are people here who hardly think of the college, but then they see someone like Ed on television, and it puts it in a whole new light."

"That's what they say," Gail admits. "But I'm not so sure."

"No such thing as bad publicity, right?" I ask.

"I'm not so sure about that, either. And in any case, is publicity the point?"

"It's useful," Annie says.

"Do you know that both applications and alumni giving

go up when a university wins a national championship?" Pops says, which is kind of what I mean about the sound bites.

But Gail is ready. "What about SAT scores?" she challenges. "Do they go up, too? Or faculty productivity, or research funding, or graduation rates, or curriculum development, or–"

"I think we get the point," Annie cuts in.

"Look at a place like Gonzaga," Pops says, obviously *not* having gotten the point. "Ten years ago no one's ever heard of it. Now they make the 'Sweet Sixteen' every year and everybody knows where it is."

"I don't," Kayla says. "Where is it?"

"Oregon."

"Washington," Gail sighs. "Spokane. Bing Crosby went there."

"See," Pops says. "Proves my point."

"For God's sake Ed, that's where Archibald Frohman is. We've collaborated on two books. I didn't even know they had a football team."

"Basketball," he says, "and *you* wouldn't have to. But for everyone else...."

Gail studies her wine glass, then the bottle, then looks at each of us in turn. "Is it just me?"

"When do we eat?" I ask, hoping to divert a total meltdown before the turkey is even carved.

"Right now," Pops says. "I'm about to serve the soup." Kayla and I carry side dishes to the table while Pops ladles some creamy squash concoction into bowls. I don't recall soup on past menus, but it smells great, and the turkey's not ready for cutting yet. Pops uncorks another bottle and refills their glasses. "O.K. for the girls to have some?" he inquires, glancing from Annie to Gail with the bottle over my glass.

"Sure," I say, "It's a holiday."

Gail shrugs and Annie frowns at Kayla. "Whatever," she says, and I quickly nod for Pops to pour.

He suggests a prayer, but no one seems to know one, so he proposes a toast instead. "It serves the same purpose, in effect," he points out.

"Camera's off," Gail reminds him.

"Now, now," Pops says, deflecting her sarcasm with his usual aplomb. He raises his glass. "We are blessed that we can be here together," he says. "Happy Thanksgiving." And that's it; he smiles brightly and touches my glass. Gail seems taken aback by his brevity, perhaps even touched.

The soup is delicious; it all is, right on through to the pumpkin cheesecake Annie made, which we get into only after a lengthy break. The turkey is succulent, the sage stuffing exquisite, even the potatoes and yams are heavenly. The rabbit, too, though the arrangement of the bones throws me at first. Mom and Kayla won't touch it, but the rest of us have seconds, and Annie marvels that any boy we'd know could put this together.

"Beginning to end," I assure her. "Emphasis on beginning."

Gail frowns at me. "He's a bit different," she confirms, then quickly puts a hand on my arm. "I meant that as a compliment."

"Of course you did."

"But has his father ever been on the morning show with Daphne?" Annie jokes. She smiles and spears an olive from the relish tray.

"No," I concede, "but he's been on stage at Wembley with Bob Dylan. Does that count?"

It's pretty much that kind of a day, mostly pleasant, with a few good laughs, even, but a fair amount of tension just beneath the surface. It reminds me of those Victorian dramas Pops watches on PBS, where all the lords and ladies are on their best behavior at table, but there's all kinds of mayhem elsewhere. I picture the scene at Nother's, and immediately feel guilty for it. But certainly it's not like here. Even when they're all together you don't get this sniping, or the edginess, like the whole thing might implode without warning, which is a definite possibility here. Kayla and Annie could go off in a heartbeat—the look she gave Kayla while Pops was pouring her wine would have knocked me over, but Kayla just sat there batting her eyelashes, just daring Annie to drag it up. And it doesn't stop with those two; Gail and Annie don't seem nearly as chummy as they have been, despite the convivial effects of the Chardonnay. There's some friction over the project, for one thing, and Gail doesn't much like anyone encouraging Pops to be...well, like Pops, I guess. And, of course, the powder keg that is my parents, well, I don't even want to go there. It's kind of amazing that we even make it through, but we do somehow, so all's well that ends well. Just past nine, following intermittent napping and *Casablanca*, Pops loads them up and there are hugs all around, and they leave with enough leftovers for a three day hike.

It is only when I have lost sight of him for perhaps the fifth time that I glean this central truth about Nother: he is entirely without artifice. Where before I had only thought him curiously unflappable, I now understand it far exceeds mere surface composure. He is at home wherever he happens to find himself, at whatever pursuit is then engaging him. I have never met anyone as comfortable in his own skin as Nother, which has me feeling that much better about what I anticipate will happen today.

It is half past noon and we have just entered the woods behind his house. I had not previously noticed the remnants of a low stone fence holding back the trees, as it is camouflaged almost completely by knee high grass and weeds, and might have tumbled right over it had Nother not steered me through a narrow opening in the crumbling rock. I'm moving awkwardly, shod in an oversized pair of thick soled rubber boots he insists I wear ("Snakes!" says I), and with a thick picnic blanket strapped to my back. Nother is jostling a bulky day pack across his shoulders, and we are walking on a spongy narrow path parallel to the edge of the forest, about twenty yards in; through the trees to my left I can just make out the open fields along the road that Nother's house is on. We hike single file with him in the lead, since the path cannot accommodate us side by side. We talk intermittently, me with questions, Nother answering, or pointing out something just off the path. The growth is thick even at this slight depth, and if something attracts my notice for a second too long, he seems to disappear before I can glance forward again. Several times I have almost walked into him, such is his ability to blend in, and I suspect at first that he is toying with me. But Nother is not a kidder, and so I begin to study him, soon noticing that he moves like a denizen of these woods—smooth, quiet, hyper-aware. He seems to know instinctively where he's at. When he stops he is all but invisible, his drab jacket melting into the underbrush, arms drawn close. It's really quite amazing, almost as if he could slip right up on any creature out here and tap it on the shoulder to ask permission before blowing its brains out. When the breeze kicks up it takes even longer to pick him out of the swaying branches, whether he's moving or not. Those rabbits, I can't help but think, never had a chance.

I try to imitate his movements but fail miserably, and soon go back to my Baltimore sidewalk galumphing.

It is now that my brain begins to extrapolate this behavior, and I take note of his universal unobtrusiveness, the result, I soon conclude, of the aforementioned lack of artifice. He blends in everywhere: his house, my house, school, The Sawmill. He'd be the last one you'd notice any of those places, if, indeed, you noticed him at all. Were it not for the bare feet, I'd have never picked him out of the pack of mourners at Ronnie Foster's funeral, and even then, I was probably the only one to take notice. I recall him departing the stage lights that night at the bar; he was immediately swallowed up by the crowd, soon anonymous beside me once again. I try to call up the name of that arctic bird that changes color so drastically, from a brilliant snowy white in winter to the dullest brown of the summer tundra, but I can't come up with it. That's him, though.

Presently the woods fall away, and we are standing beside the widest curve of Lazy Ass Creek. I recognize the bridge, though it looks much higher from down here. We pause for a minute to rest, tossing stones into the water and listening to the trucks thunder by overhead. I slip my arm around his waist and describe our inane experiment, after which he lifts his hand from my shoulder and indicates a rounded maroon protrusion sticking out of the mud bank just beside a waterlogged cypress stump. I want to dig it up for Kayla, take the whole muddy thing back to her, but he tells me I'll be packing it out myself if I do, so that's the end of that. We start off again, strolling into the shoulder high grass bumping hips and squeezing each other and stealing kisses and whatever else we can manage while upright and still walking.

We plunge back into the trees, and within minutes they have woven a thick canopy overhead, arresting the daylight, as if someone has suddenly switched the setting to DUSK. We stop in the first place the path widens enough for two, sipping water and picking out the various sounds enveloping us: the rustle of the wind in the trees; birds, of course, countless flocks of them from the sound of it, chirping, whistling, honking wildly; the scratching and scurrying of animals moving along the forest floor just out of sight. Nother begins listing the birds by their call, the unseen creatures underfoot through some process entirely his own. I move in front of him and press my thick boots onto his toes, and inquire again about the snakes, and again he assures me that the cooler weather has made them sluggish, and most likely sent them into hiding. When we are able to stop again–the path is no wider than a car tire in some places–I pick out a new sound, the rush of water, and Nother informs me we are nearly alongside an unmapped river, which I'll be able to see in another hundred yards, and we'll follow it the rest of the way. I tug his shirt front and ask how he ever found this route, as the path we're on is episodic at best. "Made it, mostly," he answers, which I probably should have guessed.

A final push delivers us to our destination, and we step into a small clearing of matted grass and pine needles about the size of my front yard, with a thin line of trees separating it from the swift current just down the bank. This aperture materializes so abruptly, and is so incongruous to the dense growth we've just exited, that I scarcely know what to make of it, though I can appreciate immediately his fascination for it. It has a solemn, natural beauty comprising every shade of green and brown, and the light filtering down is speckled and church-like. The air is thick, its scent an odd, fecund mixture of growth and decay. This is without question the most untouched spot I've ever been, and I wonder if anyone besides us has ever set foot here. We are roughly a mile from the bridge, certainly no more than two, but we might as well be on Mars.

"Damn," I whisper, despite the cathedral effect of the place. I stare up through the branches and turn slowly, the streaks of light flickering and glinting as I twirl. "Wish we'd have brought some beer."

Nother shrugs off his pack and roots through the largest compartment, finally extracting a folded sheet of plastic which he spreads dead center on the dewy lawn. "Actually," he says, stepping behind me to unhook the blanket.

I glance down at the pack. "You hauled beer all the way out here?"

"Don't be ridiculous," he says, unsnapping a pair of fasteners to let the blanket unfurl, and four cans of Bud tumble onto the plastic.

I get him pinned to the plastic and drink off half a can sitting on his chest before I let him up to open one for himself. We spread the blanket atop the ground cloth and I shed my jacket before collapsing onto it. I study a small patch of blue sky directly above us while Nother begins unloading food from his pack. He's brought turkey sandwiches (naturally) on thick slices of homemade bread, with this garlicky vegetable mixture on the meat; potato salad; chunks of melon and pineapple; lemon bars; and a fistful of vanilla creams that he tosses onto my stomach with some napkins. I set out plates and help divvy up the food and we eat, the selections all the more delicious from the hike. "What's with this turkey?" I ask after a second huge bite.

"Deep fried," he says. He takes a drink of beer. "You like it?"

"It's great. So, you cook it like French fries?"

"Yeah, except outside, and with lots more oil."

"Bet my dad would like it." I tell him about Thanksgiving at my house while we finish the sandwiches, then hear about theirs as we pick at the rest of it and open more beers. "What made you come out here the first time?" I ask when we've completed the holiday recap. "I mean, it's not the kind of place you'd just stumble into."

"I was scouting for somewhere to build a deer stand last summer," he explains, feeding me a vanilla cream. "And then I got to following something instead, and before I knew it I walked into this."

"So, there are deer back here?"

"Don't know. Never have got around to looking." He rolls onto his stomach and points low beneath some branches to an enormous patch of sunlight just past the far bank. "But I'm sure there are, and with that big clearing there, and all these shadows over here, I figured I could get a pretty clean shot if I could get up off the ground. So I started that." He points left, up to a large platform spanning several thick branches over the near bank, which I'd somehow failed to notice.

"That's a deer stand?"

"Well, most are only a foot or two square, just big enough to stand on. That's more like a condo. See, I realized pretty quick how it'd be just about impossible to pack a deer out of here, anyway. It's just too thick. I have enough trouble getting in and out myself. I more or less built that for a place to come, because I figured I'd be here a lot."

"So, what do you do out here then?"

"Mostly watch for this bird," he says. "Sometimes I read."

We're pressed up against each other by now, so I figure

we've got either of those options beat. "You ever come out here at night?" I ask. "I bet that's cool."

"Once," he says, "but then I had to stay, because there's no way to follow the path in the dark. Fortunately, I was far enough along to sleep up there." He motions toward the platform.

Which pretty much takes care of the talking for a while, other than him saying we should probably go up on the platform first, though we don't, being otherwise preoccupied right there on the ground. There's a breeze blowing across us, so the sunlight flickering down through the branches is like lots of little flashes going off, which you'd think would be distracting given the circumstances, but isn't. Occasionally a shadow blocks out the sun, and I'm vaguely aware of the sounds of birds and the wind and then birds again, and then especially this one call in particular, sort of nasally sounding and drifting closer, and then when we're pretty much all but shed of what we're wearing, and the squawk sounds like it's just in the next room, Nother sort of pulls back and says, "There," and I say, "Yeah, there is good," which comes out all throaty, and he says, "No, come on," and sort of pulls me up, but gently, and the blanket, too, and we're kind of holding our clothes on, or else carrying them and stumbling toward the trees. He boosts me onto a branch and points how to get up the rest of the way and then throws up the blanket and follows me, and we scooch over to the edge by the river and peer out through this kind of window in the branches, where across the river in the big clearing, circling slowly in the sunlight and emitting that same call I've been hearing all this time, and finally landing heavily in the middle of all that sun so that I can see totally unobstructed is the biggest bird I've ever laid eyes on that wasn't already plucked and stuffed, and I say, "Oh Lord," to which Nother says, "Yeah," and I ask, "What is that?" and he says, "It's an ivory-billed woodpecker, which is also called the Lord God bird, so you were half right already, and that's a male, you can tell from the red," and I stare for a minute at the enormous wingspan it flashes in settling and then I say, "Is that, like, totally rare, because I've never even heard of it," and Nother says, "Extinct, actually."

Which is not what I'm expecting him to say at all, but does, I suppose, make up for him stopping what we were doing, provided, of course, that it's true, and woe to his ass if it isn't. And since I have limited experience with dead species, my follow-up is a grievously generic, "Huh?"

Nother is pulling a field guide from his pack, which he has somehow thought to drag up as well, and begins thumbing through the section titled "Extinct Birds." He comes at last to a marked entry, and holds the book open just to the left of my sightline with the instruction, "See there."

The colored drawing, labeled "Ivory-billed Woodpecker" along the bottom, shows the creature in all its magnificence, the piercing yellow eyes, the glossy black and white coloring of its huge body, the vivid red of the male crest, the rapier white bill and the razor talons. My eyes flit from page to subject, and there is not a doubt in my mind that the caterwauling creature across the river and this indexed bit of history are one in the same. "I don't understand."

"There are difficulties inherent in proving a negative," he says.

"But it's right there."

"See."

"So it's not." Nother nods in agreement. "Then why is it listed like that?"

"It could be we're the only ones who know."

"Nooo...." My head ping pongs from him to the bird. "Really?"

The thing he was tracking last summer, the whole reason he ended up way out here to begin with, is this bird. Which totally makes sense; I mean, it's almost two feet tall, I'm guessing, and I've already seen how its wingspan can block out the sun, so of course you'd want a better look. The thing is, he knew from the beginning what it was; not exactly, of course, but he knew it was rare, and significant, and that it was a big deal. By the second time he knew exactly what it was, *Campephilus Principalis*–the principal eater of grubs, and what that meant: that it supposedly died out in the logging boom during the middle decades of the last century, and that it got its nickname, the Lord God bird, from the common response of those sighting it for the first time, and how the last of these sightings to be validated occurred in 1953, though there have been several credible ones since, and as such, a lore has grown up around the charismatic ivorybill among both scientists and the general birding population.

He relates all this with calm precision, in that same odd manner he employs when speaking of his father, an anomalous mixture of intimate, though studied, affection. And, naturally, being Nother, he hasn't said a goddamn thing about it to anyone til just now. Which totally flips me out, but at the same time makes me feel really good that I'm the one he told, and I definitely forgive him for interrupting things before, though I wouldn't mind getting back to it once this bird takes off again. "You need to report this, Nother. I mean, you'll be famous."

"Who'd believe it?"

"What do you mean, it's right there." It's been a good twenty minutes by now, and the ivorybill shows no signs of going anywhere. At the moment, it's pecking at the wide stump of a fallen oak tree and making a hell of a racket.

"Well, yeah. Now."

"It's not always here?"

"I don't know," he says. "I'm not always here."

"Nother." He's got this weird habit of answering questions totally literal, like that thing in History class about dead Yankees, which can be pretty funny if it's not you asking the question, but really annoying if it is. "Would you please not do that with me? Play dumb like that?"

He pauses to consider this. "We'll see."

"Now, really, why haven't you told anyone?"

"Let me ask you something; if you were still in Baltimore, and you saw a headline in the paper that said 'Mississippi Youth Claims To See Extinct Bird.' And there was my picture, what would you think?" When I open and close my mouth without answering, he says, "See," which is not what I meant at all.

"But if you got a picture or something, they'd have to believe you."

"Well, it's not really about that. I mean, it doesn't really matter if anyone else believes it or not. And do I really want a million people tramping around back here? Showing up at my house with notebooks and cameras like they do with my dad?" He glances toward the bird, then back at me. "I'd as soon leave things like they are, and he seems to be getting along O.K., too."

"Are there more?"

"You'd have to assume. Unless that's the very last one, in which case there's nothing anyone can do about it anyway."

"And you're sure it's the same one every time?"

He points out a mark on the right side of the bill that I can barely make out, and the way this one clump of feathers sticks out kind of funny on the inside of the left leg. "I don't think birds can be twins," he says. He shows me dated notes he's made on a blank page at the back of the guide, but says he quit when it became merely repetitious. Then, as if on cue, the bird performs the odd hop-step Nother has written of, and flies off into the trees on the opposite side of the clearing, as the notes also specify.

"Well, that was different," I conclude, leaning into his shoulder before turning to check out the rest of the deck. It's a pretty nice setup he's got here: way up off the ground; a short wall on each side to keep from rolling off; and a thick tarp suspended from the branches overhead, to keep out whatever rain gets through the leaves. The bottom is covered with one of those self-inflating pads for camping. All in all, it's pretty cozy, and positively ideal for observing extinct species.

"Thought it might interest you," he says. There's one of those plastic storage containers people keep in their garage lodged into the crook of two twisted branches, and he reaches into it and pulls out a down-filled sleeping bag.

"How come you never showed me this before?" I ask as he drapes the bag around us.

"Trust and mosquitoes."

"So you trust me now?"

"I've got a hunch," he says. "I just have this feeling that you won't let me down by telling even a single person, no matter what, because you know how much that would hurt me, and what a betrayal it would be after I trusted you. I just know you'd never do me like that." He's saying all this with exaggerated sincerity, because he knows he's got me pegged, totally.

"Aw man! But this is, like, so amazing."

"I know."

"And it's your secret. All yours."

He shrugs.

"And you don't care if anyone else even knows?"

"Well, yeah, I do. And now she does."

Has he got my number, or what? "That bird won't be back again today, will it?" I ask, lying back and drawing him down with me.

"Let's risk it," he says, spreading the blanket over us like wings.

"Well, hallelujah!" the first one says, raising her latte in mock salute. "It's about goddamn time."

The other one sips without acknowledging the toast. "How sweet," she replies. "It's always such a pleasure to confide in you." She had felt empowered just moments ago, almost giddy relating her news, though this feeling is quickly lost in the patronizing response.

"What, you expect a medal? I mean, what were you waiting for in the first place, Christmas?" She rolls her eyes. "You probably were."

"It's barely been a month."

"You're making my point. Another week and that poor guy would have needed a wheelbarrow to cart his nuts around."

"God, you are so nasty." She shakes her head and looks at the ceiling. "It wasn't like that."

"It's always like that."

They are at one of the small front tables at The Chickory this first Monday in December, having cut last period to sip coffee and share this news. A fierce wind is gusting outside and the sky is leaden, spritzing the pavement with

rain off and on. The first one had divined what was coming
on the drive over, having been on this same end of similar
confessions, and now finds herself alternately charmed and
annoyed at the other's evasive stammering. She is pleased
for her friend, of course, inevitable though this milestone is,
and even pretends to share her excitement, though she is
not about to let the event be sanctified. The room is nearly
empty at mid-afternoon, but still the other one speaks at
barely a murmur. "So then, is this a big secret?" she whispers back. "I'm not supposed to say anything?"

"No," the other one says in a normal tone, so that it
seems almost a shout by comparison, "it's not a big secret."

"So if Joley happens to call–"

"Let's leave her out of it."

"Fine," the first one says through a tight smile.
"I need to know, though, are you embarrassed about doing
it, or just about doing it with him?"

"What are you talking about? I wouldn't have done it at
all if I was embarrassed of him. How can you even ask that?"

"O.K., sorry. I keep forgetting how beautiful it was. But
as undercover as you guys are, it's hard to tell who's hiding
whom."

"Look, no one's hiding anything, O.K.? And I never
said it was beautiful. But Joley doesn't like him to begin
with, and no one else really knows him, so why talk about
it to them? What does she know about it, anyway?"

"I think she's familiar enough with it," the first one suggests. "It sounds like Ruckus keeps her engine running
pretty well."

"I think it's a little different with us."

"Oh, give me a break," the first one sighs. "You're no
different than anyone else. It's nice that you think so, but
everyone thinks that. And everyone else is wrong, too."

The other one stares across the table, taken aback at the strident tone. "What are you getting so mad about? I didn't even mean you."

"You probably did and you don't even know it." She swirls her latte, staring into the foam. "Next you'll be telling me you're in love with him." She starts to drink, then replaces her cup on the table. "Oh God, you are, aren't you?"

"I didn't say that. And believe me, you'd be the last person I'd tell now." But she can feel her cheeks glowing and turns away, gazing out the front window into the street.

"You don't have to, it's written all over your face."

"Oh, please," she insists, but there is nothing more she can think to add, and so for lack of a better diversion, gulps her too hot drink, wincing as the mocha scorches the inside of her mouth.

That very thought had occurred to her, in fact, later that same night–that she might be falling in love with him. That she probably was. It had made her smile then, cliché and all, and had remained camped in her brain since, eliciting a fresh smile whenever she paused to linger on it. Wasn't that how it was supposed to be? With the first boy you let make love to you. She'd rolled her eyes at the very phrase, and now dares not consider what her friend would make of it. The first guy you did it with, then, how about that? Though technically, weren't you supposed to be in love first?

But it had been special, no matter what her friend insisted, an afternoon she would never forget for any number of reasons, and quite possibly beautiful, too, in a pixilated sort of way, though she most definitely had not voiced that notion, and resented the other's mocking tone. She'd had to leave most of it out, huge chunks that she dearly wanted to share, but couldn't while still with-holding the secret of the ivorybill. She hadn't dared say where all this had taken place, exactly, nor had she described the lush beauty of the forest opening. All these details she'd managed to blur in the telling; most likely her friend assumed they'd been in Nother's house, slip-ping in undetected, or while no one else was about. In all likelihood, her friend would not have believed it could have taken place outside, or in any manner other than furtive and fumbling haste, which was most definitely not the case. And, surprisingly, she had not pressed for details, abandoning her usual clinician's demeanor, and all its concomitant impertinence, for that of the detached, world-weary confidante. Which, by this point, is fine with the other as well, as she too has grown tired of the exchange. She stares now across the table, into the first one's smirking leer. "Why did I even say anything?" she wonders aloud.

"Because you couldn't help it," comes the reply. "And I'm the only one you can tell who won't ground you or blab to everyone else."

"Must be a drag being right all the time," the other one muses, making no attempt to disguise her irritation. "Takes all the mystery out of life."

"My cross to bear," the first one sighs, taking note of the sarcasm. Then, perhaps to throw the other one off guard, she adds, "At least you had someone to tell."

"So, who did you tell?"

"The next guy," she answers with practiced noncha-lance. "And all he wanted to know was if he was better."

"Oh, Kayla." She thinks this is perhaps the most pitiful thing she's ever heard, and reaches across the table.

"Relax," the first one replies, giving the offered hand a

cursory squeeze and then picking up her cup. "I lived; I learned; everything's cool."

"Enlighten me, then," the other one requests, retracting her arm as her annoyance returns full force.

"Here it is: You're alone to begin with, and you're alone at the end, so get that goofy-ass look off your face and watch out for yourself, because no one else is, least of all him."

"Then why bother at all if you feel that way? I mean, what's the point?"

"What else is there?" she asks. "And it's fun while it's going on, so you might as well take advantage of it. Like with you, he's cute, so why not get something out of it? That's what he's doing. Just take care of yourself, is all, and use your leverage."

"Take advantage; use my leverage. Got it."

"You make fun, but it's true. And the weird thing is most people–Joley, for instance–think the advantage is from holding out, like it's still the '50s or something. But let me tell you, it's afterwards when you can really make them do tricks. I swear, you can move a guy all over the room without saying a word, like you're both the same kind of magnet. I'll show you with Tony sometime. And before you go getting all righteous on me, keep in mind that he'd be doing it to me if I let him." She stares across the table. "So, it's great that you're all happy now, and you think he's so wonderful, and you guys are different, and it'll never end. But you're not, and it will. And how you act now determines what's left of you then. I'm sorry, but that's just how it is, and you need to realize it or you're going to be roadkill."

The other one is pushed back in her chair, eyes glazed, as if to distance herself from this savage disquisition. No, she decides, amending her earlier judgment, this is the *most pitiful thing I've ever heard.* "*How do you even man-age to function in that world?*"

"*What's the option?*" *the first one asks back.*

Gail does this modified freak-out when Pops comes over Sunday to tell us he's officially giving up his post at Towson. He's even got the letter with him, and he keeps tapping the corner of the unsealed envelope on the table til she grabs it from him and slams it flat between then. "Why would you do that?" she demands. "I mean, why now? What's the point?"

"The point, I guess, is that they expect me back for spring semester, and since I'm not planning to be there, courtesy would dictate that I notify them of that."

My mother sighs mightily. "You've decided for sure? That you're staying?"

"I didn't really have to decide," he answers. "I just am." I don't even have to see her face to know that this will not go unremarked.

"Such enlightenment must be a wonderful thing," she notes. "I can see why you'd want to make such a production of it."

"Look," he says a bit impatiently, "they sent me a list of course offerings yesterday, and I'm scheduled to teach two of them." One is an intro class, he informs us for no reason I can fathom, the other an upper level course called Personal And Family Relations, the irony of which is too obvious and too immense to even elicit comment. "Anyway, I gave Jerry a call at home this morning and we hashed it out. He was totally cool about it, but he wants something in writing. To cover himself, I assume, in case I would suddenly show up."

"So he's forcing you to resign. What, exactly, is 'cool' about that?"

"First, he's not forcing me to do anything, and second, there's not really any other way. And he's going to shuffle things around to cover the classes, probably just appoint a grad ass for a semester, so the spot would still be open for fall. Which I didn't even ask him to do. So the letter's more or less a formality."

"Famous last words."

Pops shrugs. "He's being more than accommodating as it is. I should have let him know a month ago."

"Tell me, how do you even know you can stay here? I mean, Annie kind of rigged all that up at the last minute."

"She's indicated it won't be a problem," Pops says.

"Has she?"

"Gail, I'd planned to be here both semesters all along. You knew that. Why are you making such a fuss about it now? And I'm really starting to make headway on this book, not to mention some other things that seem to be opening up for me here."

"Oh, and what are their names?" she sneers, which is totally out of the blue as far as I know, and totally uncalled for. Apparently Pops agrees, since he shoots her the same quizzical look I do. The strange part of this whole exchange is why she'd care to begin with. I mean, they are supposed to be separated, right? She keeps saying that, anyway. And last time I checked, that implied some type of distance; so if she's half packed to go back already, and he's severing his ties, wouldn't that seem to play right into her hands? Unless I'm totally missing something, which is entirely possible with these two.

"Whatever that's about," Pops replies. "I just wanted to keep you informed, that's all. The more we can keep the lines of communication—"

"Spare me," she says with a dismissive wave. "Do what

you want, but save the jargon for your book."

Pops and I exchange looks. "Think I'll just wait outside," I decide.

"And where are you going in that get-up?" she barks, giving me a frowning once over.

"To work," I tell her. "I got a job. Nother's picking me up."

"What kind of job?" she demands. "Where?"

"Helping clean up at The Sawmill," I say, which explains the ratty jeans, the flannel shirt tied in the front, and even the doo rag covering my head, which is what the question was really about.

"That's a bar, isn't it?"

"Bars need cleaning too."

She looks over at my father, like she expects him to join the assault, but he merely nods at a point well made. Gail rolls her eyes. "I don't know if I want you in a place like that," she says.

"You've never even been there," I remind her. "How would you know what kind of a place it is?"

"I've never been in a cathouse, either, but I know what goes on there. And I don't think some roadhouse is any place for a teenage girl to be working. It's probably not even legal."

"They're not even open today," I inform her. "It'll just be us, and probably Sara. Usually it's just them, so they're glad for the help. And I need money for Christmas."

Gail frowns. "I don't recall us discussing this."

"Since when have I needed permission to earn money?" I ask.

She purses her lips. "And what, exactly, will you be doing in this fine establishment?" she asks, since there's really not much else she can say.

I shrug. "Wiping tables, mopping the floor, taking out the trash." I stick out my tongue and add, "Probably the bathrooms, but I'm hoping Nother will do those."

"There's a bathroom here you can practice on," she suggests. "Make a good first impression."

"I'll just wing it." I slide into my denim jacket. "I think that's him now. See you, Pops."

"Right behind you," he says, tucking the envelope into his shirt pocket and following me out.

"Does anyone even hear me talking?" Gail complains as the door bangs shut with her inside.

"Kind of hard not to," I mutter, crossing my arms to keep my jacket closed against the wind.

Pops glances over but remains diplomatically silent, then leans forward to stare around me up the obviously empty road. "Guess that wasn't him."

"Yeah, well," I say, and we both laugh. It's a blustery, gray afternoon; the wind is pushing Pops' hair all over the place, and leaves are cartwheeling across the yard. "So, you're staying," I say.

"For now, anyway," he answers, rocking slowly back and forth on his heels. He's got his hands shoved in his pockets and he's looking down at the porch steps. "Depends a lot on you guys, naturally, but it's not like I'm giving up all that much at Towson. So this"—he nudges the letter with his chin—"isn't that big a deal. And I'd like to see how all this plays out." He nods then, like he said it pretty much how he meant to. "Or maybe you could just ask Madame Marie."

"If I ever see her," I sniff. Pops looks up. "Supposedly, she's either out or with someone every time I'm there. Which is possible, I guess, but hardly likely." I shrug. "In any case, we've yet to meet."

"Huh," Pops says. "Strange. Well, one thing I do know is that I don't want to have to pick up and move again so soon." He glances sideways at me across his shoulder. "What about you?"

"It's better than it was," I say. "And as for moving, I'm still getting used to the idea that where you live is an option."

"I can understand that," Pops says, "considering we were in that same house for so long." He works some mud loose from one of the boards with the toe of his shoe and kicks it off the porch. "We moved a lot before you were born, so it's kind of old hat for us." He swivels his head to take in both halves of the house. "Things could probably be better around this place, though."

"It's fine," I say. "I'm even kind of used to it by now. And Nother likes coming over, especially hanging out on your side. He's blown away by all those typed pages. It's like, even with all the outrageous stuff he knows how to do, I don't think he ever met anyone who wrote a book before."

"Your mother," he points out. "Couple of them."

"Yeah, but yours is right there, still raw."

"That's for sure," he laughs. "But I suppose people are drawn to what's different. Like how you enjoy being at his house because there's so many of them, and they're all still around. Quite a change from this."

"Yeah, and they're all tangled up in each other's lives, too. Working together, watching each other's kids, passing stuff around." I shake my head. "Kind of its own universe."

Pops nods. "And you seem to have slipped right in. At least the working part."

"Is this O.K.?" I ask. "I mean, I guess I should have said something before now."

"Or not at all," he says. "Fine with me, though, especially if it's closed." He extracts a hand from his pocket and strokes his chin. "I've been meaning to go out there myself," he says. "Some night when Crosscut's playing."

"He and Nother are going to play on Thursday," I tell him. "And they don't perform together much, so we should go after your class."

He shoots me this curious grin. "We?"

"Hey, I work there now." He's giving me this detective kind of squint, like he knows all about it, but he's always been good about not asking questions he doesn't want the answers to. "It'll be cool," I assure him.

"All right then, it's a date," he decides just as Nother's truck rolls up in front. "Maybe don't tell your mother, though."

"Good thinking," I call over my shoulder.

Pops waves toward the truck. "That's why I'm the dad."

It takes most of the afternoon to clean the place, but the dollars per hour works out pretty nice when Sara slips us each fifty at the end of it. I doubt I could do better around here, and it beats babysitting. The doors are all propped open when we get there, but the big overhead sign and the beer lights are off, and the air drifting out is a toxic blend of stale smoke and spilt beer. The parking lot is empty but for Sara's pickup, which is angled across the front door, and a couple other cars which I assume will be picked up whenever their owners get vertical again. We park behind Sara, effectively barricading the front entrance and go inside, where the air is even more poisonous, and I'm doubly glad to be dressed how I am. The lights are off inside as well, save a pair of dim, sconced bulbs behind the bar, so it takes a minute while our eyes adjust to make out Sara's petite shape across the room. She's sitting at the bar in front of a laptop, and both registers are spitting out receipt tapes that are already curling up on the floor when we walk over.

We sip Cokes and visit for a while; Sara has this ador-
ing look on her face, like she can't believe I actually came
and she doesn't have to play janitor today. Before long
Nother slides off his stool and begins carrying huge bags of
trash to a locked dumpster out back. Sara and I swivel on
our stools and she briefs me on my tasks, all the while
gushing about how glad she is I'm here, and squeezing my
arm for proof. We carry rags and cleanser to the bar and
she shows me where to find the mop, then thanks me yet
again and heads up to the office to balance the tills. "It
doesn't have to be perfect," she says from the stairs. "Just
get up the bodily fluids."

I wipe down the bar and everything behind it, pausing
to study a couple of cheaply framed photos of Crosscut
with his famous friends, then hit the stools before turning
my attention to the tables. Nother puts on music after Sara
goes upstairs, throaty blues and gospel that fills the air and
gives the room a strange, churchy feeling.

Wiping is the bulk of the job, it seems, and it takes a
couple hours; I flip up the chairs as I go, then mop the
battered wooden floor and the storage room in back.
Nother does the bathrooms, bless his heart, then tears
down the whole stage, dusting and wiping before putting it
all back together again. We don't talk much, the music fits
too well to bother, and we're each lost in our own reverie.
He goes outside to pick up the parking lot while I rinse
glasses, knives, strainers, and the like, swaying to the music
and daydreaming that I'm the worldly old broad that owns
the place. I take a slow cruise around the room til he gets
back, pausing to wipe smooth the edges of the pool tables,
where there are crusty rings despite the signs on the wall.
The last thing I do is load all the dirty rags into the
machine in back and get it going, while Nother refills the

beer coolers. When Sara comes back down we're enjoying a cold one ourselves, and waiting for the rags to finish so we can toss them in the dryer and take off.

"Thirsty work," she says, slipping around the bar with fresh rolls of tape. She gives the place a quick once over. "Looks good, guys," she says, plucking our money from her shirt pocket and sliding it across the bar. "You be back next week?"

"If you want," I tell her, tapping the bar with my cash while she admires her unpruned fingertips. I slip the bills into my pocket. "That wasn't so bad."

"Hang on to her," she tells Nother.

It's dark by the time we leave, and there's still one vehicle unaccounted for, a beat Plymouth Valiant over in the corner. "Wonder what that's about?" I muse as we pull onto the highway.

"Couldn't make bail," Nother speculates.

I'm with Sandy when I spot this leather jacket in the vintage clothing store over by the college. I've decided it might be a good idea to cultivate a few new friendships, or at least widen my circle of class-cutting, coffee-swilling cohorts. Lately, things with Kayla just tend to get sideways too often, and I don't always have the energy for it. Sandy and I have hung out before; she was along on the bowling ball drop, and now we're finding that we do pretty well without Kayla, too.

I decide right off this jacket would be the perfect thing to give Nother for Christmas. Well, it's ninety-five bucks, and there's a small but definitely noticeable scuff on the back right shoulder, but other than that it's perfect. Sandy reminds me that he'll only be able to wear it a couple months a year down here, but then points out that this also means it should last him the rest of his life, which isn't a bad selling point, as gifts go. It's finals week at the college, so the store is deserted except for us, and it's easy enough to get the owner to hold it back with a ten dollar deposit; I don't have the money with me anyway, and I want to run the whole idea past Ruthie, just to make sure I'm not totally off base.

"Is this too much, do you think?" I ask Sandy while the woman fills out a receipt. "I mean, he won't freak, will he?"

Sandy shrugs. She's studying this beaded cloche hat she's thinking of getting for her mom. She turns it over in her hands, looking for defects, then places it on her head and checks her reflection in the mirror behind the counter. "I think it's O.K. If you got him a lot of little stuff you'd end up spending just as much. I mean, it's fifteen bucks for a CD."

"Good point."

She tugs the hat low on her forehead and makes this pouty, model-ish face. "I think it's a good choice. Like, it's big, but it's not too big. And the best part is, you're done. I mean, if it was me, that would sure as hell be it."

"Oh, yeah, definitely," I agree. "I'm going to be scrambling as it is to afford anything for my folks."

"I hear that."

Sandy is a lot funnier than I realized, and it's nice to be out bumming around with someone new. She doesn't have that whole negative vibe going, either, so even when she's trashing something, there's not that raw, paper cut edge to it, like with Kayla, even when it happens to be Kayla that she's ragging. The stress is so not there, in fact, that I mention it leaving the store, and Sandy immediately concurs.

"I know what you mean," she says as we cut onto campus heading for the library. She's decided to get the beaded hat for her mom, but needs to score some cash from her dad, who's a semi-big shot in Special Collections. "She is so vicious sometimes. And it's like every encounter is a contest, and she always has to have the upper hand."

"Exactly. And some of the stuff she does to these guys—"

"It's not just guys," she cuts in. "That's my point. She's like that with everyone. I mean, haven't you ever wondered why someone that hip and cool and funny is always alone? Except for you, who just happens to be new in town?"

"Well, yeah, but I just figured it had to do with her, um, how to say this...."

"Total slut behavior?" Which somehow comes out sounding way less judgmental than you'd think possible.

"That'll work."

"That's definitely part of it. But it's all kind of tied together. See, she's just mean, for whatever reason, and the slut stuff is just the...what's the word?"

"Manifestation."

"Right. The most blatant manifestation. And eventually she ends up running everyone off, because she treats them like shit." She glances over at me as we start up the library steps. "I mean, I know she's your friend and all, and your moms are friends, but you kind of need to know, because she's not all that reliable. And some of us are kind of concerned for you, because when she unloads, it happens in a hurry, and it ain't pretty, believe me."

"I totally believe you. I don't want to start trashing her, either, but it's kind of a relief to know I'm not the only one that thinks that." It's also kind of nice—strange, but nice—to imagine there are people I don't even know looking out for me. I kind of want to know who this "some of us" consists of, but it seems rude to ask.

"It's a pretty inclusive list, actually. And none of us want to see you get hung out to dry. So there, I said it, I'm done."

"Well, thanks."

"Sure." She pulls open a frosted door with Special Collections stenciled across the glass and we walk through a carpeted reception area to her dad's darkened office. "This doesn't look good." We hear movement across the hall and then a woman is in the doorway greeting Sandy with great familiarity and smiling warmly at me too. Sandy's dad is at the Ad Building, she tells us, in a meeting that's likely to stretch past five. Sandy curls her lip at this news, and I figure we're screwed as far as getting the cash, but after Sandy explains her predicament the lady goes back for her purse and hands over a twenty just like that, insists Sandy take it, in fact, lest the hat be gone tomorrow and Christmas fairly ruined, and they can settle up later. After acknowledging the good sense in all this, Sandy scribbles out a note for her dad to repay Melinda, which is the woman's name, and leaves it on his desk, and quick as that we're back outside, retracing our steps to the retro shop, with Melinda's cheery goodbye ringing in our ears.

"I forgot where we were," I remark, shaking my head at Melinda's automatic kindness. Without meaning to, I think of the aforementioned "some of us," and shake my head some more.

"Sometimes it's not so bad here," Sandy affirms with a nod. "That store better fucking be open, is all."

Pops parks right next to Crosscut's Lincoln and we step out, pausing, so he can survey the front of the place and basking in the garish gleam of rainbow neon from the front window, and the brilliant white of the sign on the roof announcing:
BEER LIQUOR
LIVE MUSIC

I unsheathe my camera and squat near the front tire to snap off a sharp angle photo of said sign, while Pops crosses his arms over his chest and shakes his head—his only daughter, bathed in the scarlet glow of a COORS LIGHT sign, stooped in a roadhouse parking lot. "Not a word of this to your mother," he warns again. When I stand I notice that the abandoned Valiant is still in the corner, a coating of dust testament to its uninterrupted presence. I point out the vehicle to my father, and then run through the various explanations we've thus far considered. "Did anyone think to check the trunk?" he wonders, adding yet another possibility. "Or maybe the dumpster?"

I'm hoping to get a few shots of Nother tonight, which is why I'm packing the camera in the first place, but since I'm pretty sure I don't need thirty-six of them, I walk over to get a couple of the Valiant; the yellow light over there gives it an ominous tone, and they'll be nice to have if there turns out to be some grisly mayhem involved. There are maybe another dozen cars in the lot, and I snap a couple long range shots of all that metal, neon, and gravel, with a semi plowing past in the background bleeding crimson. When I turn to come back Pops is standing by the door talking to Sara, and they're both staring at me like I've lost it. "We'll get it out of here tomorrow," she's saying as I walk up. "Don't matter so much now, but weekends we need the space. Hey you."

"Hey yourself," I say back and quick snap a picture before she can get her hand up.

"Watch it girlie," she warns, "or I'll tell Nother you brought a date."

"He's my designated driver."

"Oh, brother," Pops says.

"Is it O.K. to take a few pictures inside?" I ask. "I haven't got a one of Nother."

"Probably be all right, since it's you," she says. "But maybe ask, first. Crosscut will like it if you ask, even if he says no."

"You're leaving?"

"I don't stay during the week," she says. "I spend enough time around here as it is." She nods toward the door. "Ruth is pouring tonight."

"Oh, cool," I say. "I need to ask her something, anyway."

"See you Sunday," she says, which comes out equal parts question, demand, and prayer. "Nice seeing you again," she tells Pops. "Enjoy."

There are maybe twenty people scattered around when we go in; several of the booths are filled, with most of the rest at tables near the stage, where Nother is standing with his back to the room tuning a guitar and fidgeting with one of the amps. Two young guys in work shirts from the tire shop down the road are at the bar, on stools they've occupied since quitting time, from the looks of them. Ruthie waves as we approach the corner of the bar nearest the stage, where I leave Pops to go say hello to Nother, who is turned enough to catch sight of us and steps off the riser. He's got us a table near the wall, so Pops will have a close and unobstructed view, and I toss my coat on his to further stake the claim. We talk for a minute and then I return to the bar, leaving him to his business.

The shine we put on the place last Sunday is history. "Job security," Ruth laughs when I point this out, pausing to look up from the limes she's slicing. "Thankless, but secure." She works in the State Farm office near town, but still puts in the occasional night behind the bar. I glance around while she sets up the tire guys again; it's weird to be this familiar with the place already, especially since I'm not really even allowed to be in here.

Pops is behind the bar with Ezra, sweaty Corona in hand, taking advantage of his connection to check out the randomly arranged photos mounted on the back wall. In some, Crosscut sits regally alone, for the rest, Ezra is there to identify the others; locals in some cases, but a smattering of prominent names, too—Pinetop Perkins, Gatemouth, T-Bone Walker among them—who Pops knows of, but doesn't recognize by sight. For several, recognition is not a factor: a harmonica blowing Mick Jagger, for instance, which leaves my father bug-eyed; Crosscut dueling with the likes of Clapton, Keith, and Jeff Beck, who all share the look I see on Pops' face now; and, of course, the centerpiece of this bluesy montage, Crosscut with the man himself, Muddy Waters, up Chicago way, as he likes to say.

Ruthie slides a Coke across the bar and I take the opportunity to ask her about the leather jacket. She looks surprised, perhaps at the perceived extravagance, but quickly assures me he has nothing like it in his wardrobe already, and that he'd most certainly be pleased to receive one. "We've got a picture of him at home in a motorcycle jacket down to his knees," she says with an amused grin. "He's probably five or six, sleeves hanging down way past his hands. It's a wonder he could even stand up in it. Really cute, but damn if I can remember whose jacket."

"Probably time he had one that fit."

"If you say so." She gives me this funny little smile. "You must like him."

I nod. "Don't tell him, though."

Crosscut steps out from the back just then and joins Ezra and my father, who have been scrutinizing the same photo for a good while. Ezra motions at the picture and Crosscut stares, stroking his chin while his lips work back and forth over each other. "Baton Rouge," he says finally. "Tabby's place, that is." Pops asks when, but Crosscut doesn't recall. "Long time gone," he concedes. I love how he talks.

He's obliging when I ask to snap a few, gracious even, so after the second song I move up and have at it. He's planning to tour when the compilation comes out in the spring, it's part of the deal, I think, and so the purpose of all this is to pick through some of the more obscure ones Crosscut hasn't played in a while, and Nother's the only one around who even knows them, much less can keep up. But as I'm clicking I can tell it's not working. Even through this speck of viewfinder it's obvious that this is Crosscut's gig, and everything else more or less fades to background, even my beloved. I snap off a few more anyway, then return to the table; maybe I'll get a better chance over the holidays, at his house, maybe, or the woods. When the song ends Pops looks over and says that was quick, so I relay my observations while they change guitars. "I mean, for what I want, if Crosscut's anywhere around, you can forget about it."

"You're looking for the moon at lunchtime," he says with a slow nod. Ruthie comes by with more drinks, and this time mine is about half rum, to make up for the last one, I guess. When the first gulp pins me back against my chair, I glance over at the bar and she gazes back blankly, like: what'd I do?

When they break Pops heads over to the stage to nose around and I head to the bar. "I figured he'd check the first one," she explains.

"I'm surprised he can't smell it."

Ruth shrugs. "Good thing you drink so fast, huh?" She takes my empty glass and mixes a normal one, then pushes it across the counter. "Your dad looks better without the glasses," she says. "Younger."

I look over my shoulder toward the stage. "We've been telling him that for years, and that he should get contacts. I think he thinks the dark rims make him look smarter."

Ruth purses her lips and studies him. "Maybe," she concedes, "but what's the big deal about that?"

"Well, you know, the whole professor thing. Elbow patches, all that." I look back. "Where'd you see him with his glasses?"

"He was on TV again the other night."

"When?"

"Monday, I think it was."

"Really? Doing what?"

"Getting interviewed in front of the dorms. Talking about some program where they put the foreign students with a local family, so they can experience an American Christmas, and the college can close the dorms. I think your dad was in charge this year, or maybe the spokesman or something." She sweeps a lime wedge off the bar. "You didn't see it?"

"Nope. And usually he says something."

"Maybe he just forgot. Must be getting kind of old hat by now."

"Ho hum," I say. "Maybe I'll get him some Ray-bans for Christmas, if he's that big a star."

"Parents suck to buy for," she says. "Mine, anyway. I mean, I refuse to buy *anyone* cigarettes for Christmas." I laugh picturing Crosscut suggesting this, though I have no trouble believing it. "Like he's not going to be dead soon enough as it is."

"Yeah, I have no idea what to get him, either," I say, nodding toward Pops.

"Why don't you get a picture of him and Crosscut together and have it framed," she suggests, arching her eyebrows when I straighten on my stool. "Seems to be a fan."

"That's a *great* idea."

She nods. "I'd suggest outside, since they're headed that way anyhow." I turn to see only Nother left on the riser, and our fathers moving through the tables toward the door. The crowd parts, and a few people call out, but no one stops them, or joins the parade, and it occurs to me that a lot of them probably figure my father is in the business. "Crosscut looks better in blue light, anyway," Ruth says. "Get them leaning against his car."

"Perfect," I say, sliding off the stool to retrieve my camera. Nother is sitting on one of the amps replacing a string, so before I go out I slip in kind of crouched down and say his name low, and when he looks up I snap off a shot that I think might be what I was after. "Thanks," I call to him while he blinks from the flash. "Be right back."

My father and Crosscut are standing in the lot kicking at the gravel, Crosscut saying how he's been meaning to have it paved for about the last, oh, twenty years, heh, heh, heh, and Pops nodding and agreeing how some things are like that, and then they both kind of laugh together and breathe deep. "Let me get a picture of you guys," I say, and Pops turns to Crosscut and asks does he mind, which is kind of impressive that he thought to ask, knowing how much the idea must appeal to him, and Crosscut says no, he don't mind if Pops don't, so I take a couple while we're all still agreed, and then start moving them around a bit til Crosscut says, "Bossy little thing, that one," but laughing, and while I'm working them over near the Lincoln he starts telling Pops about me spinning into the lot that first time, throwing gravel every which way and damn near running this old man down, he says, which is such an exaggeration, I say back, now look over here, which they do and I take another one. But Crosscut has his hat pulled so low I doubt you can see his eyes in any of them, and he doesn't seem inclined to take it off, so I say wait a minute and pretend to mess with the flash or something and kind of squat down to rest the camera on my knee and when Crosscut turns to whisper something to Pops the sign on the roof illuminates his face and I snap two real fast up at an angle so I get below the shadow from his hat. Pops looks cool, too; he's got his arms hugged across his chest and is starting to grin kind of knowingly at whatever it is Crosscut just said, which I don't even care about not hearing, since one of these should come out just right, which is a damn good thing because I'm out of film.

I get totally mellow on rum after that, easing through the second set in the same hypnotic trance as everyone else. Sometimes there's a point right in the middle of a song where it's completely silent, when Crosscut has yet to pluck the next note, or unleash the next groan, and he's just holding off that extra second or two, waiting, and the joint is so hushed you can actually feel it on your skin, like some kind of magic just swept in.

They finish around midnight to a standing ovation; the tire guys are even holding up matches for one more, which has Ezra a little nervous. Nother and I step outside while things settle down, and when we come back around front a little while later Pops is waiting patiently in the Volvo, his head still bobbing. He cranks the CD before we're even out of the lot, lowering the volume only once on the ride home, to speculate as to whether Nother might join his father on the road next spring, an idea he seems to find way more appealing than I do. "I mean,

man, if I could play like that...." He sighs deeply and lets
the thought trail off.

"Then you could go, and Nother could stay here."

"I see," he says.

"I'm just kidding, Dad. The last thing I need right now
is either of you leaving."

"That's more like it," he says. "He's not interested in
that anyway, right?"

"So he says."

Pops shakes his head. "Go figure."

We zone out the rest of the way home, which is fine
since there's less chance he'll notice I'm loaded. But when
I lean over to hug him goodnight in the yard, he says, "I
knew she'd get booze into one of those sooner or later."

Every year I get it in my head that we're going to have
this really great, traditional Christmas: beautiful tree; shiny,
perfect packages; snow; the overwhelming scent of cinnamon and holly berry; and it'll be the one I remember all the
rest of my life, the template I measure each succeeding one
against, especially if I'm ever a parent myself, because I'll
want my kids to have Christmas just like out of one of those
holiday specials. But, of course, that never happens, and I
always end up feeling like I don't get it, somehow, and that
everyone else had a better time than I did, for reasons dic-
tated solely by my weirdness, which, now that I'm thinking
about it, is the whole premise for the Charlie Brown special,
so maybe my life is like TV after all, except there's grown-
ups in my version just itching to screw it up even more.

Like when my mother says, "I really don't see why we
can't just dispense with Christmas this year." Dispense, she
says, like reading the minutes. With Christmas! She rubs
her eyes. "I mean, really."

"Emphatically not," I tell her. I start to picture this in third person, *Lady Scrooge In Mississippi* or something, and I'm the latest young star entrusted to save the holiday. I focus on remaining charmingly impertinent, yet endearingly sincere. "Try to make sense, O.K.?"

"Well, I don't see why not," she rebukes. "You're not a child anymore, and I don't have the long break this year, you know. I'm not faculty anymore." She says this like she was home doing Martha Stewart projects every other year, which would be an inaccurate recollection, to say the least. "And your father's got his book." She rolls her eyes. "And his TV career."

"You-can't-just-skip-Christmas," I dictate.

"I'll bet it's way easier than you think."

"No, Mom. Now just cut the bullshit right now." Which is decidedly not a term you're likely to hear on a Christmas special, I realize, but it needs to be said. "And we're having a tree, in case that was your next idea." She opens, then closes, her mouth. "Dad and I will get it," I add. "Today. You needn't do a thing."

"Well, put it up over there. I mean, for God's sake, we're leaving the next day. There's no reason to put one up here."

"I live here," I remind her. She sighs emphatically and I wonder: Did she really expect to win this argument?

The wind blew crazy yesterday and it got real cold overnight, so at least it's starting to feel like December. I'm no big fan of winter, but I've got this notion of what Christmas should feel like, and shorts and sandals isn't part of it. Pops and I are going out later to get a tree, and I don't want to be sweating doing it, or when we're drinking hot chocolate after, which we will be, whether we're sweating or not. But first I have to pick up Nother's jacket from the retro shop, and while I'm there I see this funky silver bracelet that I decide to buy for Kayla, even though we haven't been getting along so great. She was a big help when I first got here, and even with the tension now, it's hard to imagine those first few months without her. It's not that expensive anyway, so I quickly pay for it before I change my mind.

Pops and I find a nice tree, smaller than I wanted, but perfectly shaped and with no gaping holes where you can see right through to the trunk. He suggests I try to meet Gail halfway on some of the holiday stuff, so I'll count the smaller tree as a start. He says any accommodation is a gift, but since I have no idea how to wrap an accommodation, I buy her some earrings that I see in this shop next to the diner where we get hot chocolate, which is total luck, since I only go in there because Pops is gabbing out front with someone who saw him on TV. So I'm pretty much done shopping except for Gina, but I'll wait til I get there to buy her gift; we always go after, so we can buy more stuff on sale.

"How come everyone knew you were on TV but me?" I ask when we're back in the car and headed home, our tree tied on top all festive like. "I mean, I had to hear it from someone in a bar."

Pops laughs. "Nother saw that?"

"Ruth," I say. "You know, I was on campus that night; if I'd have known I could have come watch you in action."

"Hey, I didn't even know about it til they showed up. Media Relations put the whole thing together and forgot to tell me til it was time to shoot."

"Is that why you forgot to take off your glasses?"

"Yeah," he says, glancing over at me. "They should have caught that in the run-through. And I meant to call and tell you, but things ran over and I spaced it. Sorry."

"I'm just giving you a hard time."

"I'm on tomorrow," he says.

"What this time?"

"That same morning show, but with the weekend people. It's a holiday theme; you know, they go to the mall, visit a tree lot, talk to a Santa. Bake something, probably." He says this like he totally realizes how corny it is. "I'm supposed to talk about holiday stress."

"Take Mom," I suggest.

"I think they mean how to avoid it."

"Shoot Mom."

We unload the tree and Pops carries it around back to the shed and sticks the trunk in a bucket of water. We decide to decorate it tomorrow night when I get home from cleaning. I've got a French test Monday that I'm pretty much ready for, so tomorrow's the best option. Christmas break starts Thursday, but I don't want to wait that long, and I have tests Tuesday and Wednesday that I'll need to study for big time. "Tell your mom I'm going to set this up inside tomorrow afternoon so it opens up a little before we trim it. I'll probably run the lights, too, so if she doesn't want to be around, she should plan accordingly."

But instead she says, "That's kind of a small tree you guys got, isn't it?" I have to assume she saw us unloading it yesterday, because it's still out in the shed right now.

We're waiting for Dad's show to come on and I'm standing beside a stack of boxes full of Christmas stuff I've brought in. I frown and stare down my nose at her. "We thought it might be a good idea to scale back a little this year. Um, in view of the circumstances." I've got the boxes piled against the back wall, and I wasn't even going to start putting things out til she got used to the tree.

"Because of me, you mean?" She sounds almost touched.

If she tries to pretend she wasn't serious, I'm going to wing something at her.

I shrug. "For all of us. And it didn't hurt that the best looking tree we saw all day was only five feet tall."

"A Christmas miracle," she says, but lightly, and with a hint of a smile.

Pops comes on then, sans glasses, and once again delivers the goods. The show is pretty bland, but he stays on message, and the hostess is eating it up. He speaks of give and take; that we should feel free to take what the season has to offer and to enjoy this bounty—the community, the good will, the love and tolerance; and at the same time we should be generous of ourselves to the season, make a gift of ourselves, so to speak.

"So to speak," Gail echoes as they go to commercial. She looks at me, bewildered.

"Yeah, but you've got to admit it sounds good. And if you're really being honest, it feels kind of good, too."

"And couldn't you just kill him for that," she says.

There's a knock at the door and I go to let Nother in. He was supposed to get here in time to watch Pops, but tells me he had to stop at the pharmacy for Crosscut, who's been hacking quite a bit lately, and having some tightness in his chest. "Sounded like a steam engine this morning," he says. "Thinks it might have been the change in the weather."

"He needs to go see someone," I say, recalling the oysters he was hawking up in the parking lot the other night. "Like urgent care or something."

"Only way he goes there is on his back or unconscious." He shrugs, like: what are you going to do?

"What's this?" I ask. He's got a grocery bag hanging from one arm with branches poking out the top. He sets it down on the kitchen table and lifts out a pair of wreaths, holding one out to each side, like prize fish. "These are beautiful," I tell him. "Mom, come look. Are they both for us?"

"Ruth sent one for you guys and one for your dad."

"She made these?"

"We both did," he says. "I made them, and she decorated."

Gail has muted the commercial and joined us in the kitchen. "Oh my, these are gorgeous." She reaches over and pinches a bough between her fingers and thumb. "They're real," she says.

"Hand picked," Nother says, like this is a normal thing to be doing. "There's still some sap, but I think it won't drip."

"Well, aren't you the talented one," Gail says, giving me this look like: is this guy for real? "We're keeping this one," she decides, indicating the more festive of the two, exactly the opposite of what I'd have guessed. It's got a bright red ribbon up top and these plastic gold drums and red birds set into the branches, and it's flocked with wisps of white soap flakes to look like drifted snow. The other is more elegant; a wide maroon and gold ribbon knotted at the bottom, with clumps of holly and deep red berries set into it, and a tiny strand of white fairy lights, which blink serenely when he plugs it in. Nother hands the first one to her and unplugs the other before placing it on the table, then rubs his hands on the back of his pants. "We'll have to put this right up," my mother says, setting it next to the other one.

"Oops, we're missing Dad," I notice, stepping into the living room and flicking off the mute. But they've already gone live to one of the riverboat casinos, all done up in pine boughs and flickering lights, with a chorus of carolers out on the deck in costumes from the 1800s. I look at Nother. "Sorry about that."

"We saw him the other night," he says, "talking about foreign students."

My mother rolls her eyes.. "It's a wonder they're not all coming here."

"We got one," he says.

I look over. "Really?"

"Yeah, Crosscut's idea. He got it in his head that we should do it, and Ruth called over there yesterday. There's a guy from Denmark coming on Wednesday. Rolf." As usual, it's impossible to tell what he thinks of this.

Gail looks at me. "Your father strikes again."

We watch the riverboat for a minute, then Nother and I get ready to go. "Remember, Dad's coming over to set up the tree," I tell her while he goes out to start the truck. "So you might want to leave for a while."

"We'll be fine," she says. "He'll need a hand anyway, if you're not here."

I furrow my brow and stare at her. "O.K. then, see you later." I slip into my jacket and pause at the door. "And look, Mom, if I start going overboard with the holiday stuff, just say something, O.K.?"

"Don't I usually?" she replies, which pretty much takes care of that.

I think it's right about this point that time starts to get away from me. That holiday rush begins, like the bar just clanked down on the roller coaster and you're not going to get a relaxed breath again til it's over. I'm late getting home because we stay to help Sara loop some tinsel around the bar, and stick up these cardboard snowmen and reindeers all over the place—which she assures me will all be embell-ished with sex organs by the next time I see them, and then wedge this molded plastic Santa that ought to be on some-one's lawn into an upper alcove of the back-bar, where he glows down like St. Peter. We've been listening to Christmas music all afternoon, and Sara mixes up a pitcher of holiday punch for while we decorate, so we're all pretty joyous by the time we leave. And then I probably stay too long outside when we get back to my house, but I hardly care by then, because, what the hell, it's Christmas, and I like mauling this guy in his truck.

Gail has hung the wreath right across from the door, so it's the first thing I see walking in, which is perfect, and then I notice some of our other stuff is out, too, that she's been doing a bit of decorating herself, and when I ask what brought this on, she motions with her wine glass and says, "I got tired of watching him." Meaning Pops, who at the moment is down on all fours with his head stuck in the lowest ring of branches and his ass jutting into the room, plumber-like.

He backs himself out and sits on his heels, red-faced and with pine needles littering his hair. He reaches for his wine and nods at Gail. "Try it now."

She reaches over the side of the couch and sticks the plug into the outlet and the tree lights up. He turns, gives her this "see there" look, and raises his glass, while my mother shakes her head. "Fa la la la la," she responds, which is when I notice they're a good way down one of those big bottles, which means I'm pretty much home free, and can probably even pour myself a splash, which I do. The tree is up on this thick old suitcase, so it's almost regulation, with a white sheet curled around the bottom like snow, and we get it looking really fine with bulbs and tinsel and the angel on top. Gail and I take our time putting out the rest of the stuff, but some I keep back to do Pops' side, and all in all, you couldn't really ask for a better evening given the weirdness of this house, though I'm sure it won't last.

School is a circus all week, even with a lot of the teachers scheduling tests to try to keep a lid on it. No one is into being here, except to goof off and exchange gifts and eat Christmas cookies and stuff, and half the people are wasted by the time they arrive. Kayla and I watch from our table, munching an assortment of kettle corn, candy canes and marshmallow Santas, trying to discern who's attempting to hook up with whom by New Years without resorting to asking Joley, who's apparently never seen a holiday sweatshirt she didn't like

I ace my French test Monday, even with my thick head, and Nother comes over that night to help me cram for Chemistry, which works, I guess, because I nail that one, too, in spite of it being a total bitch. Then I catch a break when my English test gets postponed til after the break, which is happening a lot as the week progresses, probably because they don't want a lot of pissed off students running around for two weeks with all that free time and direct access to eggs and toilet paper.

My mother has dinner with Carl on Tuesday, prompting raised eyebrows and a noticeable chill from me at his sudden reappearance, though she assures me it's just a friendly get together to toast the season—his idea. I decorate Pops' side that night, while he gives his last final and Nother studies for some quiz at the table. I run the remaining strings of lights around the walls and hang his wreath above Nother's head, and set up this little two-foot tree in his living room, after which I declare study time over and put off all the big lights, so it's just the colored bulbs and the tree and us, and Nother and I end up doing it right there on Pops' living room floor, just like it's a movie or something, but which I still can't believe we did.

Thursday I go with Gail to pick out a sports coat for
Pops, which he'll need another one of if he's going to
keep being on TV all the time. His picture is ready too,
so we swing by the frame shop, where I've had it profes-
sionally matted and all that, with this killer blue frame
setting off the neon and the ghostly front of the building
perfectly. Even Gail is impressed; both Crosscut and Pops
look very cool, though she hints that Crosscut could
maybe use a couple weeks of bed rest. Annie has invited
us for dinner, so we stop for wine and head over there. I
give Kayla her present early since they're driving to
Houston the day after tomorrow and I won't see her
again til I get back. She seems surprised, but I can tell she
likes it from how she keeps glancing down at it, and spinning it on her wrist with her other hand. It looks good on
her too, something she'd have picked out for herself,
even, and I think it bugs her that I did so well. "I didn't
get you anything," she says, though this admission comes
out not the least bit plaintive, but merely an expression
of the facts.

"That's all right," I reply, though it's obvious she isn't
asking to be forgiven. "It's for your kindness," I tell her.
"Before."

She looks at me curiously, as if to determine if I've just
slammed her back, then smiles slightly to acknowledge the
intended ambiguity. "Thank you," she says. "It's lovely."

I spend an afternoon making cookies with Sandy, and
another day goofing off with Pops, who is otherwise
remarkably focused on his book. He's got two chapters
outlined that he wants to write up before classes start
again, which strikes me as pretty ambitious, but he's full of
surprises lately, so who knows. I meet Rolf from Denmark,
who speaks English better than he understands it, I think,

which might be true of most people. But he's cute and fun and happy, and Crosscut just nods at him a lot and tells the rest of the family, "Rolf." I read some; I sleep a lot, sometimes on Pops' couch while he's working at the desk. Gina and I e-mail every day, making more plans than we could possibly fulfill in a month. I'm not even that excited to leave anymore; I'd rather hang out here, I think, but I'm sure it will be fun once I get there. It is sooo weird there now, she says, but without saying why. Bring pictures, she says. The days blur together; I miss half the specials I'd planned to watch absolutely for sure.

And then Christmas is here, like an ambush.

My gifts are a success; Gail likes the earrings, which I was pretty sure about, and Pops is totally blown away by the picture, which he takes next door and hangs front and center above his desk within the hour. I get some clothes and a couple gift certificates, and a really nice purse that Pops claims to have picked out himself, which I don't believe for a second. Then he puts together this great dinner; prime rib, potatoes, vegetables, and a noble attempt at a Yorkshire pudding he got off the Food Channel, which I don't care for all that much, other than to appreciate the effort.

Nother comes over at four, and I finally get to give him his present, which I've been dying to do since the second I bought it. "You got this for me?" he asks, totally serious, holding it out at arms length to stare at it, like there's been some mistake.

"Put it on," I tell him, because I'm not sure he'd think of it otherwise.

"This is great," he whispers, staring into the mirror aback the closed door of my room. "You shouldn't have," he says.

"Do you like it?"

"I love it."

"Then I should have."

He hands me a bright red sack. "Now you." There are several packages inside; a beautiful black belt that he made, with a gorgeous silver buckle and delicate weave etched into the leather, worthy of the finest shop I've ever been in. A book about the blues, which I've been saying I need to read up on, so I at least know the names. Candy. A Sawmill tee shirt. I save the smallest box for last, then lift out a gold necklace strung through a heart shaped pendant, with a small diamond glittering in its center. "It's beautiful," I say, letting it dangle from my fingers to catch the light. He takes it and fastens the chain around my neck, which is this totally great moment, and I'm thinking Gina will totally die when she sees this, and yes, I believe I do love this guy. Which I'll probably tell her if she asks. Or him.

We stay in my room as long as we reasonably can, until Gail finally raps on the door and requests—oh so casual-like—that we come out and show them what we got. She makes this face at the jacket, arching her eyebrows at me like: we should have discussed that. Then she does an even bigger double take when she sees my necklace, her lips pinching in further consternation when she's ascertained that yes, it is a diamond. Fortunately, the phone rings right then—someone in Baltimore it sounds like—so we skip over to Pops' side so Nother can see the picture. She's still gabbing when we get back a half-hour later, so we get ready to leave. I've got a couple plates of cookies to take over there, one for Nother's house, and one to bring to Seth's, which is where most of them are now. I was thinking that finally I was going to meet Madame

Marie, but Nother's just been telling Pops that he dropped
her and Crosscut back at the house on his way here
because his father was feeling poorly and she wanted him
to lie down. I do this pantomime for Gail to let her know
I'm going out, and she puts a hand over the receiver and
asks when I'll be back.

"Couple hours, I guess." I shrug. "Why?"

"Well, you still need to pack," she reminds me,
"and we're absolutely out the door at nine, so I want you
to do it tonight."

"Don't worry," I tell her. "I already know everything
I'm taking."

"I still want you packed tonight."

"O.K., I will. Relax." I go over and give her a hug.
"Good night. Merry Christmas."

"I'll be up," she says.

WINTER

"What?" I sit up too fast and immediately have to shut my eyes again til my balance returns. "What do you mean, dead?" I feel this rush of heat in my stomach and reach out to grab my father's arm, while a numbing wave of *déjà vu* washes over me.

"Last night," my father says. "I'm sorry, Teri."

"It was Christmas last night," I hear myself say, though even I don't know what I mean by this. "How do you know?" Past his shoulder I can see Gail standing in the doorway.

"Nother called."

"I didn't hear it." I look at the clock. Seven-thirty. "When?"

"He called my number."

I go to throw back the covers but Pops is sitting on them. He stands and I climb out of bed as Gail flicks on the light. "Are you all right?" she asks as I shade my eyes and push past them toward the bathroom.

"I don't know." Out of habit I begin brushing my teeth, then throw several handfuls of water onto my face. As I towel off I realize I'm crying. Gail and my father are in the kitchen when I re-cross the hall to my room, their tone grave even at that muted volume. I throw on the sweater and jeans I laid out to wear on the plane and rip a comb through my hair. They both turn when I walk out. "I need to go over there," I say.

"There's not time," my mother says.

"I'm staying," I tell her. "I can't go now." I look her square in the eye, not to be defiant, just to make sure she gets it. "I'll pay for the ticket if you want."

She starts to say something, then pauses, her lips forming a tight line. "Shower before you go," she says finally. "You'll feel better, and it could be a long time." I burst into tears at this, and, surprisingly, it is my mother who crosses the floor to gather me in her arms. "I'm sorry, darling," she says, stroking the top of my head. I nod into her chest and continue to hold on. "Go on," she says after another minute, "Get cleaned up. Another half hour hardly matters now."

Twenty minutes later I've got the keys to the Honda in my fist and I'm hugging her goodbye. "Have fun," I say, "Be safe." I've written Gina's number for her. "Don't forget to call her as soon as you land. Tell her I'm sorry, and I'll call as soon as I can."

"I left some money on the table," she says. "You should be all right. Keep your father apprised of your whereabouts, please. And tell them all how sorry I am."

It doesn't occur to me until I'm turning into Nother's yard that I haven't thought this through at all; I've been going on instinct since I stepped out of bed, the first insisting that my place is here with Nother, not a thousand miles from here goofing with Gina, the second being to get out of my house as fast as possible lest my mother decide to dig in. I'd been expecting a huge fight, one of our usual loud and ugly scenes, though much louder and much uglier this time. I'm still not sure why she caved like that, nor her reasons for being so kind in the process. From past experience I know that even when the ground rules shift, as they seemed to this morning, her tactics remain largely the same.

And now I find myself at the door, with no idea what awaits me inside, or if I'm even wanted here at this hour, or at all. When no one answers my knock I let myself in, just as another wave of apprehension engulfs me. Is Crosscut still here, I wonder, lying somewhere inside, I mean; need I gird myself to see a dead body in one of these rooms? Is Nother even here? I've been assuming his presence at my side through this, but I didn't even call to say I was coming. What are the particulars in this situation? Have I messed up already merely by coming here? The hallway smells of coffee, incense, and damp coats, adding to my queasiness. I hear voices two rooms over, and Ruthie and Esther farther off the other way in the kitchen, though I cannot for the life of me seem to move my feet in either direction. If no one comes, I dare to hope, eventually I'll starve.

But before I can determine which direction to go, or slump from malnutrition, the door to Madame Marie's office/consulting room/tent show opens, and a woman I know instinctively to be her glides silently into the hall. She is smaller than I expect, tiny almost, and clad this day–perhaps always–in loose, sweeping skirts and a black shawl; were it not for the large gold pendant dangling from her neck, and the bangles clinking on both wrists, she could easily pass for a nun of some European peasant order. She pauses, unhurried, eyes downcast, as if collecting her thoughts. We are still several paces apart when she senses my presence and looks up. "I'm Teri," I whisper. It is an odd distance from which to interact, but my feet remain leaden. "I'm very sorry."

She smiles then, the gentlest expression I've ever witnessed lighting briefly on her porcelain features, as if it is me who requires consoling this morning. And indeed, I do feel immediately becalmed, the tightness in my limbs and stomach washing away before her narcotic gaze. "I know who you are," she intones, stepping close to take my hands in hers. "I've been expecting you."

Her face is as smooth and white as marble, haloed in thick black curls with the barest hint of gray at the temples. Her features are in perfect balance, her appearance much younger than the age I know her to be—two decades and change in arrears of her husband. She will always be beautiful, I sense; hers is a loveliness that will not fade. I stare into her welcoming gaze, unsure how to address her, and even if it's rude to ask. "If there's anything I can do," I offer instead, falling back on the lamest of *clichés.* "At all."

She smiles once more, beatifically, and nods toward the voices. "Through there," she says with a slight dip of her head. She squeezes my hands, then releases them. "Thank you for your kindness," she utters, then moves past me into her room, the door closing behind her with a soft click.

I'm riveted still when Ruth emerges from the kitchen, staring at a Christmas tree music box on the hall table, paralyzed at its incongruous display at this sad hour. I determine to make myself useful the moment I can move again. Ruth crosses the hall and we hug. I express condolences, receive thanks. "How long have you been standing here?" she asks.

"Not long." I unzip my coat. "Your mom was just here." Ruth arches her eyebrows. "We met, finally," I add. "She seems O.K. About this, I mean."

"You're very brave to do that alone." She smiles to indicate it was a joke, and tugs me toward the next room. "Come on, Nother's back here somewhere."

"How are you holding up?" I ask.

She shrugs. "O.K. We all had our moments last night, but–" She shrugs again, then says, "It's sudden, but not unexpected."

"What was it?" I ask. "Have they said?" I'm not even sure who I think "they" might be.

"His heart," she states almost dismissively. We pause in the doorway of the next room, where others have congregated. "I don't know how much you knew," she continues, "but he wasn't well. His lungs were a mess; and there was a blocked artery, we just found out; he smoked; his diet was awful. He probably only lived this long out of stubbornness."

"I didn't know," I say. "It was a heart attack, then?" Across the room, Rolf taps Nother on the arm and motions toward us. Oh my God, I think, I'd forgotten all about Rolf being here. What must he be thinking right now?

"Heart failure, I think they'll call it," Ruth answers. "My guess is a whole bunch of him just had enough."

"How was he expecting to go on the road?" I ask, still a bit distracted by Rolf's presence. "Touring would have killed him for sure."

"That wasn't happening," she says. "He barely made it through the studio work last summer. It was just something to talk about."

Should I have realized all this? The rest seem to be taking it in their stride, more or less, like the curtain going down on Act Three. "Listen," I say, taking her hand as Nother approaches. "I'm here til whenever. So tell me what I can do."

"Thanks," she says, squeezing my hand, then lifting it to accept Nother's embrace. "Hug him, for now."

So I do, gathering him into my arms and burying my face in the hollow of his neck. "You're here," he says into my ear, pulling me tight, until we are pressed together from shoulder to knee.

"Oh, baby," I say.

We move through the house to the kitchen, where I stop to hug Esther. It is just after nine when Nother and I step outside; my parents have just left for the airport in Jackson, where we'll pick Gail up again six days hence. We stand staring across the yard into the trees, watching the limbs bow and shimmy in the damp winter breeze, then move beneath the carport and settle onto the cold vinyl of the displaced car seat. Nother is coatless, and still in the same shirt he was wearing yesterday; I assume he hasn't slept. I rise and walk to the glider, returning with the quilted seat cover to spread over us. We sit in silence for a long time, snuggled together beneath the covering, listening to the wind, and the faint sound of music now coming from inside, my head resting on his shoulder. If he'd sleep, I'd let him, but after a time he begins to talk, haltingly at first, and unprompted but for his own need. They had been in the kitchen, Nother seated across the smaller table from his mother, Ron and Ruthie opposite each other in the remaining places. The younger three had all recently returned, joining their mother in the kitchen to settle in for the night, talking sporadically of the day, the gifts, of holidays past, clinking tea cups and swirling ice, picking at the plates of food still out. Ron had been speaking, telling of his one wintry Christmas, a family trip to Wisconsin when he was eight to visit his grandparents. Nother had happened to glance up in time to see his mother's face tighten, her eyes pull sharply into focus, her jaw set itself grimly. "Your father," she said across the table when she saw that he was watching her, and he knew.

He'd told Ruth to stay with their mother and gone immediately to Crosscut's bedside, though he was certain, upon entering the room that any further haste was unnecessary. He'd checked for a pulse, then wiped a spot at the corner of his father's mouth, noting each time that the skin was still warm to his touch. "Eleven-seventeen," he says now. "I remember seeing the clock over my mother's shoulder when I got up." He nods slowly, his chin dipping to touch the cover. "Funny the things that stick." The ambulance had come straight away, but silently, as there'd been no need for sirens or lights, the paramedics confirming what was already known. As they loaded the body onto the gurney, he'd watched Ron bend to shut off the blanket.

They'd notified everyone within the hour, despite the lateness, lest there be bad feelings today. Rolf had already gone to bed, so they let him sleep, pulling the door closed to the small back room where he snored on the day bed so their movements in the coming hours would not disturb him. The others had not been overly surprised, the news received more as summation than announcement. Ezra went to the hospital to see to things there, and arrange for the body to be moved to the funeral home; those who could came to the house. It was strange, Nother says, how the grief dispersed itself among them, the lack of focus somehow mitigating their singular pains. When the hugging was complete they'd begun bumping around the house, talking in pairs, then groups, then all together, before breaking off again to begin the process anew. They took turns crying and consoling, laughing and remembering.

They'd drank, briefly, around two, but no one's heart was in it; there'd be ample opportunity for that in the coming days, they all suspected, when news of this passing reached the music world. They settled what few things they could at that late hour, and then waited for daylight.

Nother had dozed around four, he thought, but by then the difference between sleep and consciousness had blurred. He'd been the one to tell Rolf, who'd taken the news visibly harder than any of them, as if he were somehow to blame. "Then I called your house," he says, "And then you were here."

I turn and kiss his cheek. "I'd have come last night," I tell him. "You should have called."

"I know you would have. That's why I waited." He shifts to look at me. "I think we needed that time alone," he adds. "Not that we didn't want you here. Everyone asked, and everyone knew you'd come."

"What made you call Pops?"

"I knew he'd tell you," he says. "It occurred to me that your mother might wait til you were on the plane. And I knew that wouldn't be good."

"You'd have been seeing that on CNN," I confirm, settling back to ponder this. "But I think she would have said. At the least, she'd have told my dad, and he'd have told me, no matter what she thought." I look over at him. "But that was pretty good thinking for seven A.M."

We've been out here long enough for several more cars to arrive, spouses and grandkids from the sounds of it, though we are blocked from view by Crosscut's hulking Lincoln, and so remain undisturbed by the new arrivals. The phone rings at regular intervals, and I note additional communications via cell phones, as the siblings alternately step onto the patio to make and receive calls. The activity seems to be picking up by the minute, so we get up and go back inside.

"Here they are," Rachel says, more of a general comment than one directed to anybody in particular. We hug since she wasn't here earlier. "Where were you guys?"

"Just sitting," Nother tells her. He looks around the kitchen, then to me. "What can I get you?"

"Coffee?" He pours us each a cup from the industrial/church picnic sized percolator steaming on the counter, and we stir in lots of cream and join Rachel at the table. "What're you doing?" I ask, indicating the papers and legal pad she has spread before her.

"Funeral stuff," she says. "There's some things we want, but right now I'm trying to make sure everyone knows who needs to know." She taps her pen on the list she's compiling on the legal pad. "The last thing we need is a bunch of old, pissed off musicians."

There's to be a viewing tomorrow night, and another the following morning, then the funeral service that same afternoon, followed by what sounds like a combination reunion/wake/jam session for whoever shows up, possibly here, but more likely at The Sawmill, which will remain closed until then. The family are all local, excepting a few on Madame Marie's side, who are spread out around New Orleans, which is still pretty close. Were it not for several of the far flung bluesmen who will undoubtedly want to come, the whole thing could be concluded tonight.

Nother and I make a run to Bodean's at eleven, to pick up the order Luke is phoning in. The house is full now, but the casseroles have not yet begun to arrive, and most of this crowd hasn't eaten since yesterday. There are new arrivals every few minutes, so we'll need to pick up more sodas and some snacks on the way, along with paper plates, cups, and napkins. We take Daniel along to help carry stuff. At the Winn-Dixie several people approach Nother to offer condolences; apparently word has gotten out to the local stations. Then, in Bodean's, the owner refuses our money, insisting we take the huge order–along with a wide assortment of sides and desserts we haven't asked for–with his compliments and deepest sympathy. Nother is gracious to a fault to everyone, as is Daniel to the several who recognize him as one of the clan, and I marvel at their composure and civility.

"Teri!" Ezra barks as soon as we walk in, "Come here! Quick!" We scramble through the house, crowding into the back room with all the rest, who are arranged around the television. I hear my father's voice and my eyes dart around the room, until Nother puts a hand on my shoulder and motions toward the set.

Onscreen I see Pops, standing in front of our house with a silver-haired man in a network blazer, the station number and the caption "LIVE" spread across the bottom of the picture. Pops is in a polo shirt and jeans, his writing attire most days, and unshaven, which contrasts rather well, I think, with the scrubbed and shiny reporter. Resting on the porch railing behind them, propped precisely between the two bobbing heads, is the photo of the deceased and his current champion. Only on local TV could you get away with that. "The anomaly in a situation such as this," my father is saying into the mike, "is that we tend to think of the artist as a citizen of the world, belonging more to his craft and his fans than to any one place. Still, he does, in fact, have to call somewhere home. And so for those of us fortunate enough to have a person of this calling amongst us, to know as a neighbor, and perhaps a friend, the loss is doubly poignant. For not only have we lost a giant talent and inspiration, but one of our own, too, a husband, father, neighbor."

There is a quick cut, and suddenly we are staring at Crosscut's dapper profile from way back, clean shaven in a white shirt and tie, with his name and the term of his life beneath it, while a voiceover from the studio repeats the news. Elizabeth stares at the screen. "He hasn't looked like that in a while."

"Shit, he never looked like that," Ezra says, as the room begins to empty toward the kitchen.

"I can't believe they don't have a more recent photo." Elizabeth complains.

"They never paid any attention to him," Ezra reminds her. "Only time they ever mention him at all is when we sell underage at the 'Mill, or someone gets cut up." He flicks his hand dismissively. "Only reason they're on it like this now is that it's slow for news from Christmas. Else he'd be dead a week before they'd even mention it."

"That was nice what your dad said," Ruthie tells me. I smile and begin helping arrange buns on a tray to put with the meat. "He always sounds so good on there. I almost forgot he was talking about Crosscut."

"He can talk all right," I agree. "But I know in this case he meant it."

"Hey, I didn't mean anything against your dad," Ezra says. "That was nice, him saying all that."

"That picture on the porch was new," Luke says. "Where'd that come from?"

"Teri took it, didn't you?" Sara asks. "Couple weeks ago."

"How do you rate?" Luke wonders. "Nobody could even look his direction with a camera yesterday."

"Crosscut took a shine to her," Sara tells him. "I never knew him to take to anyone so quick."

"This one either," Ezra says, motioning toward Nother with his sandwich, which, to my annoyance, makes me blush.

"I'll bet those are the last pictures of him," Ruth says. "Did anyone get any yesterday at all?" A survey of the room yields shaking heads all around. "I think he knew," Ruth says.

"I'll get some made, then," I offer. "I just figured you had lots."

People come and go well into the evening, and the day passes in an odd mixture of muted bereavement and barely restrained conviviality. Visitors arrive sober-faced, with eyes downcast, their greetings given in hushed whispers, accompanied by prolonged hugs and head shaking, as if the processes of this life have suddenly been rendered inscrutable. Most come bearing some offering of food, and the kitchen soon fills with mountains of fried chicken, tubs of salads, beans, biscuits to feed an army. Bottles are presented, many the largesse of patrons known best to Sara and Ezra, who have made their way here upon being displaced by the locked door out on the highway. All, in turn, are lifted from their gravitas by one of the family, who return each greeting generously, with a smile, an intimate nod, a few soft words. Chairs are offered, refreshments; introductions are made. Bottles are unsealed, stories traded, warmth soon shining from reddened faces to join the familiar throaty blues wafting from the speakers, which should be macabre, given the circumstances, or at least inappropriate, but isn't at all.

"Call your father," Ruthie says at one point, an idea I've considered and dismissed more than once already. "Tell him to come eat, at least. Have a drink." I nod and glance at the clock; if he's writing I'd just as soon wait, but it's after five now, so I'm sure whatever he might accomplish today is completed by now. I should have had Ruth call, but I don't want to chase her down now, so I do it myself.

By the time he arrives, packing a flower arrangement he picked up God knows where at this hour, there is a van from the ABC affiliate in New Orleans parked in the yard, and the producer has one foot stuck in the door trying to convince Ezra to let his crew in to record the scene, *Real World* style. The passing of a blues legend is not treated lightly in the Crescent City, he avers, and the drive up was no picnic, either. But Ezra is having none of it; it's a privacy issue, he explains to the incredulous newsman, and instructs them to set up out back if they want, where someone will join them soon.

Which turns out to be Pops, not surprisingly, who has witnessed the encounter in the doorway and has yet to meet a camera he wasn't at home in front of. "Would you like me to speak to him?" he offers, when it becomes apparent that no one already present is of a mind to. He's still holding the flowers, which Ruth finally takes from him in exchange for a glass of ice and a nod toward the makeshift bar set up on the counter. "It's no trouble," he assures Ezra, in a voice that sounds oddly like he's the one asking a favor. "Least I can do."

Ezra shrugs and pours him a couple fingers from a bottle of Wild Turkey. "We'd be obliged," he says.

I follow Pops out back, where he begins speaking to the skeptical producer, who seems baffled, still, to have encountered so many camera-shy people in one place. Pops has brought several of the local bluesmen out with him, dragged with their instruments and glasses from the gathering inside, where they've been paying their humble respects and wetting their whistles. Once he has them

seated and comfy and picking, Pops turns to discuss lighting with the crew, and camera angles, and how best to
convey the tone of this singular gathering. Which is when
I go back inside, wondering where, exactly, he picked up
all this.

Shortly thereafter we are gathered in the same tight circle, watching my father on television (again! today!), as he
somberly places the passing of Crosscut Martin in its
proper light (red chili pepper, apparently, provides the
requisite lurid feel), and details the healing process already
begun for the family joining together inside (us! here!). He
speaks in more general terms than this morning, as the
audience he plays to now is much broader, while behind
and slightly out of frame, the bluesmen play on, Titanic-
like, oblivious, to all appearances, of the media event at
their backs, while farther still across the yard, the trees
sway in the evening breeze. It is, I have to say, the perfectly orchestrated scene; soberly reverential in its delivery, gothic for its haunted trees and dirge-like soundtrack,
yet alluring all the same for its crimson-tinted *dishabille*.
As I stand watching the screen I can barely accept that it is
being played out a scant thirty feet away, compliments of
my father and his newfound sorcery. Crosscut, I have to
think, would be pleased.

The family is grateful, in any case, as am I, simply that
we can be of some small use to them at this time. Lord
knows they wouldn't ask. As much sympathy and comfort
is being given as received, I can't help but notice. Still,
they do seem to appreciate their father being eulogized in
this high regard, a near reverence that has come suddenly
after somehow managing to elude him in life. He was
known locally, in that odd, almost dignified manner of the
once famous, a silent film star, perhaps, or a long turned

out senator, or in the near-famous terms of a local diamond phenom who had withered in Triple A. The encomia spilling from my father today are words they have
heard only sporadically, and in these few instances only by
die-hard fans, fellow practitioners, and half-bagged
emcees, so that they had only half-dared believe it. And so
it is that my father's sober appraisal now, given under the
cloak of academician, outsider, and keen social observer, is
perhaps especially welcome.

He is thanked heartily upon his return inside, his glass
refreshed with another splash, more ice; softened eyes
beam gratitude. I join him at the table while he attacks a
plate; I suspect he hasn't eaten since noon, and then
merely picked at leftovers and sweets. He devours chicken,
a pile of pork barbeque, slaw, corn muffins, as if raised on
this fare. He's given a beer, a slice of pecan pie, then
Nother joins us at the table. "My mother would like a
word," he tells Pops, "when you're finished." Pops nods,
finishes, goes. The music is now gospel; "Amazing Grace"
fills the house. My eyes brim.

The kitchen refills; visitors continue to come and go.
We cannot possibly eat fast enough to stem this tide. When
Pops returns much later, many of the new arrivals recognize him from TV, greeting him with smiles of mild aston-
ishment, like he *is* someone. "Oh my," I say to Nother,
noting my father's ease and affinity with such treatment.

"Might need to get used to it," he suggests.

I corner Pops a little later, when he's studying a wall
photo in the hall. "Muddy Waters," he says as I slide up
and lean on his shoulder. He's bent slightly, his face inches
from the ancient photo, as if it's some relic in a European
cathedral. "Muddy," he says again, as if anything else
would just be pointless.

"Thanks for doing that, Dad," I tell him. "It means a lot. To everyone."

"It's nothing," he replies. "An honor to do it."

"Well, thanks anyway." I kiss him on the cheek. "There is one thing, though." He looks over, his face suddenly anxious, as if I'm about to inform him of some egregious, unintended *faux pas.* "Rolf," I say.

"Rolf?"

"From Denmark."

"Oh yeah, Rolf. Oh."

"Yeah," I say. "We need to get him out of here. I mean, for everyone."

"You're right." His lips tighten, then relax. "We'll take him with us, I guess."

"I was hoping you'd say that."

"He can use my room, and I'll sleep over on your side."

"And during the day he can hang out on my side, so you can write."

The hardest ones to convince are Nother's family, who find the whole idea ridiculous at first. It is only after Pops suggests to Nother and Ruthie in a hushed voice that it might be easier for *Rolf* that they begin to come around. "Maybe it would be for the best," Ruth admits. "I hadn't really thought about what it's like here for him."

"Well, if he wants to be here, we'll sure bring him, but it would probably be good to have somewhere else if he needed it."

And with that last bit of logic they cave, and when we leave, Rolf is part of the caravan. He is confused by the arrangement at first, as any normal person would be, but charmingly so. He stops in the yard to study the duplex, as if that might help. But it doesn't, of course, and his eyes dart from one door to the other. "Separate," he says finally, his extended finger arcing from door to door. "Two homes."

"Exactly," Pops says, placing a hand on his back to usher him to his side while I run next door to check the messages. When I join them a few minutes later Rolf is already planted on the couch with the remote, a college basketball game flickering on the set, and I know things will be fine. I call in to my father that Gail made it all right, which he already knew but somehow failed to mention when I somehow failed to ask. He walks out and sets his shaving kit and gym bag on the table, then goes into the bathroom.

"This arrangement," Rolf asks, "it is normal and common?"

"Neither," I assure him. "Very abnormal, in fact." He turns from the set and smiles expectantly. "It's a little late," I tell him. "How about I explain tomorrow, O.K.?"

"No problem," he says, aiming the remote like he's shooting ducks. "What number is MTV?"

The next day is more of the same. I hang with Rolf for a while in the morning, drinking coffee and hearing about his research in land reclamation, which I guess could prove useful in Denmark, then drop him at campus. I head over to Nother's from there, though it's not like I feel particularly useful. This family is doing remarkably well, I can't help but think; even if Crosscut's demise was not unexpected, the grace with which they've assimilated the loss is extraordinary. Which is not to imply that their sorrow is not immense and genuine, but rather that they seem to draw strength from their distress, and turn it outward, somehow, in a generosity of spirit that saturates the house.

Still people come, the deluge of food continues unabated. Others phone to ascertain the calling hours this evening and tomorrow, or the particulars of the service to follow, and, of course, the welfare of the family. A collection of old men have gathered by mid-afternoon, their guitar cases piled in a corner of the back room while they sit or stand or lean, exchanging muffled greetings, handshakes, recent exploits, and sipping brown medicine over ice. I speak briefly to Madame Marie in early afternoon; she thanks me for Pops speaking so finely of her husband—as if I had anything to do with it. When she tells me they are both good men I smile and agree. She is so very sweet, her voice hushed and lilting, so that I bask in her presence, as if beneath a full moon. But at the same time she is somehow remote, and I sense a distance between us that makes me anxious before her gaze. I ask if there is anything I might do for her, anything she needs that I might get, though her children and stepchildren have been overly-solicitous throughout, and I realize I am talking mostly to fill the silence. She assures me that it is enough that I am here. And this seems a good note upon which to take my leave, so I say, "Well, then, I best get back," and leave her to her musings.

At five I pack up dinner for Rolf and my father and go home. The viewing is at seven, so we'll go together from here, then probably back over there for a bit. Pops has called to say he's on campus, and so will retrieve Rolf on the way. They are both there when I arrive, on our side for some reason, with open beers and a bowl game blaring from the set. I warm the food, set it out, call them, and go to shower and change.

The viewing turns out to be not so different than the past two days at the house, other than the lack of food and drink, and the addition of a dead body. It is a sober affair for the most part, necessarily so, I guess, though the lack of warmth here in comparison to events at the house is a bit disconcerting for me, perhaps bringing home the finality of the passing. Madame Marie has been and gone prior to our arrival, yet her absence now goes unremarked.

By nine we are on our way to Nother's, where the guitars are unpacked and an impromptu jam session appears imminent out back. I recognize Buddy Guy from that first night, though Pops has to refresh me on the name. He points to another old guy settling himself near the bonfire that Nother and Daniel are fanning. "Gatemouth," he utters, which obviously means more to him than it does to me, though I nod appreciatively, since it looks like it's taken everything Gatemouth has, and then some, just to be here. "Oh," Pops says when Ezra has stepped over to join us, "before I forget, there's a segment about your father on *Nightline* later." Ezra goes in for one of the televisions, on the assumption, probably correct, that none of us is likely to remember several hours hence. He returns and sets it up on the picnic table, muted and tuned to the proper channel. Ezra is nothing if not proactive.

A fair sized group has made the trip out from the funeral home, and before long most are outside. A bar is set up beside the television, a beer-filled cooler placed beneath the table. The chilis are turned on. In what seems like no time at all, the crowd loosens up. People begin to dance on the bricks, or sway where they stand, smoking and sipping their drinks. The old men, half a dozen or so, move in and out of the circle, picking their way through Crosscut's repertoire, or their own, riffing on extended solos that have the crowd clapping, hooting, calling out needless encouragement. Were there a way to trap the smoke at eye level, it would be just like another night at the 'Mill.

The performance is mournful, heartfelt, feverish; a beautiful tribute, haunting in its simplicity. When Nother sits in, it becomes sublime; though not their equal, his right to sit among them is unequivocal, and for this one night at least, the older men are content to follow his lead. It is after the last of these selections, as Nother is slipping off his father's venerable Fender, that Daniel, who to this point has been planted at the edge of the group, intently monitoring the fretwork and silently fingering his own guitar, glances sidelong at the television and calls out, "I think someone's talking about Grandpa," into the momentary calm.

On the screen, Ted Koppel peers out, his mouth moving in its usual deliberate fashion through this muted delivery. Across the bottom of the screen is a red banner with the words "Blues Legend Mourned." The camera pans up and right and two windows appear beside Ted's head, the labels beneath them reading Delacroix MS and New York City, respectively. In the first is my father, dressed as he is now beside me, with an open, helpful smile on his face; in the other, garbed in bedouin-gypsy chic and pulling on a cigarette for all he's worth, is Keith Richards, eyes focused off camera, head bobbing. Daniel turns up the sound just in time for us to hear Ted doing his intros. Around the patio people glance from the set to my father and back; it seems to take a moment for most to reconcile this, perhaps due to the drinks, which have been flowing liberally. "Well, that explains how you knew that," I say to my father out of the side of my mouth. The two guests now fill the screen, and I cannot pull my eyes from this odd and unlikely pairing.

"Yeah, well," Pops says.

He is being described as a professor of sociology, author, and family friend of the late bluesman by Ted's disembodied voice, which is more or less accurate, I suppose, though perhaps a bit presumptive with the author bit. "And you've written on the subject of popular music as well," Ted says.

"Yes," my father replies easily, "though it's not an area of particular expertise, I should point out." In truth, he's written exactly one music-related article that I know of; a brief, disjointed piece that appeared in a very minor journal eons ago. I can't wait to hear how he even got this gig. "I'd simply call myself a fan," Pops adds.

"Well, in that context, then," Ted continues, "and certainly as a learned fan, let me ask you to place Thaddeus Martin in the blues ledger. Is he one of the greats?"

My father is nodding thoughtfully, his face tight with concentration as he follows the tortuous question crackling through his earpiece. In the next panel Keith smokes vacant-eyed. "My gut reaction is yes," Pops replies after a brief pause. "But of course, I was privileged to know him, and certainly biased from that. It's difficult to judge these types of things anytime, though, given the subjectivity of it. I think perhaps 'essential' would be a more appropriate term. And more accurate."

Slightly in front of us, seated and bobbing his head, the one called Gatemouth repeats, "'sential, that's right." Around the group, others nod approvingly at the set.

"There's a significant segment of the music-listening population that has never heard of Crosscut Martin, after all," Pops continues. His face disappears at this point, as does Keith's, replaced full screen by an ancient file photo of Crosscut. "He's not a household name, in the sense of a Muddy Waters or a B.B. King, but I think that's missing the point. Like most art forms, music is a tapestry." We're now looking at my father and Keith again. "Certainly you have your big names, that's always going to be the case. Picasso, Shakespeare, Mozart. But to appreciate any form in its entirety, to become what Hemingway would have called an 'aficionado,' you have to look at the big picture, to recognize the interchange and contribution of all the players—all the threads of the tapestry, if you will. And in that regard, Crosscut emphatically belongs, is undoubtedly essential to the big picture." Pops shrugs. "And if you want to call him 'great,' too, I sure won't argue."

"Mr. Richards, your response," Ted prompts, and as absurd as this formal address comes out, he might as well have called him "Bishop."

"Yeah man, he's great." He laughs to himself. "I mean, yeah." He pauses again, wipes his mouth. "The perfesser's right, it's all the music, man. Like now, that's what's left." His face clouds briefly, as if perhaps contemplating his own long anticipated demise, then beams. "Yeah, what he said."

"So then, you would acknowledge a debt to this man?"

Keith takes a long drag, then flicks his hand through the cloud. "Sure man, that's how we started out." He laughs, coughs, laughs again. "We stole from all those cats. Everyone did." He shrugs, takes another drag. "Wish he was still here." He nods. "Wish they all were."

Ted engages him in talk of the early days, reprising the influence of American R&B on the vanguard of the British invasion. Names from both sides of the Atlantic are tossed about: Muddy, Howlin' Wolf, Elvis, Lennon, McCartney, Clapton. Keith tells of a day on a train platform, of seeing

Mick with an armload of blues recordings. "The start of us," he says. Crosscut in that stack, no doubt.

"Final thoughts," Ted says to my father.

Pops shrugs. "Wish he was still here, too. What he said."

Keith nods in his frame, crushes out his cigarette, smiles tightly. "Amen to that."

Ezra clicks off the set and we are left with the sound of shuffling feet, swirling ice, stray chords floating on the wind. "How you know him?" one of the old guys asks, leaning his head back to address my father.

"Never met," Pops says. "It was just a hookup for TV."

"Where were you, anyway?" I whisper.

"The studio on campus."

His questioner is nodding, fingering, taking in the answer. "Still should have brung him," he decides.

The session goes free form after this, and it is well past one when we leave.

We are quiet on the first half of the ride home, Pops and I up front, Rolf a little bagged in back. "Do you realize you were on national television with one of the Rolling Stones?" I ask. "I mean, when this day started...."

"It didn't really hit home til I saw it now," Pops says. "I mean, it was me and a couple camera guys in the studio. I was mostly just trying to hear him."

"Well, it came out O.K.," I tell him. "And I'm sure they were thrilled. I think they'd like to see him get his due, no matter how low key they act."

"So would I," Pops says.

"You think Mom saw?"

He shrugs. "I don't ever recall her watching *Nightline*. To tell you the truth, I didn't even know it was still on til they called." He purses his lips. "Maybe, though."

"She'll die."

Pops nods. "Might."

I skip the second viewing. It feels wrong not to be
there, but several of them noticed how uncomfortable I
was last night, and Nother calls early to insist I not bother.
It isn't necessary, they all agree, and there's still the funeral
to get through this afternoon. "Well yeah-uh!" Joley confirms when she calls a little later, "I mean, dead people
totally creep me out too." Which does not manage to provide the comfort I suspect was intended.

I goof off with Rolf again; we go for coffees and then
drive around while he tells me about Denmark, which seems
incredibly foreign as I picture it through his accent, and
about as far as you can get from here. There are actually
American style blues clubs in Copenhagen, I'm surprised to
learn, and that he had, in fact, heard of Crosscut before he
ever arrived here. "It really is a small world," he says.

"I guess so."

When we get back I send Gina this long-ass, way overdue
e-mail, explaining everything that's happened here since I
failed to get on the plane to go there. I'm assuming she's
pissed, because she hasn't e-mailed me, either, so I give her
all the details, to make it seem like my hands were tied as far
as leaving. Which doesn't really matter, because if Gina
decides to be pissed, she's going to be pissed no matter what.

I have it pretty much done, but unsent, when Gail calls.
I fill her in on most of the same stuff I've just written, and
warn her about Rolf, who's really taken to our sofa and
television. I end up repeating a lot of it because she keeps
saying "What?!" and demanding further clarification. I
have to assure her several times that Rolf is definitely *not*
sleeping over here, though it seemed perfectly clear the first
time I said it. She's already heard from several people there

about Pops being on *Nightline*, but doesn't seem to want to discuss it, even though she's the one who brings it up. "What are you wearing to the funeral?" she asks.

"That same blue thing I wore last time, I guess. It's the only dark dress I own."

"Maybe we'll look for something when I get back," she says, though we both know this won't happen. I think she just feels left out because there are things going on here that she can't interfere with from way up there.

"I'm pretty much counting on not needing to do this again for awhile," I say, though it seems I said that the last time. "And at least it's not summer."

"Is your father going?"

"Yeah."

"He's not conducting the service, is he?"

I sigh. "Not as far as I know."

"I'm sure he would if they were broadcasting it."

"How's it going up there?" I ask, just because I don't want her bagging on Pops the whole rest of the call.

"It's cold," she says, which hardly seems worth mentioning. It's Baltimore; it's December; it's going to be cold. She names several people she's seen from Hopkins, and tells me of her plans for today. One of her regular research partners is working on something exciting, and wants her in on it, so they're having lunch to talk about it. "So that's something," she says. "It's good to see them, in any case, no matter what I decide."

"Good," I say. "So, um, how does it feel to be back there?"

She sighs. "Honestly, Teri, it feels pretty good." There's a long pause, and in the silence I sense she wants to say much more than that, but doesn't. "Just cold."

We both kind of laugh, to get her off the hook. "Well, enjoy it, Mom. And you don't need to apologize for it."

"Don't I?"

"Mom, look, do what you need to do, O.K. Go buy a new coat, maybe. Sounds like you might be needing it anyway. Make Marian go with you. She's a shopaholic."

We laugh again. "Maybe I'll do that," she says.

I hang up a few minutes later and hit SEND to launch Gina's e-mail, then log off. I've had about enough of Baltimore for one day. That's all another world to me now, like Rolf's version of Denmark, or the moon.

I go to the closet and pull out my dress; Gail did end up having it dry cleaned last time, so I take off the bag and check for wrinkles, then hang it on the back of the door since it's too early to get ready. I stand there kind of dumb; it's the first free time I've had in days, and I'm unsure what to do. I could start taking down some of the Christmas stuff, but that seems kind of rude with Rolf out there. Christmas seems as distant as Baltimore though; I can hardly believe it was only three days ago—it seems like weeks.

Staring at the dress gets me thinking about Ronnie Foster's funeral, the first thing I was part of here, not counting the paint job that may or may not have led to it. That day seems so long ago, too, like from another lifetime. Other events come to mind; weird occurrences at school, goofing with Pops in one or another of the nowhere towns on a Saturday, bickering with Gail over something neither of us even gave a shit about. I think of Kayla for the first time in days, and wonder if she's back from Houston, and, if so, whether I'll see her later today at the service. I could call, but I don't. If she's in town then she's certainly heard, and whatever she decides is fine by me.

My thoughts stray to the evening Pops and I limped to a stop in front of Nother's house. The image is striking in its clarity compared to the others, a distinct watershed in my tumbling mental narrative. A succession of memories fill my head, needless of any prompting, heedless of any restraint. I am immersed here, I understand with immediate certainty; my life is exactly this. Which accounts for all else now seeming so foreign, so difficult to hold in my mind, and these past months filling up like a lifetime, steamrolling along under their own momentum, and the hazy speculation that it's not always good to think too much.

"Probably," I say when Pops asks if I'm sitting with the family. "I think Nother wants me to."

He nods. "Good. You should, if he asks." He slows to turn onto the road leading to the church, the same one Ronnie Foster departed from, as it happens.

I let out a long breath. "It's closed coffin, right? I mean, if I'm going to be up front, I'm not going to have to stare at him the whole time, am I?"

Pops gives me this really strange look. "He's been cremated, Dear. There is no coffin."

"What?" I say. "No."

"I think so," Pops counters. "That's why the service is so late." He glances into the rearview mirror. "Isn't that what Ezra said, Rolf?"

"Yes. Cre-mated," Rolf answers.

Pops looks over and nods. "There might be an urn up on the altar, depending on what the family decided to do. But that would be it." I let out another long breath and slump back in my seat, thinking of Crosscut being incinerated while I was eating lunch, but ultimately grateful not to have to share space with his waxen corpse. "Relieved?" Pops asks.

"Yep," I admit tersely. "Am I total scum, or what?"

Pops winces. "No one enjoys it, Teri. It's a ritual you get through as best you can." He reaches over and squeezes my arm. "That's why they're so formalized, so no one has to think too much." I stare at him dubiously.

But it turns out not nearly so bad as I feared. I do end up seated with the family, in the front pew, with Nother, Ruthie, Ron, and Madame Marie. I'd wondered, briefly if she'd even be here; she's been all but invisible so far. But here she is, just to Nother's left, covered in black, peasant-looking garb; thick, layered, and formless, encased in her grief. The other children, those from the first marriage, I eventually comprehend, are in the next two rows with all the grandchildren, several of whom cannot sit still from the sounds of it. There is an empty pew, then Pops, Rolf, and everyone else. The small church is nearly full, which surprises me, though I'm not sure why, given how many have made their way out to the house. In the last few rows I spot several of our classmates, which touches me deeply. Peg Lawson, the principal, is here, and I wonder how often she is obliged to perform this sad task. Though there are seats open, many of the old men stand in back, coughing and shuffling their feet, as if leery of being caught out (or, in this case, in) by the master of the house. They appear lost without the shield of their instruments, and as if their very presence threatened the integrity of the building. Most look ready to take flight at the first opportunity.

The service is blessedly short; a few readings, a brief eulogy attesting to Crosscut's sinfulness and grace, but ultimately reckoning in his favor. The family is strong; any weeping has already been done, or saved for another time. I, too, survive, determined for the sake of the family to hold it together. The lone bad moment comes during the playing of a Mahalia Jackson recording of "Precious Lord," which, I suspect, does not leave a completely dry eye in the place. It is during this mournful rendition that I first notice, through brimming eyes, the urn sitting up on the altar rail. It is the size of a small trophy, a loving cup, I think they're called, with the appearance of black marble, and trimmed elegantly in gold. How I've failed to see it for this long is beyond me, as it now becomes as conspicuous as a giraffe. It commands my attention from then on, so that when the service has ended, Nother has to reach over for my arm to exit the pew.

We stop in the church yard, where a group of our classmates have gathered, including Sandy, whom I hadn't seen inside. She touches Nother's arm and leans in to speak into his ear, which he thanks her for, then turns and gives me a hug. "You doing O.K.?" she asks.

I nod. "Yeah, thanks. And thanks for coming."

"Sure," she says. She reaches out to touch my necklace. "Nice," she says.

I smile. "I didn't see you inside."

"I made sure I was directly behind you, in case one of us started bawling."

We talk apart, while Nother chats with the others. I don't know why I'm surprised they've come; he's not disliked, after all, and he has known some of these people his whole life. Maybe I just think of him as a group unto himself, though I can see he's glad they came.

It begins to rain en route, but the heaviest of it holds off til we are back at the house. Food is laid out, drinks are poured, a CD of samples from the upcoming compilation is produced and cued up. Some of us gather under the carport after we've eaten; it's hot and crowded inside, and several want to smoke. Nother gets a wood fire going in the sawed off barrel and we sit around it on the car seat and the glider soaking up its warmth and listening to the rain on the roof. Nother is picking at an acoustic guitar, which sounds pretty good with the rain. Presently, we are joined by my father and Buddy Guy, who lean against the workbench with their drinks and listen along with us. "Play that one," Buddy says after a while. "You's playin' it that one night from inside." Which turns out to be "Love In Vain," which Nother figures out from just that, and starts into it nice and slow, with Buddy and my father nodding like those toy dogs people used to set in the back window of the car.

The skies open almost immediately, though Nother seems not at all put off with the competition from above. "Ver' nice," Buddy growls when it's over. "All jumblin' with the rain like that. Yessir."

Ezra steps out and lights up. "Damn," he says, staring into the deluge. "Conjure that." He turns and seeks out Nother. "You tell them what Dad would have said about weather like this?"

Nother shakes his head. "Some other time."

"Oh hell," Ezra says. "Funeral's over." He turns to Buddy. "Soon as it stops we'll head over." The party is moving to The Sawmill, is what he means, and he goes back inside to roust the others. "Tell 'em, boy," he calls back to Nother just before the screen door bangs closed behind him.

"Might be good to tell it," Pops suggests helpfully.

"Not really even a story," Nother says.

"Still," Pops says.

"Crosscut had a thing for sitting outside listening to the rain," Nother begins reluctantly. "Like tonight, he'd have been out here for sure. That's how this got here." He pats the car seat. "I used to sit with him a lot, but before me it was Ezra, and this came out of some car he wrecked way back. He and my dad set it up like this so they could sit out here, and then Ezra was gone and I came along, so I started sitting out here with him. Wasn't like we did anything, didn't even talk usually, just looked at the rain. Harder it rained, the better we liked it. Sometimes you could hardly stand the noise, but we did, and we'd sit here watching all the holes in the driveway fill up, and then the tread lines, and sometimes the whole drive would be underwater, and there'd be this kind of grayish river out to the road. Or we'd turn the seat and watch it beat on the patio, how the rain would bounce up sometimes, or if there was hail it'd bounce all over. Crosscut really liked that. Sometimes it was so heavy the backyard would start to fill up, and we'd just sit here, him smoking, and watch the puddles grow bigger and bigger til they'd start connecting so it was like a lake. And we'd watch it rain on the lake. And at some point he'd walk to the edge over there, so he was almost out in it, and he'd just stare. And so I'd go stand with him"–he gets up and walks to the edge of the carport, and we all brace ourselves for it to get real poignant now–"right about here, I guess, and we'd check the breeze from how his smoke was blowing, and point out how the leaves were turned inside out, and there'd be that hissing sound if it was summer and hot, and how it smelled different and why was that, which we never did clear up. And sometimes we'd see animals come out of the woods through the backyard, nutria, maybe a snake, a deer one time that practically walked under here with us. And if it got where it was like this, we'd have to stand right next to each other to hear, and at some point Crosscut would half-turn and put his hand on my shoulder, like he'd just then figured it all out, and he'd kind of nod like he did and say, 'Son, it-is-raining-like-a-motherfucker-out-there.'"

No one says anything. It's pretty much all nature while we gape at him, just the rain pounding down and the fire popping and the wind, with a little of the glider creaking. I'm still staring when he sits down and looks at me. "I tried to tell you," he reminds me. "Or not tell you."

Then Buddy starts laughing, a soft low rumble at first, but growing steadily til his whole middle is shaking, and the workbench is dancing in time to his convulsions. And then Pops is laughing too, maybe remembering he was the one that encouraged the whole telling in the first place, and then it kind of goes around the circle, til even I'm cracking up; all except Nother, who sits there staring into the flames, but not minding us getting off on it.

"Lord have mercy," Buddy says when he can speak again. "We have lost a great man."

I sleep in way late on the twenty-ninth, right through the alarm, which I never do. But we didn't get out of The Sawmill til well after two, so I've got cause, and no pressing reason to get up anyway. It turned out to be an excellent jam; about half the crowd was either family or musicians, the rest regulars who've been waiting for the place to reopen, and a couple tables who had the blind luck to stumble in. By nine o'clock I doubt anyone was remembering the sad impetus for the gathering, which was more or less the point I think. A pack of Rolf's friends blew in about eleven, and they were all still parked at a back table when Pops and I left.

The house is quiet when I go out. I pick up in the kitchen a bit, then go for a mocha to clear my head. I bring back a latte for Pops, who I find sitting gamely at the keyboard when I go over. "Can you even work?" I ask, handing him the steaming cup. We were in there a long time last night, and he knocked back more than a few.

"Probably won't know til tomorrow," he replies, taking the latte and immediately setting it down on the desk. "Thanks." He looks at the monitor and frowns. "Hopefully some of it will be salvageable."

"You're a better man than I," I tell him, dropping onto the couch. I take a sip of my coffee and notice the door to the bedroom is open. "Rolf hook up?" I ask.

"One of those was his girlfriend."

"Girlfriend?"

"The one in the black sweater, I think." He highlights a long paragraph and deletes it. "Much better."

"Wait a minute. What's he doing here if he's got a girlfriend in town?"

"She just got back," Pops says. "That whole bunch went to Disneyworld for Christmas. But Rolf needed to work, and he's broke." He types in a line, eyes it, shrugs. "He'll probably come by for his stuff today." He substitutes a semi colon for the period, adds a clause. "Guess I forgot to mention that."

"No problem." I sit finishing my drink while Pops struggles on. Finally I stand. "I'll let you work, then."

"I was afraid you'd say that." He stops typing, sips, spins around. "What're you up to the rest of the day?"

"I think I'm going to take down Christmas stuff," I decide as I'm saying it. "Because I can't even believe it's still December."

"Wrapped up kind of early this year," he agrees. "You want that tree out of there?"

"No hurry," I say.

"Well look, I'll come over later and help." He glances toward the screen. "Something tells me this is going to get old quick."

"I'm getting tired just watching you."

"Nother coming over?"

"No, he's going to spend the day with his mom. And I've probably been over there way too much, anyway."

There's an e-mail from Gina when I get back:

> Hey,
>
> I'm sooo sorry about all that. You must be so sad! How is Nother doing? O.K. I hope! Did you have a good Christmas, otherwise? Or do you just want to forget?
>
> You're so excellent to stay like that (even though it meant blowing us off!!). I think I might have bailed.
>
> I saw your mom. She said you're coming up this spring to check out schools. Cool!!!
>
> What's up for New Years?
>> Love/Miss Ya!
>> G

How was Christmas otherwise? What's up for New Years? Other than the natives, how did you find Montana, General Custer? That girl is something else, and any response will have to wait for another day, like maybe til after I find out about this alleged spring trip, which is news to me.

I take my time putting things away, a couple days, in fact. I rise late, work slowly, and take lots of breaks to run errands or goof with Pops. I'm kind of in a daze from all that's been going on, and not having any schedule to follow since school's out, and Gail not here breathing down my neck. At some point Rolf returns for his things, though I'm out when he comes. Nother and I see a movie one night, and afterwards neither of us can even decide if we liked it or not, so he must be in a bit of a funk, too. Gail calls several times, which is O.K., actually. She's not nearly as strident from a distance, I'm discovering, which bodes well for the rest of my life. I talk to Sandy, apologize for being so out of touch. She invites us over for New Year's Eve, four or five couples is all, nothing major, but still I decline. I think we'd put a damper on things, and I'm not sure Nother would feel right about it so soon. She understands—she always does—but leaves the invitation out there if we change our minds.

I almost call Kayla a couple of times, but I can't seem to get myself to do it. It's been a weird week, and I'm finally getting some sort of balance back, and I know if anyone can screw that up in a hurry, it's her. Plus, I think she should call me, given the circumstances. I'm positive she knows about Crosscut by now, so isn't that just polite? Which is a juvenile argument, I realize, but the call still doesn't get made.

And what about Joley? Other than that one call, I don't hear from her, either. All that time I spent over there when I barely knew her, and now when it's sort of turned around, she's nowhere to be found. I don't call her either, needless to say.

Pops might really be on to something with this bad behavior angle.

"Tell me again why I have to do this?" Ezra carps, star-*ing at the smooth surface laid across his stepmother's worktable, and the odd assortment of items arranged there.*

"You're the oldest."

"Rachel's the oldest," he corrects. *"And it was her idea."*

"Well, she's not here, is she?" Sara points out. "Now just do it already."

"How convenient is that," Ezra grouses, wiping a spot clean in the center of the table with his sleeve. He lays the urn flat and carefully dislodges the lid, using the top to direct the vessel's contents into a small pile, which he ponders uneasily. "This is pretty weird."

"You know, you'd be done by now if you'd quit bitching and cut," Sara says.

Ruth is watching from a chair in the corner, ready to intercept her mother should Madame Marie suddenly enter. "Actually, it is pretty macabre if you think about it."

"See there," Ezra says, lifting the Death card—entirely by chance, this—from the top of the deck and motioning toward his stepsister. "It's not just me."

"Then don't think about it," Sara instructs.

The idea, Rachel's brainstorm, is to divide the mortal remains of the father amongst his children, reserving a separate share to the black urn for the widow. Each child, in turn, is free to retain or disperse their portion as they see fit. An inspired idea, all are agreed, not least Madame Marie, who, though reserved, is not an ungenerous soul, and is particularly cognizant of the symbiosis between this life and the next. A bit of closure, in any case, rendered a touch more personal. How, exactly, the division of said remains was to be effected remained undetermined.

Ezra pauses, the card poised just above the center of the pile. He frowns. "Why isn't Luke doing this?" he queries, resting the card again on the table. "I mean, he was the cokehead of the group back in the day. He could probably divvy this up down to the gram in no time."

"Oh, for Christ's sake," Sara sputters, stomping to the table and grabbing up the card. She slides a corner of it into the pile and shovels several clumps back into the urn, which she turns upright and closes emphatically. Then, with a few deft movements she levels the pile to a height of perhaps a quarter-inch, squares the edges, and cuts a tic-tac-toe pattern into it. "There," she says, snapping the card back onto the table, so that a small whitish plume of their father mushrooms into the air, "think you can take it from here?"

"Whoa, nicely done, Scarface." He scoops up one of the sections with the card and carefully sifts it into a small Ziploc bag, returning several times to include any residue before sealing the opening and placing it in a white business envelope.

"I don't think it has to be that exact," Ruth suggests. "We're not dealing with the Colombians here."

Ezra pops open the second baggie. "Everyone's a fucking critic," he laments.

Now that the process is underway, and despite Madame Marie's knowledge of it, they hope to complete the particulars without attracting her notice. Though her composure these preceding days has been extraordinary, the children are certain the loss is having its effect, and wish to mitigate any additional heartache. As Ezra proceeds at snail's pace, the two women exchange looks of exasperation. "Chop, chop," Sara cajoles. "No pun intended."

"Look, unless you want to take over, fucking shut up," he replies distractedly, his gaze locked on the task.

"Touchy."

"What are you going to do with yours?" Ruth inquires of her stepsister, just to change the subject. "Any ideas?"

Sara frowns. "I have this little, kind of stone jar at my house I might use." She shrugs. Or maybe figure some way to have it out at the 'Mill without that being too weird. What about you?"

"I think I might buy a rose bush for just beneath this window." She indicates the one opening onto the front yard. *"Then spread the ashes in the hole when I plant it, so like, when it blooms, part of Dad will be in there, too. Maybe?"*

"Ohhhh, that is sooo sweet," Sara moans. *"Oh, God, it's perfect. And for your mom, too."*

"Does it actually work like that?"

"Shut up, Ezra," Sara barks. *"Unless you have a better idea."*

"I've got a couple," he informs her, leaning the fifth envelope with the others.

"Doubles your life total, then."

In a few minutes the task is completed. The room is quickly set aright, the parcels divided among the three for delivery. Madame Marie's portion, already returned to the onyx vessel, is replaced meticulously on the mantel.

Pops surprises me by saying he also got invited to a New Year's Eve party; not that you wouldn't want him at your party, but my parents have never been big on going out that night. It's some woman from the TV station who's throwing the party, one of the associate producers, and he decides to go for a while because they've all been working together a lot lately, and he thinks he should at least make an appearance, though he waits to tell me until he's sure I've got plans, and says he'll likely be home before midnight.

"Don't bail early on my account," I tell him. "I mean, if it's good, just stay." I'm going to Nother's, is all. Maybe we'll stop over at one of the siblings', but it's not going to be anything major.

Which turns out to be the case. We watch a year-end wrap up on CNN with Madame Marie, and then when she excuses herself, we drive over to Esther's with Ruth and Ron. It's fun, and we even pop some not so great champagne at midnight, but I'm still home by one, which beats my father's arrival by a good hour, at least.

We're in Jackson at eleven the next morning to meet Gail's flight, and back home again a little past noon. The trip went well, it seems; my mother managed to see everyone she knows up there from the sounds of it, though she answers several of my father's queries with a cryptic, "We'll talk later," which I assume means when I'm not around. Which is fine; I can't be walking on eggshells just because she doesn't know what's what. Hopefully, she'll tell me when she comes to any decisions, but I've got enough on my mind as it is without having to worry about her, too. Like right now, I need to get over to Nother's house. He says he's got something we need to take care of today, and even though he wouldn't tell me what, I promised I'd be over as soon as I could slip out. He said to wear my Doc Martens, so I'm assuming we're headed into the woods.

He's waiting under the carport when I get there, his day pack bulging on the car seat, and we set off across the yard into the trees. We're on our way to the usual spot, he says, which I assumed, and which seems like a nice enough place to start off the year. It's a beautiful day for hiking, cool and dry, with a bit of a breeze zipping through the trees, and we walk at a good pace, talking easily and absorbing the sounds of the woods. I'm enjoying just being outside again after all that's been going on, and it's nice that it's just the two of us. The path has firmed up nicely from the rains of a few days ago, the day of the funeral, I recall. We stop at the bridge to drink some water and skip a few stones, then plunge into the thick growth toward the clearing.

We've made a few trips out here since that first time; the monster bird has shown twice. Nother tells me about a show he saw the other day on the coelacanth, another supposedly extinct species that turned up very much alive in 1938. The fuss caused by that discovery only seems to have cemented his resolve, and he claims to have no desire to become an ornithological footnote, which, when he puts it like that, I can't really blame him. I kind of hope we see it today; it seems like a sighting might bode well for the coming year.

We stop once more for water; I pick leaves from his hair, kiss his cheek. I'm curious what he's got in his pack, but he won't say. When we get to the clearing he unshoulders it and pulls out a picnic blanket, which we spread in the middle of the clearing and sit down. I unlace my boots and rest my feet in the cool grass while Nother takes off his jacket and begins digging into the pack. "This is kind of weird," he says, drawing out a bulky white envelope. He tells me they've divided up the remains of their father; his portion is in the envelope laying between us. "I put some in the body of a guitar he left me," he says. "But the rest,"–he indicates the envelope– "I didn't know what to do with. I kept thinking of this place, for some reason."

I nod.

"Anyway, I don't want this just sitting around my room, not even in a vase or something. So I was thinking I'd scatter the ashes here." He makes this motion to take in the clearing. "What do you think of that?"

"That sounds fine," I say.

"It's the best thing I can think of to do with it."

"I think it's one of those things that has to come from the heart, whether it makes sense or not." I scrunch over and take him in my arms. "I mean, I'm no expert, but I think if it feels like the right thing, then it probably is."

He nods and stands up. I hand him the envelope and he begins moving around the clearing tossing pinched clumps of ash—his father, I marvel from the blanket—into the air, like some biblical character sowing seeds. He moves deliberately, in a counterclockwise circle. It takes longer than I'd have thought, perhaps ten minutes, and then he rejoins me on the blanket. He takes a rag from his pocket and wipes the last of it from his fingers, then returns the rag, along with the envelope to the same pocket.

He reaches again into his pack, this time extracting a sweating bottle of champagne and two plastic glasses. "It's over now," he says, working the wire cage from around the cork. He aims the bottle toward the river and lets the top fly, while I catch the foaming liquid. We hold up the glasses in a toast. "Crosscut has left the building," he says, and we drink. We knock off the whole bottle, in fact, in pretty short order, resolving to abandon our sadness when we leave here today, and to celebrate his father's life and music, rather than mourn his passing.

Then we climb onto the platform, where we remain until the fading light dictates we leave. We do not see the ivorybill; I scarcely remember it til we're back on the path.

After the events of the past week, it is almost a relief when school resumes. The distraction alone is a welcome respite from the emotional roller coaster I've been on, and, as odd as it sounds, I'm looking forward to not having to think so much. The routine will be good for me, and Nother, too.

I swear it feels like months since I've sat out here, almost like the start of a new school year again. I decide I should make a list of all the things I should be getting busy with, school-wise, which is what I'm doing when Kayla walks up. "Homework already?" she asks, letting her purse drop onto the table across from me.

I set down my pen and look up. "Not exactly." She's wearing the bracelet I gave her, I notice right off, which pleases me more than I'd like, though I guess I'd feel worse if she'd just stuck it in a drawer. We haven't seen each other since before the break, and it's only when we start catching up that I realize how out of touch I've been. Neither of us mentions the lack of contact, which would have been unthinkable just a few months ago, but there's enough residual weirdness in our conversation to make it obvious that we're both aware of it. "How was your trip?" I ask.

"O.K.," she answers flatly. "Weird family stuff, but other than that...." She shrugs. I nod back and we sit for a minute without speaking. It's another dry, cool day, the kind that's perfect if you're wearing the right coat. Kayla takes out her cigarettes and fishes the last one from the pack. She frowns, looks over at me. "Split it?"

"No, go ahead."

She lights up, does that elegant Garbo exhale, flicks ash off to the side. "I'm sorry about Nother's dad," she says. "Was it bad?"

"For them, yeah. For me," I pause, "yeah, too, I guess, because of them." Which is about as touchy-feely as I decide to get. I give her a rundown of the past week or so, trying to keep in mind that she probably doesn't care much. I leave out anything that hints of human sentiment; how Nother and I came together more, for instance; and how I've grown closer to his family because of it; and what it felt like being in the middle of all that. She doesn't want to know, really, and it's only something that would get thrown back in my face someday, anyway. It's a pretty spartan version, then, mostly a summary of events that doesn't begin to tell the story. But, like I said, it's not like she gives a shit. "I think everyone's ready to move on," I conclude.

Kayla nods, takes a last drag, crushes the butt on the side of the table. "Good," she says, sounding equally disposed to let it go. "That's good."

"You still see that guy?" I ask. "From, whatever that other school is?"

"Psycho Brian?" she replies. "Yeah, I guess we're together."

But before she can expound on this, Joley appears, jogging the last ten yards with a loaded pack and rounding the table clumsily to wrap me in her arms with a long, "Ohhhh."

Kayla and I exchange looks. "Hey," I say when she finally unwraps herself from me.

"You poor thing," she moans, plunking down next to me and dropping an arm across my shoulder. "Are you doing O.K.? How's he? Was it too, too sad with the holidays?" I open my mouth to answer, but I'm not quick enough. "Did you sit with them at the funeral? Oh,"–she reaches over to finger my necklace–"is this from him?"

I wait a beat, to be sure she's done, taking note of Kayla staring at the stone around my neck. "Yes, fine. He's O.K., too. Very sad. Yes. And yes."

"You weren't at the funeral?" Kayla inquires.

Joley takes her eyes from me and glares across at Kayla. "You either, I take it."

Having made her point, Kayla gets up to leave. "Let's do something," she says to me.

"Sure."

"You know, unloading her would be a great New Year's resolution for you," Joley suggests.

"Not til I hear about Psycho Brian."

"Ugh. What is with her? That guy is like, dangerous."

"Really? Like, physically?"

"Yeah," she says. ""The only reason he's even still in school is he's on parole. I mean, it's school or jail."

"What'd he do?"

"Auto theft, disorderly. Punched a cop, I heard." She shakes her head. "He's bad news." She continues shaking her head until Kayla disappears into the crowd. "Her, too, for that matter. So, tell me about it," she says, returning her attention to me. "We can compare notes."

I give her a slightly expanded version. I don't really believe she cares any more than Kayla, but the kinds of details she wants are precisely what Kayla didn't want to hear: like how the family treated me; and what all went on with Nother and I, even though she still doesn't think much of him. So it's almost a parallel rendition of the first one, shorter on names and places, but lots more emotional content. Again, I leave out about the clearing–no one needs to know about that, or the ashes, but I kind of hint at some singular moments between us, so she pretty much gets the idea. It is only later that I realize all these specifics will become the template for the tale as it will be remembered, what particulars I've left out easily supplied by the oracle beside me.

It also occurs to me that I'm saying all of this–both versions–more for myself than either of them. I still haven't got a lot of it settled in my mind, so I'm taking advantage of these opportunities to think out loud. As long as I don't get too detailed it will probably be harmless, and I might get a few things straightened out in my head. I like the version of things I relate to Joley; it seems, well, *significant*, I guess, almost like it couldn't possibly be my life we're talking about. There's love and death and family, and even a little bit of celebrity, as Crosscut's fame is now becoming apparent, and my own father is achieving a bit of talking head status himself. Joley likes the drama of it, and I guess I do, too. I don't know that I've ever felt more alive, though I don't say this to her, of course; she'd just look at me weird, or say yeah, she knows just what I mean, and then add something about ten miles off the mark that would just piss me off.

To be entirely truthful, it does bother me that neither of them care more than that. I mean, I know it wasn't *my* father who died, and neither of them really knows Nother, let alone Crosscut, so it's even more removed for them, but it's also pretty obvious that it's a big deal for me, so you'd think they could at least try to treat it as more than just the latest round of drama. Then again, they're both behaving pretty much to form, so why am I surprised, and what right do I have to be upset? Maybe it's just that after all the genuine sentiment I've witnessed this past week, their cursory interest rings a bit too false by comparison.

Joley gathers up her things to go; she's not much for quiet reflection to begin with, and now she can go start spreading this news. She gives me another hug. "Hang in there," she says. "Be strong."

I watch her walk off, knowing that deep down she means well, though deep down might not even apply with her. She stops after a short distance and turns. "I saw your dad on TV," she calls back.

I wait for a second to see if there's more. "Hollywood," I say, and she gives a thumbs up before heading off again.

I begin to get annoyed at myself for thinking ill of her. She did come around, after all; late, certainly, but still one of the first to acknowledge these events, and express condolences. I think how embarrassed I'd be for Nother to know my thoughts, as he has behaved so impeccably throughout this ordeal; never has he been petty, not once has he responded less than graciously to anyone. In truth, he's imparted as much comfort as he's received, and I cannot imagine him sharing my selfish thoughts toward Joley and Kayla.

The day passes uneventfully. I even turn down an offer to cut out early with Sandy to get coffee, figuring I ought to hit all my classes the first day back, for which I am promptly buried in homework. I search out Nother twice to make sure he's doing O.K. Normally, we don't see each other a lot at school, our paths just don't cross much, but I do want him to know I'm thinking about him. He doesn't seem to mind me stalking him, and I'm glad to notice that several people approach to express their sadness at the news of his father's demise. A couple of my teachers even mention it to me, so I guess we're more widely known than I thought. None of them asks after me personally; rather, they ask how he's doing, or the family—Ruth in particular, or some other stray question about Crosscut. I refuse to let myself take this as a slight. I'm not one of the family, after all, and they don't know the degree of our involvement, or if we've even survived winter break. Most of what is directed at me is in regards to Pops. Quite a few people caught one or another of his spots, and a lot of them seem to have assumed he's some sort of regular TV personality, which I'm sure he'll be amused to find out.

The rest of the week is more of the same, including the homework. "Nother seems to be more public now,"

Sandy points out when we finally do take off early for coffee.
"I mean, I see him talking to more people."

"Yeah," I agree. "Just kind of weird it took that for people to notice him."

"How are you doing.?" she asks.

"O.K.." I shrug. She sips and sets her cup down slowly,
which seems to mean: continue. "I think I'm still a little
overwhelmed. I mean, here I was, expecting this kicked
back Christmas, then Baltimore, with lots of goofing off,
and it didn't turn out like that at all."

"That's for sure."

"And what's really weird is, except for his dad dying,
most of it was good. We got a lot closer, which I wanted;
his family and I got close; hell, I even bonded some with
my dad. And even now, people are being really nice to
Nother, which I love, and seeing what a good guy he is,
which is about time, and that it was kind of special that his
dad lived here, which is about time, too. So that was all
really cool. But then I think that at the heart of it was this
really tragic event, and that we'd all give all of that back if
Crosscut was still here. But that's not happening, of course,
so like, what am I supposed to think?"

"Whoa," she says. "And who told you *I'd* know this?"

Pops almost gets on MTV. They decide to do a snippet
about Crosscut for *MTV News*, which is kind of amazing
since about ninety-nine percent of their viewers have
never even heard of him. But this guy calls, and ends up
talking to Pops for a good half hour one afternoon, and
then says he'll call back to set up a video feed, but then
never does, so we figure that's the end of it. And then I'm
flicking through the channels one night and I stop on
MTV because maybe somebody got arrested or filmed

naked that I might need to know about, and instead there's a picture of Crosscut next to the announcer's head, so I quick yell to Pops, and as we're watching he tells me that everything coming out of this guy's mouth is straight from that phone call, though all of it goes unattributed now. And then there's a segment with Buddy Guy, who pretty much confirms everything Pops said, and then just Buddy's voice over a picture of The Sawmill, talking about the sendoff they gave him.

"What a rip," I say when it's over, figuring Pops will be kind of pissed, or at least disappointed.

"It's not about us," he says. "Just so the man gets his due."

He makes out better with the article he wrote for the local paper. The daily in Jackson ended up running it, too, and it got out on the wire from there, and made it into twenty or thirty other papers, including the *L.A. Times,* where part of it got incorporated into a longer article, and Pops ended up getting quoted right alongside Tom Petty and B.B. King. Which is all playing great at the college, needless to say; Annie is beside herself with the exposure it's generating, and Pops has a lunch date with the Chancellor next week. He's handling it pretty well, though, not getting all big-headed or anything. He's managed to stay focused, too; he pounds on the book every day, and I just this evening proofed the syllabus for his class this spring. So I guess there's not much point in detailing my reservations about good things coming out of tragedy to him.

Gail, on the other hand, has been pretty distracted since she got back. I thought at first that some aspect of her trip went sideways, but she insists that everything was fine. So now I'm wondering if she's made some sort of decision and just doesn't want to tell me, or, more likely, she's leaning hard one way, and the thought of committing is freaking her out.

I've got to give her credit as far as dealing with Pops, though. I figured she'd be all sarcastic with the attention he's getting, and how it's a big deal over at the college; I mean, it's got to bug the shit out of her. She's been busting her ass for twenty years making a name for herself in her field, writing books and delivering lectures and all that, and now here's Pops on network TV yakking with Ted Koppel just because he can deliver a juicy sound bite. I find it a little hard to believe myself, sometimes. But she's been cool about it. She's stopped well short of praise, certainly, but has managed to hold her tongue with the catty remarks, and she's grudgingly admitted that the attention is probably good for the school. "I mean, for what it is, it's fine," she's told me, which pretty much sums up her feelings on the matter. "And there are way worse than him out there." Which probably sums up her feelings about Pops.

"So like, this guy carries a gun?" I ask. "I mean, that's what I heard."

Kayla laughs, pleased, from the sound of it, that this is going around. "Well, he *has* a gun," she clarifies, "and sometimes he keeps it in his car. But it's not like he's always packing or anything."

I wince involuntarily, not really comforted by this slight refinement. We're sitting in her room this Saturday afternoon, sipping Cokes that she's laced with Jim Beam. I haven't been over here in a while, mostly because Kayla doesn't particularly like it here, either. She's sitting by the open window, dangling her cigarette outside between puffs. "And this would be the car he stole?" I query.

"Stole is not quite accurate, either," she answers, pulling her arm in to take a long drag, which she then turns and exhales out the window. "My, my, though," she says, "you certainly seem well informed." This does not appear to bother her, either.

"I hear things."

"Especially things like that, I'm sure." She tosses the cigarette into the side yard and pulls the window closed. "Actually, it's his uncle's car. Who he lives with. And it's pretty much Brian's to drive, since his uncle has a new one, but every now and again they get into it, and his uncle takes the keys back. So Brian finally figured out he should get another set made." She flashes this wicked grin, and it is obvious she means this was her idea. "Which he did. And then this last time, right after Thanksgiving, they got into a huge blowout. Like, they were shoving each other and shit, and Brian ends up taking off in the car, and his fucking uncle went and had him arrested." She settles back into her chair and draws her legs up. "So yeah, technically, he stole it. But it wasn't like, 'get outta the car, motherfucker!'"

"I can't say that you're putting my mind at ease," I tell her.

She shrugs. "You asked."

"So where are his folks?"

"Dad was never around, mom couldn't handle him. When Max came around, she took off, too."

"Max is the uncle?"

She nods. "So it's not the best setup. Although Max is actually pretty cool. I mean, it's not even his kid, and he tries really hard anyway. That's what getting him arrested was about. Max cut this deal with the judge to suspend the charges if they'd order Brian to stay in school as a condition of not prosecuting him. Which has kind of been working." She shrugs. "Of course, he doesn't think it's so great."

"Which would explain the gun, maybe?"

"I doubt he'd ever use it. He just likes to act like a gang-banger. He heard some clown was selling a pistol so he bought it. Doesn't even have anywhere to keep it."

"And the part about punching the cop?"

"Well, yeah, he did that."

"And what, exactly, is the attraction here?"

Kayla takes a long drink. "Well, he's cute. And unpredictable. But he's pretty easy to control, too, because he's not all that bright."

"You sure about that? The control part, I mean?"

She shrugs. "He's definitely got an anger management problem. But a little danger's O.K. Reminds you you're not dead."

"And that you easily could be."

"He's only dangerous to himself," she says.

"Til you decide to dump him."

She purses her lips. "Which could happen." We hear the front door open and then Annie calling for Kayla. "Plus, *she* hates him," she adds, without bothering to answer.

"Better and better," I say, and she arches her eyebrows to concur.

What's funny is Kayla doesn't see how well-matched they actually are, aside from the intelligence disparity. She could have been describing herself right there; she's every bit as temperamental as she makes him sound, and probably more dangerous. And now that I think about it, if she's hanging around a guy with an explosive temper who has ready—sometimes immediate—access to a gun, how the hell smart is she? I used to marvel at this stuff when she'd tell it; I remember it seemed like she was thirty years old sometimes, back when we first met. But now it just seems indulgent, like she's just some spoiled kid who feeds on people that let her get away with it. Like this Brian guy, and me, probably. We're just entertainment to her.

There's a rap on the door and then it swings open. "Oh, hello, Teri," Annie says. "I wondered who she was talking to." She shifts from foot to foot. "How was Baltimore?"

I glance at Kayla. "Oh, I ended up not going. Um, a friend of mine, his father died, so I stayed here."

"Oh, I didn't know that." She looks toward Kayla, but without actually looking at her. It occurs to me that she must know about Crosscut, since he's the primary font of my father's television access, but doesn't associate that with what I'm saying now. "I'm sorry to hear that."

"Thanks. I guess Mom had an O.K. time, though. Sounds like she did."

"Yes, I guess so. Hope we don't end up losing her."

"Um, yeah." Apparently Annie gets more of the scoop in that regard than I do, though it's kind of weird Gail wouldn't have mentioned me not going. Kayla either, although they hardly talk to each other as it is.

"Your dad's making quite the splash, eh? A regular TV star these days."

"He does seem to keep turning up," I agree.

"Well, we're really proud of him. And it's great for the college, let me tell you."

"He's going to be doing a weekly column for the Jackson paper," I inform her. "And they might give him a recurring segment at the TV station, but that's still up in the air."

"Wow, that's great," Annie says "He's really busting out, isn't he?" Suddenly her face tightens. "Hope we don't lose him, either." She shrugs and turns for the door. "Let the Chancellor worry about it." Kayla exhales loudly as the door clicks shut, like she's been holding her breath the whole time.

"So like, you guys don't talk at all?" I ask.

"It just seems to work better that way."

Later, driving home, it occurs to me that her inane attraction to Brian is not unlike mine for her; the thrill of reckless behavior, some bizarre need to step right up to the edge and peer over, to feel the hot rush of adrenaline that does, in fact, remind you that you're not dead. I suspect I'm only growing impatient with her now because I've found a new source for this; in which case I can hardly hold it against her.

Gail is at the table when I get home Monday afternoon, which is a bit of a surprise; that the table is covered with papers and other work-related detritus, less so. She spent most of the weekend on campus, so except for a rushed breakfast out yesterday, I didn't see her at all. "This is getting done by Friday," she declares. "Enough is enough."

"Good for you." I sling my pack onto the couch. "Then what?"

"Daiquiris."

I get a Coke from the fridge and lean against the counter. "I was thinking a little more long term."

"Oh, one thing at a time, Teri," she says, which is kind of funny in that she has at least three things going now that I can see from here. She looks up and exhales fitfully. "I've got a conference at the end of the month, and a lot of little things I've been putting off because of this." She gives the table an exasperated nod. "And hopefully, there will be some time for us."

"That'd be different." It just kind of slips out before I can stop it.

"It can't be helped, I'm afraid. Sorry."

"That was mean, Mom. I'm sorry, too."

"At least you still care enough to be bothered," she says, though I have no idea what that means. She picks up her cell phone and pushes a button. "Now when did she call?"

"Who?"

"Annie. I told her to leave me alone til Friday."

"She's probably just checking that you're still here." Gail gives me a curious look as she sets down the phone. "She's worried you're going to leave."

"She said that?"

I nod. "Since your trip."

"Honestly," she sighs. "All I said was 'Don't be surprised by anything.' She always assumes the worst." She rolls her eyes. "But, I guess if Kayla were my daughter, I would, too."

"It does tend to save time." I get a glass and some ice and return to my spot. "So then, you're staying put?" I ask. She hasn't said, at least not to me, and I'd kind of like to know, since it is of some consequence.

"I haven't made any decisions yet," she answers, setting down her pen and looking up at me. For once, it feels like I have her full attention. "To be honest, Teri, I haven't had time to spit since I got back, so I've put it on the back burner til this gets done." She nods again at the table and smiles weakly. "I do appreciate the position this puts you in, Dear, but again, it can't be helped. I promise to let you know the minute I decide anything."

"O.K. then, I'm going to hold you to that. And I hope you do. Stay, I mean." She smiles more warmly as I gather up my pack and start for my room. "And good luck with that."

"Let's pick up something to eat in a little while," she calls after me.

"Fine, let me know."

Which turns out to be the last thing we do together all week, which is kind of O.K., since I know about the deadline, and I have a big-ass Chemistry test to study for, anyway. We're not all that different from Kayla and Annie when it gets right down to it, which is pretty sad. If anything, Annie is around more than my mother; I mean, Kayla is having to work at ruining that connection, while in our case, if I shut it down, that would be it–over, done, no questions asked.

Which could easily happen, depending on what she decides. I know I'm not always the easiest person to get along with, but I've been cutting her a lot of slack for a long time now, and she's going to have to start meeting me part way. I mean, Pops is busier than both of us, and he still manages to make time. And if she bails, forget it.

One night toward the end of the week Nother and I decide to get ice cream, and when I go next door to see if Pops wants anything, I'm surprised to find that he's not there. "Funny he'd be out," I tell him as we get into the truck. His lights are on by the time we return, and when we get back inside I can hear talking through the wall. I kind of want to go check it out, since it's definitely a female voice over there, but I know Nother would give me one of those looks. After about twenty minutes the door opens on his side and the voices move across the yard, so, Nother or not, I go to the window to check it out. When I peek through the blinds, Pops is standing with some woman beside a red Honda that I somehow failed to notice when we pulled up. They're kind of joking around, laughing, talking too loud, and I see her reach out and touch him on the arm a few times. Pops is just standing there waiting with his hands in his pockets, and she's taking her sweet time leaving, standing with her door open and twirling her hair. Finally she gets in and Pops moves over and says something into the window. As she pulls out she taps the horn and Pops extracts a hand to wave after her. He starts back toward the house, then pauses to stare up the road at the receding tail lights.

"Well, well," I say, turning back from the window.

"Who was it?" Nother asks, barely glancing up from his book.

"No idea."

He reads a few more lines then marks the page and closes the book. "Where are you going?" I ask when he starts to gather up his things.

"Well, look, your test is tomorrow, and there's no way you're going to get another second of studying done til you go over there. So I might as well take off, because the sooner you do, the sooner you can get back over here."

I open my mouth to argue but he's exactly right and we both know it. "You could wait," I suggest lamely.

"How about you tell me tomorrow?" he says, so I shrug and see him off.

Pops is at the computer when I walk in, looking at a website on Seasonal Affective Disorder. "Hey," he says.

"Hey yourself." I plunk down at the table. "Who was here?" Subtlety and patience are not among my virtues.

Pops laughs as he scrolls down the page. "She's from the station. Her name is Cloud."

"Cloud? Like–" I point up.

He nods. "Parents were hippies, I think. She's one of the producers." He glances over. "She was the one who had the party."

"Oh. So, like, are you guys hanging out now?" I'm sure I just asked my dad that! But man, you have to ask if you expect to find out anything.

"We work together a lot," Pops says. "She's fun."

"You were working?" God! I am such a nag.

He nods at the screen. "We might do a piece on this," he says. "You know, about people who get depressed in winter because there's not enough daylight."

"I think I've heard of it," I say. "She's kind of young, isn't she? How old is she?"

"I don't know, twenty-eight, thirty. How old does an associate producer need to be in your world?"

"What-ever, Dad. I mean, it's not like you couldn't have looked this up without her. And she didn't seem to be in a big hurry to leave, if you ask me."

Pops has this amused grin on his face. "Which I didn't," he points out. "And what makes you say that, anyway?"

"Well, when I looked out there she was just bopping around the car all happy and chattering away. I didn't think she was ever going to get in and go."

"And this upsets you, why? Because I really can't see apologizing for my friends."

"Yeah, well, if that's all it is."

"Well, even if it isn't, I'm still not sure that necessitates an apology, either."

I sigh mightily at his equivocating. "O.K., Dad. What-ever you say. But I know what I saw, and I don't want to see you end up in your own book is all."

"I'll keep that in mind," he says. "And I'll try to behave."

"Everyone tries," I warn.

So, all told, more questions get raised than answered, and if Nother figured I'd be doing any more studying tonight,

he was way off the mark. It's the whole Carl thing all over
again, even if he is making it sound like there's nothing
going on. He wasn't doing a whole lot of denying, either, I
noticed. And as for her, I see that goofy little dance every
day at Decatur, so you're not telling me she isn't after it. I
go to bed before Gail gets home, because it's just as easy to
freak out in the dark.

I manage to get it together for my test, which is a lot
easier than the last one. I just force myself to focus, if for
no other reason than to keep from thinking about Gail
possibly leaving and/or Cloud possibly staying. Which
seems to work, because I'm pretty sure walking out that I
nailed it, and probably locked up an A for the quarter,
which would kick ass, not to mention get Gail off mine.

Kayla is at the table with some guy when I go out, and
it seems I've walked square into the middle of a spat, as
neither of them is saying too much, and Kayla has this
look on her face like she wishes he'd crawl in a hole. "This
is Teri," she enunciates tersely as I unload my books on the
table. "This is who he was waiting for. Not me. Her. Just
like I said." She looks across the table at me and rolls her
eyes. "Brian," she explains with a sideways jerk of her
head. "You just missed Nother."

"Hi," I say. I flash this half smile, which feels pretty
ridiculous given the scowl each of them is wearing.

He sort of grunts and bobs his head, though more
toward the table than at me, then looks away. Kayla snorts
at this display. "That means 'Pleased to meet you,' in
Neanderthal."

Brian continues to stare off, while Kayla grins and
makes faces at me. He is kind of cute, in a comic book sort
of way, with these curly ringlets pasted to his forehead and
dangling over his ears. After an awkward and extended

silence he swings one leg over the bench. "I got to go," he says in a guttural drone.

"Good. Go," she says with a wave of her hand, like the Queen dismissing Alice. He's straddling the bench staring at her, but she won't even look at him. His face is locked in the tightest expression I've ever seen, equal parts rage, confusion, and longing. His eyes are vacuous, his gaze riveted precisely on her ear. Then, and totally improbably, given how things seem to be going, he leans toward her, his arm rising to pull her to him. She turns away, but he's got her by the back of the head now, and he's planting one half on her lips, half on her right cheek. I stare, unable to move, while they struggle. Then, equally improbably, her face jerks suddenly toward him, and she starts grinding her mouth onto his, her tongue going like a pry bar on a stuck window. There's nothing tender or loving about it, and they stay locked like this for too long, Kayla with an expression of blank industry, him looking like a fish on ice. Neither seems to care that I am here; there's a point to be made, evidently. Then, abruptly, Kayla pulls away, and out of his grasp. "There," she says sharply, wiping the side of her mouth while he stares slack-jawed. "Now go fuck off, why don't you."

"Nice meeting you," I mouth as he stalks off. I feel kind of bad joking about it, but it is funny.

"My man," Kayla says as he disappears across the parking lot.

"Interesting."

"Well, we're not going to be 'Couple of the Month' like you two, but it's not without it's moments."

"And was that one of them?" I inquire, ignoring the dig. Kayla's one of those people who think she's allowed to rip into anyone; family, friends, boyfriend, it doesn't matter, but if you so much as look funny at them, she's all over your ass.

"One of many," she sighs. "But at least he hung around til you got here."

"Was there a scene or something?"

She shrugs. "Not really. I mean, when I came out, Nother was sitting at the table by himself, waiting for you, I assume."

"I just had a big test. He probably wanted to see how I did."

"Well, anyway, he's here, and doofus is just standing over there by that tree, like he can't square it in his head why the person here isn't you or me, 'cause he knows this is where we sit. I kind of wave him over, but he just stands there like some kid lost at the mall. So I sat down and started talking to Nother, like, the hell with him, and he's over there getting more and more pissed, til finally I went and dragged him back here. Then he just sits here fuming, not saying anything until Nother finally takes off, probably because he can't stand it, either." She shakes her head, like: how come these things always happen to me? Even though she orchestrates most of it. "Then you came."

I frown picturing Nother's unease. What I want to say is, "He knows a train wreck when he sees one, why stick around?" But that would just make her defensive, and I'm too wrung out from my test to deal right now. "Why was he here, anyway?" I ask instead. "I mean, don't they have school today?"

"He cut," she says, lighting up a Kool. "He pretends like he's coming around because he wants to see me, but what he's really doing is checking up. I think seeing Nother flipped him out." She exhales bounteously.

Poor Nother. He doesn't like being around Kayla much to begin with, so getting caught in the middle of one of her episodes probably wasn't what he was looking for this morning. He's never come right out and complained about her, even when I rip into her, but I can tell. It's the same old story; she likes to fuck with people just to see them squirm. Like, if Nother and I are sitting there, she'll start flirting like crazy with him, just to piss me off, and to see if she can embarrass him. She goes on and on about sex, or some guy, or whatever, or she'll start asking one or the other of us really personal questions, usually him. And she's always talking like she's ready when he is, and then laughing about it when he doesn't just come across the table and jump her bones, like he's too shy or straight-laced to take her up on it, because it never for a second occurs to her that he might not want to.

I think she's starting to catch on, though, because he pretty much avoids her now, which she treats as equal parts victory and insult. But she's still annoyed that she hasn't been able to get more of a reaction out of him. Nother's pretty adept at deflecting her shit, which annoys her, too. So it's probably no coincidence that Brian's coming around like this. I wouldn't be surprised if it wasn't Kayla's doing entirely, because she's going to have her fun one way or the other, and if Nother won't take the bait, this Brian character certainly will, even if it means risking jail. I'm sure he doesn't even realize how over-matched he is, and Lord only knows what she's filling that empty head with.

"So, what's up?" she asks, ending the long silence while mashing out her cigarette. As if I haven't been here for ten minutes already.

I shrug. "Aced my test." She makes a lazy circling motion with her finger, like: big whoop. And I wonder again why I even bother.

I stop by the Chem lab after lunch to see if Mr. Lowell will grade my test, because for some reason I really want to know. He's been working on them already, and he sifts through the pile on the floor next to his chair and holds up mine. "Nicely done," he says, a hint of humanity coming through his normally analytical tone. He's probably a nice guy, but how the hell would you know? "You forgot to render the by-product for question seven," he adds, which cost me four points, I see, "and seven moles minus four moles leaves three, not two."

"I knew that," I joke, though if he gets it, he doesn't let on. But I don't care; I'll take a 93 any day. "And that would have been...carbon?"

"Asking me or telling me?"

"It's carbon."

To my shock, he gives it to me, redlining the 93 and scratching in a 97 over it. "Can we expect this from now on?" he asks. Like most of the faculty here, he assumes if your parents teach at the college you're automatically a brain.

"I'm hoping," I say.

"Just decide," he instructs, returning my test to the pile. He glances up one last time, and I see my twin reflections in his glasses. "Good day," he says, and goes back to the test before him.

"Bye," I answer with a sheepish wave at the top of his head. "And thanks." I snag Sandy and we go out after fifth period to celebrate my good fortune. We take hot chocolate to the park and drink it outside, which is perfect for this blustery day. We're balanced on one of the teeter-totters and she's imposed the no-cherry-bomb rule til we finish our drinks, so we just kind of sit there, suspended, sipping in silence. The park is empty but for us, and one old man in a snap brim cap way across the lawn, and all I can think is: this is my life. My boyfriend is great, but misunderstood; my supposed best friend has a death wish; my dad may or may not be dating someone named Cloud; my mother is likely leaving town soon; and I'm sitting in the park, in the cold, on the seesaw, drinking cocoa like I'm five years old again. Is it any wonder I can't remember to render the fucking carbon?

I've been telling Sandy about Kayla and Brian's little set-to, and then how it didn't get much better after he left. "So, like, 'Couple of the Month,' what the fuck does that mean?"

"It means she's jealous of you guys and she's being a bitch about it."

"Why, are we that obnoxious now? You have to tell me if we are, Sandy."

"You and Nother?" she hoots. "Obnoxious how? You're practically invisible."

"You're sure?"

"Trust me. I mean, you are more visible now, but that's only because you were totally off the radar before. Besides, you handled the 'death in the family' drama really good, so people are looking to cut you slack."

"Yeah, that's what I'd think, too. So why is Kayla being such a bitch? I mean, we're friends. At least we're supposed to be. We were, anyway. I think. Shouldn't she be happy for me? If she hooked up good, I'd be happy for her. So what's the deal?"

"The deal is, she's a psychopath," Sandy says. "There's no chance she's going to hook up good and she knows it. And seeing you two only highlights how fucked up her situation is. How all of her situations are. So what she does is, she picks at yours."

"That's pretty jacked up."

DAVID RACINE

"Yeah it is, but she can't help it," Sandy replies. "Like I said, she's a psychopath."

"I'm not disbelieving you," I assure her. Sandy's really into this Psych class she's taking, so this kind of stuff comes up all the time, since I already know most of the names and buzzwords from listening to my parents spar. Kayla's in the class, too, so Sandy has a tendency to attach just about any pathology they happen to be studying to her, whether from cause or merely proximity.

"I wouldn't even talk to her about any of that if I were you. If you're happy, it'll just annoy her, and she'll feel compelled to try to ruin it. And if you're not, she'll just say, 'I told you so,' which will annoy you. And then she'll start dragging you down, too."

I nod slowly. "I could see that."

"She's done it with everyone else who's tried to be friends with her. And every single person has ended up backing off, because ultimately she's only tolerable from a distance." She tosses her empty cup on the grass. "I mean, you and Nother should just do your thing, because whatever works for you is all that matters. Forget what she thinks about it, because she's just like"—she flicks her hand dismissively—"well, whatever she is."

"A psychopath," I suggest.

Sandy jumps off, totally ignoring the no-cherry-bomb rule, but I manage to get my feet set, so I don't bounce on my ass at least. "I wasn't done! You are such a cheat."

We toss the cups and drive around, since she can't go home until school's supposed to be over because her mom's there. She tells me again about this big Psych project that's due at the end of the semester, which she's getting to be a real pro at not finishing. "Don't worry, I'll get it done," she promises. "I've still got two weeks."

"I'm not worried," I tell her. "Honest, I could give a shit."

"My pal," she says. "Oh, and listen to this. He just today told us that we each have to do a ten minute presentation in class. Does that suck, or what?"

"Rhetorical, right?"

Pops buys me dinner for nailing my Chemistry test; we go out for Chinese and then I don't see him for three days. I catch him on the tube Saturday morning, though, thanks to the reminder he leaves on our machine. It's the "not enough light" disorder, and he more or less supplies an overview of the malady, then answers a few softballs that the host lobs at him. I marvel yet again at his aptitude for this; I seriously doubt he'd even heard of this condition a week ago, but you'd never know it watching him now.

Gail and I keep tabs on each other by sound; I hear her in the kitchen; pacing, making coffee, talking stridently into her cell phone, swearing; she talks at me through the bathroom door, or the shower curtain if I forget to turn the lock. She doesn't quite make her deadline, which means another weekend on campus, and then all of Monday afternoon summarizing for Annie. But Annie doesn't really get it, and so drags Mom over to the Chancellor's office on Wednesday to repeat it to him, which doesn't go well, either, since all the Chancellor wants to talk about is Pops, which has Gail ready to rip his throat out, and still fuming when she gets home. "I swear to Christ," she says as she storms through the door. She drops her briefcase onto one of the kitchen chairs and lets her laptop slip onto the table from her shoulder, then thwacks the two-hundred or so pages she's composed these last few months loudly beside it. "Urrgghhh," she snarls, looking around the kitchen like she could spit tacks. Her eyes come to rest on me,

watching with mild interest from my perch on the couch, and
she sighs fitfully. "And why aren't you old enough to drink?"

"Poor resource management early on."

Twenty minutes later we're at Casa Ole, where the food
is only moderately palatable, but the margaritas are top
notch. Gail knocks back one-and-a-half of the fishbowl
size, while I handle the rest in a couple of timid sample
tastes, and one pretty big glug when she goes to the can.
We work through a bowl of chips and salsa and a couple of
appetizers that are surprisingly not awful, while she goes
off on her meeting with the Chancellor, and then the college in general, which she variously describes as Podunk,
no account, and shallow. I let her rant while I wrestle with
our several cheesy concoctions; it seems to be helping, and
I doubt there's a chance the conversation can turn til she's
had her say. "I swear, if Walmart made me an offer
now...." She lets the thought trail off, an indication that
she's losing steam. "Now what is this here?"

"Quesadilla," I tell her as she pries a wedge of tortilla
loose from the plate. "Kind of a Mexican grilled cheese." I
reach over with a knife and flick-sever the strings of pep-
per-jack, so she doesn't lose an eye.

She takes a bite and chews thoughtfully, her glance flitting around the table. She shrugs and spoons salsa onto the
remainder of the wedge. "So, how are things with you and
your friend?" she asks, this breezy inquiry about on par,
interest-wise, with the one preceding it. She looks across
the table at me, her eyes a tad unfocused, and wipes mar-
garita salt from the corner of her mouth.

She means Nother; he's the only one she refers to like
that. I think how nice it would be to just tell her, to let go
and just say all the things clogging my brain these last few
months. I'd like her to know that the girl she dragged

down here is not the person sitting across from her now; that the landscape and the rules have changed. But it would be pointless. She's half in the bag for one thing, and it could get really loud really fast, which we'd both regret later, and the Ole family more immediately. And she's only asking because it's her turn; I let her vent, so courtesy dictates she return the favor.

"Good," I say. "You know. Good."

"That's nice," she replies, like this should cover it. And soon she's off again, something about airfares for the upcoming conference in New York.

When I pull in at the house there's a red Honda parked in front of Pops' side, and I get this feeling in my stomach that you'd only ever expect would be accompanied by a mushroom cloud. Worse, the door is opening over there as we cross the porch, and Gail heads straight to the front window once we get inside. To my relief, there are two of them making their way across the yard with Pops, which is better, strangely enough, rather than twice as bad. One is Cloud, of course, the other a mousy looking woman who appears to be about my father's age. I speculate silently as to what she might be called: Fog? Misty? Occluded Front?

"Now, who's that?" Gail demands, like she's already expecting to be annoyed by the answer.

"I think they're from the TV station." I pause briefly to watch her. Pops is between the two women, and it all looks harmless enough. "Dad might be getting his own segment," I tell her.

"Oh, please," Gail moans, reaching for the cord to snap closed the blinds. "Hasn't this gone far enough?" She marches off to her room without waiting for an answer.

I move to the front door, which is still open, and watch through the screen from several paces inside. The other woman is in the passenger seat now, and Cloud is talking to her through the window, about Pops, it would appear, as she is stroking his back while she speaks. She gives Pops a final pat, more ass than back, I'd call it, and climbs in. Pops glances over on his way back across the yard and gives this little half-shrug, though I'm not really sure he even sees me. When he's for sure back inside I nudge the door closed with my foot and take off my jacket, not sure exactly what to think about all this. One thing I know is there's a good chance of things getting really ugly before long. I mean, if Gail had seen that, she'd be out there tearing Cloud a new one right now. My father, too, most likely.

Pops is already at his desk when I walk in Saturday morning with doughnuts. He's still zeroed in on the book, even with all the other things he's got going on. Two chapters left, he told me the other day, and then a last one to sort of pull it all together. He's writing awfully fast, so I figure he's got some work ahead of him revision-wise. "Ahhh," he says when I walk in, "breakfast. Perfect timing." He run's a long diagonal line through the page he's been typing and joins me in the kitchen to get another pot going. "You're up early," he notes as we settle at the table.

I glance at the clock. "You making fun?"

"No, just you got in late," he says.

Damn. Gail doesn't even roll over when I get home, but I always seem to forget he's just over here. "I was just at Nother's watching movies," I say casually. Which is true. "I called Mom to tell her," I add, which isn't.

"That's fine," he says, taking a big bite out of the crème filled I brought for him. "Just surprised you're awake, is all." He picks up his empty cup and frowns into it, then shoots an impatient look at the coffee maker.

"Hey, guess what? They're moving up the release date for Crosscut's CD."

Pops nods and swallows. "Yeah, I heard."

"From who?"

"Ezra. He asked me to proof the liner notes, and if I want to add anything they might use it."

"Wow," I say, trying to envision Pops and Ezra working this deal. "That's cool. Are they paying you for that?"

"Nah." He gets up and walks to the cabinet beside his desk, returning with a CD in a black case. "He gave me some outtakes though," he says, setting it on the table. "Probably worth more than they'd have paid, anyway. Is to me."

I pick up the disk. There's a date scratched on it near the center, but nothing else. Bootleg Crosscut, I muse. We finish the doughnuts and Pops pours coffee. "So, how goes the book?" I ask. "Are you writing to publishers or anything?"

"No, nothing like that yet. But I have an agent now."

"An agent? I didn't even know they did that for academic books." Gail doesn't even have an agent.

"Well, it's kind of a package deal. See, Cloud knows this woman—"

"The one who was here the other night?"

"That's the one," he says. "I was hoping that was you watching from the shadows."

"Don't you figure you'd know by now if it was Gail?"

"Good point. Anyway, this woman handles mostly TV people. The ones on the regional stations down here—New Orleans, Baton Rouge, Little Rock. But the agency, which is in Dallas, has people who handle everything: books, music, screenplays, all that stuff. So if they represent me, they'll handle all of it."

"All of what?"

"It's all about creating buzz," Pops says, obviously mocking someone. He brings his hands together so his fingers cross. "We're talking synergy, Teri."

"I might puke," I warn him.

"Yeah, that's pretty much what I said. But then Cloud pointed out that I've gotten some decent exposure just by accident, and that's worked in my favor, so why not run with it, see what happens?"

"Wait, why is Cloud hooking you up with an agent if she works for the station?"

Pops shrugs. "I guess she figures everyone benefits." I roll my eyes huge, like: how dumb do you think I am? "Anyhow," he continues, "when this woman said they'd do the legwork for my book, I figured: why not? I mean, I like the TV stuff; I wouldn't mind doing more of it; and I want to sell the book. If they can help me with all that, *and* probably get me more money, why shouldn't I let them?"

"Well, when you put it like that." I shrug.

"Right. Otherwise I'd have to do it all myself. So let her take a shot."

"O.K., O.K., I'm behind you all the way," I say. "But I'd leave out the bit about 'synergy' when you tell Mom." I gather up the bag and napkins. "Got to run; Nother's coming by in a little bit."

"What's your mother up to now that the big project is finished?"

"No idea," I tell him on my way out the door. "Haven't seen much of her since she started having all this time for us." Which comes out as more of a complaint than it actually is. I mean, it is a complaint, but mostly theoretical. I'd just as soon be hanging out with Nother anyway, or cutting with Sandy, so Gail not hovering all the time is probably a good thing. But that still doesn't absolve her of the negligence, or, if that's too strong a word, then her woeful lack of attention to all things me. I should be way more pissed than this. I mean, if it wasn't for Nother, she'd really be hearing it.

I'm circling the living room talking to myself when Nother pulls up. We drop Ruth off in town and decide to hike out to the clearing; actually, that's been the plan all along, but the sky is slate colored, and we're both assuming a downpour is imminent. But we head out anyway, and on the way I start unloading all my family shit on him. Which he doesn't get, of course, growing up in his family. How could he? I point this out to him, the innate connection they share—*all* of them—that commonality that isn't spoken of; like religion, almost, among the truest believers. It's like...well, like they just know.

"See, we don't have that at my house," I try telling him. "When my mom blows me off for six weeks straight, I start to wonder. It's not like the connection's just...*there*."

"How do you know?" He's walking in front of me and asks this over his shoulder without slowing down.

"What do you mean, 'How do I know?' I'd know automatically. Like you guys."

"It's not automatic," he says. "It's mostly trust, in fact."

"Well, they haven't shown they can be trusted," I say back.

"You could trust them first," he says. "Someone's got to start."

"And then what, just wait?"

We emerge into the clearing and he slows to let me catch up. "They're your family," he says. "I mean, who else have you got?"

I squeeze him around the waist. "You."

He squeezes back. "What if that changes?"

"Is it?"

"No, and I didn't mean that. All I'm saying is I wouldn't go cutting loose your family for some guy you've only known a couple months."

"What about that trust you were talking about?"

"If you've got enough for me, then you've got enough for them." He tosses his backpack up onto the platform and boosts me up.

"They're not like you."

"Well act like they are. Maybe they'll come around."

"I'll think about it." I reach down to help him up. "You're sure we're O.K.?"

"Way better than O.K.," he assures me.

A little later I'm more convinced. We stay curled up in the blankets and sleeping bags, napping, talking intermittently, and listening for the bird. The tarp stretched above us responds beautifully when the skies finally open, the few drops that do reach us coming in from the open sides, when the squall is at its most pitched. As the storm kicks up around us I burrow further into his chest. Finally, nestled in this warm cocoon, I begin to relax.

Things have been so good with us that even thinking they could go wrong hardly occurs to me. Since Crosscut's death we're together all the time; even at school we see each other a couple times a day. Joley has even quit trying to push other guys on me, though she's stopped short of giving the relationship her sanction. We seem really in sync to me, like things are totally meshing, and a lot of what passes between us feels automatic–not unlike what goes on in his family, now that I think about it. The closeness is amped up since Christmas; he's more or less woven into my life now, like I want it.

Which is why the "What if that changes?" comment landed like a gut punch. It's not that I think it's going to last forever. I'm not a total idiot. Who knows what it'll be like in six months, let alone forever. We're only sixteen; I realize that. But right now it's still new, and it's working, and things have turned up a notch, so why start talking about it being over?

Nother tenses next to me. "Listen," he whispers, and after a moment I hear it too, the nasally call of the ivory-bill. We sit up slowly, bringing the covers with us, and peer over the low wall across the river. Beneath the wide branches of the lone tree on that side stands the bird, wings fidgeting in an attempt to flush the water. The rain has slowed to a thin drizzle, I notice only now, the steady thwacking on the tarp reduced to a barely audible patter. Nother tenses again, his head cocked to one side. "Up there," he breathes, his bare arm emerging from the folds to point up through the branches.

My eyes follow the line of his arm, and through the leaves I see another bird circling lazily downward into the clearing to join her red crested mate. I squeeze his arm. "There's two." I say.

"Almost had to be," he says back. "But where's this one been all the other times?" He turns to look at me, eyes rounded. "We really can't say anything now. There'd be a million people back here with nets."

We watch for half an hour before they circle off again to wherever it is they go. Nother figures they move to even deeper growth, and that perhaps they came to the clearing today to dry out and escape the sodden drippings of their hide-away. Which makes sense, I guess. It sounds good, anyway.

We spend the evening at his house, even slipping into his room for a while when Ruth and Ron go to a movie, and Madame Marie is otherwise engaged. I get home by midnight though, in case Pops is still up. His light is on but I don't go over, and as I lie in bed waiting to sleep, I wonder what he would make of our sighting. If I could tell one person, it would probably be him.

When I get home from The Sawmill the next afternoon, crusty from cleaning and reeking of stale smoke, Gail is at the table prattling into the phone to Annie about something or other. The table is covered with papers, and on the counter are two Styrofoam containers giving off a pungent, peppery aroma. Gail flashes a tight smile and indicates the food, then gives a hopeless look at the phone. I mouth the word "shower" and she nods before going back to her conversation. When I come back out the papers have been piled on a chair, replaced by the steaming containers of spicy noodles.

"You've been seeing a lot of that boy," Gail comments as we load up plates.

"I like him," I say. I recall the conversation with Nother yesterday, something he said about making the first move, but tonight I'm just not up to it. I shrug, and congratulate myself for not adding: at least he's around.

"So I've noticed," she says, which can't be all that accurate. I mean, she couldn't have noticed much, and it sure has taken long enough. "I'm just wondering if—"

"Mom," I say, cutting off this inquiry with a firm look. "Just...don't."

"O.K., now, this is going to be, like, really weird," Sandy says. "But, here goes. We're doing our presentations in Psych this week, right, and—"

"Did you go yet?"

"Yesterday," she says.

"How was it?"

"Good," she answers distractedly; I've thrown off her train of thought. "I was nervous, but it ended up being O.K. I mean, people asked lots of questions, and I answered all of them. So it was cool."

"Great. Did Kayla go?"

"Today," she says, "that's kind of what I'm getting to."

"Uh oh."

"Um...yeah. So, like, she starts talking about her project, and it turns out to be a case study, based on this theory she made up, about people or couples sometimes trying to get along better by placing...artificial constructs, I think is what she said. They place things between themselves to keep from dealing with, like, the real issues."

"That's hardly original," I say.

"I thought that, too. But anyway, she has this case study, like I said, this couple she's been observing the last few months who did that. And so she's telling about it, right, and it all starts sounding really familiar, you know. And then, she even comes up with this name for it, for this example, or condition, or whatever. She calls it"–Sandy glances up from her cup to look me in the face–"Duplexity."

"What?!"

Sandy nods. "I about shit. She never, like, mentioned you guys by name or anything, but once she said that–"

"Well, yeah!" I shriek. "I mean, anyone who knows our situation at all would figure that out." I can physically feel myself getting more pissed by the second. I start drumming my hands on the table, hard enough that Sandy grips her cup to stop it from dancing to the beat. "I can't fucking believe her."

Sandy purses her lips in this helpless expression. "I can," she replies after a minute. "Dumb name and all, it's just like her."

"You're right," I admit. "And I knew it, too, that's the fucking thing. I noticed almost from the beginning how she used to just hang around watching them. And always asking these really open-ended questions to get me to talk about it, and what our house was like."

"I think you're referenced rather liberally," she says. "I mean, it almost has to be you."

"It's me." I shake my head wildly, remembering how freely I'd spilled the beans all those times, and how Kayla used my discontent to get what she needed. "I just thought she was strange, was all. Or nosy. Or maybe she was just trying to fuck with me by asking all those personal questions, knowing I'd go off like I did." I pound the table and my cup does a full quarter turn. "I am so fucking stupid!"

"Come on," she says. "Don't start beating yourself up. No one could anticipate that."

"Man, if she was here right now...." I stare across the table at Sandy. "I mean, you'd be prying my hands off her neck."

"Or not." She looks out the front window of the coffee shop, then back at me. "I even asked her, 'How could you fucking do that to Teri?' And she's all, 'What was I supposed to do? I didn't know he was going to make us give oral reports. I thought it would just be him reading it, so like, who cares? He wouldn't know who it was.'" Sandy shakes her head. "Like that would have made it O.K."

"Yeah, never mind totally betraying our friendship." My head has been going side to side this whole time, entirely out of my control. "Fucking Kayla."

Sandy nods sympathetically. "It wasn't all that bad, just so you know. Not that that excuses her doing it even for a second, but it was really clinical sounding; you know how she is when she's trying to act smart. And I'm not sure how many other people in there even know about your parents, in which case they probably weren't even listening. Plus she had that one shirt on, so all the guys were staring at her tits."

"Whatever," I sigh, suddenly very weary of all this. "I mean, thanks for saying that, and you're probably right. Not very many people know. But shit, it's not even about that."

"Right." We sit for a couple minutes in silence, not even looking at each other. She asks, "So, what're you going to do, do you think?"

"I don't know." My rage has already cooled markedly. I'm still really pissed off; this anger/betrayal/disappoint-ment/sadness isn't going away any time soon, I can tell already, but the urge to break things, preferably Kayla, is dissipating steadily. Soon it will be a frigid black hole. "I mean, I'm more stunned than anything. How could she just *use* us like that, my parents especially?"

"Yeah. The only kind of bad thing that sticks out is she predicted they'd split up for good, eventually."

"She said that?"

Sandy nods.

"In class. About *my* parents?"

"Yep."

I let my head fall back and stare up at the thick wooden crossbeams, where ancient enameled coffee pots dangle beside historic advertisements for long gone blends. I exhale abundantly. "Maybe Psycho Brian will let me bor-row his gun." O.K., so maybe I haven't cooled off as much as I thought. I look over at Sandy and arch my eyebrows.

"He'd probably do it for you."

What I end up doing is pretty much...nothing. I keep away from our table the whole week, but I don't seek Kayla out for answers or retribution. I'm so disgusted with her I don't even want to be in her presence, let alone risk interaction or hair pulling. There's nothing I have to say to her at this point. Nothing that wouldn't come out as a lot of screaming, which would just end up suiting her more than me, anyway. Joley becomes an annoying presence again; she can't shut up about it when she finds out, though her enlightenment does not come from me. "She is like, so...I can't believe her." Which is about as analytical as Joley gets, though she seems to have limitless ways to express this one non-sentiment. And apparently Kayla's been missing in action at the table, too, though I'm not sure whether this is to avoid me, or the indignity of sitting alone, or maybe she's out in the parking lot with psycho boy. "You guys are going to lose that table," Joley warns, in what passes for advice and support from her. "I mean, that's a primo spot."

"Collateral damage," I reply, which Joley comprehends not at all.

Nother doesn't have much to say when I tell him, though he doesn't seem overly surprised, either. I get the impression he finds it really foreign, like I was describing life in Mongolia, and what could he possibly add. He seems surprised that *anyone* would do it, more than the fact that it was Kayla. "That other one's right about the table, though," he agrees, so I return the following week. I mean, it is a good spot when she's not there.

"I'm amazed Annie would let her do that," Gail says when I finally tell her a couple days later. She's packing for her conference, so it seems like a good time. I decided they both needed to know, but I had to cool off myself first. Not that I expect, or even want, either of them to do anything, but it's out there, and it's mostly about them, so they should be aware of it.

"She probably doesn't even know," I inform her. "Those two don't talk."

"Well, maybe she should," Gail says, smoothing a dark sweater she's placed atop a pleated skirt in her suitcase. "Do you want me to call over there?" She frowns at the bag, then looks over at me.

"No. I mean, I didn't tell you so you'd do something. I just thought you should know."

"Well, you better believe I'm going to say something when I get back," she declares, more to the suitcase than to me. She fwumps the thing closed and leans on it to run the puckered zipper. "That little shit is not going to be messing around with me." Which might be even more ominous sounding if I didn't know she'll forget all about it by then.

Pops is a little more concerned; he at least thinks to ask if the revelation is a problem for me. "What I mean is, I don't feel the need to justify my behavior to anyone not directly involved," he says, leaning back from his desk, "let alone a bunch of high school kids. But I'm wondering if it's been a problem for you?"

"Not really, other than wondering if people are staring behind my back, which I doubt. Most of them still don't even know me, and half didn't realize who she was talking about, anyway. Second, it's not near as bad as a lot of them have it at their own houses. So it being out there isn't that big a deal. It's the fact that she did it *at all* that bothers me."

"Yeah, that is rather disturbing," he says.

I nod at his manuscript. "You could put her in your book. But don't, 'cause she'd probably like that."

"It does fit," he says.

I find myself feeling strangely protective of them, that I've brought all this down on us, and they're the targets of the finger pointing. But I think mainly I feel guilty about running my mouth in front of Kayla all through the fall, when I was still really pissed at them, and being here.

Maybe I'm trying to displace my self-loathing on her. Not that she still doesn't deserve it, but I probably should have kept all that to myself to begin with, and none of this would have happened. But at the same time, my parents are as much to blame as I am; they're the ones who decided on this ridiculous arrangement. How was I not going to talk about it? My mistake was trusting Kayla, and not meeting Sandy earlier.

By the middle of the week I'm starting to get over it, or at least it isn't slipping back into my thoughts every five minutes. Nother says just take the high road and let it go; nothing has really changed, after all. People knew before, and there was nothing to keep them from spreading it around then. Plus, I have new insight into Kayla now because of it, which could prove useful down the road. Joley, of course, wants drama, and she's probably responsible for more people knowing than Kayla or me, since she's tried to turn it into this big morality play. She's half-annoyed at me, too, for not playing the wronged innocent, or at least not projecting to the back rows.

Which is how things stand on Wednesday when Kayla finally reappears at our table. I'm working on some French homework, and I'm surprised when I look up to see that it's her. I have to squint because the sky is so bright behind her, but rather than raise a hand to shade my eyes, I simply stare for a second and then go back to my French.

"I take it you're still not talking to me, then?" she asks, in this tone that suggest *she's* somehow tired of it. She slides her pack from her shoulder and sits down.

Right, I'm thinking, it's my fault, now. I'm the one with the explaining to do. I feel all the anger of the past week coming back, but I refuse to give her the satisfaction. "Why?" I ask, looking up only after I've completed the translation in front of me, "do you have another report due?"

She smirks and looks off, then fishes her cigarettes out of her bag and pulls one out, tossing the pack toward me, offering. She lights up and puffs casually while I go back to my work. "So, like, are you expecting me to apologize, or what?" she asks finally, like I'm being tiresome.

"I don't think anyone ever expects anything from you."

She takes that last, signature drag and mashes the butt on the side of the table. "Well, I will say one thing, bitterness has certainly made you wittier."

"Seems there's no end to the ways I can entertain you," I marvel.

"Right there again," she notes. Another uncomfortable silence passes. "So, go ahead," she offers tiredly. "Rant, scream, let it out. 'How could I? What's the matter with me? Who do I think I am?' I'm sure you're ripping me to everyone else."

"I've told Nother. That's it."

"Right."

"Whatever," I say. I've got two sentences left to translate, then I think I'll leave.

"So, like...what?" she says. She can't stand being ignored, and the irritation is evident in her voice. "We're feuding? Arch-enemies til I apologize?"

"You're not getting it," I say. I pause to finish accenting the sentence just written. "I don't want your apology, or your friendship, or anything else from you, because what does being friends with you even mean? Pretty much nothing, right?" I glance down at the last sentence, which should be the hardest one, but which I do instantly in my head. I close my book and shove it into my pack. "And I just don't care enough to feud." I stand up. "So like, you can have the table, that's only fair. I might still sit here if you're not around, but if you want it, just walk over and I'll leave. That way we won't have to deal with each other at all." I sling my pack over my shoulder. "And I'll tell Nother, so you won't have to worry about him coming by looking for me and freaking Brian out."

Kayla frowns. "Some days that's the only entertainment I get."

"You know, he might not be so jealous if you'd explain it to him sometime."

"Why would I do that?" she asks as I start to walk off. "It takes months to get an idea in there to begin with."

Nother is at my house the following afternoon, staring out the front window while I look for my keys, which I just had an hour ago when I let us in. "So how is your dad going to meet us at Bodean's if his car's parked out front here?"

I snap my fingers and pull open the front door. "Good question," I say, yanking the keys from the lock and shoving them in my pocket. "Ready," I announce, and he steps past me onto the porch while I get the lights and fish my keys back out to re-lock the door.

Grades came out this morning and I nailed a four-oh, so I called Pops around lunchtime to give him the news. It's not like it's a huge deal, I've done it before, but I figured I could weasel dinner out of him if I called early enough. Which is just what happens, and he even invites Nother along because he hasn't seen him in a while. We agree to meet up at six, since Pops isn't sure how his afternoon is going to play out, though I have a sneaking suspicion how it is he'll be arriving. On the way there we run into Ruth and Ron at the drug store and I invite them

along, so there are four of us leaning on Nother's pickup
yakking when Cloud's Honda pulls into the lot. "This is
him," I say, starting over toward the car.

Pops introduces us—he calls me Einstein—and we shake
hands; Cloud, rolling her eyes at his lame joke, calls me
Teri. I think if it wasn't for Nother and Ruth I could just go
ahead and be a bitch right now, but I'd feel so putrid with
them watching that I can't, and I wonder if Pops was
counting on this when he invited Nother. She's neither
overly friendly, in that nervous, trying too hard way, or the
least bit timid, like she's afraid I might bite her head off.
The other three somehow know to give us a minute and
remain at the pickup, which is closer to the door anyway.
They've been at the studio in Jackson, Pops tells me as we
approach the others, going through archival footage of
Crosscut as it turns out—what little there is. Further introductions are made; Cloud is Pops' "friend" from the station, and she seems quite pleased to be meeting two of
Crosscut's children. "Nother?" she repeats when Pops says
his name, but only to be sure she's heard it right. When he
nods she says, "I won't ask if you don't."

Nother smiles; he's heard much worse. "Deal," he says,
and we all go inside. "How about that big round one,"
Cloud suggests as we stand huddled eyeing the room.

Bodean's is one of those places where you know what
you want going in, so we don't even pick up the menus
while we wait for our server. Instead the talk is of Crosscut.
Pops wants to do a half-hour show to coincide with the
release of the CD, and they've spent the afternoon trying
to storyboard it. Cloud seems a bit amazed to be meeting
his kin now, in the flesh. "That kid sitting on top the
piano," Pops says to Cloud, then nods at Nother. "Probably five or six back then."

"Damn," she says. "This really helps." She speaks to the table. "You look at the tape and it's just, well, tape. But meeting you guys...." She lets the thought fade and begins to outline ideas, shaping the show as she speaks. There's nothing bossy in her tone, though she sounds familiar enough with control. My father watches her with this strange look on his face, his head moving up and down in silent agreement. By the time the waitress arrives Cloud has charmed the table.

While we eat, I tell Ruth the whole story about Kayla and her project, right through our little set-to yesterday. She seems as confounded as Nother, but appears to comprehend the meanness more readily than he does. "No loss there," she determines when I've finished. "Good riddance."

"I'm just glad it's over."

"I wouldn't be too sure about that," Ron warns. "She doesn't sound like the forgive and forget type."

"Teri's the victim here," Ruth points out. "It's her that would be the one to do that."

"Don't sound like that would matter to her," Ron says.

"What was it Faulkner said?" Pops asks, "Something like 'The past isn't dead. It isn't even past.'" He looks around the table.

Ron lifts a forkful of slaw and chews thoughtfully. "Sure," he says.

Ruth rolls her eyes. "He's right though, Teri. I'd still watch out for her."

We kick around in the parking lot when we've finished, enjoying the cool air after all that food. "Are you going with them?" Cloud asks Pops. "Because I need to hit it." They're standing pretty close together, and she tugs his coat sleeve playfully when she asks, which I'd probably find sweet if it wasn't my dad.

"Yeah," Pops says, then looks at me. "Is there room?"

"Sure," I say.

"Well then, it was nice meeting everybody," Cloud says. "Thanks for dinner," she tells Pops, who sprang for everyone. She smiles at me. "And thanks for being so smart, Teri."

"Anything for free food," I reply with a laugh. Much as I don't want to, I think I like her.

"So then, I'll be by to get you at...ten, did we decide?" she asks, turning again to Pops.

"Ten, the-thirty," he says. "We're diving up to Clarksdale," he adds for the rest of us. "Nose around a little bit. See if maybe anyone has anything to say about your dad."

Ruth nods. "Might," she says.

"My aunt has a bed and breakfast up there," Ron tosses out, drawing an absolutely withering look from Ruth.

"I need to get my briefcase," Pops says to Cloud, turning her by her shoulder toward the car.

"Ron, sometimes, I swear," Ruth says when they're out of earshot.

"What?" He looks from face to face, then kicks at the gravel til the awkward silence gets to be too much for him. "Your dad's girlfriend seems nice," he tells me.

Ruth groans. "Honest to God."

Friday is a half day at Decatur; still, Pops is well up the road by the time I get back just past noon. Nother is assisting Luke with livestock-related matters this afternoon, which I could help with, I suppose, or at least watch, but I kind of feel like being alone for a while, so we decide to hook up later this evening. But now that I'm rattling around here all by myself I kind of wish I wasn't. I think of calling Sandy, but I don't want to drag her over here just to keep me company.

I mean, how lame is that? I sit down and read Chemistry for a while–at least I won't have that hanging over my head all weekend, and then log on and shoot Gina an e-mail. She might even be home now, and still sober.

> Hey,
> How goes it up there? One cool thing about here is it's in the fifties already, which is nice for January. Gail's up in NYC probably freezing her ass off.
> Kayla and I had this jumbo falling out. It's too ridiculous to tell here, let's just say major weirdness on her part. So we're not friends anymore (as of Wednesday). Plus she's dating a lunatic who packs.
> Been hanging out with Nother A LOT. That's going REALLY good. I like his family better than mine, I think.
> Pops might have a girlfriend!! He says no, but he's probably lying, or she just hasn't told him yet. More major weirdness.
> Got a 4.0 this quarter. What do I win?
> My new best friend here is Sandy. I may have mentioned her before. Very cool.
> I think Gail's going to bail out of here.
> Which makes me the best behaved one in this family!
> What's new?

I hit SEND and go to the kitchen for a Coke. The mail comes right then; I hear the heavy footsteps on the porch and the creak of the mailbox, and after she leaves I take my Coke and walk outside, where I sit and read our junk mail with a scrutiny neither it nor I can bear. The sky is nearly white, blindingly so, thin wisps of clouds the

width and breadth. I get chilled and go back inside; Gina
has delivered:

> Hey yourself,
> It's 25 degrees here. Which sucks, by the way.
> Too bad about Kayla. I want to hear it sometime.
> The guy sounds interesting, though.
> A boyfriend you can actually stand?? Very
> impressive! I like everyone's family better than mine.
> So who hooked Ed up? Yeah, ask HER, he'll be
> the last to know.
> Woo hoo! Nerd!!
> O.K. then, I'll meet Sandy when I come.
> Good for her.
> Who's fucking fault is that?
> It's cold. Ice is like, totally impossible when you're
> drunk! On foot or driving. Grades are Tuesday here, no
> 4 point on this end. Matt got beat up at a party last
> weekend. *Merchant of Venice* rehearsals start Monday.
> Suz drinks waay to much, and that's coming from me!
> > Be bad. I mean it.
> > G

More of the same, in other words. I clean the house for
a while, solely out of boredom, then take a nap on the
couch with the front door hanging open, so that when I
shiver awake again the house smells really fresh and out-
doorsy, but it's about fifty degrees in here. I crank the heat
and get in the shower, where I decide to take Gina's
advice, so when Nother calls I ask can we go out to The
Sawmill tonight, and he says sure.

We sit at the bar getting loaded, me a little more focused
on it than him, and it's nice to know I won't have to worry

about dodging Gail when I get home. Nother and I slow dance, hanging onto each other through a series of mournful, weepy tunes, and on the way home, very late, I doze on his shoulder. He walks me inside and even yanks off my boots before he leaves, and I recall vague instructions regarding aspirin and my own bed before crashing on the couch.

Which is how it is that I happen to see Cloud's Honda sitting out front big as the world at six the next morning when I get up to pee. Which, I know also, is significant, even through the fog of my hangover, but which still doesn't keep me from conking out again til about eight, by which time the car is gone, causing me to wonder if I only imagined it, but if not would certainly put to rest the whole "girlfriend" question.

I focus on recovery for the next few hours–shower, aspirin, lots of water, blessed silence. I want to go over and quiz Pops down right now, but I'm having trouble holding thoughts in my head for more than a few seconds at a time, and I'm so cranky I'd probably just go off on him big time before he could even get his mouth open. And if we did start arguing, my brain would totally explode. I fry up a thick ham and cheese, just for the grease, and eat it with a Coke before I grab the keys and take off. Pops will walk over eventually, and I want to be ready when I see him, or at least more alive than I am now.

I find myself on the same country road that eventually curls back on the 'Mill, the one I drove that day last fall when I was so pissed about something else, when I saw Crosscut leaning on his car smoking. Which now doesn't even seem part of this same lifetime. The sky is bone white again, the landscape all but colorless as well: dull, flat fields of turned, latte colored earth; clumps of washed out turf here and there, with only the merest hint of green; skeleton trees amid islands of sodden gray leaves; blackened splintered fence posts shouldering drooping barbed wire. It's good this way; with nothing of interest to distract me, my mind is free to run with thoughts of my father and Cloud, Gail in New York, and motes of Crosscut spread over half the county.

But I should have got coffee first.

By the time I circle back into town I'm feeling better, but I'm not really dressed well enough to stop anywhere. I'm thinking I'll stop by at Sandy's for a while, and then see about going out to Nother's. I pull up beside the house and slip inside to change out of my sweats and tee-shirt. I put on jeans and a knit top, then notice there's a message, so I let it play as I yank on a hooded sweatshirt. It's Gail, her voice overly magnified by the machine, just checking in. All is well there, she says, then mentions several colleagues whom I've heard of but never met. A bunch of them are going to a show tonight. She's got a meeting with her department head–from Johns Hopkins, she means– Monday, and she'll see me Tuesday.

So, then, nothing really. But at least she thought to call. I'm lacing up my boots and wondering if I need to buzz Sandy first, or if it's just O.K. to drop in, when I hear Pops coming up the stairs. I take a deep breath as he pulls the screen door open and remind myself that he hasn't done anything he has to account to me for. It would be nice if I had a little better idea of certain facts, though, like what time I got home last night, for instance, and whether the Honda was already there or not.

"You're back," he says, pushing the door closed behind him.

"Yep," I reply, "but not for long." Another couple minutes I'd have made it. "Did you hear that?" I ask, nodding at the phone while I pull my jeans down over the laces.

"Yeah, but I didn't get any of it."

"Mom's doing good. She's seeing everyone, going to a play, meeting with Dr. Martin on Monday and back here Tuesday. She might miss us, but she didn't actually say."

Pops nods slowly. "Sounds about right."

"I really think she's going back," I say. "I mean, just the way she phrases things. Like, she called Dr. Martin her boss, but Annie's her boss, really." I look at him and raise my eyebrows. "You know."

"Indeed, Holmes," he says. "You're very observant."

"Oh yeah," I tell him, and get a slight frown for the tone of it.

"Well, it wouldn't surprise me, I guess, from some of the things she's said."

I sit back and shove my hands into the center pocket of my sweatshirt. "What would you think of that?" I ask.

"I'd wish it were different," he says. "I think it would be a big adjustment for us."

Adjustment. For God's sake. "I meant you, specifically," I clarify.

"I can only think of it in terms of all of us," he replies, sounding like he might have guessed where this is heading. "Sorry."

"Well, like, it might even make things easier for you. With this whole Cloud thing, for instance."

"There is no 'Cloud thing.' Except maybe in your head."

"Pops, who's fooling who? I mean, do you really not know, or do you just think I'm that stupid? 'Cause like, when she spends the night, that's kind of a sign, O.K."

"She didn't spend the night. Not how you think, anyway."

"Well, her car did, because I saw it parked out front this morning. And like, when you're out in public and she's touching you all the time, and you spend whole days together, and you have these private jokes. I mean, even if you don't think there's something going on, she does, and anyone else with eyes. Come on."

He exhales emphatically. "Look, I can't really do anything about how she seems to be acting to you. Or anyone else for that matter, though I don't really care about that. And second, I can't exactly tell her to stop doing something I don't even think she's doing."

"Dad, her car didn't *seem* to be sitting out front at six o'clock this morning. It was. That's not really a question of interpretation."

"Listen. We went up to Clarksdale, just like I told you. It was a good day; we got some great footage and picked up a lot of stuff we should be able to use. And it was fun, I won't deny that, either. It was four or five by the time we get out of there, we're pretty happy about things, so we get a couple for the road; then we stop a time or two on the way at these roadhouses and call it research, so we're a little bit loaded by the time we get back. Which isn't the smartest thing, either, but there you go. So we get some food and come here around nine, nine-thirty, and drink a few more since...well, we just do, and listen to that CD of Crosscut's, and by about midnight she isn't driving anywhere." His lips tighten and he does this little half shrug. "She slept on the couch; I slept in my room; when she sobered up, she left. It was either really late or really early, but it wasn't all night."

"O.K. Dad, think about this. She drinks with you all evening, comes to your house, drinks more, listens to all those songs. Do you really think she planned to spend the night on the couch?"

"I don't really want to speculate on her intentions."

"'Speculate!' 'Intentions!' Pops, you're not on TV now. It's me. Your daughter." His face drops and he looks at me with the most injured expression I've ever seen, like I've hauled off and slapped him, and I am immediately back pedaling. "I'm sorry. Really. That was mean. Please, forget I even said that. All I meant was: if she was comfortable enough with you for all that, and given how you two acted the other night, it could have...happened. I mean, whether it did or not."

"I said it didn't." He still sounds really hurt. "I wouldn't lie to you about it." I can't believe I've become the heavy.

"And I'm saying that's not really the point. It could, easily. In her mind, it's going to, I'm telling you. So it will have to be you who stops it if it's going to get stopped. I mean, just so you know." This all comes out a lot bitchier than I meant it to sound.

"I'll take that under advisement," he says, which is this phrase he picked up from some lawyer show on TV that he uses when he gets advice he hasn't asked for, usually from my mother. I see now why she hates it.

"Fine," I reply. "Whatever. You're the behavior expert."

"What then?" he demands with a deep sigh. "Am I supposed to get your permission?"

"No," I tell him, equally exasperated. "Do whatever you want. Or what she wants."

"Meaning?"

"Meaning, that's what's going to happen anyway, because whether you know it or not, you have this knack for attracting...demanding women."

"One more than you think," he suggests.

I notice I'm hugging one of the couch pillows to my chest, though I don't recall picking it up, and I lift my chin from it to glare at him. "It might be best if we finish this another time."

"I'll stop by later," he says, leaving without further comment, while I continue to stare at the wall. I recall the first time I talked to Mom about her and Carl, it was way louder than this, but I don't remember feeling nearly as bad. I was more concerned how Pops would take it than the threat of any romance actually developing. But him doing it is different, which I suspect accounts for the sick feeling in my stomach right now. Because Pops and Cloud could actually work. She's just old enough, and she seems really cool, much as I hate to admit it. And she's into my dad, too, no matter what he says. You can tell from a block away. Which is why he's taking it slow, I'm sure, or trying to. Pops isn't the type to just trip into something like this, and he wouldn't want a lot of raw nerves over something that wasn't going anywhere. The very fact that he's denying it speaks volumes.

So I don't really know what to think; I mean, they've pretty much created this mess, so why should I get all stressed worrying how it plays out? The more I think about it, the more I decide the best course is to *not* think about it. Gail's up in New York working some kind of a deal or other, you can be sure of that, and Pops is down here doing God knows what with a woman named Cloud. And I don't notice either of them overly concerned how any of it affects me, so why should I be the only one worrying? They're both going to do what they want anyway, so I might as well just keep the hell out of the way and worry about myself.

I sit on the couch for a long time, rocking slowly with the pillow clutched to my chest, pondering all this. In time, I hear the phone ring through the wall and just from his tone I can tell who it is. Now that the quiet is broken I shift into action. I'm hungry again, so I eat; yogurt, a soda, some crackers. I brush my teeth and grab my jacket and a CD. I decide to blow off the visit to Sandy's and just go to Nother's. It is on the way over that I decide to spend the night. We consider camping at the clearing once I've convinced him I'm staying, but I want to be home at first light, and the hike out precludes that. We go into town instead, run into Sandy and some others eating pizza, and rent movies. Though Ruth and Ron are here–they even watch one of the movies with us–and Madame Marie, of course, staying is not a problem. I do not crash on the couch.

It is just after six when I pull in at my house, and the phone begins ringing the moment I get inside. "Come over here now, please," my father says.

The door is open so I just walk in. Pops watches me enter from the armchair, a blank look on his face. His hair is disheveled and he is already–or still–dressed. "We need to talk," he says evenly. I sit in the chair across from him and fold my arms over my chest. When he realizes I'm waiting on him, he says, "It seems we need to re-establish some ground rules."

"I'm sure that can be worked out," I say. "We're all adults here."

"No, we're not," he replies. "So we might as well get straight on that right now. You're sixteen, Teri. You're my daughter. You're still my responsibility, and I'll decide what's acceptable behavior."

"That's awfully convenient," I say. "You guys just do whatever you want, no matter how I feel about it, or what I think, but then, I act the same way–not even as bad, actually–and it's some major crime all of a sudden. That's really fair."

"First, fairness doesn't enter into it. You and I are not equals. What is O.K. for me is not necessarily O.K. for you.

And I know you understand that, so lets not waste time debating it. Second, your staying out all night has always been a 'major crime,' as you put it, so it's not all of a sudden that I'm coming down on you."

"It wasn't all night," I declare, though it doesn't give me near the satisfaction saying it that I'd anticipated. It seems kind of silly, actually. "I crashed over there and I left either really late or really early."

His mouth draws into a tight line, and this odd mixture of disappointment and annoyance slides across his face. "I probably deserve that," he says after a long minute. "And if this was to get back at me for that, please say so."

"Partly," I admit. "I don't like you mincing words with me, Dad. We've never been like that, and I deserve better."

"Agreed," he says. "I apologize. It was an awkward situation for me, and I took the easy way out. I'm sorry. Now, let me say this. You are still my little girl, and I was worried sick wondering if you were upside down in a ditch somewhere, or sheared in half by a telephone pole. And I deserve better, too, whether you're put out with me or not."

"Agreed," I echo. "I'm sorry."

"Not only that, it was disrespectful. Which, I assume, was intended. You've made your point."

"Respect goes both ways."

"Go on."

"Well, you know, things have changed a lot this past year, and sometimes it seems like you think I'm ten years old and I have no say in anything–like moving here, for instance. And then other times, nobody's paying any attention at all, and it's like we're just three people sharing a house. This should be a triplex, by rights; it might as well be.

Like, half the time it's 'run your own life,' and then suddenly I'm your little girl again." I pause for a minute and
he leans forward in his chair, but I continue before he can
speak. "And you know what, that's been getting old. If
we're all just going our own way, then I ought to be able to
make my own rules, too."

Pops is sitting with his elbows on his knees, his hands
folded out front. "I see," he says when he's sure I'm
done. "Well, I'm not entirely sure why you feel that way.
You've always been pretty independent, Teri, and we've
always given you a lot of leeway. But there were always
limits, and you always seemed to know what they were,
even as you pushed them. But it seemed to be working,
too. We've always thought that you've shown good judgment, and respect for our authority and our rules. If you
think we've ceased to hold up our end, that's a problem.
Like I said, I haven't really noticed that, at least for
myself. I know I've been a lot busier this year, but I think
I've been there for you, too. I can't speak for your
mother, because I don't know. But I do know that even
though it's been a rough stretch, we both love you as
much as we ever have, and we're proud of you, and we
expect to remain part of your life. If you've felt slighted,
I'm sorry. It certainly wasn't my intention. Or your
mother's I'm sure. And I certainly don't mean for my
friendship with Cloud to come between us; I wouldn't let
that happen. All we can do is try it again from here, but
at the same time, we're going to have some rules, too.
And you being home at a reasonable hour is still one of
them, so I don't expect a repeat of this." He pauses and
stares at me.

"All right," I say. It's not much of a concession anyway;
I'd never get away with this if Gail was around.

As if reading my mind, he says, "Can you imagine if your mother were here?"

"I doubt she'd be too pleased with either of us," I point out.

Pops nods slowly, his face contorted like he's sucking a lemon. He settles back in the chair and continues to nod. "There is something else," he says after a minute. "And I'm just going to ask. Are you and Nother sleeping together?"

My lips press together, and I pause for just a second so my voice will hold. "We have," I answer evenly, making sure to meet his gaze.

"Well then, you are," he says, "because you don't just stop."

I shrug. "O.K."

"Do you think that's wise?" he asks.

"It just is."

He nods slowly and chews his lip, and I feel just like you'd think. "Thank you for telling me," he says finally. "Are you taking precautions?"

"Yeah."

"*Every* time?"

"Yes."

"Well, that's good to know." He exhales abundantly. "Though I don't approve, I feel obliged to tell you. I think you're way too young. I think you'll both end up hurt. You could get pregnant anyway...." He lets this last item linger. "At the same time, I don't expect this will make much difference. No one ever thinks they're not ready. And you can't really put the genie back in the bottle."

"Are you mad?" I ask back, because, other than agreeing with his final point or two, I don't know what else to say. "Disappointed? Totally disgusted?"

"No."

"'Cause like, I didn't do it just to do it. I mean, he's not just any guy."

"I realize that," he says. "I don't have a problem with your choice in partners. I just want you to understand it's a big step. And any consequences are going to be very real, and very adult. There's no going back to, 'I didn't know,' or 'I didn't mean it.' That's done with. Do you realize that?"

"Yes."

"Well, you don't, actually. But you've been told. So we'll have to settle for that, I guess." He runs his hand over his mouth. "When you play grown up–"

"We're not playing."

"–it can explode on you big," he finishes. "Really big."

"We think we can handle it."

"Everyone thinks that," he says, showing me his palms. "But O.K." And somehow, when he says this, it's all back on me, even more than if he'd gotten all pissed off, or disowned me. He looks into his lap, and again at me. "Does your mother know, speaking of explosions?"

I laugh, which comes out nervous sounding. "No."

"I didn't think so. Were you planning to tell her?"

"I wasn't planning to tell *you*."

"I take it that's a no?"

"I will if she asks. But I'm hoping *you* won't say anything."

"All right. But I'm hoping *you* will."

I knew he was going to say that. "Can we just see how it goes, maybe?" I ask.

"You decide," he answers, like I knew he would again. "But I can't go behind her back about anything." We both seem to understand the various implications of this, and I nod while leaving it unremarked. "So, I guess this changes everything, and changes nothing," he concludes. "We're both still here for you. I hope you know that."

I nod. I want to leave, and glance at the clock in the kitchen. "You should get some sleep, Pops." It's barely seven.

"That's the plan," he says.

I could stand a few more hours myself, though my brain can't seem to slow down enough for it. It's nice that he didn't lose it, though I didn't really expect him to, and that he doesn't feel obligated to tell my mother, which I was a little concerned about. Because I certainly won't be telling her any of this unless she straight out asks, which isn't likely. And all that stuff I was telling him about feeling ignored and left out, which I probably should have been saying to her–it won't get repeated, either.

Gail returns and we enjoy several weeks of relative peace around the house; that is, we all keep out of each other's way, and no one behaves too badly too obviously. She's pretty happy about the 4.0, and I even get another dinner out of it the night she gets back, though she is quick to inform me that she expects nothing less. And while we're still on the subject of school, she broaches the idea of a trek east at spring break to look at colleges–the same trip Gina heard mention of six weeks ago. Gail may need to go back anyway, her third trip in as many months, but who's counting. It seems that while she was at this conference she got herself roped into (her description) some research project, and if she gets her preliminary stuff done down here, she may fly up to help finalize the rest of the study. "I may be gone most of the summer, too," she mentions quite casually as we're picking at pasta in a garlicky restaurant near the college. "We're hoping to get our data collected between semesters, when everyone has more time."

"So, Mom, what happened to your big interest in administration? I mean, I thought you wanted to get away from doing research? And, can you even leave like that? All summer? Isn't your job year round now?"

"Well, technically yes," she says. "But then, I still have the position up there, too, if I decide to go that route. So I've got some leverage if I need it. Annie would have to approve it on this end, but I think we'll be able to work it out."

"Next question, then: Are you even coming back?" Gail licks her lips and swallows, then sips her wine. "You can tell me, Mom. I wish you would, in fact."

"I haven't decided," she says. She pushes some food around on her plate and then sets down her fork. "But I have to say the conference was really invigorating. I felt an excitement that I haven't experienced in a long time. And just talking about this new project with Robert and Claire got my juices flowing again." She's been staring into her plate the whole time, like this is some embarrassing confession. She looks up. "The work I've been doing here is unsatisfying."

"Really?!" I gasp.

She rolls her eyes. "I feel I'm wasting my time and my talents." She lets out a long breath. "I may have made a mistake coming here."

"It's O.K., Mom," I tell her. "You're allowed to every once in a while." This is quite the concession for my mother; she doesn't have a lot of practice admitting she's wrong. And even though it's pretty obvious now that she'll be back to Baltimore next fall, I decide not to push her to say so. I mean, this research excuse is totally lame. Most of what she's talking about could easily be done from here; she's got access to the Hopkins mainframe, and all kinds of research and conferencing software. She could do it from Mars if she wanted, though I refrain from pointing this out—even though she would if it was me making these arguments. "If you think you want to do that again, go for it," I say.

"Yeah," she replies airily, her gaze drifting off over my head. She quickly refocuses and allows herself a slight shrug. "We'll see."

Which is pretty much it for the next couple weeks. I have no idea what her schedule is anymore, and usually when I find her home, she's either on the phone back East or hammering on her laptop at the table.

"Keep trying," Sandy coaxes when I again contemplate giving up on Gail. I've started going to the Chemistry lab for study hall, rather than the table. The room is empty then, so unless Sandy or Nother comes by, I'm left alone.

"Why, she's bailing anyway."

"You don't *know* that. And you don't want her saying you didn't try."

I drum my lab book with a pencil. "You're going to have to do better than that."

"You don't want to be like Kayla," she proposes.

"No fair."

Pops has a lot going on, too. He and Cloud are pounding on this show about Crosscut. The release date for the CD is the end of February, and they've been splicing together tape and doing interviews and voiceovers a couple hours a day. Buddy Guy is on board, and several of the Clarksdale luminaries. A record executive or two. Pops interviews Ezra and Sara throughout, since they spent the most time with him. Rachel gets some airtime, being the oldest, but the rest beg off, including Madame Marie, who receives and declines the overture by proxy, namely Nother.

I can only imagine how it is with Pops and Cloud as the weeks pass, but at least he has the good sense to keep her away from the house. It seems weird that they'd put this much effort into something only a handful of people are ever likely to see, so I'm wondering if it might just be an excuse for them to hang out together, a question I pose to my father one night.

"Not at all," he answers quickly. "Though that is a nice side benefit. I imagine Cloud wants something meaty for her portfolio, so she can get out of here, eventually. And the resources are so localized, it almost has to be someone here that picks it up."

Meaty, I think, odd word right there. "And for you?"

"I think it's a worthwhile project. Simple as that. I admired the man, and this is my way of paying tribute." He pauses. "If this was Jersey and Springsteen had just croaked, would you be asking me why?"

"Point taken," I concede.

I don't see Kayla at all after our face-off. Actually, I can see her fine from the window of the Chem lab; our table is just across the driveway in open view. Brian is still coming around, I notice, and she's still making his life hell from the looks of it. She tries to corner Nother when she can, but he figured that out pretty quick, and just takes the long way around.

Which is how the bulk of February passes. It rains almost every day, but the temperature beats the hell out of Baltimore, where this would all be snow. I begin to develop a serious coffee habit. Nother and I are together most evenings to study, gab, make out. We see the ivory-bills one Saturday, then stay too long and hike out in near darkness. Sundays we clean the bar. He carves a wooden jewelry box for me for Valentine's Day, with gold hoop earrings inside. I get him a plant for his room, a big cinnamon candle, a shirt. It's a good day, a semi-charmed life in some regards. A triplex, and I might shut up for good.

But, of course, it doesn't last. My father and Cloud—and others, to be fair—finish up their work with three days to spare. "It's in the can," he announces when he calls over one evening near the end of February. It's a Monday, around seven-thirty, and I'm sure he assumes Nother is here to receive the news, too, which he is.

"And seventy-two hours to play with," I calculate. "Way to be safe, Dad."

"Seventy-three, actually. And we had it all the way."

"So when can we see it?"

"Thursday night, same as everyone else."

"Fine," I grouse. "Be that way."

"Got to go. We're all heading out to celebrate. See you tomorrow."

The release is set for Thursday; there's a big bash at The Sawmill, where the compilation will first be available. Already, a stack of them are locked in the office, save the one playing on my boom box right now, and a second in Nother's truck. Had I taken the one Ezra has for Pops, he'd still be getting it Thursday, since he won't let us see the show early. The documentary, *Delacroix Stomp*, after the title of the CD, will have its debut in the 'Mill as well, two days before its first scheduled broadcast. Very Harry Potterish, I decide, at about one millionth scale.

Later, after the last song has played out, we sit on the couch studying the cover art and the libretto sandwiched inside. The lyrics and credits are there, of course, along with encomia to Crosscut from his peers and disciples, all laid over photos of local color bled to a nostalgic sepia just

right for the contents. I point out sections of the liner notes
I recognize as my father's. "It's good," I say. "I'm no
expert, but I think the song mix is good, and the packaging. They did him right, I'd say."

Nother nods. "Yeah," he says. "I think so too." He picks
up the case and stares at the cover, a collage of delta
scenes set behind a progression of photos of the local eminence. He shakes his head and sets the case on the table.
"All that polish to pick up all that grain."

"I expect Pops' show will be more of the same," I warn
him. "But Thursday should be fun. We could do with a little excitement anyway." The front door bangs open just
then and I about jump out of my skin as Gail barrels in.
She stomps across the kitchen and unloads her stuff on the
table to maximum volume, then pulls up short with a
harsh, "Oh," when she notices us.

"What's the matter with you?" I ask.

She starts to speak twice, but doesn't, then exhales an
emphatic, "Nothing," as she exits the room. "It can wait."

"Careful what you wish for," I chide when the door to
her room closes.

"It was you that asked," he reminds me, leaning forward to stand up. "I'm gone."

"Coward." I help him pack up and see him out, and
when I return Gail is in the kitchen, leaning with her back
against the counter, her arms folded across her chest.
Apparently it can't wait for long.

"Guess who I just saw?" she demands.

From her tone, it wouldn't even be a guess. "Who?" I
ask back, to avoid any suggestion of complicity.

"Your father," she informs me, in a tone that can only
be described as restrained menace, and just barely.

"I'm guessing this was unplanned," I reply. "Where?"

"The Bistro," she says. "Where I'd been dining with Annie, where we'd gone to discuss some mutual concerns. Where we saw your father in the bar, with a woman—not me and not you, but who might fit exactly between us, age-wise. Who Annie pointed out quite casually, as she's apparently seen them together before."

"It's probably someone from the studio," I say easily. I don't know why I'm covering for him, or even which of them I'm trying to protect, exactly. "They're finishing up that piece about Nother's dad."

"I don't care if they're re-mastering *The Godfather*; half the faculty eats in there, and he shouldn't be crammed in a corner booth with some child doing God knows what!"

"Like eating, maybe? Having a drink? It was probably the woman who's producing the show. We saw her here that one night. Was she blonde? Like, hair to about here?" I make a sawing motion about shoulder length.

"Christ almighty, am I the only one in town who didn't know about this?"

"Mom, there's probably a—"

"Well, if he thinks I'm going to stick around and be the laughingstock of this mud hole, he better think again."

"—perfectly reasonable explanation."

"Oh, grow up," she snorts. "I know what I saw. It was a back booth, in the bar, with drinks, and from the look on their faces they sure as hell weren't discussing scene framing or fadeouts." She sighs. "There was a candle."

"Fine, Mom. Whatever. Don't ask. Don't clarify anything. Just make your assumptions, make your excuses, and bail. That's fine."

"Oh, I'll ask, don't you worry. I've got plenty of questions for him when he comes home. *If* he comes home."

I exhale loudly. "Well do it over there, because I don't

want to hear it all night." I start toward my room, then turn back. "I'm sorry you're upset, Mom. I really am. But don't you dare use this as an excuse to leave. I mean, don't even! At least not to me." My door bangs closed only slightly louder than I intend.

They do get into it, but not until Wednesday, and I'm blessedly not there to hear it. Pops is giving me the blow by blow that evening, and he still looks a little haggard. "So yeah," he concludes, "be glad you weren't around."

"And you be glad you didn't come straight home Monday, or you wouldn't have any eyebrows left. Just think if she wouldn't have had two days to cool off."

"I'm through thinking about it," he says. "I had my say this afternoon, and I sure as hell got an earful from her. So we pretty much know where things stand, and now whatever happens, happens."

"And where do you stand, exactly?"

"I'm right here where I've always been," he says. "I want to work this out. That's why I came here."

"And her?"

He shrugs. "I couldn't really say. Half the time it sounded like the world's greatest treachery, and half like she was already gone." He shakes his head forlornly. "I'm not sure *she* even knows at this point."

"And how does Cloud figure into all this?"

"Cloud is not an issue," he says summarily.

"Does she know that?"

"She does."

Which really has me confused now, especially with the way Gail was describing things the other night. But it doesn't sound like I'm going to get any more out of him. "Is she coming to the party tomorrow?"

"Yeah, they'll all be there."

"One last question about the other night, Dad. Where were all 'they' when Mom saw just you and Cloud?"

"Well, there are only six of us to begin with. Two went home—they have families so they didn't come at all. Two came for a drink and took off. Which left us."

"Just math, then," I suggest.

"You're out of questions," he says. "Hey, did I tell you the Walmart over there is bringing in a big screen TV for the showing?"

"I heard."

He frowns. "Well then, did you hear we're going to be on *Nightline* tomorrow?"

"Who is?"

"Me. Ezra." He shrugs. "Ted's a fan."

"Ezra?!"

"Well, it's kind of news, the compilation coming out. And they want to do a follow-up from last time I guess. Probably just a few minutes at the end, but they may show part of our film. Cloud is pretty jazzed."

"They're going to do this from the 'Mill?"

"No, Ezra and I are going to Jackson in the afternoon. He should be funny in the studio."

"Very cool," I say.

The release turns out to be a way bigger deal than I anticipated; the place is packed. Technically, it's a private party, but as near as I can tell, all that means is if you're a private citizen, you're invited. Twenty bucks will get you in—open bar included; another twenty and you get the collection, too. The CDs run out before we even get there, except for the one on continuous cycle pulsing from the speakers, and Ezra immediately has Nother and I run to Wal-Mart for a stack of theirs, which they can't start selling

til tomorrow, anyway. Cars are still piling in when the documentary starts, and Ezra ends up showing it again an
hour later, which even the early arrivals don't seem to
mind. All the local channels have remote units in the parking lot, but it's Cloud's posse that gets all the primo sound
bites. A crew from New Orleans rolls in about ten-thirty,
and Nother and I watch from a monitor in the van the
scene from the House of Blues down there, where a con-
current bash is in full swing, hosted by Buddy Guy, it
would appear. Sara keeps tabs on *Nightline* from a small
set under the bar, and when Crosscut's segment comes on
she zaps it onto the big screen, and we all get to see Pops
and Ezra, combed and polished and yakking breezily with
Ted from a couple of armchairs. There's a brief clip from
the documentary, and when Ted asks if there's a national
broadcast planned, Ezra strokes his chin cagily and says
no, not yet, anyway, but maybe Ted could get that done.
Cloud, who is watching wide-eyed next to me at the bar,
almost passes out. When that concludes the live entertainment starts up, and it seems like half the crowd is suddenly
unpacking guitars. Nother joins in, pumping out a dead-on
version of Crosscut's signature ballad, "Tailwalkin'," which
brings down the house and has Sara glassy eyed, and Ezra
gazing slack jawed from behind the bar. "Good wine after
bad," one of the previous players observes from just
behind me, though to no one in particular. "Like Canaan,
that is." It's twenty minutes before anyone dares follow.

Two evenings later I watch the broadcast premiere of
Delacroix Stomp with Madame Marie. It's less over-
whelming at normal volume and viewed regular size, and
without a hundred of my newest best friends hooting and
chugging all around me. But it's impressive nonetheless.
Pops' script is fluid, engaging, and only approaches

obsequious maybe once. But it's the production values that stand out in the cold light of day—or at least the pale lamp light of Nother's living room. Cloud's handiwork, in other words. I mean, this is network quality stuff; the pacing, the camera work, the transitions. Even the captions are first rate. There are episodes of *Biography* that aren't this polished. Which does not go unnoticed in the room. "Very nice," Ruthie determines as the credits roll. "Makes me wish I'd known the guy." Madame Marie nods silently, that Mona Lisa smile on her face, then quietly slips from the room.

"Can we take that as a thumbs up?" I ask. "My father will be curious."

Ron nods. "For her, that's a standing O."

The show airs in New Orleans the following week. Then Houston. The agency now representing my father makes a big push. Pops appears on several cable news shows, the lighter side segments near the end. He trades quips with Aaron; banters with Greta. Can Larry King be far off? Sales of the CD spike following each broadcast, and the side-door outfit that is distributing the CD comes on board. A deal with VH1 is rumored to be in the works. Synergy, I whisper to myself. Fucking A.

Amidst the chaos Pops announces that he's finished his book. Awe would not be too strong a word to describe my reaction. He's on quite a roll, other than his wife about to flee town, and maybe even counting that. I congratulate him heartily; unlike some of the rest of this stuff, this is truly an accomplishment. I offer to proof it if he wants, he just has to print me a copy, but he says there isn't time. His agent already has it, is attempting to peddle it as we speak. She is intent on striking while the iron is hot, apparently, grammar be damned. And though his

TV stuff, particularly this latest round as Crosscut's champion, has nothing whatever to do with his book, she's trying to link it all up anyway, intent, I suspect, on obtaining exclamation filled blurbs from all his new media buddies. Pops even uses the term "product placement" in front of me, without blushing, I might add.

Gail finds all of this quite unnerving; she claims she's afraid to switch on the television for fear of being greeted by Pops image beaming back at her, which is a little overstated, but not all that much. The book news in particular wigs her out, though I'm not sure if this is due to the presumptive packaging of what could well turn out to be a banal, or more likely, incomplete, piece of work, or the mere fact that he finished it at all. "How do you not have time to proofread a manuscript?" she demands, which crossed my mind too, I have to admit. But clean copy or not, he's going to garner a lot of attention for it around the college, which she'll have to witness, and suffer graciously, all the while wondering when next she'll bump into him and "that TV person."

I almost feel sorry for her.

I am wiping down the bar one Sunday, gabbing with Sara and listening to *Delacroix Stomp*, when Ezra strides in holding an envelope aloft and grinning ear to ear. "Finally, that son of a bitch," he says, clicking up to the bar and slapping the envelope in front of Sara.

She pulls out what appears to be a business check and whistles softly.

"Yep," Ezra says, "the bastard."

Sara grips the check at the sides and pops it twice. "The advance," she explains with a head thrust toward the speaker nearest us. "Like, two weeks *after* the release."

"How's that work?" I ask. Funny, but in all the time I've known Nother, I can't recall any of them ever mentioning money. Which seems weird now, albeit less so because it's them, though I wonder now why *I* never thought to ask about it. I mean, if Pops sells his book, you can bet your ass I'll be asking. And even with the way she's snapping that check I can get a clear look at the number; a hundred and a half, Pops would call it.

"How it works is, we should have had this six months ago, but the conniving little shit that runs that place"–the record label, he means–"kept putting Dad off, because he knew Crosscut would let it ride for a while. Probably figured he'd never have to pay."

"Ezra got a lawyer," Sara says.

"Hell, he owes us more than this already," her brother barks. He looks over at me. "The album is selling good," he says. "I'm a little surprised, but not really. I know we earned this back."

"We," Sara repeats.

"Well," he says, "we're the ones going to spend it." He takes the check back from her and returns it to the envelope, which he tucks into his chest pocket. "What did we decide about him?" He thrusts his head at the door, through which Nother has recently passed to clean up the parking lot.

"I told you what I think," Sara answers. "He's got the most sense of any of us. Pay the man."

"All right then." Ezra looks over at me. "We were thinking we might put Nother's share in a trust account til he's eighteen."

"Oh, no," I reply immediately. "I'm with Sara; pay the man."

"Uh, huh." He heads out to talk to Nother. After he leaves, Sara fills me in. Ezra is the executor of Crosscut's estate, such as it is, and the final arbiter of any issues regarding his music. But the money, at least to begin with, was all Madame Marie's, being the surviving spouse and all. She's decided, however, to consign two-thirds of it to the children, keeping the remainder for herself, and the upkeep of the property. The kids will split their share equally, with Ezra again handling the particulars. "It only makes sense," Sara explains, "he's got the mind for it, and the temperament. He's the one got after the record guy; didn't waste a second once Crosscut passed, and didn't fuck around doing it. Hell, he should probably take an extra cut for himself, but don't tell him I said that."

"Good deal," I say. "And good for him."

She nods. "He's the one got back the rights to all those songs," she says. "Dad didn't even own half of them. 'Course, they weren't worth much, either, but at least now we're not having to pay out every time we sell another CD."

"We," I repeat.

"Damn, now he's got me doing it." She shakes her head. "Plus, there's been two calls at least from people asking could they do a cover. That's money in our pocket, too." She makes this sideways motion with her head, like it's the damnedest thing. "Pity he didn't live to see it. Never a dime to show for any of it when he was living. Every penny to keep things up. Gone half the time just to cover the bills. I'm not calling him an angel, but he lived up to his responsibilities, I'll say that for him. He was a man about it. Now it's going to roll in and he's gone." She knocks the bar twice. "There's a song for you right there."

"Yeah it is," I agree. "What about this place?"

"Ezra and I bought it years ago. Hardly worth it less we run it ourselves. I mean, it gives us a decent living, but that's about it."

"Clean, though," I say.

Nother fills in the rest on the way home, and it turns out Ezra might be sharper than even Sara knows. He'd convinced Crosscut to forego a big lump sum up front in return for an overly generous royalty rate, which the label had only agreed to, Ezra figured, because they could dance around any significant payouts with some shady bookkeeping, and questionable production costs, and most likely Crosscut wouldn't ever know, or would just let it slide. But Ezra already had power of attorney, effective the first of the year, had Crosscut lived to see it, at which time Ezra planned to unleash an assault on the label the likes of which they'd never seen. Which all became moot on Christmas Day.

"Now it looks like we're going to clean up," Nother assesses. "But I think Ezra figured that, too, that Crosscut was one of those cult types everyone had heard of, but no one had any of his records. And while he was still alive, it didn't really matter. But now he's dead, so he's hip again, and now everyone's just buying *Delacroix Stomp* because they don't have any of the other ones, and it's easier than trying to find them." He looks over and shrugs. "Which is fine with us."

"Cha-ching," I summarize. "Ezra thinks it's already earned back the advance."

"I'm sure Ezra knows exactly how much it's earned."

I push over closer to him. "So, what are we going to do with our share?"

"I was thinking pizza," he says, glancing over dubiously and hanging a right into town.

"What *are* you going to do with your share?" I ask more seriously when we're settled into a booth. The place is almost empty, so I don't feel too weird bringing it up again. "I mean, have you thought about it at all?"

"Some," he admits. "Promise you won't laugh?"

"I swear."

"I was thinking maybe college."

"That's a great idea," I reply. "Why did you think I'd laugh?"

He shrugs. "I'm not really the college type."

"Now, why do you say that?" It's exasperating to know he thinks this, given how much he has going for him, and how many total jack-offs are enrolled as it is.

"Well, none of the rest went. Not even beauty college. I'd be the first one in our family."

"That doesn't matter. Maybe they never wanted to. That doesn't mean you can't, especially now that you can afford it. You could all go now."

He laughs at this. "Maybe the grandkids."

"What would you study?" I ask. It's kind of a vague prospect, I've got to admit. It just seemed from the start that he'd be staying here. Probably for the same reason he just said, because all the rest of them did. And it never seemed that Crosscut or Madame Marie were the type to push college on anyone.

"No idea," he answers, shaking his head dejectedly already. "I mean, that's another thing. I don't even know what they have."

"You don't have to decide yet."

He looks up. "You don't?"

"No," I tell him, just now beginning to realize how lost he is here. "Some people take years to decide. I mean, there are all these required courses the first two years, anyway. And then, you can always switch if you change your mind."

"Really?" He looks more at ease hearing this. Our food comes, and when the waitress leaves he says, "I didn't know that."

I plate a slice and hand it to him. "Yeah, you can take a whole bunch of the intro courses the first year and see what you like." I sever a wedge for myself. "Lots of people do that. Then they switch anyway, sometimes a couple times." I take a small bite and smile at him. "You'd be fine."

"Interesting," he says, chewing slowly. "I thought you had to be really focused right when you got there."

·"Not at *all*," I assure him. "Trust me." I watch him turn this over while we eat. "And I'll tell you what else, there's probably not a better way to spend that money. Except on me, of course."

"Right," he answers distractedly, still mulling it over.

"You've never thought about this before?" I ask as he dishes up more pizza. "I mean, ever?"

He shakes his head. "College was always just this thing that was out there that other people did. There was never any money for it, so we just never considered it."

"Well, you ought to now," I say. "And since that's not an issue anymore, you should just do it." We sit for a while in silence. "Have we ever even talked about money before?" I ask, because I can't recall another conversation like this.

He swallows and washes it down with a swig of Coke. "Money isn't worth talking about," he informs me.

SPRING

March starts out very wet, but between downpours it's actually quite nice; cool still, but for someone used to East Coast weather, it's a welcome change. Nother gets totally fixated on this college idea; every day he's got more questions, which he just assumes I'll be able to answer. And most of them I can, just from growing up like I did: How many in a class? (it depends on the class); Do you have to have a computer? (it's probably a good idea); sometimes I just guess. He's so earnest I can't help but grin at some of the things he asks—it's like he's joining the priesthood or something, and he has to be totally sure. Some of the stuff he doesn't know is astounding. He thinks college is like really intense high school; when I tell him that there's nowhere that you check in every day, like with home-room, and no study halls, he doesn't believe me at first, and I wonder how much else he thinks I'm making up.

We spend a lot of time at the computer scanning web-sites and ordering catalogues, which are soon scattered all around his room, and he's wearing this look like he's getting away with something. He's already asked me to help him with Chemistry next year, which I suggested he take, along with Calculus and a writing course. Other than that he's fine; he's over a three-point, so there are a lot of places he can get in.

It's kind of weird thinking ahead like this, after taking it day-by-day so far, and now that we're talking months, even years, ahead, it gets me thinking sometimes. Not that we've decided on anything past me helping him with Chem, but it's going to come up sooner or later. For now though, I'm just glad for his interest in moving on, and pleased to help when I can. Plus, he's really cute when he's being earnest.

Gail flies East for several days in the middle of the month, and this time when she returns she announces that she'll be resuming her position at Johns Hopkins in the fall. "I wanted to tell you first," she informs me on the ride back from the airport. "I didn't want you hearing it second-hand from Kayla once I tell Annie." She somehow manages to relay this with an air of magnanimity, like she's bragging on the severance while she's canning me.

"Not much chance of that, but thanks," I reply, tightening my grip on the wheel. "I think I knew it was coming, though." This comes out in kind of a dead voice.

"You can tell me what you're feeling, Teri," she says when I don't continue.

"You'd think so, wouldn't you," I say. "But I can't, actually. I mean, I'm not sure yet." I feel kind of hollow, but that seems a little too trite to say. And edgy. Suddenly I'm very agitated. There's a warm, adrenal flush in my stomach, and my knuckles are white on the steering wheel, which I'm now strangling with both hands. I stare out the windshield at the flat strip of road winding beneath us, and the barren landscape, not wanting at all to be next to her in this car, as it somehow compresses. My unease catches me off guard, at least in its intensity. I had, truly, anticipated this turn of events, had begun to assume its inevitability, and believed I'd reconciled myself to it, though her departure is not something I necessarily wanted.

Now that I'm thinking of it, I realize I've just been blocking it out, focusing on other things, mistaking denial for resolution. Jesus, I sound like her. "Does Dad know?"

"Why would he know?"

"I don't know. You could have called him or something."

"I'll tell him tonight." She glances over at me. "If he's even around." She resettles herself and looks out the window. "I assume he'll remain here."

"That's a pretty safe bet."

"Which just leaves you."

Which is one explanation for the flip-flopping in my stomach. "I'm not moving again," I tell her. "Even if he does chase you back there."

"Oh, really."

"Really," I answer, my tone quashing further discussion.

We complete the trip in silence, and then when we pull up at the house she doesn't even come in, just asks me to carry her suitcase inside and then takes off for campus. I decide right then and there: fuck it, I'm writing her off. I tried; I really did, but fuck it. She's taking care of herself; I'll do the same. We can be civilized til she leaves, pleasant, even, but I'm taking it for what it is from now on. She has her life; I have mine. I'm not going to hold it against her, I kind of even understand her side of it, and I sure don't want her around all next year laying some big guilt trip on me because she hates her life, but I'm through accommodating her. If she thinks she needs to be back there, then maybe she does, and that's fine; but it doesn't mean I have to pick up and go with her. Again. And I'm all but sure Pops will stay, which is why I even said that to begin with. He's got less to go back to than I do. And probably as many reasons to stay.

I'll give her credit for anticipating Kayla, though. On the first clear day after several very sodden ones, when I have it on good authority that she isn't at school, I spread out at our table to enjoy the fresh air and knock off some French. Halfway through the period, however, Kayla and the psycho stroll up from the parking lot, making her no longer absent, just exceptionally tardy.

"Hey," she says, setting her books on the table and sitting sideways across from me.

"Hey," I say back, assuming she's taken my presence as an olive branch. "Hi, Brian," I add, then go back to my homework. He grunts or maybe says something.

"I'm late."

"Yeah, I thought you weren't here."

She flicks her hand like, no big deal. "The car conked out. Again." I can feel him sulking at this revelation without even looking.

I shut my book and stick it in my pack. "Well, at least you made it." I sling my pack onto my shoulder. "See you, sorry about the table."

Kayla glares at me. "What? Are you mad I was right?"

"About what?"

"Your mom taking off." She smiles tightly. "I could have told you that."

"You should have. You told everyone else."

I go to the Chem lab to fume and finish my homework, and when I enter the room Sandy is at the window gazing out. "I wondered if you'd come here," she says with a quick glance back. "What was that about?"

"Her being a bitch." I set my books down and replay the particulars, then join her at the window when she spots Nother outside. We watch him skirting a wide perimeter around the table, but then Kayla catches sight of him and signals him over. He stops a couple feet from the table, obviously not wanting to be there, but she keeps talking nonetheless, with great animation, while Brian sits glowering.

"Jesus Christ," Sandy says when Kayla pushes up her skirt and motions at some mark way up on her outer thigh. Nother looks briefly, then looks away. "That other guy is ready to explode," Sandy notes, which is obvious even from here. "Why does she *do* that?"

"You answered your own question." When Nother walks away a minute later, Brian stares daggers after him, ignoring whatever it is Kayla is saying. Sandy pronounces it the most stone evil look she's ever seen. A minute later he stalks off.

"That guy is going to kill her one of these days."

I walk back to my seat and pull out my French book. "You're just trying to make me feel better."

When I ask my father what he thinks about Gail going back to Baltimore, he shrugs and says it wasn't unexpected. "The signs were all there," he points out. When I ask about his plans, he pushes back from his desk and sighs. "That depends largely on you," he says.

"How so?"

"If you go back, then we all go back." He turns up his palms. "Simple as that."

"And if I stay here?"

"Then I'm here, too."

"Is that what you want?"

He shrugs.

"Look, just tell me, Dad."

"I plan to be wherever you are," he says. "That's where I want to be. I'd like all three of us together, but that appears doubtful here."

"O.K., let's say it was next year, and I was leaving for college anyway. Away from here and away from Baltimore. What would you do?"

"In that case I'd probably stay here," he answers. "I *would* stay here."

I nod. "So then, if I said I wanted to stay here, it would work out O.K. for you, too?"

"Definitely."

"Good. Because I was staying either way."

"Actually, I knew that," he says. "But I do want to stay here."

"Actually, I knew you did, too, which is why I got so hard ass with her."

"Such an open family," Pops says.

Nother finds this all quite amazing, that my mother would just up and leave, and Pops and I stay here without her. And he's right, up to a point, but there's so much that's jacked up about our family situation that it's not really that surprising at all. Nothing about us is logical, so you can't very well hold this last bit of foolishness against us, either. Then there are the outside factors, which I try to explain to him, like the fact that I'll be moving out myself in another year, so we'd end up separating then, anyway. And that Gail has a lot at stake, which he may or may not appreciate. If she doesn't return in the fall, she'll have to give up one of the primo positions in her field, one she's not likely to match very easily, and certainly not around here. So if she's dissatisfied with what she's got now—which she definitely is—then it's kind of a no-brainer that she get her butt back there before it's too late. Even Pops is in agreement on this; he never went for the whole "administrative" bit she was preaching last year, and he knows how well the Hopkins post suits her, and all she's done to earn it.

As for him, well, he's done a lot to set himself up here, and there's no reason he should have to sacrifice it just because she's not happy. And if things keep going for him like they have been, he'll be able to write his own ticket in a year or two. So yeah, it will be weird with her up there and us down here, none of the details of which have been worked out as far as I know, but all things considered, it's probably for the best.

"Well, maybe," Nother allows after pondering it for a good while on the couch. "We never made those kinds of arrangements in our family. We're just not as modern, I guess."

"Modern," I repeat. "That must be it."

Through this, Nother and I spend even more time together, though I'm not sure how that's possible. I certainly don't have anything else going on, though, save the occasional afternoon skip session with Sandy which threatens to become chronic as the weather warms up. Neither of which is a complaint, by the way.

Gail is so distracted these days that even when she's around, she's not really here. She's in daily contact with Hopkins now, and she's still got her work here, which she'd never blow off even though she is leaving. She's got shit piled everywhere, the table is now permanently covered with her academic as well as administrative detritus, which makes her easy to keep track of, at least.

My father is busier than ever. He's doing ten minutes on the Sunday morning show now, and usually at least one other segment during the week, commenting on some bit of breaking news. Add to that a column he cranks out every week or so for the local paper, and the occasional quote regarding Crosscut he's called on to make for any number of the larger dailies, and his dance card is pretty full.

He hasn't cut a deal for the book yet, but it's making the rounds at all the big houses, and they're telling him it's only a matter of time. So despite his gallant decree to remain here for me, I've seen precious little of him since. We talk sometimes at night, get ice cream, laugh at videos, but he's gone a lot in the evenings now too, though I don't ask where, and he doesn't say. Cloud is mentioned only in passing, and no longer comes around, which pretty much tells me all I need to know.

My squabble with Kayla resumes, though "continues" is perhaps more accurate, as she seems determined to feud whether I consent to play along or not. She still thinks I overreacted to her use of me and my family for her Psych project, still contends it wasn't her fault she had to present it in class, and still thinks it's the incident, specifically, rather than the principle of the thing, that upset me. Avoiding each other only works if we both commit to it, and lately she's not holding up her end. We have these ugly little snits every couple days now, always after she finds some pretense to bump into me and make a tentative attempt at contact, which I invariably rebuff with meticulous courtesy—though to be fair, I suppose this could be taken for indifference, which is when the ugliness starts. If she wants to rag on me, that's fine; call me stuck up, childish, petty, whatever. I can get it all back just by walking away, by doing nothing at all; retribution has no easier form. But she's been eavesdropping on our moms again, and she's found out about Pops and Cloud—whether there's anything to actually find out being largely beside the point—and begins casually disseminating this news to anyone who happens to be around, even though it's no more their business than hers, knowing it will circle back to me eventually, with attribution, especially when she plays her trump card and tells Joley.

"She says what you're really mad about is her being right about your parents," Joley dutifully reports. "And your mom running out on you. She says it's...I forget. Something."

"Transference?"

Joley snaps her fingers. "That's it." Her face screws up. "Maybe."

"She's the expert."

"And she's saying the college doesn't care if she goes or not, so long as your dad stays. That he's the one they're worried about losing."

Even I wince at this. Only Kayla could manage to create sympathy for my mom under these circumstances. "Then they lucked out, I guess."

Joley sighs, almost as disappointed, I suspect, as Kayla will be that I didn't take the bait. Which is difficult, I have to admit. She doesn't fight fair, and it's a drag having my folks sucked into it just because she's pissed off at me. But going off on her would be playing right into her hands, not to mention dragging me down to her level, which is just what she wants. So long as I take the high road, I win; but the minute I adopt her tactics, it's all her.

It gets doubly hard when she pulls Nother into it. I mean, if there's one person ever who's above this kind of shit, it's him. But like I said, Kayla doesn't play fair, and she doesn't stop mid-battle to count the bodies. She flirts with him every chance she gets solely to annoy me. She has no interest in him other than to get at me, but that's reason enough. Any snide comment she can make to put herself between us, you can bet she'll let fly. And the fact that he stays even more removed from it than me irks her to no end, so that even while she's sucking up to him, she trashes him privately, which makes no sense, and then says she's going to take him away one of these days, just for the exercise. Which makes no sense either, except possibly to her. The thing is, half the time when she's performing, Psycho Brian is right there tripping out on it, which she does nothing to correct, since messing with his head seems to be the only reason she keeps him around.

Then, today, to show you how absurd it's gotten, I'm at the window in the Chem lab waiting out the last five minutes of study hall, when I see Kayla get up from the table–she's alone today, psycho boy nowhere in sight–and walk into the parking lot, where she shoves something into the cab of Nother's truck through the slot of open window on the passenger side, and then saunter back into school when the bell rings. When we go out later, there's a paperback edition of *Othello* laying on the seat, which must be what she threw in, since it doesn't belong to either of us, and there are no other extraneous items about. Plus her name's in it, which I'm sure I saw her writing just before she did it. Nother has no comment when I tell him what I observed from my perch, other than to note it could have been worse.

"Still time," I caution.

And sure enough, it gets weirder when she calls my house that night. "Oh, hi," I say, rolling my eyes as I mouth her name for Nother.

"Hey," she says back. "Um, like, sorry to bug you, but I lost something and I thought you might have picked it up off the table."

"I don't go out there anymore. Sorry."

"Oh." She pauses dramatically. "I wonder where it could be?"

"Beats me."

"Hmmmm."

"Well, sorry again...."

"It's just that I really need it." Still, I don't ask. I wouldn't ask her for water now if I was on fire. "It's a copy of *Othello*," she says finally, with an emphatic sigh to convey her annoyance.

"Oh, that. Nother has it."

She giggles. I swear. "Oops," she says, in a manner that could only be described as coquettish, then giggles again.

"Yeah," I say. "Remember, you shoved it through the crack in his window right at the end of study hall today."

"Is that what he told you?" Man, she is *good*.

"No, I told him, actually. It was right after you wrote your name in it." I pause, then say, "I'm really surprised you don't remember. Good thing I saw you, huh? 'Cause, like, I was standing in the window of the Chemistry lab and watched the whole thing." I should just stop right here; I mean, I can feel her embarrassment right through the phone, and I've been totally steady til now. She can't even be mad at me, she's got to be so pissed at herself. But I can't resist. "Plus, he'd never have anything to do with you in the first place, so even if I hadn't seen it, I'd have known nothing was up."

"Your trust in us is refreshing," she oozes.

"Fortunately, I only have to trust one of you."

There is a long, toxic pause. "You sure about that?" she asks, more a threat than a question. "Maybe you ought to ask him."

"Maybe I did." There is another poisonous stretch of dead air. "So if you have to go fucking with someone's head, call Brian."

She sniffs loudly at his name. "He thinks I'm studying Shakespeare," she says, "til late."

The lump in his pack feels significant, consequential, authoritative even, though he is not the type to think in such terms. "A fistful of whup ass" is how he might say it, but even he understands the stakes far exceed this crude description. His shoulders are thrown back this morning, the weight at the bottom of the pack jostling his kidney as he strides purposefully behind the girl, having no trouble matching her pace this day. She does not know, further pleasing him.

They are late again; only she is late, actually, he is absent, though not even from here. Which is confusing to him as he thinks it, though it will cease to matter soon.

They have just come from her house, having dallied til her mother left, then stayed long past the first bell at Decatur. There had been words, and more. He had marked her, most likely, his grip on her arm viselike as he raged for answers, apologies, other things, before shoving her heavily onto the sofa. There have been countless versions of this same scene, but even she had seemed to discern the difference this time, the blackness of tone, the heightened propensity, perhaps even desire, for violence. And still, he'd gotten no answers; he never did from her, at least not of a kind direct enough to interpret. Questions bred only questions in return, or cryptic replies that hinted at answers he might not want to hear, followed by her bitter laughter. But she had not laughed today. The apology, yes, that had come, as sometimes it did. But it was harsh, as always, equivocal, almost an indictment of his asking, as if the asking had been the offense; she'd sat disheveled on the couch then, rubbing her bicep, glaring hatefully up at him. The rest of it he simply took. Right there, despite her protestations. Her atonement, in his eyes; for him, vindictive need.

She, of course, sees it differently, realizes now she has finally run her course with this lout, has only to contrive a *way to be rid of him. And so she has let him follow now, has led him here, perhaps, all but handed him the rope to do the deed himself. A scene here and he's back in the can, til twenty-one most likely, by which time she'll be long gone. So let the stooge have his moment, and then they'll all be quit of him.*

She stops at the table, dumps her books heavily, sits. She lights up, not offering one to him, then blows smoke dismissively across the table. Her arm still burns where he'd gripped her, and she touches it lightly now through the sleeve of her sweater, her defiance returning. "What now?" she prompts. He is still standing, and she rolls her eyes as if to say: you are totally hopeless.

"Shut up," he says, but the edge is draining from his voice. "Shut your stupid fucking mouth or I'll shut it for you." He sits now, dropping to straddle the bench across from her, his pack resting between his thighs, his head swiveling above slumped shoulders, squinting from the parking lot to the girl.

She laughs at him, provoking. "Big man," she says. "They're inside," she mocks, mashing out her cigarette and laughing again. "Take a look at the script sometime." He is seething, she can tell. She glances around at the other tables; plenty of witnesses should he go off now. Good. She'll take one, she has decided, across the chops if she has to, it's probably even better that way. He seems confused enough already, having expected to stride into a showdown of some sort, she imagines, though who knows for sure what goes on in that head. Still, coaxing him to take a poke at her should be simple enough.

And then, well off to her right, she catches sight of Nother Martin circling wide around them toward the parking lot. She says nothing, having decided to keep this drama confined to the table, but then the head across from her jerks suddenly, and she knows he has seen him, too. His face goes taut as he follows the other silently, his neck corded, his eyes slits. Yet he does not move, makes no attempt to follow, and she smiles dismissively. "Oh, there's Nother," she says airily. "I need to–"

"You set right here," he says. "You don't fucking move."

Nother is at his truck now, bent into the open passenger side digging behind the seat. The two at the table watch him with varying degrees of scrutiny. "Seems we're both 'setting' right here," she notes, convinced now that he will not confront the other. Nother emerges from the cab, a book in his hand, and slams the door. He begins to cross the lot toward them.

He has been getting increasingly agitated watching the other's movements. His left foot is now pumping almost of its own accord, so that he has to place his hand on his thigh to keep his whole body from shaking visibly. His mind races, unable to hold a clear thought as the other approaches. His pack, he is surprised to notice, is now unzipped, the tips of his fingers resting just inside the gaping zipper. His breath comes in quick, shallow bursts, his teeth grind at the back of his jaw. Nother is now strides away, having left the pavement for the grassy patch upon which the table sits. His approach is nearly soundless.

"Hey there," the girl coos when he reaches the table.

"Teri says this is yours," he answers, placing a copy of Othello on the table and continuing on without stopping.

And immediately, for the other one, the world lapses into slow motion. The particulars tumble together in his mind; very calmly he puts together the pieces. This guy, with her book. Shakespeare, til late. And now this clumsy lie right in front of him.

It is as if he is underwater. "Hey you," he hears himself say, his voice distant to his own ears, the words garbled, as his arm slides into the pack. A precise click and the safety is off, the gun emerging in a smooth arc as he stands, still straddling the bench. His target has begun to turn, is fully around and facing him as he levels the gun, holding it sideways, knuckles up, like every urban hood in every movie he's ever seen. At the corner of his vision he can see the girl's face go ashen, while before him his target stares back expressionless.

The sound is muted in his ears, as if from far away, more of a pop than the explosion he'd anticipated at the end of his arm. The girl screams, and there is a tear in the other one's shirt as he jerks back, then crumples to the ground. His mind is working in such a way that he realizes the scream could not possibly have preceded the impact, but he does not know what to make of this, or if it is important.

Heads snap around at nearby tables, all eyes suddenly turned toward him. Others stop in mid-stride, gazing back at the commotion, indifferent at first, then with wide-eyed confusion. His victim has fallen without a sound, buckling right where he stood, like a precisely imploded building. The girl continues to scream, which, he realizes now, is drawing most of the attention. He could silence this easily enough. There is a round in the clip for her, too, and a third for himself. That had been the plan. But instead he lowers the gun, which til now he's continued to hold straight-armed before him since discharging it. He notes the smell of sulphur; an ache in one of his knuckles as if he's punched some ungiving surface; a rising cacophony of panicked movement.

The girl is gaping at him, anguished, now directing her words at him, which he must wait on, he notices, as they seem to slip out by degree: "What-have-you-fucking-DONE? You-fucking–fool!" Now there are voices all around him: "Oh God!" "Holy shit!" "He's got a gun!" "Run!" People begin streaming away from him toward the school, awkwardly half-stepping with their heads turned back, expressions of sheer terror, as if they expect the next one right between the shoulders. The girl is now standing over his victim, staring at the motionless form, then at him, then back. "God-damn-you!" she screams. "God-fucking-damn-you." She cannot even pronounce his name, he observes.

A man in a dark suit appears at the nearest door–thirty yards, the shooter calculates–urging the stampeding students inside, waving wildly at those trotting toward the front doors to hurry, to get inside. He calls to the girl, yells her name several times, then starts toward her, stopping when the shooter glares at him. The gunman sees all this in slow motion: the escaping swarm, the horrified girl, his fallen rival, and now this teacher, unable to decide how badly he wants to be a hero. His eyes take in the building, the windows rapidly filling with faces, hundreds of fingers pointing down at him. In the nearest room, just above the corner door from which the teacher has emerged, he spots a lone figure in the center pane of glass, staring down on the scene, her fists pounding the surface above her, the reflected light shivering with each blow, until finally the glass gives way, shards raining down into the shrubs behind where the teacher stands frozen.

His composure seems to shatter with the glass, and instantly he is aware of everything at once, but can make no sense of any of it. The noise is suddenly deafening, shouts from countless open windows, crying, horror-stricken screams from the students bunched at the doors staring back at him. He is sweating, he notes, is covered with it, the stark breeze now cold on his wet skin, his forehead dripping. The girl stares malevolently, her face twisted in hatred, the color gone from her skin. At her feet lies the body, a dark spot beside it widening into the grass. He thinks to kill her now, but doesn't, and his mind begins to race. He cannot stay here, he knows, but cannot end it as planned.

He steps over the bench, lifts the pack and slips the fisted gun through one of the straps, hoisting the bag onto his shoulder. He begins to back away, the weapon hanging near his hip, then turns and makes for the parking lot. As he does, the teacher comes to life, moving across the grass toward the girl, stopping again a few paces short when the gunman stops. He stares at the teacher, discerns that he is not in pursuit, wants only to reach the girl, and continues on, zigzagging between the cars. He throws open the door and tosses the pack onto the seat, then flings the pistol out before slamming the door. He revs the engine, grinds the wheel til his knuckles are white. When he hears sirens in the distance he pulls quickly down the row and out of the lot, heading west away from the sirens.

The teacher envelops the girl, asks if she is hurt, ushers her away from the body, then goes back to check the slumped form for signs of life, though he senses already there is no need. As he rises from his futile attempt to glean a pulse, another girl flies out the door, moving headlong toward them. He steps between the girl and the corpse, thinking he will catch her in his arms and spare her from this nasty business, and is knocked sideways off his feet for his effort, while the girl slumps, wailing, onto the body, her repeated cries of his name going unanswered as she presses against his soaked torso.

In the car the shooter gulps air, checks the rearview mirror, slams his flattened palm on the side of the car. Wind blasts through the open windows, papers swirl about him, the straps of his pack dance. He cannot think, his thoughts racing like the sirocco blowing around him. He checks the speedometer without knowing why, accelerates for the same reason. Ahead in the distance is the overpass marking the edge of the county. He can continue to drive, prolong the inevitable, perhaps goad a helicopter into the chase, but why? For the one precise thought he has, the one which stands out with perfect clarity among all the others, is that his life is over. He has sacrificed it to her. Foolishly, he sees now; too late, he understands, as is always the case.

The overpass is approaching. He can see faintly at this distance the red markings scrawled there. Her and the other one. Last fall. So she'd claimed, anyway, showing him one night, proudly. They'd even stopped, gotten out and hopped the culvert to check her handiwork in the glare of the headlights. Something about a zero welcome; inexplicable, he'd thought.

He has an idea, probably his last ever, to erase her artistry, annihilate it beneath a wide scar of blue. The ditch is not wide, a good run-up and he's easily over it. He accelerates, his jaw frozen as the car gathers speed. He holds his line through the curved approach, floors it one last time, jerks the wheel. The contact is deafening, car hitting concrete at ninety miles an hour, so that even this glancing blow, for he has miscalculated the angle, renders the vehicle a crumpled mass, flat and overturned in the ditch, wheels spinning.

He has miscalculated further, though he will never know this, being deceased, as well as a blockhead. For the road is perfectly flat at this juncture, and, as the words were applied at slightly above shoulder height, the impact of car to concrete is several feet beneath, and so misses its desired effect, serving, rather, to underscore most spectacularly what it had meant to obliterate.

I awaken yet again to the crushing awareness of death near at hand. I sigh deeply and feel a hand slip into mine; I squeeze it but do not open my eyes. This is not my bed, I think, though surely it is one, for I am undoubtedly horizontal and well tucked in. I open my eyes to dim light, and the sight of my mother's concerned face gazing down at me. She smiles sadly and strokes my hair, then says my name. I press my lips together, the closest I can manage to a smile, and feel a tear roll to the corner of my jaw, where she catches it with a brush of her thumb.

I'm in a hospital room, obviously, private, at least for tonight, as the other bed is unoccupied, though how I got here, and the why of it, are mysteries to me. There is gauze wrapping and tape below my right elbow, quite a lot of it, and the hand my mother is gripping feels swollen, and would undoubtedly ache were I not drugged to the eyeballs.

"Nother's dead," I say, the words coming out in a harsh, choked rasp. My throat is parched and tastes of something horrible.

My mother's lips press together and she blinks twice, quickly, then confirms this with a nod. She reaches to the table and brings a plastic cup of water with a straw to my mouth. My lips nearly shatter as they close around the straw, but the water is cold and delicious in my throat. "I'm so sorry," she says, and I cannot doubt her. She looks like glass, the most delicate crystal, and I fear breaking down myself for what it might do to her.

"Yeah," I whisper.

"Are you in pain?" she asks. "Shall I call the nurse?"

I shake my head no. In truth I ache all over; my eyes feel like fried eggs they're so swollen, and a sharp pain flares deep in my shoulder when I attempt to shift positions. "Where's Dad?"

"He was here," she says. "He went to the Martins." I almost begin to cry thinking of them, visited yet again by death, and that I should be with them, that I want to be, for them and for me. "Sandy is here," my mother says. "She has been all day. Why have I never met her before?"

When I shrug I swear my arm about falls off. "Is it still Thursday?"

She nods, checks her watch. "Nine-fifteen."

The door opens with a soft click and Sandy slips in, palming her cell phone into her purse. She smiles slightly when she sees I'm awake, moves to the other side of the bed to take my free hand. "Hey," she says, squeezing lightly, "how you feeling?"

I curl my lip, but even that hurts. "Thanks for being here."

"No problem," she says. "You've been no trouble at all."

"I'm going to call your father," Gail says. She pats my arm and smiles at Sandy. "Will you two be all right?" Sandy nods and she takes up her purse and goes into the hall.

"What happened?" I ask as soon as the door closes.

"What do you remember?"

"Brian shot Nother," I say. "He's dead."

"Yeah," she says. "I'm so sorry, Teri. And I'm sorry you had to see it."

We're both crying, softly and immediately. She leans over the bed and hugs me, repeating the words, "so sorry." I hug back with my left arm, then release her. "What happened to me?" I ask. I touch the gauze with my other hand.

"You cut yourself pretty bad when the window broke," she says. "That's mainly why you're here. Do you remember that?"

I nod.

"There was lots of blood."

"I think my shoulder's broken." I look at her quizzically.

Sandy covers a smile. "You knocked Muzzo on his ass getting to Nother. Remember that?"

I shake my head. "Not at all."

"He was trying to catch you when you went running out, but you pretty much bowled right over him."

I wince. "Don't remember. Is that why my hand is swollen?"

"No, I'm guessing that's from when you broke Kayla's face."

"I did?"

Sandy pantomimes a haymaker of heavyweight magnitude. "They were trying to pull you off Nother, and you were pretty much out of it by then, but when you saw it was Kayla, that seemed to register, and you got this totally crazy look and POW! I mean, I swear I felt it."

"Where were you?"

I was just coming into the lab when you broke the window. You don't remember going past me on your way out?"

I shake my head.

"I said your name, and then I just ran after you 'cause I figured something was up, and you were bleeding like crazy. See, I didn't know about the shooting, yet, because I was in the hall."

"It was like a movie, I swear. It didn't even seem real. I mean, I saw him pull that gun, and Nother stop, and I just knew. I swear I even heard her scream, but it might have been me. And there's this flash from the gun, and Nother just dropped, I mean...dropped. And then I was pounding the window and screaming, too. And then there was glass everywhere." I pause, press my lips together, try to concentrate through the painkillers. I shake my head. "That's the last I remember. I don't even know how I got outside, let alone here."

"You were pretty hysterical by then," Sandy says. "But, I mean, who wouldn't be. Everyone was losing it. It was totally crazy for a while, I mean, just...crazy. I think that's why Muzzo tried to stop you; you looked totally gone. He probably meant well, is what I'm saying. And then when you punched Kayla, everybody just backed off, because the police and the ambulance were getting there, anyway. You fell back on Nother, then, crying and hugging him, and there was blood all over you guys. When they went to put him in the ambulance you wouldn't let go, and then they saw you were bleeding, too, so they took you both, and I rode over in another one with her."

"Kayla?"

"Her nose is busted for sure, maybe her cheekbone, too. But she wouldn't take her hands away to let them check, and she was bleeding, and hysterical, too. So they pretty much figured she ought to come along."

"Remember me telling you how she uses Nother to mess with Brian?" She nods, but with this quizzical look, so I tell her about Kayla planting the book in Nother's truck yesterday, and then the phone call last night, and how she told Brian she'd be studying Shakespeare til late. Sandy shakes her head, like she doesn't even want to hear the rest, but I tell her anyway. "So this morning, the book is on the seat when he picks me up, and I tossed it behind us with all his other crap, like: who cares. But I meant to get it when we got to school so I could give it to her, but Nother and I were talking about something else and I forgot. Then later, he comes by the Chem lab, and we saw them outside so I asked him for the keys so I could go get the book, because it was my fault we forgot it to begin with. And he says no, he'll go, because I'm doing homework. Which didn't really make any difference, because I was at the window the whole time watching. Brian's all pissed off already, I could tell from there, and she was messing with him, it looked like, and then Nother walks by and leaves the book without even stopping, and that's when it happened."

Sandy lets out a long, pent-up breath. "That would explain it," she says. "I mean, the whole way to the hospital she kept saying, 'Oh God. Oh God.' Which I couldn't figure out except maybe her face hurt a lot. But you could tell it wasn't that, because she was, like, wailing almost." She pauses, then says, "Damn."

"I served him up," I say. "I delivered him." I begin to cry again, really letting go this time. Sandy is holding me, crying too, though probably for me.

"It's not your fault," she insists, talking right into my ear. "Please don't think that. You can't. Teri, please."

"It is."

"She'd have brought it on no matter what you did," Sandy says. "And he was crazy. It wasn't you at all. You were the least of it."

"What am I going to do?" I bawl. "I don't know if I can stand it." I pull back from her and wipe my nose. "I swear my heart is breaking." Even in my state I hear how soap opera this sounds, but I think it just the same.

She hands me a tissue, kisses my forehead, strokes my wet cheek. "It'll be O.K.," she says. "I promise."

I take in a huge, wet breath. "I'm sorry." I take another tissue and blow. "Sorry," I say again, wiping my eye.

Gail steps back into the room. When she sees our tears she moves between us, a solid presence, putting an arm around Sandy and taking my hand. Who taught her this, I wonder? Since when?

"You should go, Dear," she tells Sandy, "it's getting late."

Sandy nods and smiles feebly down at me. "I'll come tomorrow."

"I'll be home," I say. I look up at my mother. "Won't I?"

Gail nods.

"I'll bring coffees," Sandy says with a wink. She hugs me. "See you."

"Thanks."

"I like that one," Gail says when she leaves.

"Yeah," I say. "You should go too, Mom. You must be tired."

"I'll stay for a bit," she says. "They'll probably give you something to sleep soon, anyway."

"Is it on TV?"

She nods. "Of course."

"Dad?"

She nods again. "He read a statement from the family a little bit ago. I saw it at the nurses' station just now. I'm pretty sure he wrote it for them."

"They might have asked him to."

"Right," she says. "I don't think you should watch anything tonight."

The remote is well out of reach, my mother's doing, I'm sure, but I don't protest. It's excruciating just picturing it in my head; the way they'd sex it up would probably flip me out all over again. "What have they said about Nother?"

"All good things," she says, smiling softly and taking my hand. "The things you already know." My eyes glass over, and then hers do, too, and we're just kind of there, holding hands, perfectly meshed in this dim, silent room, an odd, serene moment on the worst day of my life. Presently, the nurse comes with a pill, and I fall asleep shortly thereafter, in the comfort of my mother's gaze.

I am roused by the sound of gentle snoring. The horror of yesterday returns suddenly as I remember where I am, and my heart proceeds to break anew. I roll my head toward the sound and let my eyes drift open. I become aware of my raging throat and my father's recumbent presence at the same instant, the first dry as parchment and infusing a bitter taste onto my swollen tongue, the second perking softly on the other bed, a jacket half-covering his face. I almost smile but my lips won't allow it. Turning the other way I reach for the cup on the nightstand, pulling water through the straw until I am producing sounds not dissimilar to his.

I feel awful, lumpish and stiff, a blob of skin and tissue that hasn't moved in years. My head throbs. I determine to get to the bathroom, perhaps splash water on my face. It's a start, anyway, and I need to look ambulant to get out of here. I swing my club arm across my chest and rotate my legs off the bed, then drop to the floor, which, I note, is impossibly cold. I'm wearing a hospital gown that gapes in back and my underwear, and I wonder if I've been aware of this before this exact moment. The walk to the bathroom is teetering, but I manage it mostly upright, grateful, though, for the handicap rails framing the sink and toilet. I sit, catch my breath, evaluate the damage. My arm is beginning to throb from the cut, but my hand seems a little better, more so after I work it open and closed half a dozen times under a stream of warm water. My shoulder is O.K. if I keep my arm down, which shouldn't be a problem.

I rinse my face and check the mirror, fearing I look as repulsive as I feel, but finding I've still underestimated by half; I'll have to rally just to look like shit. I flatten my hand at the base of my neck and press, stretching the skin taut, to no positive effect. There seems a blankness in my reflection that I cannot pinpoint. While I am still staring, now pressing at the bags beneath my tumid eyes, then pulling my good hand through knots of hair before wiping the crust from the corners of my mouth, the full weight of my life as it suddenly is settles upon me, and when I can no longer stand to gaze on my pathetic, ravaged self in the glass, I slump onto the bowl and begin to weep convulsively.

I don't know if it is my sobbing that wakes him, but almost immediately my father is at the door, tapping softly and calling my name. I wipe my nose on the gown and go out, stepping into a giant hug, where I continue crying into his chest. Pops just stands there holding me, which is perfect. We rock silently, shifting foot to foot for several long minutes while he strokes my back and tells me it's O.K. over and over in a low voice. He leads me back to the bed and helps me up, where I settle lotus-style, the gown bunched down between my legs. "Mom went home?" I ask.

"Around midnight," he says. "I sent her."

"How's Nother's family?"

He shrugs. "As well as can be expected, I guess. I mean, they seem to be holding up." He pauses. "But much...sadder."

"Yeah." A lone tear drops from my cheek into my lap. "I almost can't believe it." I stare up at him. "I feel like I'm dying sometimes."

Pops smiles weakly. "I'm sorry, Teri. Really, really sorry."

"I need to go over there," I tell him. "I want out of here and then I want to clean up and go."

"How do you feel?"

"Like I want out of here."

He picks right up on the futility of debating it. "Why don't you rinse off and get dressed, and I'll see if the doctor is here yet."

"Where are they? My clothes?"

He hands over a shoulder bag from the floor beside his bed. "I brought some," he says. "And a hat; your mother said you'd want a hat."

"How *did* she know?" I take the bag and slide to the floor. "What time is it?"

"About seven."

"Will they release me this early?"

"Don't know," Pops says. "I don't see why not, if the doctor signs off."

"Can they make me stay?"

"Don't know that, either." He pauses at the door. "I'll see if I can hurry them up. Try to look healthy."

We're out by eight; home by eight-thirty. My cut is newly dressed–it isn't nearly as gruesome as I'd imagined, but pretty deep nonetheless–and I have a yellow bottle of antibiotics and another of Darvon, so I'm set. I've got instructions to keep the dressing clean and dry–I'm supposed to stick my arm outside the curtain when I shower, or wrap it in a garbage bag–and an appointment for Monday to have it changed. While I gather things together, the physician pulls my father into the hall for a private chat, I assume regarding whether I'll flip out again.

"One step at a time," Pops instructs as we walk into the house. "Nice and easy."

Gail is on the phone when we enter, and rises from the table to give me a hug with her free arm, the oddest multi-tasking she's ever done, I'll bet. She smiles distractedly and strokes my back, her attention split between our arrival and the phone. It becomes clear that Annie is on the other end, and presently she announces into the receiver that I'm back home, though her expression seems to indicate that she doesn't know what this might portend.

I dig out a garbage bag and round up some rubber bands and join Pops at the table. We begin experimenting with my arm until Gail holds up one finger to tell us to wait. She says her goodbyes and promises a return call when she knows something, then hangs up.

"Sorry about that," she says, walking over to give me a two-armed hug. "How are you this morning?" she asks, pulling out the chair next to my father.

I shrug. "O.K. at the moment," I tell her. "Though I expect it'll get worse. But at least I'm out."

"I'm curious how you managed that," she says, watching us continue to fuss with the bag and my arm. "Before you do that," she says, touching her hand lightly to my shoulder, "we need to clear some things up."

"What happened now?" I ask, perhaps a bit flippantly; what could be worse than what's already happened?

My mother picks up my pills to examine the labels, then sets them at arms length and sighs heavily. "Kayla tried to kill herself last night," she informs us.

Pops' face is startled, and I feel my own draw tight. This is certainly *not* what I expected to hear, though how, at this stage, can I let anything she does surprise me? They're both staring at me, watching for any reaction, any indication of what this might signify, but it would be impossible to say how I feel about it. After a very long minute I throw up my hands, feeling a sharp twinge pierce my shoulder, cutting the movement short. "I don't know," I say, though neither has asked anything, and my voice cracks saying it, though I'm not sure why. I don't even know what I mean. "How?"

Gail reaches for one of the bottles, begins tapping it on the table. "She swallowed thirty Percodan." She shakes her hand, rattling the pills. "The whole bottle."

"At home?"

Gail nods. "Fortunately Annie was checking her every few minutes, and they got her back to the hospital in time."

My parents both show surprise at my equanimity, but really, how am I supposed to feel? I blame her for everything; what fate would be too harsh in light of this? "You don't seem overly bothered," my father notes, more as a prompt than a criticism.

"She killed Nother," I declare. "How bothered should I be?"

"What?"

"The dead boy killed Nother," my mother says. Her eyes narrow with concern. "You must be confused."

"What?!" I shout. "*He's* dead, too?"

"Oh, that's right, you wouldn't know that," Gail says. She exhales, as if to acknowledge that all this death is getting way out of hand. "Yes, him too."

I place my pointed finger to my temple. "Suicide?"

"He drove his car into a bridge abutment," Pops says. "Doing around a hundred, they figure."

"Apparently he tossed the gun before he ever left the parking lot," my mother adds. "They found it under another car."

"Stupid til the very end," I marvel.

"Now, what's this about Kayla?" she asks. "That's what I wanted to talk to you about. Annie is beside herself."

I tell them the whole story, not everything I know of her, but enough so they can piece this together and believe it.

"She's a very disturbed person," I say by way of conclusion. "I don't know what it all stems from, but she's got major issues."

"I suspect you're feeling a lot of anger toward her right now," Pops says, causing my mother to roll her eyes in disbelief.

"I hate her," I tell him.

"I'm going to have to tell Annie," my mother says while Pops goes to answer the phone. It occurs to me that this is the longest we've all been together in months, probably since Christmas, though it doesn't explain why he's answering our phone.

I stare at my mother blankly. "I have no loyalties to either of them."

"Just so she knows what she's dealing with."

"It's Sandy," Pops calls in from the living room.

"Tell her to come over."

"You need to take it easy," Gail says. "I want you to rest today."

"I'm going to Nother's house," I tell her. We both seem to notice that I say it like he'll be there. She purses her lips, but does not argue.

Pops returns and we seal off my arm. "I'd still keep it out of the spray as much as possible," he advises. "I don't know how good that is."

"My hand is tingling, if that's any indication."

Surprisingly, Pops is still here when I go back out. A door slams on the street and I continue straight from the hall to the porch to greet Sandy, who's crossing the lawn with four coffees balanced on a corrugated tray. "Hi," I say, holding the screen door open for her.

"Hey." We go inside and dispense the drinks, mochas for us, tall lattes for my parents, who gush effusively at her thoughtfulness. Sandy pushes a lock of hair behind her ear. "You look better," she says.

"You should have been here twenty minutes ago."

"Oh, wait," Gail says, reaching down to the floor for her purse. She scrounges inside and comes out with her hand fisted. "Here." She drops the necklace Nother gave me into my upturned palm.

My empty hand goes immediately to my throat. I'm horrified to realize I hadn't even noticed it missing, though perhaps it was this absence I perceived when I studied myself in the hospital mirror. I stare into my palm. "Why did you have it?"

"I was afraid you'd lose it yesterday." She pauses, then adds, "You were a bit wild at times, so I took it."

I make a face. "Thanks," I say as Sandy takes up the chain and refastens it. "Kayla tried to kill herself," I announce, then immediately cover my mouth before I remember I don't really care. "Is that all right to tell?" I ask Gail.

"It's going to have to be," she notes. "But maybe you two could keep it quiet, at least for now."

"I won't say anything," Sandy says. I point at her coffee and motion toward the hall.

"You're not the one I'm worried about," Gail calls after us.

"It just keeps getting weirder," I say when we're in my room.

"You heard about Brian?"

"Yeah, but just now, from Gail." I stare at her. "I'm sorry, but I just can't feel bad about it."

Sandy nods. "I'd say that's understandable. You know, there's a rumor going around that you tried to kill yourself, too."

"What?"

"Yeah, slit your wrist on Nother's crumpled body. Like, totally *Romeo And Juliet.*"

"You're lying."

"No, I swear. I heard it from Joley this morning. Probably right after she thought it up."

"I wouldn't doubt that." I shake my head. "So school's open, then?"

"There's teachers and counselors there, but no class. She called," Sandy explains, meaning Joley. "She's dying for information. She made me promise to come get her if I came here."

"And you did? Promise?"

"Sure. What kind of friend would I be." We laugh, probably a little longer than it deserves. "So, are you doing better, or just not thinking about it?"

"Not thinking about it. I'm trying to hold it together in front of my mom til I get out of here. Plus, I'm not quite so drugged up."

"Well, it's nice to hear you laugh," she says. "And I can take you when you're ready; I mean, if you want."

"O.K., thanks."

But we don't go right away. We sit in my room for over an hour talking. It's mostly me talking, lying on the floor staring up at the ceiling, babbling in this tired monotone except for the times when my voice cracks, while Sandy lies stomach-down on the bed, chin resting on her hands, looking down over me, quiet, nodding, saying all the right things. When I rant, she lets me, seeming to understand that it matters not a lick if what I'm saying is right or true. I need to get it out, and so she takes it, listening without interruption, except to agree whenever I pause to demand, "Right?"

I begin recalling things about Nother, times we had, things we said, quiet moments. All of which must be monumentally tedious for her, like watching someone's jerky, rambling vacation videos, especially with me sniveling every five minutes when I remember something else. But still, she has a patient smile for each vignette, a hushed exclamation, a gooey, tender, "Ooohhhhh...." I'm reminded of the times at Joley's house right after Ronnie died, and know I must sound just the same, and hate myself for it. I become more insistent, as if this will serve to separate me from Joley, that my loss is somehow different on some real and very basic level. Which must be nonsense, I realize, to anyone but me; the losses are precisely the same, it is Joley and I who differ, and it is this distinction I seem determined to establish now. And Sandy, bless her enormous heart, allows it.

When I begin to repeat myself, I know I'm just stalling, drawing comfort from Sandy's unwavering sympathy, basking in her undivided attention. I need to be at Nother's, but my earlier resolve has given way to a more clear expectation of what awaits me: an entire household of fellow mourners, branch after branch of extended family who grieve as deeply as I do, more, perhaps, though this does not seem possible. Any comfort will, of need, be shared, the pain perhaps magnified. Just past ten, I decide to move.

"I need to go," I tell her, though I sound like I'm trying to convince myself as I climb up from the floor. "And stop torturing you."

"I'm fine," she insists. "When you leave I have to go to Joley's." Which is perhaps the only contingency that allows me to believe her.

I rinse my face—how many times is this?—and apply makeup. It's certainly not the best I've ever looked, but

I'm not expecting a fashion show from any of us. "A black sweater?" I ask, recalling that the day was blessedly cool earlier. Sandy nods and finger combs my hair after I pull it on, gently arranging the necklace outside the cowl neck. I slide into some black flats and turn toward her. "O.K.?"

"Perfect," she says, pinching a stray thread from my slacks.

We go out, and I'm amazed to see that my father is still here. They've made more coffee, even, and are in their same spots at the table, drinking refills from the cups Sandy brought. I conjure a long lost image of Baltimore, but shake it off. "I'm going to go," I say.

My mother looks me up and down appraisingly and nods. "You look nice," she says, walking over to tuck some hair behind my ear, a remarkably intimate gesture for her. "Do you want one of us to come?"

I shake my head. "I'll be fine. And I think for now I should go alone."

"Take the Volvo," Pops says. "I can ride in with your mother."

"Sandy's going to drop me off."

"I'd rather she not drive if she's taking medication," Gail says. She plucks the two pill bottles from the table and hands them to me. "Don't forget these. And try to remember to take them when you're supposed to. The antibiotics, at least."

I slip them into my purse. "Thanks."

"When will you be back, do you think?" she asks. "Dinner?"

"I don't know." I haven't really tried to picture it, other than to brace for the worst, emotionally. "I was thinking I'd play it by ear."

"You should eat something before you go."

"No chance."

"Well, we'll both have our phones, so call if you need a ride. And let me know if you're on your way."

"I may swing by later on, if that's O.K.," Pops says, looking at me expectantly.

"That's fine," I tell him. "I'm sure they'd like that." I let out a long breath. "O.K., then. See you." There are hugs all around, Sandy included, and we go.

"Egg shell city," Sandy says as we cross the yard.

"Yeah," I agree. "I wonder when Gail rehearsed? I mean, she's never like that. It was weird enough seeing them in the same room."

"They're trying." She pops the locks with a press of her thumb, then pauses at her door to glance around. "O.K. day, at least."

I look up at the overcast sky, a thin scrim of clouds blotting the sun. It is still cool. "What's the date?" I ask when we're settled inside.

"April first." She starts the engine and looks over at me. "Seriously."

"I totally believe you," I say, letting my head fall back. "If only."

We ride in silence, and when we pull up to the house Sandy offers to see me inside. While I'm still considering this, the nearest door, the one which gives entry into Madame Marie's lair, opens, though no one leaves, or appears to fill the opening. "Whoa, Addams Family," she says, sounding like she's beginning to regret her offer.

"Closer than you think," I reply. "I suspect that's a summons."

"You want me to wait?"

"No, it's fine." I turn to her. "These people are the only ones who feel like I do now. Her especially."

I glance at the open door. "I belong here." Again, I sound a little too much like I'm convincing myself, but this time I know it's true, and I'm ready, or as ready as I'll ever be. I open the door and put one foot out. "Things happen for a reason, right?"

She looks over, curiously. "Do they?"

I chew on my lip, then nod toward the door. "I'll ask."

"Call if you need anything."

"Thanks." I step out and lean around the door. "Did you *want* to come in?" I ask. "I mean, you can."

"I do, but not now."

"O.K. Thanks again, for everything."

"Good luck."

I shut the door, recalling as I do where she's headed. "You, too," I mouth through the glass, and she smiles.

I pause in the driveway until she's gone, then for a few added moments, taking deep breaths and feeling the cool air on my face. O.K., I say to myself, and cross to the open door. I mount the two steps and enter without knocking, since it seems I'm expected, pausing partway through the door to say hello before letting the screen door close behind me.

"Come in, Dear." The voice is low and steady, kindly, Madame Marie's I know with certainty, though I cannot yet make her out in the dimness. As my eyes adjust I begin to pick out objects; a pair of candles flickering on the mantle, curtain tails wafting lightly in the breeze, one of the cats perched on a straight-backed chair in the light from the open door. And finally, a figure in black, seated facing away from me, bent slightly forward over a low table.

I move into the room, over next to her, where I bend to pull her close and press my face to hers. "I'm sorry," I say, my eyes instantly wet. Her shawl-draped arm encircles my waist and she hugs me to her. "I should have come sooner. I'm sorry."

"You're here now," she says graciously, intensifying her grip for just a moment before releasing me from my awkward stance. "We're glad for that." I can hear movement, voices through the inner door, though I doubt any of them know I'm here. There are cars in the yard; several of them are here now. Madame Marie nods to the chair across from her. "Sit," she says, so I do. She gazes across the green felt surface at me. "You were injured," she prompts.

I nod and push up my sleeve, which seems unnecessary even as I'm doing it. "Cut myself," I say, wishing immediately to be done with this demonstration. "Pretty deep, but I'll be O.K." She smiles and I roll down my sleeve. "Did I interrupt?" I ask, motioning toward the table. She shakes her head and we fall silent. "Did you know?" I ask presently, prompted by the over-sized deck of cards in front of her. "I mean, is that even the kind of stuff you know?"

"It was foretold," she says, "but long ago."

"Does it help to know?"

"Death is always sudden," she says. "One is never ready." She reaches down to straighten the deck. "There was to be a death. For months I knew that, and I feared it was the one foretold. But then, when my husband died I assumed that to be the premonition I'd had, and my guard was lowered." She pauses, her lips drawn tight. "I had not considered it might be both." She shakes her head. "I was foolish."

"I'm sorry," I say again, my hands clasped tightly in my lap. We begin to speak of Nother; me haltingly, plaintively, my thoughts and voice wracked with emotion; Madame Marie with a sure and calm sincerity, her even tone in no way mitigating the intensity of her loss. It is homage, encomium, utter sadness. "I don't know how you can bear it," I confess.

"One does," she says. "You will, too."

"I'm not so sure," I say. "There is such a hole in my life."

She nods, takes up the deck, begins to shuffle the cards slowly. She stares across at me, rubbing the top card as she does with the ball of her thumb, a deliberate, circular motion, then turns it onto the table. Venus on the half shell. "You will love again," she says.

I gaze back at her, trying for hopeful, but managing only skeptical.

"I had worried that my gift would forsake me upon his death, as it had visited me with his birth. But it was truly a gift, I see now, as his love was to you. And so we will both go on."

I pull my heels onto the chair, clutching my knees to my chin, and stare down at the card between us. It is surreal, and not a little hokey, and I wonder if perhaps she has set the deck while I was still outside. But I see also the attraction of the quest, the reason so many come here, unbidden. "Where do I start?" I ask, rocking slowly.

She nods toward the inner door. "They're waiting for you."

And so I stand, move around the felt to engage in another awkward embrace. I kiss her cheek, thank her, fumble to say more, but can't. I start across the room, pause beside an ancient wingback chair, turn. "Do things happen for a reason?" I ask, remembering.

Madame Marie sweeps the card back into the deck, looks up at me, smiles depthlessly. "Of course not," she answers, though gently. "But it can help to think so."

I stand alone in the hall pondering her words, recalling the memories lately spoken of, vaguely aware of the others just out of view. The big TV is on, the final portion of some inane game show, annoying despite the low volume. There are quiet voices in the kitchen, several, and then Ruthie is coming through the archway, and stops when she sees me, smiles, calls over her shoulder, "It was Teri. She's here," and advances to wrap me in her arms. "We were wondering who she was talking to, if anyone," she explains, laughing a bit nervously. And then we are both crying softly in each other's arms. This sobbing has got to stop, I tell myself; I have too many others to speak to, I can't be breaking down like this. But it is Ruth who steps away, wipes her thumb beneath her eye, says, "Sorry, I promised myself I wouldn't." She smiles sheepishly.

"Me too," I tell her. "So far, I'm oh for today."

She escorts me into the kitchen. Rachel and Sara are there, staring at a small TV on the counter with the sound muted. Esther is at the table with Luke, Seth in the other room where the big set is blaring, minding the kids. When we've all hugged, sobbed, and again settled ourselves, Sara hands me a Diet Coke and asks of my injury. I display the wrapping, a repeat of my show and tell for Madame Marie, offer a lame joke, do what I can to make light of it. They all seem to have regained their composure, even Ruth after her shaky start, and the attention is now on me, my well-being the focus of concern. It appears that again they've made their peace before my arrival; unfortunate for me, in that I would like to learn this trick. The tears I've just seen are for me, for my sadness and suffering, not their brother. There is a knock at the back door and a casserole arrives, not the first, either, as I now begin to notice the familiar assortment of mourning food that before long will crowd us out. It is Esther who greets the neighbor; grateful, gracious, dry-eyed; it is she who

dispenses kind words and comfort, rather than the bearer
of this noodle concoction. The others smile, offer thanks
from where they sit or stand, nod thoughtfully. Seth walks
in, greets the neighbor with a hug, then sees her back to
her car, murmuring in soft agreement that indeed, the
Lord does work in the most inexplicable ways.

"Turn that up," Luke says, motioning at the flickering
set. "News is on."

I glance at the clock, surprised to see that it is midday.
The studio goes immediately to remote, where the day-
time anchor stands somberly before an enormous mound
of flowers that I notice, by and by, has buried our table.
The anchor recounts the news of the shooting—for what,
the hundredth time?—and the ensuing chaos. It has
become all too common a story, he suggests, and indeed,
it does seem eerily scripted—the sudden, inscrutable violence; the shock and anguished tears in the immediate
aftermath; the inevitable makeshift memorial; the futile
whys and wherefores. The film cuts to an overturned car
in a culvert, a wicked gash of blue paint specifying its
exact course to this inverted end.

"Jesus," Esther breathes.

"Jesus had the day off," Luke says.

Back at school the newsman motions off camera and
The Law steps into the picture. "Principal," I say. She is
speaking in clichés, catch phrases, gauzy aphorisms,
though still clueless, it appears, as to just what has
occurred on her watch. She does not deny responsibility so
much as defer it. The shooter was not a student here, it is
pointed out, as if this really matters. Does that not, perhaps, make it worse? But the newsman does not go there,
allowing her to direct this set piece, nodding sympathetically, dispensing bromides of his own when she's finished,

before dragging two of my classmates forward to blubber in Lawson's arms. Back at the desk, the studio pair begin to backfill; they tell of rumors of bad blood, a brewing feud, a love triangle, perhaps. Two girls have been hospitalized–that is established, one re-admitted last evening; a suicide pact has been suggested. "Good Lord," I moan.

Sara mutes the sound and they wait. It is only now that I understand that they are as clueless as The Law, the newsmen, the real cops, even. All but the few I've told, and Kayla, and two who won't be talking. "O.K.," I say, "here it is...." It's the full version this time, all of it; they have a right to know. I tell it slowly, haltingly, with all the necessary sidebars and tangents. It takes forever, making no sense, and perfect sense, in this telling, til by the end it's like a horror movie: you know what's coming and there isn't a damn thing to be done about it but scream til it's over.

They listen mutely until I've finished, a grimace or down turned glance the only betrayal of emotion through this whole sordid litany. "Ezra said she was trouble," Sara mutters after an unnerving moment of silence. "That first time, in the bar. 'Stone evil,' he said. 'You could tell.'"

We stretch, fidget, move about; my account was lengthy in the telling, like a sermon, and now there is little to say. We talk in fits and starts, trivialities, stray comments; we don't speak of Nother, I suspect on my account. The doorbell chimes regularly, or someone just appears, invariably bearing some steaming dish and a flushed, pitiful expression. They are invited to sit, comforted, thanked profusely as they exit. Around three we eat; until then no one has touched the mounting assortment of food, but once the suggestion is broached the response is swift. I am embarrassed at my consumption–not that I eat so much, but that I partake at all, and then with such relish. "How can I eat?" I demand of Ruth, more accusation than inquiry.

"When did you last?"

I have to guess at this. "Probably Wednesday."

"Well, then," she says.

These people are amazing, I think, so generous, so lacking in artifice. I am entirely at home among them, even at this horrible time. But Pops was right; it is different than when Crosscut died, this being eminently sadder, almost profane. There has been little laughter today, at least since I arrived, no backslapping, no ribald stories. And suddenly I wonder, and turn to Ruth. "Is it all right, my being here?" I ask. "I mean, I didn't even call."

She looks sweetly incredulous. "You're family," she answers softly, so as not to draw attention and perhaps embarrass me. "Which is why we didn't call, either. We knew you'd come." She pauses and shakes her head in what looks to be amused disbelief. "You're always welcome here, Teri."

"Thanks," I say quickly, so I don't cry again.

"All last night we kept saying how weird it was without you here. Ezra and Sara were going to go to the hospital til we talked them out of it."

"Where is Ezra?" I ask, which I've been wondering anyway.

"Arranging things," she answers vaguely. She glances at the clock. "He's got Ron with him, so who knows? I thought they'd be back by now."

Which is the first mention of these necessary details, oddly enough, probably another concession to my presence. "Is there a viewing?" I ask, thinking, for the first time, that this might not be advisable, or even possible, given the circumstances. A picture of Nother laid out flashes in my mind and I twitch, though I'm trying hard to bear up.

"Tomorrow," she says. "And then Sunday evening. The service is Monday." She squeezes my hand.

"I'm O.K.," I tell her. It suddenly occurs to me that I could help. "What can I do?"

"There's not much besides that," she says. "And I think Ezra needs to do it or he'll go to pieces." She pushes her plate back and wipes the corners of her mouth, then places the napkin on the plate. "So just be one of us," she says. "Maybe help with your classmates who come. And sit with us in church."

"Sure," I say, a hundred images suddenly racing through my brain, the most vivid being Ronnie's stifling sendoff last summer, when Kayla (her!) and I had barely squeezed inside. I bite my lip, recalling–entirely without warning–that this was also where I'd first set eyes on Nother. I pull in a sharp breath. "I can do that."

"Perfect, then," she says. "Let's get dessert."

She's trying again to distract me, but I soon notice that they're doing it to each other, too. None of us, it seems, can face this loss just yet. I half-expect him to walk in, and I catch myself scanning the room for him too many times to count. The looks I note in the eyes of the others tell me I'm not alone in this mental lapse. With Crosscut, we could take comfort in his grizzled, hovering presence, calling him to mind again and again in story and song to keep the specter at bay; but with Nother, none of us can bear to look at his passing straight on. These will be days of deflection, I see now, the quotidian details of mourning a decorous exercise in avoidance, with any reconciliation to come much later, perhaps when the shock has worn off. The stories will be kept for another time; the guitars will remain tipped into corners, silent.

By late afternoon the house begins to fill. The nieces and nephews arrive, released from school with the prospect of two free days ahead, thus bringing laughter and loud voices into a house in sore need of it. They speak openly, like children do, unafraid to address the topic of their newly departed uncle, the reason, after all, for this hasty gathering. Rachel emerges from her mother's room, where she has been this past hour relating the circumstances leading to Nother's demise. Ruth looks up when she enters the kitchen, and Rachel mouths, "She's fine." Ezra and Ron return at five, having swung by the 'Mill to check on things. "I'll go by later," Sara tells him when they confer. "When it slows here." Her face pinches in a heartsick frown. "Probably need the distraction myself by then."

My father arrives at six, accompanied, to my utter surprise, by my mother, who follows him into the kitchen carrying an enormous, foil covered serving dish, as if she were just another normal person. "That's my mom!" I tell Sara with bald shock. I hurry across the kitchen to relieve her of the platter. "Mom! What's this?" Whatever it is, there's a shitload of it.

"Crab cakes," she says, turning to take a covered bowl from Pops, who is already in two separate conversations. She follows me to the counter, where I unload the dish heavily. "Take it easy," she says. "Your arm."

"What are you doing here?" I never expected her to come; in no way do I associate her with this group, this house, this world. Pops, yeah; he's practically the family consigliore, but I figured her about as likely to show up as Crosscut.

She shrugs. "I wanted to come," she says, her eyes darting around the crowded room. "Did you take your meds?"

"Oops."

"Do it now." She reaches for my purse and waits.

"Who made these, you?" I ask after gulping the pills. I love these things; it was one of the few dishes I'd eat growing up, so we had it all the time. It's the one thing I really miss now that she doesn't cook anymore.

"Of course, me. Did you think we found them on the side of the road?"

I tear off the foil and the kitchen fills with a briny, oniony aroma that gets everyone's attention. I begin loading paper plates. "Try these you guys," I demand of the room. "My mom made them and they're great." As they step up to be served I introduce her; Gail smiles, shakes hands firmly, offers condolences and cocktail sauce with equal grace. Soon she is tucked in a corner, talking animatedly with Rachel and Ruth while the others await their audience, just one of the group except for the tweed skirt and jacket.

The crab cakes—and Gail's appearance—are a huge hit, the lone happy surprise in an otherwise bleak day, and set off another round of eating. While I'm helping fix plates for the kids, Gail slips off with Rachel to acquaint herself with Madame Marie, an encounter I'd give my front teeth to witness. As soon as she leaves the kudos begins, the siblings suddenly surprised at my celebrated distance from this charmer. To this I can only shrug, smile, ladle more casserole. I get with Pops when everyone's been fed, curious as to how he convinced her to come.

"All her," he says. "The crab cakes, too, or we'd have been here a lot sooner." He shrugs. "She has her moments."

"So, what did you do all day?" I ask him. "I kept expecting to see you on the tube." I give him a rundown of the rumor mill his station has become, which makes him wince, sigh, roll his eyes.

"To tell you the truth, I spent half the afternoon arguing with Cloud about that very thing. I mean, they really want to run with this, which is understandable, I guess. I mean, how often do you get a story like that around here? The thing is, they expect me to deliver it to them, you know, through you, the Martins, even Kayla. There's no sense over there that it's real people they're dealing with, other than the sympathy hook. And when I said no, well, they didn't understand at all."

"Wasn't there a shooting around here a few years back?" I ask.

"In fact there was," he says. "In Pearl, I think. But none of the people at the station now were around then. At least none of the on air people or producers. It's just a jumping off point for them. They all want out of here, and some of them are figuring this could be their ticket." His face screws up. "Hell, I think Cloud would be badgering your mother if it wasn't for—" I glance up as he cuts the thought off, almost laugh at his slip.

My parents hang around til after nine, and when they gather their things together to leave I go with them. There are watery eyes at the door, the first in many hours, and we make vague arrangements for tomorrow. Again I catch myself glancing around for Nother, still unused to his profound absence. Ruth catches me at this, is able to discern from my darting eyes and the sudden twinge what has just happened, and steps across the gravel for a final hug.

"It gets better," she comforts, then, as if to share in my troubles, she asks, "Right?"

"I fucking hope so." And we give each other the same melancholy smile.

I can't recall the last time we were all three in the same car. There have been times where it's been impossible for

us to be in the same house, so this is something. "Thanks
for coming, you guys. I really appreciate it, and I know
they did, too." I say this mostly for my mother; if it were
just Pops and I, it probably wouldn't even occur to me to
thank him. But with her along I'm reminded that he's
gone out of his way as well. "The crab cakes were a big
success, Mom."

"Yeah," she says, tapping the empty dish in her lap with
a fingernail, "they went fast." I watch her head nod distractedly while she stares out the window into the blackness. "Glad I thought of it." She turns to my father. "Did
you even get one?" They are, I recall now, a favorite of
his, too.

Pops shakes his head. "Next time."

My mother hoots at this. "Don't hold your breath," she
warns.

The emptiness returns as soon as I get inside. The light
is blinking on the answering machine and I think, Nother,
before recalling that this is impossible. It's Sandy, actually,
who I should have called from over there, but didn't, and
probably won't tonight. I sink onto the couch, sigh tiredly
though I've done nothing all day, kick off my shoes. I
begin to understand that it will be like this; that he is gone.
There is a giant hole in my life that he used to fill, and how
this is to be remedied is entirely up to me. But right now, I
just can't deal, and my eyes swim.

Gail reminds me to medicate. It's been four hours; four
I won't have to suffer again, at least, so that's something.
While I'm swallowing under her watchful eye, she asks,
"So what did you think of your father's news?" I toss down
the Darvon and make a face. "About his book," she adds.

"What about it?"

"He got an offer. Didn't he tell you?"

"No!"

"Huh," she says. "Yeah, not long after you left this morning, in fact. He was on the phone when I left, and still on when I got back." She mentions the publisher, a big one, says he'll probably take it.

"Well, I would think," I say.

"His agent may try to bid it up," she says. "They might not be the only ones interested, it sounds like."

"Go, Dad," I say. "He could have told me, though." I pull my jacket into my lap. "Maybe I'll go over."

"I think he's on the phone again," she says, which appears correct, as we can hear him talking through the wall. "I hope so, anyway."

She moves to the counter and sets the serving platter in the sink. "Leave that," I tell her. "I'll get it." She arches her eyebrows. "You guys need to quit being so thoughtful. It's weirding me out."

I put on the TV to look at the news; nothing has changed, but that doesn't seem to have discouraged anyone. An impromptu prayer vigil has broken out at Decatur near our table, scrutinized in all its tedious detail by the somber anchor, who for some reason feels compelled to whisper like a golf announcer. There is a lot of dripping wax and hand holding, with the Jesus Nazis leading a swaying pack in some tuneless dirge. I sigh painfully.

"They're just doing what they need to do, Teri," my mother says, sounding way too much like my father until she adds, "Or what they think they need to do."

"Mom, they're only there 'cause there's nothing better to do. It's Friday night, so they're out. Half those guys are drunk."

"Teri, honestly."

"Mom, I swear, if they panned that camera on the side

of the school, there'd be half-moons of piss the whole length of the building."

She sighs. "Could we try to be a little more charitable?"

I watch as long as I can, then channel surf til I find something I won't get embarrassed watching with her. Gail is at the table, laptop out, but she's mainly watching me, I can tell. "So, what did you think of Madame Marie?" I ask.

She purses her lips. "Is that what they call her, too?"

"Or Mom, but usually that."

"Hmmm. Well, I'd say she's severely depressed, for one thing, which is entirely understandable. For instance, she's distracted, melancholic, completely disengaged; her speech patterns take forever. She's functioning almost in a dream state. They should probably keep an eye on her."

"She's always like that," I tell her. "I talked to her this morning and I think it's the most lucid I've ever seen her."

"Really," she comments, and I fear I may have revealed too much, that it might spook her on me going over there. She taps the table deliberately with her index finger. "Interesting."

The weekend is unbearable. I cry once during the night, a soft, exhausting whimper, and again briefly at dawn, before rising to face the day, and the dire prospect of seeing the sole love of my life now lifeless before me. This will be the worst moment ever, I know, worse even than the event itself, for I have time to consider it, to suffer the pain in advance, and incessantly, as well as in real time. If I can make it through this, the rest will be manageable. If I can bear up now, perhaps the healing begins. And I have no choice, really, it has to be gotten through; that is the way of this life, I'm finding. I recall Gina's blithe advice from long past: Go numb.

And so I do, as much of need as by choice. My method becomes a mixture of torpor, habit, and distraction, my movements performed rotely, or in a state that closely mimics sleep-walking. I call Sandy just to hear another voice in my head. "Talk," I say, and she does, the tumble of words a needed diversion, however brief. "The viewing is at four," I tell her, and she promises to be there. "I didn't mean," I say.

"I want to," she replies, then asks do I need her to come by before, or now, and I tell her no, it isn't necessary. I ask if she went to the vigil at school. She did, but she left. "Posturing," she says. "Geeks." I nod, like she can hear this, then say I figured.

Pops comes over at ten, and the three of us go out. I order, but don't eat, push French toast around the plate, let Pops tell me about his book deal. I want to be excited for him, try mightily, perhaps succeed. Again, the flow of words is soothing, the buttery breakfast odors, too, the busyness and clatter. Coffee is welcome, the surfeit of syrups wondrously consoling, even Gail's carping about her omelet is music in my addled brain. We go to the outlet mall. I purchase a black dress, quickly, knee length, then hose. When we get home I shower, rinsing the oleo scent from my hair and skin and slip into my new dress. I medicate. The bandage looks tawdry, but it's clean, mostly, so I forget it.

At two, Pops drives me to Nother's. "Now, when is it?" he asks.

"Four," I say, "til seven. We might go early."

"When should I come?"

"Don't come early."

He bites his lip and considers this. "O.K.," he says. "Call if you change your mind." When he hugs me across the seat, I think to cry, but don't, which is easier than you'd expect.

We bump around the house for an hour, mumbling and straightening ourselves. I feel progressively worse; but for the company of these people I'd surely lose it. I may anyway. A little after three we go, a procession of vehicles trailing Ezra's big Ford, where Madame Marie is perched waxenly beside him.

When we are assembled the coffin is brought in, and it is as if all the air goes out of the room. Liza, Seth's youngest, begins to cry, and Meredith takes her out. I am breathing through my mouth, as if trying to hold down one too many tequilas, wishing to be taken out myself. Ruth clasps my hand and I squeeze. "O.K.?" she whispers. I nod, possibly smile. We watch Madame Marie at the casket, standing with her hands touching the sides. She is motionless, utterly composed, draped head to toe in black. After several moments she steps away, head dipped, to a spot along the wall, where she crosses herself. A rosary is knit in her fingers, and she raises it to her lips and kisses the crucifix. The rest of us begin to step up, alone or in pairs; the children stand with their parents. Sara and I go together, after Ruth and Ron. When Ruth's shoulders clutch in what I know is a stifled sob, I almost break down. At the coffin I stare at the lower portion first, below the chest, and then force my eyes to move up until I see collar, neck, chin, smooth darkened lips, a beatific expression, closed eyes, tousled hair. Sleeping, I think, just like everyone always says. I feel a warmness as I stare down at him; this is not awful at all. It should be, but it isn't. He is lovely still, as he was in life. There is no other way to say it. And, apparently, I have said it, out loud, as Sara looks over, nods, says, "I thought that exact thing." The difficulty now is in stepping away, out of this wondrous presence. But I do, finally, well after Sara has moved away, my eyes locked on the floor, folded hands pressed to my mouth, where I am biting down hard.

My parents arrive precisely at four, just missing Madame Marie, who has taken her leave without apology or explanation, to the surprise of no one. My eyes go glassy when my mother hugs me; it is these odd moments that set me off. The routine, I can take, all else brings agitation, bizarre thoughts, tears. She tugs a stray thread at my collar, presses a tag flat behind my neck, tells me again that she's sorry. I bite my lip, sniff loudly, and thank her.

The procession of mourners is slow, but steady. Neighbors at first, many who were at the house yesterday, some second or third cousins from farther away, even a classmate or two. The Law arrives, and then stays too long; several teachers, too, who must know of Nother and me, as they are overly-solicitous to me. Sandy arrives, behaves perfectly. I introduce her to the family and she joins us near the door. At six she leaves to get Joley, who is not the mourner we've been led to believe. I shoo my parents off with her, and they go unwillingly. I'll catch a ride with Sandy, I tell them, and Gail reaches into her bag for my meds, then stays til I've swallowed them in her presence.

The floodgates open at six-thirty, as my classmates begin to arrive in droves, or, at least, in loud clumps of four or five, their voices dropping precipitously as they cross the threshold, questions of food and movies giving way to those of a higher order. They are clean, powdered, dressed for the night to come; the room fills with the scent of shampoo. This stop is of necessity, a brief interruption to allay any nagging fears that they may be shallow, self-centered, heartless. It is only a few minutes, they realize, and then something odd to recall later, while pissing out their half dozen beers: "Like, dude, what was with that fucking music?" And dude can explain, "Totally!"

At quarter to seven Joley bursts in, makes a beeline past the others to envelope me in a grandma-sized hug. She begins dripping platitudes, and expressing dire concern for my well-being, oblivious, it would seem, to the equally deserving blood relatives surrounding us. I gaze past her shoulder, where Sandy is just now entering, as she has not seen fit to skitter dramatically across the lot as well. I cross my eyes and Sandy's hand goes to her mouth, this ridiculous scene nearly causing her to laugh out loud. "Thank you," I say, then say again when she still doesn't release me. I step away when her grip slackens, tug at my dress. "It was good of you to come." She begins to blather full volume, like we're at study hall, so that I have to pull her away from the others out of respect for the deceased, whom Joley has still not acknowledged. At seven precisely she begins to check her watch, discreetly at first, then less so.

"We should get out of here," she says as Sandy walks up. I see Ruth glance at Sandy, arch her eyebrows, and Sandy shake her head reproachfully. Two others join us from the casket; Patti touches my arm and whispers condolences, Linda (I think) smiles sympathetically. I thank them both for coming.

We are ushered outside soon after by a stiff, dark-suited employee. I will not take Joley to the Martins; they've suffered quite enough. And so we make our good-byes until tomorrow in the parking lot, and I invite Patti and Linda (definitely Linda) to follow us to my house. Both halves are dark when we arrive, so that I fumble on the porch letting us in, then almost break my neck crossing the front room to the lamp. I get them settled with sodas and go to change out of this dress. There is talk of pizza, and then Joley discovers the remote and cranks MTV, which is loud even through the wall of my room. Gail arrives, raps at my door, enters without waiting. "How'd it go?" she asks.

"O.K., I guess." I throw on a sweatshirt, having already decided to stay in if they head off somewhere later. "A couple rough moments, but O.K." I dig out shoes, then toss them back in the closet. "Where were you?"

"We got a bite to eat."

I nod. "I think we're getting pizza."

"I'll buy," she offers, then shrugs when I stare at her. "Well, you never have anyone over."

We go out and I introduce Patti and Linda. She already knows Joley somehow, maybe just from hearing me talk about her. "Gail's buying pizza," I announce. It takes the requisite twenty minutes to settle on toppings, and the guy at the place has just answered when Joley lets out this paint-stripping scream that makes me slam down the phone.

"OMIGOD! You guys! Look!" She's on her feet, pointing at the set, almost hyperventilating. "OMIGOD!" she screams again, bouncing up and down and biting her hands, like those chicks at the airport when the Beatles came.

We all turn to the screen and Linda says, "Holy shit," then glances at Gail. "Sorry."

"That isn't them, is it?" Sandy asks, stepping closer.

But it is, of course, I recognize Ray from here, even through the make up. "These guys are from here," I explain to my mother, who must be wondering what the hell everyone's fussing about. I lower my voice in deference to Joley, though I think she's catatonic at this point.

"That guy who crashed his car right after we got here, Joley's boyfriend? That's his brother."

"Ahhh," Gail says. She observes Joley clinically, then takes the scratch paper from me. "I'll call," she says. "She's not going to scream like that again, is she?"

"You're the expert," I remind her.

"Are you guys hearing this?" Patti asks. "He keeps saying 'Kayla,' I think." So we all shut up to listen and sure enough, right in the middle of the long string of girls' names that comprise the chorus, is hers, clear as a bell, and rhymed, in stylized wailing homage, with Layla, the ultimate rock goddess.

"Damn," I sigh, "The Hogs on MTV." I look over and Joley is still staring wide-eyed at the screen, her cheeks glistening, hands clasped to her mouth.

As the song winds down the credit appears in the corner, making it official, and we all sit back except Joley, who remains stock still, like she's seen a ghost. I mute the set and the rest of us watch her in silence, in an unbalanced battle of wills to see who'll cave first. Which is Joley, of course, who's way too anxious to solidify her centrality, undoubtedly shocked that she's been thus blessed on a night that might otherwise be solely mine. "I was just wondering," she says in a quavering voice, "if he even knows yet. About Ronnie, I mean." Her voice catches dramatically on Ronnie's name.

"They're in L.A., not Tibet," Linda reminds her, "How could he not know?"

"Well, I don't know," she says, wiping a hand across her cheek. "He never called me."

"Well, if he's working down that list it might take a while" Linda suggests. Which is two good ones in a row, I'm thinking, and draws a particularly vicious look from Joley.

"So like, he did all those girls then?" Patti asks. "I mean, that's supposedly what the song's about?"

"Isn't that what most songs are about?" Sandy asks back.

"You guys!" Joley whines. "That's nasty. And this is really hard for me."

"There, there," Linda says flatly.

Joley sighs emphatically. "I mean, I just keep thinking...." She lets the thought hang there.

"That explains the difficulty," Linda says.

"How can you joke when Teri and I are so upset?" Joley demands. She moves, finally, to where I'm perched on the arm of the sofa and loops an arm across my shoulder. "Just ignore her."

I smile for any number of reasons. "Go rinse your face," I say softly. "You'll feel better to eat." She smiles pitifully, like some dying child in a movie whom I've just promised a home run, and moves down the hall.

"Now let me get this straight," Linda says, staring after her.

Sandy turns to Patti. "Is she always this on?" she asks, meaning Linda.

"Pretty much."

Sandy nods appreciatively. "Good to know."

Joley recovers sufficiently to scarf down her share of pizza, and while we eat we critique the production values of the video (decent), the song (we need to hear it again), Ray (yeah, pretty hot), and wonder how rich the Stereo Hogs are now, and if Ray might show up on *Cribs*. Patti thinks she can download the video and promises to forward copies around.

"I wonder if Kayla's heard it?" Linda muses.

"Have you seen her?" Patti asks Joley.

She nods, but addresses the report to me. "Broken nose, like, tape across here." She makes an X centered between her eyebrows. "Swollen cheek, two black eyes." She outlines half circles under her eyes. "Um, sore jaw. I think that's, no, a loose tooth, too, that'll probably be O.K."

Linda lets out a low whistle. "Damn, Tyson."

"Kind of wish I could remember doing it," I say, glad, though, that Gail has gone to her room.

"And now this song," Patti says. "Bad week for her."

"Payback's a bitch," Linda points out.

They hang for a while after we eat, talking about school. I get various versions of what went down Thursday after I left; who said what, who freaked, what teachers did what. The consensus is that it didn't seem real, like they were all watching in a daze, waiting for the commercial so they could flick to something else. Monday will be weird, it is agreed, and probably the next couple weeks. "No homework," I say, remembering after Ronnie, and everyone kind of nods: oh yeah, right. I won't be there Monday for sure, not with the funeral to get through. At the moment, I'm not sure when I'll go back.

Linda and Patti leave first, to a party, I think, but they politely don't say. Sandy and Joley stay another half hour, then leave too. I make sure to fuss over Joley, thanking her effusively for being there for me, for her bravery. Sandy I just squeeze extra tight, for everything.

Surprisingly, I sleep. I think I'm just totally spent, emotionally; crying wears me out, and I've been doing way too much of it the last few days. I think, too, that I was really stressing about how I'd handle seeing Nother laid out, and just the relief of having that behind me helps a lot. I remember looking over at the casket a couple times, thinking: I did it. Which is a totally weird thing to think, I realize, but I really wanted to handle it O.K. I knew the family would hold up, there was never any question of that, and I wanted to do as well. Because there really is a right and a wrong way to behave, I'm starting to believe, that it's not just doing what you want, or what's easiest, or what feels best. There's virtue simply in doing the right thing, even when it's hard—especially when it's hard. That's what it is about them that stands out, what makes them...noble, almost. And even if I am just trying to emulate them right now, I could be doing a lot worse.

At noon I borrow Pop's car and drive to the bar, having hung my old blue dress on one of the back seat hooks and tossed some dark shoes on the floor. The viewing today is four to six, and I'll go crazy if I just sit around. I cry softly on the way, knowing Nother won't be there with me. This is my first solo, the first of countless routine things we did together that we'll never do again, the first of many, I'm sure, that will catch me unaware, and set off the tears. I don't even know if there will be anyone there to let me in, but I'm betting so, and if not I'll just keep driving.

When I pull up the door is open and Sara is behind the bar running the tapes when I step in. Crosscut is on the stereo, and the air is pungent with smoke and stale beer, just like always. If you didn't know better, you'd think it was just another Sunday. Sara looks up as I cross the floor, appears entirely unsurprised to see me, but says, "What are you doing here?"

"Same as you."

She smiles knowingly, her eyes warm. "Right." She draws me a Coke and I sit across from her. She's looking past me out the door, her hands shoved into the pockets of the loose house dress she's wearing, which makes me think she might have arrived here without entirely meaning to.

She looks old today, and I hope it is only temporary, or that I'm just wrong; I can't bear to think of her wearing this sadness like a mask, hiding the beauty beneath it. We let the music swirl over us, every note perfect for this day, this place, as if written just for us, perhaps about us. After a while she turns and tears off the register tape, which has finished without my noticing. "I'll come down in a little and help," she says. "You be O.K. by yourself?"

"That's the million dollar question," I reply, pushing the glass across for her to put in the sink. "But yeah, for now."

She steps around the bar toward the stairs, a tail of tape fluttering behind her. "Well, holler."

I get to work, glad for the distraction, the physicalness of the task, the clarity of purpose. I wash, wipe, sweep, easily able to tell where I've been and what is left to be done, wailing along with the more familiar songs, feeling them burn into my soul. A shadow blocks the door at one point and I barely look up. "We're closed," I call out, swiping determinedly at the table and sounding like every wronged and wearied woman Crosscut ever met, and the shadow moves on. Sara returns and we finish by three-thirty, having decided to let the parking lot go this once. I bring in my dress and change in back, while Sara goes upstairs to pull on a dark sweater and run a comb through her hair. I wash at the big sink, straighten my part, shadow my eyes a bit, apply lipstick. "O.K.?" I ask when she returns.

"Perfect," she says. "Me?"

"Very nice."

She pours two healthy slugs of peppermint schnapps and slides one across the bar. "Can we toss one down for him?"

I lift my glass. "I think he'd be cool with that."

We arrive at the funeral home right at four, where it is only family so far. I have a bad moment right off, when I first see Nother laid out again. Has he been in that coffin with the top shut since yesterday? Or is there a cooler back there, or did they take him out and slide him into one of those slots like they have in the morgue on every TV show? And if so, did they have to take him out early to warm up again, like how you set a frozen chicken on the counter to thaw? I don't know why it even matters, but it kind of freaks me out wondering about it, even though he looks exactly the same as yesterday. I'd really like to ask someone, but I won't. It seems like the kind of thing I should already know, especially with all the death I've been around lately.

It's not as bad after that. I'm kind of in a daze, and there are a lot fewer people than yesterday, especially classmates, most of whom wouldn't be able to take off afterward, since it's a school night. Sandy stops in briefly, just to say hi and make sure we're all O.K., and then Gail and Pops walk in about five-thirty, even though I told them it wasn't necessary. She's dropping him off, actually, on her way to meet Annie, who's having a rough weekend with Kayla, apparently. So he'll just come home with me at six, which still doesn't explain why they had to come at all, but it's still nice, especially when she stays the rest of the time, too.

"So, is the TV station going to be at the funeral?" I ask on the way home. "'Cause that's kind of messed up."

Pops shrugs. "My hunch would be yes," he says, "though I don't know for sure." He glances over. "It *is* the biggest story in town."

"You can go on if you want," I tell him.

"We'll see."

I sleepwalk through Monday. I go totally numb for the funeral, which is at ten. Through some weird kismet I wind up next to Madame Marie, on the far right in the front pew, both of us cloaked in black, neither entirely steady. My parents are behind me—Gail is really starting to trip me out with her attention, and I spend a few quiet moments before the service starts wondering if I could have endured this scrutiny throughout my childhood. The church is small enough to be full; Sandy is here, of course, Joley, Patti, and Linda. The Law is near the front, across the center aisle with quite a few of the faculty and staff from Decatur, which I'm not sure now is even in session today. The entire back half is students, who I can hear shuffling, coughing, clunking the kneelers up and down every ten seconds.

I do whatever it takes not to listen; even the readings might set me off, and I've vowed not to lose it in front of everyone. It's not like I want to remember this day, anyway. The urn bearing Nother's ashes sets on the altar rail, and I focus on that for a good part of the service, though only for something on which to lock my gaze, not as the vessel of my lover's mortal remains. My mind goes briefly to the thought of his incineration, causing my grip to tighten on the hand I'm surprised to find clasping mine. I think of Baltimore to clutter my mind with something else, anything else, recalling old classrooms, trying to name every student, desk by desk. I picture hallways, each staircase, review every class I've ever had, until, finally, the service is over.

I stand outside with the family, thanking people for coming, accepting hugs, kind words, condolences, agreeing that it was a beautiful service despite not having heard a word of it. My parents watch from nearby, Pops eyeing the

TV van parked on the road. Now that it's over, I feel really lame for blocking it out, though my current actions are still performed by rote. Sandy walks up and we hug, the first thing I allow myself to feel. "Thanks," I whisper, my voice almost cracking. Many of our classmates loiter amongst the cars in the side lot, so I can assume school is in session despite the presence of The Law and much of the faculty.

Joley strides up, arms thrown wide, a moan of commiseration bellowing from her rounded lips, as if I've just fallen and scraped my knee. She enfolds me in a matronly hug for all to see, then steps back and says, "I'm *so* sure she came!"

"Joley!" Sandy says.

"Who?" I ask, but who else can she mean? I scan the lot and finally detect what is surely the unnamed topic of this exchange. Across the grid of cars, Kayla and Annie are long-stepping the ditch to their car, which is parked on the road just down from the TV truck, despite there being ample space in the lot. Annie has a hand on Kayla's near shoulder and an arm across her back, as if to steady her. They are proceeding slowly, I notice, and it appears that Annie is having to urge her along.

"They were at the back," Sandy says in a quiet voice.

"I totally cannot believe her," Joley huffs.

"She wanted to come," my mother says, moving over to stand beside me. She rests a hand on my shoulder, squeezes.

I don't say anything for a moment, as my mind struggles to accommodate the shock of her presence. I watch from a distance as Annie opens the passenger door and settles Kayla inside. In another minute they are gone. "Is that what they wanted you for?" I ask.

My mother nods. "She needs to get through this, too."

I let out a long breath as the group makes a move to go. "I can't really worry about her needs right now." Which I think is pretty even-handed, all things considered.

We drive to the Martins, where the family is gathered to be together and try to work through the mountain of food in the kitchen. Ruthie has suggested that Nother's ashes be dispersed in the woods, which has been deemed agreeable by the rest, and now by me. Perhaps I know a place, Ruthie speculates, and I nod. Just the place, I tell her, and ask will she come, too? Of course, she says, she meant to, and we say perhaps tomorrow, we'll see how it goes.

At one we leave, dropping Gail at the house so Pops and I can go to the hospital to have my bandages changed. "You going to be able to do that?" he asks as we wait in one of the examining rooms for the nurse.

He means with the ashes, and I shrug. "I think so, if it's just Ruth. And if one of us freaks out, who'll know?"

My cut is healing well they say, and in another twenty minutes we are out. There's going to be a scar for sure, but on the inside of my elbow, so not very noticeable. Thinking back, I'm lucky it wasn't my head that went through the window.

"The cameras weren't too bad," I say on the way home. They were filming from up in the choir loft I heard Ezra tell someone, but they kept away from us afterwards, which you wouldn't expect these days. "I'm surprised they didn't drag you over."

"I think they're boycotting me," Pops says.

"That sucks."

"Yeah, but I had a message from *Nightline* this morning, so it evens out."

"Really? About this?"

He nods. "School violence is still news." His forehead creases. "That's good, I guess."

"You going to do it?"

"Same ground rules," he says. "If they agree, then yeah."

"Man, Cloud will be pissed."

"She's already pissed."

I see parts of the service later on TV, even catch the back of my head a couple times near the edge of the frame. I go ahead and listen this time, having a good cry by myself at the solemn intonations of the preacher. Oddly, it seems more real watching it now than it did when it was happening, which is probably some sort of indictment of my life.

The story is pretty much out by this point; the station has managed to cobble it together from my loudmouth, camera-struck classmates, and the newscaster is telling it now. None of the surviving principals or their families are talking, but the corroboration elsewhere is pretty over-whelming. They'd probably be on shaky ethical grounds naming us, since Kayla and I are minors, which is not to say they won't do it anyway. Later on, I see the front of Decatur on CNN, and hear a sketchy version of the love triangle theory while the camera pans right to show the mound of withering flowers covering our table.

I get a call from Gina around six; I let the machine get it, then pick up when I hear her voice. They've caught wind of it up there, and she's calling for details, though still unaware how directly involved I am. I tell her the whole story, but a quick version, while she gasps and mutters "Omigod!" over and over again. "My dad might be on *Nightline*."

"Damn," she says. "I mean, damn."

I sigh into the phone. "Pretty much."

"*Nightline*. Damn."

I hear Gail on the porch and sense an exit. "Someone's here," I say, "got to go."

Gail has pasta, which she insists I eat with her. And I'm starving, actually, though I don't realize it til I start eating, and then I wolf it down. "How can I eat?" I moan, even as I'm forking up another mouthful. "I am so lame."

"What has that got to do with anything?" she wants to know. "You're hungry; eat."

She checks the dressing on my wound, nods approvingly, like she'd know good doctoring from bad, and we settle in watching old movies on the classics station, one with Ingrid Bergman, and then some really old screwball comedy with two famous leads I should know but don't. Pops comes over late, and the three of us watch him on *Nightline*, trading thoughts with Ted about gun control, youth violence and the like, while neatly dodging Ted's queries into the particulars of this latest incident. Nother is mentioned–his name is out there, being the victim. Crosscut's demise is recounted as well, the burden of this double loss to their family duly noted. There are the usual concluding bromides to healing, closure, moving on, and then it is over, leaving me to marvel that this chunk of my life has gone out to the whole world.

I look over at Pops. "The station will be sucking up by morning."

"Whatever," he says, getting up to go.

Gail watches him leave, then goes to lock the door behind him. "Television completely baffles me."

I click off the set. "You expect too much, Mom," I tell her.

"That's probably it," she agrees, putting out the kitchen light and following me down the hall. "I do that."

Gail wakes me at nine the next morning, I guess simply because she's leaving, as there is no other logical reason. School has already started, so she must assume I'm not going, and there's nowhere else I'd need to be this early. "I have meetings all day," she says from the foot of the bed. "Sorry."

"I didn't expect you'd be here," I tell her.

She studies me thoughtfully. "What are your plans for today?"

"I'm not sure yet. Maybe something with Ruth."

"But you're not going to school?"

I shake my head.

She bites her lower lip, then says, "O.K."

"I'll be fine," I assure her.

"O.K.," she says again. "I'll take your word for it. Call if you need anything." She moves up the side of the bed and bends to give me an awkward hug. "And take your meds, please. You need to finish all of those antibiotics."

"Got it."

"And don't stay in bed all day."

"I'm up as soon as you leave," I promise.

I drop Pops on campus and get to the Martin's by noon. Ruth is in the kitchen, transferring food into Tupperware, foil, plastic wrap. Some of the bowls and pans are already washed, and beside each, stuck to the counter where they are air-drying, is a post-it bearing a name and whatever food the container had held. A dozen more have already been wiped dry and are stacked on the table, with identical notes stuck inside. I take up a towel and clear the counter while she finishes rinsing, and before long all the cookware is stacked and labeled.

"I'll write some," I say.

"That's O.K.," she says. "Sara's coming to help, and they wouldn't know you anyway."

"I'll just sign, 'The Martins.' How about that?"

"All right then, thanks." She splits a stack of note cards and we have at it. "You don't need to go crazy," she says. "Just 'thanks for the whatever in our time of sorrow.'"

I hold up the card I've just finished. "'Thank you for your kindness during this difficult time. Your generosity is appreciated more than you can ever know. The children, especially, enjoyed the lemon bars. With sincere thanks and affection, The Martins.'"

"Perfect," she says. "Leave that one out." Sara arrives shortly and we knock out the whole bunch by two o'clock. "I figure we drop a few off at a time," Ruth says. "If everyone takes a couple every time they go out, it'll eventually get done."

Sara nods. "At least the hard part's finished." She drops the last small envelope into an upturned bundt pan. "I figured that'd take all week."

"Me too," Ruth says. She sits back in her chair and lets out a long breath. "I just want all this done, so I can get back in my routine. Just have it normal again."

Sara is bobbing her head absently, tapping the side of the cake pan. "So, how you doing?" she asks me.

"Still numb," I say truthfully. "And I might just ride it for a while. 'Normal' seems like a pipedream."

"We might take the ashes out, if you want to come," Ruth tells her sister. She looks at me. "We're still doing that, right?"

"Yeah, let's." I turn to Sara. "You don't have to, though."

"I think I'll pass," she says. "Maybe sit with Mom for a while." She stares off, and does this whole body shiver. "Sorry."

"Wear boots," I advise when Ruth goes to change.

"You're still coming Sundays, right?" Sara asks.

"Yeah, I was planning to, if that's O.K."

"Definitely O.K.," she says. She locks her eyes on mine. "We want you to keep coming around, you know that, right? I mean, I hope you know that, but if not, I'm telling you now."

I smile and stare at the table. "Thanks."

"You better fucking come over," Ruth echoes, clumping back into the kitchen and placing the urn on the table.

"Lady Sunshine," Sara says.

I swallow the last of my Coke and carry the glass to the sink. "Ready?"

"Let's do it," she says.

I hug Sara and we're off. We cut through the yard and into the trees. Ruth has the urn towel-wrapped in Nother's backpack, which she insists on carrying. We follow the thin path just inside the tree line to the bridge, then turn into the deep woods past Lazy Ass Creek. "Do you know where we're going?" I ask when we stop for a water break.

"Nope. I haven't been in the woods in ten years, I'll bet." She hands me the water. "He practically lived in here til you showed up, always trying to drag me along, too. I wanted to feel sorry for you, but I was too glad it wasn't me."

"Well, this place we're going is pretty outrageous," I tell her as we start off again. "It was his favorite spot." I wasn't even sure at first that I could find it, but all of a sudden I've got, like, radar. Just before we reach the clearing the sun breaks through overhead, so that when we step from the thick trees, the opening is dappled in this golden, filtered light, just like the first time I walked into it.

"Whoa," Ruth says, gazing up at the fingers of light streaming down. "Nature Club." She doffs the backpack in the middle of the clearing and we just stand there for a minute taking it in. "This is perfect," she says.

"This is where he spread Crosscut's ashes, too" I tell her. "I can't believe I just now thought of that."

"Even better," she says.

"So, um, should we?" This could get kind of weird, I'm starting to think now that we're here, and I'm glad it's Ruth that's with me.

She reaches into the pack, but instead of the urn she lifts out a bottle of wine. "I was thinking maybe a toast, first."

"That's why you wouldn't let me carry it." I run to the platform and drag down one of the blankets, and we spread it in the middle of the clearing and sit. Ruth fills plastic cups and we toast Nother in turn, happily, sadly, lovingly. We cry telling each other stories, but the crying just seems part of it and we don't really mind. I tell her of watching him spread their father's remains, which reminds us why we've come. We begin strolling around the clearing, tossing the gritty powder into the air, watching it drift through the slanting bars of light. A shadow passes, then, a moment later, another, and then I hear a familiar, nasally screech.

Ruthie jolts her head upward. "What the hell was that?"

"Oh God, come here." I grab her arm and pull her to the platform, pointing out the footholds so she can climb up. I follow and direct her to the far side, where I point into the opening across the river and instruct, "Watch."

It takes a few minutes, but finally the pair lands, lazily circling the open field, their massive wings spread wide. They are facing us as they hop to a landing, almost like they know we're here watching. "What in the world...." She goes silent, awestruck.

"Ivory-billed woodpecker," I say. "Long considered extinct. Rediscovered by your brother last summer."

Her mouth opens and closes several times. "I totally believe it," she says finally. "And then he made you promise not to tell."

"Exactly."

"And you weren't even going to tell me now, were you?"

"Ruthie, I swear, I totally spaced it til that one shrieked. I swear it. I mean, I wanted to tell *so* bad, but today, with the ashes and stuff, I didn't even think of it." We stare across at the birds. I point to a clump of rotting, old growth stumps and explain that the ivorybill's preferred food source is found there, some type of grub, and how logging has hastened the species demise. "I sound just like him."

"Yep," she says. She turns slowly to face me. "So, you might as well swear me, too."

"Yeah, you can't tell," I say, not knowing til just this second that I would be making such a demand. I sound like I'm ten.

When the birds fly off we climb down. Ruth has this idea that we should cross over there and spread the remaining ashes in the stumps, that maybe, somehow, the birds will take in bits of this, of him, and Nother, in a manner of speaking, can rise from his own ashes. Which is ridiculous, of course, though I agree to it immediately, and even wish I'd thought it up myself. We find a dead tree bent over the river slightly farther downstream and edge across on our butts, having to ford the last bit of shoal on foot to reach the far bank. We spread the ashes like fairy dust, sifting it with our fingertips into the honeycombed bark, so that the birds' banquet now looks powdered with confectioners' sugar. We wipe our hands with the towel the urn was wrapped in, then sit on the sturdiest of the limbs and finish the wine, without tears this time, but rather to fortify ourselves for the hike out. I take a final look around as I drain my glass, knowing I'll not be back here again.

Gail rouses me early on Wednesday, in time for school, I note, but again I decline to go. She frowns down the length of the bed at me, a look of concern tinted with mild annoyance. "Teri, I really think–"

"Mom, don't, O.K.?" I rub at one eye, loosening some grunge. "We're doing so good lately."

She stares down on me for a long minute. "Tomorrow then," she declares. "For sure."

"We'll see."

"Teri," she says preemptively.

"O.K. I will make every attempt to go tomorrow, I swear."

She knows there's not much she can do, that this will have to suffice. "Do you need anything?" she asks by way of surrender. "I can't stay."

"No. Thanks."

"What will you do?"

"I have no idea," I tell her, firmly though, like I've planned it this way.

"O.K., I'm going." She steps up to give me a hug, unable to resist adding, "I still think you'd be better off in school."

And she's right, probably. The distractions alone would be enough to justify the effort, and I'm sure the day would pass faster. I'm starting to feel edgy already; by ten I'll want out of my skin. I take a long shower, wash my hair, put on my softest clothes, which helps a little, briefly. I make tea and carry it outside, where it is cool and quiet and still. The street is empty, the sky overly bright with a wispy white layer of haze that bothers my eyes. I go inside and put on Crosscut's CD, leaving the door open when I return to the porch. The music is soothing to me, which I can't figure, exactly. It calls up everything I've lost, after all, but somehow it's O.K., calming even. I stay for a long time, glad at first, for the solitude, the time to myself, the lack of weather to disrupt my thoughts, the throaty blues. But slowly my agitation returns; the whiteness of the clouds becomes blinding and I squeeze my knees to my chest, rocking as if in pain, which, eventually, I decide I am.

I go inside, lock the door, lie flat on the floor with the remote. I flick on the television, muted, just for a place to rest my eyes. On the screen a reporter squints into the camera from in front of a church, speaking in what surely must be a somber tone as a flower draped coffin is being hunkered down the front steps. This is local, I realize, and quickly silence the music and un-mute the TV. I understand, suddenly, what I am seeing, and my stomach clenches. It is as if I've been kicked, and were I not already on the floor, I would surely have crumpled here. It is Brian in that shimmering box; the psycho, the killer, receiving the same righteous send-off as his victim, and equal attention. My thoughts are so scrambled I cannot even make out the words. Beyond the newsman's shoulder are mourners in black, some sobbing, others holding them in support. *What kind of world is this?* my brain screams. *Why is this news? He murdered the best person I've ever known; why are tears being shed for him? How dare they?!*

I flick off the TV; the silence is deafening but I do not restore the music; even Crosscut cannot soothe this ache. I stare at the ceiling, eyes blurred with tears, wanting to go crazy, hoping to die. The worst thing that's ever happened to me is five days gone; how can I feel worse now? How is that possible? By rights, I should be immune. I've watched the person I loved most on earth killed before my very eyes, seen him laid out in a suit of clothes he'd *only* be caught dead in, then spread his powdery remains in a place I will never go again. How have I managed to endure all that, only to be subjected to this anguish now, rendered fetal on the floor, squeezing as if to force the last bit of breath from my lungs, sobbing uncontrollably. When does it end?

I awaken from my tearful slumber considerably later, to loud knocking at the door, and Sandy calling my name through the small glass window. I sit up crookedly, wipe my mouth on my arm, holler for her to come in.

"It's locked," she calls back, jiggling the knob.

I lurch to my feet and stumble over to let her in. "Sorry," I say, sweeping my hair from my face. I must look a fright from her expression. "Be right back." I run to the bathroom and wash my face, rubbing briskly with a towel to generate some color. There's still a rug pattern on my cheek when I go back out. "Rough morning," I say.

Sandy arches her eyebrows. "I brought lunch," she says, holding up a bag from the sub place. We sit down at the table and I tell her of my morning. "And I thought calculus sucked today," she says when I finish.

I get up for Cokes and ice. "The thing is, there was a minute there where I really, honestly thought I wasn't going to make it; I thought I was going to totally flip out, or just, like, die. I'm serious." I set a glass and can before her. "And then, when I realized I wouldn't, I couldn't decide if that wasn't worse."

"Don't talk like that," she says, pausing to coax a tomato slice from her bread. "It scares me. I mean, I can't pretend to know what you're going through, but I know it gets easier. It just takes time."

"I think I know that, too. Hopefully, it was just a bad moment." I shake my head. "Gail told me I should go to school. I fucking hate it when she's right."

"You ain't missing a thing," she assures me. "Oh, except did you hear about that in Minnesota?"

I carry our dishes to the sink. "What?"

"Some kid shot three people at a school up there."

I turn and lean against the counter. "Killed them?"

Sandy nods. "It's all over the news now. You must have just missed it."

"Good." I let out a long breath. "I don't want to watch it, O.K.? I can't deal."

"Me either. That's partly why I left school. Want to get coffee?"

We sit outside at The Chickory so as not to have to hear the TVs, both of which are locked on CNN and full of more sobbing students, frantic parents, and really serious cops. "I don't know," I say after we've been sitting for a while in silence, "maybe catatonic is the way to go, 'cause when I start thinking about this stuff, I start going crazy."

"Whatever works," Sandy says. "I don't know about long term, though."

"Long term," I repeat softly. "There's a concept."

There are messages from Pops when I get home; all these dead bodies strewn along the Mississippi are proving to be a gold mine for him. He says to watch *ABC News* tonight, that he's probably getting forty seconds, and then later he's back on *Nightline* with his buddy Ted. Which is pretty amazing to be leaving in a thirty second message, at least I think. Then he calls back to say he's

going to be on one of the Fox news shows, trading
thoughts with one of those loudmouths for a whole segment. That's around seven, he thinks, but I should check.
By now I'm thinking this next one must be *60 Minutes*,
but actually he's called apologizing for not seeing me
today, and to say he doesn't mean for all this to get
between us, especially now, and promises it won't, but
today just got out of hand in a hurry, and if it's not late
he'll stop by when he gets home. Which is pretty amazing
for him to think of, let alone bother to call.

I watch it all, and thankfully he does fine; he's not even
on the *News* long enough to screw up, and at Fox he
pretty much agrees with one of the other panelists who
dominates the segment. He does get to plug his book,
though, which I'm figuring should seal the deal if he hasn't
signed already. My father comes across as a really decent,
down to earth guy on TV, the type any publisher would
want in their stable, especially when he's already getting
this kind of airtime.

Gail blows in about nine, back on her old schedule, it
seems, "I heard," she answers when I give her the rundown. "Everyone I saw on campus is talking about it." But
this comes without the edge she's had in the past, more
like it's some harmless absurdity now, or a freakish bit of
weather, than a stone in her shoe. She walks in from the
kitchen with a carton of yogurt. "Did you tape it?"

"Shit! I never even thought of it. I'm sorry." Though
even if I had thought of it I probably wouldn't have, since it
would never have occurred to me that she'd want to see it.

"No big deal," she says.

She settles at the table to finish up a few things, and I
do French on the sofa until *Nightline* comes on. Neither of
us mentions waiting for it, but we both are. Pops makes a

nice showing here, too, though again I wonder where they're filming. He and Ted have a nice rapport, and unlike most of the other shows, Ted actually lets his guests finish their thoughts. He's looking for links this night, common threads in this not infrequent subset of youth violence, and he asks Pops now whether it's even useful to look for recurring patterns. My father nods as Ted coughs up this mouthful, his right hand pinned to his ear where he's being fed the question.

"Where is he?" I wonder aloud. "That backdrop looks like someone's basement."

"That's the campus studio," Gail says. "It's in the basement of the Language Arts Building, actually."

Onscreen, Pops says, "Well, Ted, I think, unfortunately, you'd be able to find whatever you went looking for. The thing to keep in mind regarding gun violence is that the very nature of the act tends to suggest a commonality that might, in fact, be limited *except* for the nature of the crime itself. I think what we need to be looking at here is the breakdown of the social contract. In a healthy society, we allow ourselves certain assumptions regarding acceptable behavior, an unspoken agreement, if you will. What these types of acts serve to evidence is the breakdown of these basic tenets, in these examples, among the youngest segment of society. What we need to establish is *why*, exactly, these standards are being violated, or simply ignored."

"So, you wouldn't specifically target this as a 'gun problem' then?" Ted suggests.

"Not at all," Pops answers. "Or at least not exclusively. There are countless ways to inflict similar damage. Other types of weapons, alcohol, drugs, drunk driving. The common thread here, perhaps the pertinent similarity, is the youthful nature of the perps, and their dissociation from society. More to the point: What is it that allows these young people to view their actions as acceptable, or at the very least, logical? I think an answer to that difficult, and much more complex, question will go a lot farther toward curbing this type of carnage than merely focusing on access to firearms."

I look at Mom and raise my eyebrows. "Dad just plugged his book, I think."

"Did he have to use 'evidence' as a verb?"

"Happens."

Ted seems pleased, though, and the exchange continues evenhandedly for several more minutes; he doesn't even upbraid Pops for failing to trash the gun lobby—which has released its usual assortment of inane observations—and calls him 'Professor' as they go to commercial.

"Now, see, did anything get said there?" Gail asks. "I mean, wouldn't the average person be able to figure all of that out for herself? Or just know it already?"

"I think you're missing the point."

She sighs. "You should go to bed, since you're going to school tomorrow."

"I took a nap," I inform her, but go anyway when I'm sure Pops is done. Who knows how tomorrow will go.

Thursday is much better, but it would almost have to be. I can tell people are watching me, and I even hear some of the whispering in the halls as I pass, but everyone is exceptionally nice to my face, especially the teachers, who all make a point to address me privately during class, and let me know they're available if I need them. Classmates I've hardly spoken to offer support and condolences, call it a tragedy, tell me how brave I am, that they couldn't do it. The Law sends for me mid-morning to offer more of the same, making all of the resources at her disposal available to me. We chat then–she insists–which isn't so bad, really, until she notes in passing that it's been one week, to the hour, since the "tragedy," this to point out how well I'm doing. My eyes get glassy and immediately she apologizes for this blunder, circling her enormous desk at lightning speed to embrace me; she didn't mean to cause me additional suffering, she only meant.... It's all right, I tell her haltingly, really. These things happen. I'll be fine. She smiles weakly, says she'll make tea(!), even produces fancy cookies from a desk drawer–her private stash, she calls it, and I compose myself while she chatters on, our cups steaming between us.

"Outrageous," Sandy says when I tell her. "Tea with The Law." We're outside at the table, cutting class, technically, but there's not much going on inside anyway. Decatur is still in recovery mode, meaning every class dissolves into a healing session, each more ridiculous than the last, especially if I'm in it. There are students all over the lawn–those that haven't already left, sprawled casually, or cross-legged in tight circles, enjoying the spring sunshine and this unexpected reprieve. "What kind of cookies?" she asks.

"Guess."

"Milanos."

"Amazing," I say.

Friday is more of the same–a six hour study hall. Kayla has been out all week, I'm told, the hot rumor going into the weekend is that she won't even *be* back, at least not the rest of this year. "Well, shit," I tell Sandy, "it's not like she'll miss anything, at this rate."

"I'm not complaining," she says, turning her face up to the sun.

"About her not being here, or screwing off?"

"Pick." She moans luxuriously and blinks open her eyes. "Hey, I saw your dad on TV last night."

"Kind of hard not to, anymore." The story from Minnesota gets weirder by the day, and the cable shows are eating it up. Pops was on CNBC last night, which I didn't even know we got; I'm not sure I even knew it existed til Pops showed up there riffing on the risks inherent in an open society. He mentioned the Old West at one point, which is when he lost me.

Sandy insists I go out for pizza Friday night, so I do, just to keep her from worrying, and because it will get her off my back for the rest of the weekend. We hang for a while at the pizza place, watching the guys act like idiots and the girls not eat, which is amusing I guess, but I still get the feeling that my presence is a downer, and I start to wonder how many of them might disapprove of my even being out again so soon. It's one thing to show up at school, I'm supposed to be there, but out on the weekend might be a little much at this point. Plus, I keep thinking how much better it would be if Nother was here, which rips me wide open. I'm back home by ten; we pull in right behind my father, and the three of us stand chatting outside for a while before Sandy heads off. Pops was at school working on an article for the Sunday paper, and he looks kind of relieved to know I haven't been sitting home alone all evening. We make plans to have dinner tomorrow, since I have some reading to do in the afternoon and he has book things to take care of, and the article to finish.

Grades come out again next week, I just found out. I mean, I knew, but I spaced it. I'm pretty sure I missed an assignment or two this last week, maybe even a test, but no one's said anything, so I haven't either, and if I end up getting sympathy credit this time I'm just going to take it and shut up. I've decided I'm going to really try to re-focus this last quarter and make straight A's; it'll help when I start applying next fall, but more immediately it'll help take my mind off everything else. And now that I'm caught up in French, it's just Chemistry that might be a problem, especially if the two chapters I plod through Saturday are any indication.

I'm snoozing on the couch, in fact, lab workbook over my face, when Pops walks over to go eat. He apologizes the whole way to Bodean's for being away so much, even though I insist it's O.K. I don't want to be treated like glass, I assure him, or like I might collapse any second. He seems relieved, tells me his agent insists they strike while the iron is hot, and not let this opportunity slip by.

"Opportunity!" I bark. "That's what she's calling this?"

"Well, she means for me," he says, because it's in his nature to put the best light on things. "She doesn't mean it's good." He takes a hand off the wheel and turns it palm up.

"Lemons. Lemonade," I say.

"More or less," he concedes. "Law of Unintended Consequences."

"Which is?"

"Pretty much what it sounds like; you never know how things are going to turn out. One person's misfortune is another's big break. The lead actress has a sore throat one night, and the stand-in becomes a star. Or the quarterback. The Russians boycott the Olympics, and we get Mary Lou Retton on the Wheaties box. The news director in Houston is a blues fan, Cloud has a new job."

"She does?" I ask, snapping my head left to look at him. "I mean, is that true?"

"Yeah, just this week. I've been meaning to tell you that."

"Is that O.K.?"

"It's great for her. It's a top ten market."

"But her moving?" I say.

"She can't do it from here," Pops says.

I roll my eyes and stare out the window.

"We were just friends," he says. "It's not a big deal."

"Then why was she so mad?"

Pops sighs. "Whatever."

We order up monster burgers and he tells me they're ready to sign the book deal, maybe Monday. The publisher wants another chapter, though, on school violence; specifically, the spate of deadly shootings the past several years. Which Pops is uneasy about, since it doesn't really fit in all that well with the way the rest of the book is set up. Which is true, but when he tries to point that out they either don't see it or, more likely, don't care. He knows it's just a marketing scheme; that they're going to promote the whole book on just this one tacked-on chapter, the way record companies used to with a hit single. And to my father's credit, he's wary of going this route, but it doesn't sound like he'll be able to do much about it, either.

"The whole problem I'm having is that it *almost* fits," he tells me. He takes a big bite and chews slowly. "I mean, the book is about deteriorating behavior, and, well, that's a pretty solid example right there."

I nod.

"The thing is, it's likely to take over the rest of the book, which then becomes about youth gun violence only, and no one pays attention to the rest of it."

"Couldn't you sort of lead up to that?" I ask. "Maybe make it the last chapter, sort of like, here's what could happen at the logical extreme."

He takes a swig of tea and purses his lips. "That could maybe work," he says. "That's kind of what I've been doing most of the afternoon–trying to figure a way to give them what they want without collapsing everything else around it. And it does have to come at the end, you're right about that. I just don't want that to seem inevitable, like, all types of rudeness lead to murder. Because then people will conclude, 'Well, if no one got hurt....' Which totally misses the point. You see the problem?"

"And all without blowing the deal."

"Exactly."

"Think you can do it?"

"Oh yeah," he says. "But I want it to be something I can live with, too."

"Which must have them totally confused."

"They don't seem overly familiar with the concept," he concurs.

I tell him about being back at school. He asks about Kayla and I tell him she hasn't been back, nor have I seen her, or know where she is, nor do I care. "If that sounds harsh, oh well," I tell him. "I was almost going to say, 'I'm sorry,' but I'm not." I've finished eating and slide my plate back. "Right now I hate her, and I don't care what happens to her."

Pops starts to say something, then holds off. He gets out a twenty and sets it on the check. "That's understandable," he say. "For now, anyway."

"Now, always, forever."

Pops slides out of the booth, having decided further commentary would be futile. "Ready?"

His article turns out pretty decent and I read it to Gail the next morning. As usual, he's hit all the salient points, often with a clever turn of phrase, while managing not to say anything too controversial, or needlessly ruffle any feathers. "Filler," my mother pronounces it. "I'm sorry if that's mean, but it is. Though apparently there's a place for that, and your father's managed to settle into it quite nicely." She blows on her coffee and sips. "So, good for him."

"He does seem to have hit his stride."

She nods. "They're making his position tenure track," she says. "Did he tell you that? At the rate he's going, he'll get it next year, then he's set."

"How do you know that?"

"Annie. They're ready to make him king." She says all this very evenly, so it's impossible to discern exactly how she's taking it.

"Well, that's nice, right? The security and all."

"I suppose," she says. "I mean, of course it is. And based on the visibility he's gotten the college, they probably owe him that."

I stare across the table at her. "Which is not necessarily the same as earning it," I note.

"You said it, I didn't."

"You sort of did."

She grins slightly. "Well, he seems to like it here. And they could certainly do a lot worse."

"Law of Unintended Consequences."

She looks up from the paper. "Big time."

I follow Sara to the Martins after work, just to say hello. I want to get in the habit of going by regularly, so it doesn't get all weird. I stay half an hour, talking with Ruth in the kitchen. When Sara goes across the hall to see her mom I stick my head in too. Ruth asks me to stay for dinner but I beg off; I need to get home, I tell her, my parents are still kind of jumpy, which is just plausible enough, I guess.

They invite me to Esther's on Wednesday; Deacon turns eleven and most of them will be stopping by for cake. I promise to come, so Ruth says she'll wait here for me, and shoots me this little passive-aggressive grin, which is nice somehow, coming from her.

I sleepwalk through the next two weeks, surfacing but occasionally from my self-imposed torpor. I do go to Esther's for Deacon's party, where Daniel tells me that he's been given Nother's favorite guitar, which is hanging from his shoulder now, by the strap Nother made for him last fall. I begin to sense how things move on in this family, emerging out of the past, like flowers blooming in rich earth. He plays for me, picking one of the same tunes I watched Crosscut teach him that night last fall. He's good, even I can see this, will probably be better than Nother soon, if he keeps at it, which seems assured given his lineage. It's sad thinking of the other two gone, missing this celebration, and Daniel's progress, but at the same time they don't really seem gone at all, and I begin to understand, finally, the dry-eyed nature of this family.

I get the same sense in The Sawmill, that somehow Crosscut, and even Nother, remain, have seeped into the walls like turpentine, their presence almost visceral. And yet, this feels more soothing than haunting, and it is here that I allow my defenses to rest.

Otherwise I am on autopilot. I sit in class scribbling notes, unaware of all else, and move through the halls in a daze, though no one, save Sandy, bothers to look close enough or long enough to notice. The Law pulls me aside twice to see how I'm doing, and I con her just as easily. Even she can't see I'm just going through the motions, mouthing what I know she needs to hear to release me back into the swarm. Joley is oblivious; she talks to hear herself talk. As long as I nod occasionally, and utter the random, "Oh," or "Really," she'll continue to prattle. I hear Kayla's name time to time, but don't rise to the bait. She remains absent, a spectral presence, the continued source of rumor. I even think, fleetingly, that the days are getting easier, but in truth they just get less. Less stimulus, less response, less feeling. I am adjusting by subtraction, though no one seems to notice.

Grades come out and I make all A's, at least one of which is a gift, but that's fine. My parents are pleased, of course, and take it as a sign of my continuing recovery, conveniently ignoring the fact that the quarter was all but over when Nother was killed. There are no dinners this time; I don't feel much like celebrating any aspect of this life just now. When Gail hugs me and prompts, "Keep it up," I think ahead to June, and wonder how I'll make it to then.

It's not the best way to go, I realize; Sandy is right on that count. It's like being dead myself, or dying, but right now it's the only way. Otherwise I just think of him, and miss him horribly, and wonder why it has to be like this. I feel sorry for myself, angry at the world, hatred for Kayla. My evenings are black holes, knowing he will not come. Weekends mean nothing, but for the few hours with Sara, and now Ezra, at the 'Mill. My father keeps tabs, but I can fool him too. He wants me to be all right, so when I say I am he backs off, for both our sakes, and I sink further into myself. I can't blame him; he's trusting me to be honest with him and I'm not, so when he gives me the space my answers dictate, and I feel like I'm adrift at sea, whose fault is it but mine? Gail is in and out at all hours, working even when she's here, though what, exactly, she is up to, and why she continues at this frenetic pace is beyond me. She asks after me regularly, more than before, to be sure–How am I doing? Is there anything I need? Do I want to talk about anything?–but her attention seems cursory, like a waitress with too many tables. She has a lot on her mind, too. Her life is as much of a mess as my own right now, but at least she's trying to straighten hers out. I should follow her lead, actually, and begin trying to work through this, but I don't. At the very least I shouldn't hold it against her, and resent her for it, but I do.

"I think you just need to start letting people back in," Sandy tells me one day as we circle the mall parking lot in Jackson. "I mean, not everyone's as big a pain in the ass as me, and they're not going to keep bugging you like I do. Couldn't you at least meet us halfway?"

"You're not a pain in the ass," I tell her.

"This is pretty rude."

Which, maybe it is, seeing as how she's dragged me along to help her look for a prom dress. But she's the only one my age I can stand to be around for more than ten minutes, and it's the least I can do considering how much of my shit she's had to put up with. Chosen to put up with, actually, which is more amazing. And I don't mind coming, really, it's a nice distraction, and she's excited to be doing it. "Let's try there," I say, pointing toward one of the anchor department stores. She nods and we take another lap looking for a good spot. "It's easier my way," I say.

She sighs. "If you say so. But think about it; who are the only people you like seeing now? His family, right? And who are the only people you *really* talk to? Them." She pulls into a slot and looks across the seat at me. "That's not just coincidence."

"It's different with them."

"No, *you're* different with them," she says. "And how do you even know that, if you don't give the rest of us a chance? I mean, you could open up a little."

"I don't know," I say skeptically.

She grabs my arm and shakes it, whining like a four year old. "C'mon, Teri. Pleeeease! For meeee...."

I stare at her til she stops. She's the only one left who'd try this kidding with me. "Maybe. For you. A little." We get out and start for the store. "But I'm absolutely not doing the prom. We're clear on that, right? You've told Joley?" I probably wouldn't be going even if Nother was still alive, but I don't let myself think about it long enough to decide for sure.

"I told her," she says. "But I'm not making any promises."

I sigh. "Could you have parked any farther away?"

I make a modest effort the following week, but it's only marginally better. With the people I don't know well, it's awkward, and I can't help feeling I still make a lot of them uncomfortable. Joley only wants to talk about the prom, so she's easy once I convince her I'm serious about not going. Pops and I are back to normal, though. The difference with us now is how *he's* changed. The book deal goes through, so right now he's really distracted with trying to wedge in that extra chapter, but otherwise we've struck a nice balance. He does try a little too hard sometimes, but I can't really hold that against him.

On the plus side, my grades should kick ass this quarter, even though I do cut a lot with Sandy.

I'm flashing through the channels one Sunday morning when I see Pops in a roundtable discussion on the local station. Gail looks up from the table when she hears his voice. "I thought he was *persona non grata* over there," she says, then adds, a bit testily, "Must have made up with what's her name."

"She left," I tell her. "Took a job in Houston."

"Really?" she says. She stares at the program, which I've muted. "Kind of a mixed blessing," she notes before going back to her work.

"What is it you're doing there, Mom? I mean, it's eleven o'clock on Sunday morning. How come you have so much work, and why do you even care, if you're leaving?"

She sighs and sets down her pen. "Actually, this is what I'm supposed to be doing at the office, but I've been spending so much time with Annie that I end up having to drag it home just to stay caught up."

"Shouldn't she be working with someone else by now, for like, after you're gone?"

"Actually, I'm helping her with Kayla. It's got nothing to do with the college."

"*You're* helping *Kayla?*" I demand. I punch off the set and stand up. "You're over *there* helping *her,* instead of *here* with *me*?! Is that what you're trying to tell me?"

"Those two are a mess," she says. "It is about the most dysfunctional relationship I've ever seen. Kayla, especially, has her problems, and now, because of this shooting, she's in therapy half the day, and blasted on tranquilizers the rest of the time. Annie is at her wit's end, and she asked if I could work with the two of them in the evening to see if that might help. So I said yes, for her. Because she's my friend."

"And I'm your daughter," I remind her. "And while you're over there, helping the person responsible for my misery, I'm sitting here by myself trying not to lose it. Does that picture make any sense to you at all?"

"I think you're overreacting, Dear."

"I don't believe you, Mom! I mean, what about ME?!"

"What about you?" she asks back. "You've been through a very traumatic event. Your father and I have done all we can to see you through it. WE'VE DONE ALL YOU'VE LET US. We've tried to get you to talk, to open up to us. But you've resisted; what chance do I have when you've even stone-walled your father? So we've given you your space. That works for some people, and we thought that might be best with you. You've certainly given us reason to think so. Though it sounds now like that's not the case. But of course, there's no way we could have known that, is there? And hovering around while you act like a houseplant didn't seem like something either of us would care for."

I sigh emphatically. Houseplant! "I knew it wouldn't last," I say, my eyes blurry with tears. "All that concern, you being around for a week, the crab cakes, even. Now it's back to business as usual."

"That's what we thought you wanted. How were we to know, Teri?"

I'm half-crying now, gulping air, wiping my nose on my wrist.

"You know what I really thought?" she says, not at all meaning for me to guess. "I thought you were heroic. That whole night in the hospital while I watched you sleep, all I could think was how awful it must have been for you."

"It was."

"And then, over the next days, I watched you hold up so beautifully. I knew you were dying inside, that you must be. But you kept it together. You turned outward for those days, comforting us." Her lips press into a thin line. "It was marvelous to see. I was so proud of you. And then you retreated again, and we let you. You seemed to know what you wanted, you acted like–"

"You?" I accuse.

Her face tightens. "I don't know if I could have done that," she says after a minute. "I was amazed. You seemed all grown up." She shrugs. "There didn't seem to be anything more for us to do."

"So you went over there?" I say, unable to let this pass. "And that seemed all right to you?"

"Teri, it wasn't something I did to hurt you. That girl is very sick. Her mother is one of my oldest friends. Why are you drawing lines like this?"

"I can't help it," I tell her. "And I can't understand how you can be so clinical. You know what she did. And you know what it's done to me. Didn't you think of that at all, of what it would do to me? Do you have any idea how betrayed I feel right now? Do you?" I stare at her hard, feeling the pain etched into my face, wanting her to see it, demanding she look. "How could you?"

"Teri, what you have to under–" But that's all I hear before my door slams shut on her. There's nothing she could say that would appease me now, no explanation would suffice. I am furious, hurt, humiliated; I feel like I've just been dumped. I don't even want explanations; anything she'd say would only stoke my rage. I sit fuming at her callousness, mystified at how she could even entertain the notion that this was all right. I picture her at their house, cajoling them across the coffee table, coaxing that odd pair to health, followed by warm hugs at the door, and fulsome expressions of gratitude for her selfless humanity. I feel stabbed imagining this, my stomach suddenly flush with a queasy heat. I get up and pace; stalk, actually, like a big cat at the zoo, a really pissed cat in a too small cage. At noon I throw on jeans and a flannel shirt and stomp out, moving past her through the door without a word and drive off. I don't say where I'm going, don't even ask to take the car, if she might need it. Let *them* give her a ride, since they're all such good friends now. At The Sawmill I rant to Sara, who makes sad faces but says little other than to suggest my mother's heart is in the right place, which helps not at all. But my ire is to the bar's benefit; when I finish you could eat off the floor, though Sara says she would still be loath to recommend it.

"Don't fight tonight," she requests as I am leaving. "Promise me, O.K.? Stay with your dad if you have to."

"I was thinking I'd go over there, anyway."

"Anything you might say tonight, you can still say tomorrow," she reasons, spreading her arms for a hug. "Taking it back is always a little trickier. Promise?"

I nod into her shoulder, grudgingly.

I leave the car out front and walk directly to Pops' side, where I enter without knocking. "Ah, the car thief," he says through the pencil clenched in his teeth. He glances down to finish typing a line, then removes the pencil and swivels to face me. "You're back."

I flop into the chair across from him and grimace at his amused smile. "I'll stay here a while if you don't mind," I say tersely. "It's been suggested I avoid contact with her tonight."

"Good suggestion," Pops says. "She's out anyway." When I look up he adds, "Took the Volvo. You're not the only one with two sets of keys."

"Where'd she go? No, never mind. I don't care."

"She's having dinner with the Chancellor," he says anyway. "That could have been a real mess if I'd been gone."

I shrug.

"Look, no matter what you think, rudeness is never the correct response to a real or perceived slight. It's one of the shittier aspects of being an adult, but there it is."

"I'd call this more than a perceived slight."

"Still."

I give him this perturbed look, so that he'll know he's not helping. "What did you make?"

"Chicken soup," he says. "I hadn't cooked anything in a while, so I picked up some stuff on the way home. I was hoping you'd join me."

"Sure," I say listlessly. "I'm going to go shower since she's not there." I display my grimy hands. At the door I pause. "You looked good on TV today."

When I walk back over twenty minutes later the computer is off and he has the soup warming on the stove. "Better?" he asks when I walk in, pulling open the oven to slide in some rolls.

"Cleaner." I sit at the table. "Were you working on the book?"

He nods and carries bowls and spoons to the table. "That last chapter wasn't so bad. It was tweaking the others that was a pain." He sets down a pitcher of tea and shakes his head. "Hope it works, anyway."

He serves up the soup and we sit quietly facing each other while it cools. "Did you know she was doing that?" I ask.

"Annie mentioned it."

I stir my soup, feeling the steam on my cheeks. "So, like, am I totally out of line, or what?" I can feel my eyes getting wet, which pisses me off. "Because Dad, I feel so betrayed, I can't even tell you. I'm just...." I can't even finish the thought; I don't know what I'm just....

"It would be hard for me to say," he concedes. "I can

only imagine how you must feel losing Nother like that. And I can see how you might feel the way you do."

"Might? How can I feel any other way?"

He spoons up some soup, taking his time. "Teri, this whole thing was a tragedy. There isn't a part of it that wasn't awful beyond belief. Your mother and I realize that. Annie realizes that. I think by now even Kayla sees it."

"Yeah, well, it's a little late for her."

"It's pretty late in the game for everyone," he says. "Your mother is only trying to make the best of a very bad situation. I know that sounds trite, but when Annie came to her, your mother saw the chance to salvage something out of this mess."

"Yeah, save Kayla instead of her daughter."

"You didn't need saving," he says.

"So why do anything for me, right?"

"She'd already done plenty for you," he says, his voice rising so that I look up from my bowl. "How is it, do you think, that you handled that so well? Where do you think that came from?" We stare at each other, and then he continues. "I'll tell you where, then: It came from sixteen years of being your mother's daughter. From watching her handle one problem or difficulty after the next. Seeing her strength, her resolve." He points at me with his spoon. "You had all that going in, and you didn't even know it. Eat."

I stir my soup. "So I'm supposed to be grateful now that she wants to help the person responsible for me feeling like this. I don't think so."

"You know, your mother doesn't even like Kayla. She didn't like her when you did. She knew she was trouble from the get-go."

"Then why didn't she say something?"

"Would you have listened?"

I shrug.

"Of course you wouldn't have. Just like you won't listen now. It's part of your charm."

I make a face, perhaps even a charming one.

"She trusted you to decide for yourself, and you did figure it out eventually. But it was already too late."

"So it's my fault?"

"It's not any of our faults. It's the fault of some goofball with a gun, thinking he could blast away his problems. Your mother is just trying to help Annie. I doubt she's any happier about it than you are, but she believes it's the right thing to do."

I taste my soup. "You're taking her side, then, is what you're saying?"

"What I'm saying is: *There are no sides.* There's only deciding what's best now, which is something we each need to do for ourselves. And I think if there's a flaw in your logic, it's in thinking that you have the right to decide that for your mother, or anyone, just because you've suffered more."

"Well thank you for at least noticing that."

"We all noticed, Teri, and we're feeling the pain right along with you, whether you believe that or not."

"So why does she get the moral high ground, then? When is it my turn?"

"When you realize it's not a contest." He motions toward my bowl with his spoon, indicating I should eat. "A lot of it will probably clear up then."

When I come in late Wednesday afternoon the house is filled with a wonderful, sweet-spicy aroma. Gail is at the table with her address book out, loading numbers into her cell phone, I think. We've pretty much avoided each other since Sunday, hardly spoken at all, in fact, though the tension seems to have dissipated somewhat. We exchange bland hellos as I cross the tile to look under the lid of the pot bubbling on the stove. "Is Dad here?"

"No," she says without looking up from the number pad. "Why would he be here?"

"Who made this?"

Now she glances up. "I did," she answers, which is a lot less obvious than she makes it sound.

"You don't cook," I remind her.

"I can, though."

"Hmmm, Dad's cooking again, too. Maybe 'cause he's done with his book." I replace the lid. "What's this called, again?"

"Ratatouille," she says. "It needs to cook for a while yet."

I nod and head for my room. "Smells good."

And it tastes good, too, when we sit down later to eat it. Real good, in fact, though I'm less effusive in my compliments than I might be. We don't say much during the meal, it's as if we've both decided it's too tasty to risk one of us having to stalk off halfway through. But when I offer to clean up she stays at the table with her wine while I carry bowls and silverware to the sink. "Put some of that in a container for your father," she says, which is amazingly domestic for her. "You can take it over later."

"Not all of it, though," I reply, partly to make up for skimping on the praise earlier. I keep expecting her to pull out work, or her laptop, all of which is piled nearby, but when I glance back she's just sitting there, turning her wine glass by the stem, lost in thought. "What?" I ask.

"What?" she says back. I turn a soapy palm up, shorthand for: *Why are you still sitting there, and what is it you*

have to say, and why haven't you said it? She lets her
hands rest flat on the table. "I've decided to stay here
another year. I've met with the Chancellor and we're getting the last few details worked out." She lets out a long
breath. "I think it's for the best," she adds, though she
makes it sound like she's been caught at something.

"For whom?" I rinse out the big pot and upend it on
the counter. "Not you."

"Maybe for all of us," she says. "I was thinking it
wouldn't be that big a deal if I was back there, but now I'm
not so sure."

"Mom, don't do this on my account," I say, though I
get this strange sort of rush thinking that's the case; I
mean, it's about time I started to figure in her plans. But
then I get this picture in my head of her bitching all next
year because she "couldn't" go back, in which case I'd be
as miserable as her. "I don't want that hanging over my
head."

"It's not like that," she says. "I've just decided that my
place is here."

"Mom, if you're going to leave anyway, you might as
well go now, while there's still something to go back to."

She sighs heavily and stares at the ceiling. "I've considered that," she says. "You'd prefer it, I suppose. That's
what you want, isn't it?"

"Don't lay all this on me. I haven't said a thing either
way."

"Well say something now. What is it that you want from
me?"

I throw the towel I'm holding onto the counter,
annoyed that she's forced me into this. "What I want is to
know where you were before, the whole rest of my life,
when I could have used your help? Where were you then?

What, do you think now you can cook a few dinners and hang around another year and everything's suddenly O.K., that we're all even again? Meanwhile I get to hear you blame me all next year. Forget that." I slump heavily against the counter and cross my arms. "Don't do me any favors. I mean, why start now?"

My mother looks stricken, but recovers quickly enough, and her eyes again flash defiance. "Actually," she says, her tone stern and deliberate, "I thought it would be O.K. to go because you could take care of yourself. I watched you adjust to the move, and you did fine. There was some carping at first, and that ridiculous stunt with the spray paint."

My jaw drops. "You knew?"

"Of course I knew. You spray paint just like you print. I could dig out some of your old papers and get you arrested."

"But...." I don't even know what I was going to ask. "Does Dad know?"

"Of course not, or you'd have gotten a chapter in his book."

I pick up the towel. "Why haven't you said anything til now?"

"My assumption was always that it was Kayla's idea. It just didn't seem your style. But I wanted to see if you'd develop a taste for it; that happens sometimes. But right off, that fool crashed his car and you seemed to snap out of it. Your grades came up, you started seeing that boy. I figured you'd be fine, even with only your father here, who, by the way, wouldn't have recognized that scrawl if you'd spray painted it on his forehead. And since you never seemed to care if I was around or not...." She shrugs.

It's my turn to roll my eyes, which I do, emphatically.

"Then this happened, and I really started having second thoughts. It just seemed wrong to leave you now. But again, you did so well—at least I thought, that I decided it would still be O.K., especially since you'll be going off yourself in another year, anyway."

"So, go. Don't let me stop you." This comes out perhaps a little more hateful sounding than I'd intended.

"Oh, but you are," she says. "I see now that you're not as far along as I thought."

"Oh, really?" I snort.

"Really," she confirms. "We all realize you've been through a lot, Teri, but that's no guarantee you've learned anything from it. You've still got some growing up to do."

"Fine, stay then." I cannot believe she's reaming me like this, like I signed up for this life. I decide immediately to change tactics; I'm going to pin her down on this, since she's being so high and mighty, and hold her to it. I don't believe for a second she really wants to stay, any more than I want her here now, but if she's going to insist on playing the martyr, she's going to pay the price. I glance over at the clock on the stove. "Too bad it's so late in Baltimore already; you could call and let them know right now."

She rolls her eyes. "That's exactly the type of thing I'm talking about."

"Bad behavior is Dad's department," I remind her. I dry off the big pot and replace it atop the fridge, then wipe the counter and drape the towel over the handle of the oven. I pick up Dad's bowl and turn to her. "And you're not staying here. Who are you kidding? Not for me, anyway."

"Watch," she replies. She has this funny look, though, like she's playing it all back in her head to see how it's come to this.

"You want me to get you the phone before I go?"

She presses her lips together and her forehead tightens.

"I'll take care of it, thank you," she says evenly.

I grab my backpack from the couch. "Right," I sneer on my way out the door.

The atmosphere in our house grows toxic. Though we are hardly speaking, are almost never in the same room, even, and barely acknowledge each other's existence, it is all but intolerable. How we can live this way for another year seems impossible, though what must happen to change it seems just as unlikely. It feels, finally, as if we are equals, and though the situation is far from ideal, I experience my newfound leverage almost tactilely. I vow not to let her off the hook; if she regrets her decision, which I know she must, she will have to come to me with it. For a week we circle each other, like evenly matched fighters, sure of our strengths, yet still wary of the other's. This is what power feels like, I decide, as I begin to understand its allure.

We are at an impasse, a standstill. My mother pretends it is business as usual, that her decision is final and irrevocable. She's ready to just move on, she says, but a little too often to be believed. She has not made the call, I know—she'd announce it, I'm sure—and I catch her taking anxious glances at the calendar. There are still professional courtesies to be considered, after all; if she does hope to get out of here again one day, she can scarcely afford to burn her bridges so recklessly now. There is a certain satisfaction in watching her squirm, though it stops well short of pleasure. Truth be told, I'm somewhat ambivalent about all this, not least because I'd rather she go; it's nothing short of foolish that she's placed her career on the line like this, risking twenty-odd years of accomplishments just to be contrary, to make a stubborn and ill-advised point on my account. I don't want that blood on my hands, but at the same time I cannot bring myself to extend the olive branch. I've waited too long for this, for the hefty bulk of an equal; backsliding is not an option.

My father has not been spared this nonsense; we've both made our cases over there, forcing him to endure our sorry intransigence in measured doses. And, in a commendable show of fairness, he seems equally disgusted with both of us now, which, in some perverse calibration that could only apply to us, serves to reconfirm for me my enhanced stature. Which is not to imply that he's cutting me any slack, quite the opposite. He thinks Gail is being foolish—I've heard them through the wall—though he hasn't directly challenged her motives. Even allowing for her good heartedness, which I assume is the conceit that she's staying on my account, he's suggested that it has become so poisonous on our side now that no benefit is possible in this arrangement any longer, for either of us. And so, Pops says, she might as well go. She's just being stubborn, he says, afraid of what people will think, and I'm just being mean.

"How is it my fault?" I demand one afternoon when he again takes me to task. "I said she should go to begin with, if you recall. She's the one acting like Mother Teresa, like if she doesn't stay I'll go all to pieces. All I did was call her on it."

"And so you feel good about that now? Did you win?"

"No, not really. I feel lousy about it, actually."

"That ought to tell you something," he says.

And so, again, I feel like shit. Our side remains virulent, but now there is not even respite through the wall. He's not mean, but just being around him makes me feel petty and contemptible, and who wants that? The best case scenario becomes his side when he's not there, which eliminates the likelihood of Gail breezing in before I can take evasive action, while still not having to endure his disappointed gaze, though I cannot imagine executing this little *pas de trois* for the next twelve months.

"I think I should ask her," Annie says. "It's my idea, after all, and my kid." They both glance back into the room, at the catatonic child curled fetally in the overstuffed armchair. "It's not the sort of thing you should have to do anyhow. She resents you enough as it is."

"No, I'll speak to her," the other one says." I don't want to bring a third party into our issues at this point, or have her feeling pressured from another adult." She smiles briefly, ruefully. "And she's going to blame me anyhow, so it hardly matters which of us asks."

Annie sighs. "Gail, I'm sorry, but I just don't see any other way."

She nods, pausing with her hand on the knob to give her friend's arm a reassuring squeeze. "I suspect you're right," she says, stepping through the door. "I'll speak to her tonight."

On the ride home her mind drifts evasively from the task at hand. She recalls with odd clarity a professor from her undergrad days, a crotchety old bastard, probably long dead by now, but notorious campus-wide in his day for his severity. He'd taught one of the required upper level courses at an intellectual pitch so high that he'd been forced to recalibrate the grading structure to get anyone enrolled at all. (Every fourth term the course was taught by someone else, resulting in a land rush to the registration table.) But for three terms out of four, 70% was deemed

worthy of A; 60% would get you a B; and merely assimilat-
ing half of what got tossed out earned you a passing grade.
"I'm not the best instructor by a long shot, and I don't
know that I care to be," he'd told them quite bluntly while
passing out the syllabus. "And the scope of this class is far
beyond the capacity of any one pedagogue, anyway. But I
do know a few things, and if you can manage to retain half
of what you hear, you'll have done quite well for yourself."

And she had, improbably, adopted this same inane
logic in the rearing of her only child; perhaps because she
herself had shone under these harsh strictures–she'd
earned every point of her 69, the highest in the class that
term, and uncomplainingly accepted her B, and the mantle
of a rising star. It was this course, in fact, the toughest of
her academic career, which had pointed her irrevocably
into her chosen discipline. So if she was predisposed to an
exaggerated scale of performance regarding her daughter,
at least she'd come by it honestly.

She has always expected–no, demanded–a lot of Teri,
has always held her to standards beyond her years, knowing that even when the girl fell short, inevitably in most
cases, she was still well ahead of the game. And it had
worked, brilliantly, she thinks now, if her daughter's
behavior these past months is any indication. This despite
their most recent go-around, and her husband's constant
machinations to thwart her boot camp brand of love with
leniency and appeasement, to force her always into the
role of bad cop while he got the grateful looks. (She notes
the useful balance to this, of course–she is, after all, a psy-
chologist–but resents him nonetheless.) As regards her
daughter, though, she could not be prouder.

If she is guilty of anything, it is of imposing standards
too harsh, of failing to adjust the curve sufficiently.

But again, Ed has seen to that, and it has often been necessary to redouble her efforts solely to counteract his, all to
keep her daughter's brain from going to mush. It is a tendency of hers to expect too much; others have said so,
Teri herself most recently. And the trouble with this–the
impossible demands, the harsh scrutiny, the toughest
love–is that you can never let on, lest the method be
exposed, and the strategy ruined. So now she must do it
again, make this one last demand of her daughter, to push
her, perhaps, the last little bit into adulthood.

But is she finally asking too much? The girl is sixteen,
after all, and has suffered mightily of late. She chooses to
wait, and spends the remainder of the evening contemplating her options: say nothing and attempt to regain the
uneasy peace, then pass another tedious year enduring the
truce they have brokered; cease with her demands and
content herself with her daughter's growth to this point.
Or, conversely, stay the course through this one last trial,
press this one, ultimate demand, hold the girl's feet to the
fire a final time.

And what if Teri agrees to the visit, impossible though
it seems? What then? Would this not, in fact, free her to
return East as she'd planned til just recently? Her lips draw
together into what is almost a smile. Yes, this could all still
work out.

But immediately she is guilt-stricken, loathes herself for
putting her own concerns before those of her daughter.
And so her course is set: to make the request of her daughter, and to remain here no matter the outcome. She cannot
in good conscience demand a selflessness she is not willing
to match. And so it becomes settled in her mind, and if
nothing else, she will at least have determined where she
stands as a parent.

The week passes glacially; Sandy, I'm certain, is sick of my constant carping, though she lets me rail nonetheless. I decide maybe, possibly, finally, to cut my mother some slack. I can forgive and forget if she can, but she has to start.

"I think that's very wise," Sandy commends.

I begin to think Gail is working along the same lines when I arrive home one afternoon to a semi-cheery message on the machine saying she'll be home around six with takeout from the China Garden. The orange chicken is an obvious peace offering; my favorite for years, but a dish she cannot stand. I wait patiently through the meal, intent on helping if she makes the effort. She finishes before I do and cracks open a fortune cookie. "'Be receptive to new ideas,'" she reads, then places the scrap beside her plate with a frown. I take up the other one and break it open, but it is empty, which somehow seems fitting. We both begin to laugh.

"Have mine," she says, sliding it across the table. "I want to propose one, anyhow."

"I figured something was up."

Her jaw tightens, just perceptibly. "First, I wanted you to know that I'm not working with Annie and Kayla anymore, if that makes a difference."

"I didn't know you still were."

She nods. "There's nothing more *I* can do over there, it's become apparent."

I nod, too, almost curious to know more. Kayla has become the great enigma at Decatur, and any info I could provide would be treated like spun gold. "Well, you tried."

Her lips press together and I wait, knowing there is more to this. Perhaps now she feels cleared to leave on all fronts but ours, and I wonder if she is about to broach the idea of her returning to Baltimore. "I'd like to ask you to do something for me," she says, which is not how I figured this would start.

"If it's about you leaving, Mom—"

"No, it's not that," she cuts in. She pauses and stares across the table til I look up to meet her gaze. "Teri, I'd like you to go see Kayla."

"What?!"

"Teri—"

"Are you out of your mind?" My mouth opens again, but words fail me.

"I don't know if anything else will work." It's like she doesn't even hear me.

"NO!" I scream. "Never. How can you even *ask?*" I want to do something dramatic, sweep everything off the table, perhaps, but it's all Styrofoam and paper, so there'd be no crashing satisfaction to it. I stand abruptly and my chair clatters onto the tile, which helps a little, then stalk from the room. "I don't fucking believe you!"

I move trance-like through the passing days, largely unaware of what is happening around me; the hours slide by, I move rotely through them. Sandy is there, but even we don't speak beyond essentials. I've told her of my mother's request, and she seems to appreciate its effect. My parents I avoid entirely, only venturing from my room when I'm certain they'll not be there. Sara is ill on Sunday, when I might speak to her; I could go see Ruth, I suppose, but it would feel too much like I'd gone there solely to unburden myself, and I don't want that. Ezra is there to let me in at the 'Mill, but I'd feel foolish speaking of any of this to him. He'd listen kindly, I'm sure, but what would he think? My mother and I barely able to inhabit the same town, while he visits his *stepmother* almost daily. Either of us able to end the impasse, but neither willing. Instead, we'll stay in the same house, a condition neither of us wants, one perhaps even ruinous to her, hating our lives and, eventually, each other. He'd find it all insane, I'm sure, and he'd likely be right.

Through all of this I continue to mourn, to suffer the all but unendurable loss that has ripped my soul apart. I think, perhaps, that this has been forgotten in all the side-line drama—the fights with Gail, the mystery that is Kayla, the public luridness of the whole event. But I miss him still, horribly and daily: his benevolent, calming presence most of all; but the soft timbre of his voice, too; and his arms around me. There is a yearning now constant within me, as much a part of my being as the intake of breath, so that to even speak of it seems superfluous. He is what I need to get through this, he would know what to do, what to say; that his absence is what has brought it about seems a cruel and excessive joke.

Gail announces one morning that she is flying to Baltimore the following day. She claims to be merely reminding me of this, it was all planned weeks ago and concerns the research she's lately involved herself in, though I don't recall hearing of it before now. I am also informed, rather pointedly, that she will be advising all concerned of her intentions to remain here, which I cannot help hearing as an accusation. My father has been trying to talk her out of this, she says—the announcement, not the trip, and when he walks over a few minutes later they take it up again, and he rides into campus with her in a further attempt to change her mind.

Once they're gone I decide to bag school. I've got his car, so I drive around beneath gray skies, grateful for this unexpected time alone. I begin to look forward to her absence, and determine to use the time well, to get my shit together if at all possible, and gird myself for her inevitable return. But this leads only to further speculation, and as I imagine how this next year will play out, my resolve wanes inexorably to despair. By mid-afternoon I am slumped on the porch steps, watching a thunderhead roll up like a Bible epic, as angry a cloud as I have ever seen. When it lets loose I sit there, the huge drops pounding my skin and clothes, matting my hair to my scalp, until I cannot tell the rain from my own tears, nor my sobs from the groaning of the wind in the trees. With any luck, the earth would open and swallow me whole, but luck does not seem to know me anymore, and so I sit, drenched, the rain and my life crashing around me.

When I cannot possibly get wetter, I rise from the step and slosh across the yard to the Volvo. There is a hand towel on the back floorboard, slightly stiff, that I use to wipe my face and arms. By the time I reach the Martins' there is a small puddle rolling back and forth on the plastic mat at my feet, and rivulets of water are coursing from my hair onto my face and shoulders. I slowly negotiate the pitted driveway, avoiding the many brimming craters, and roll to a stop near the carport. The rain has all but quit, so I cut the wipers and stare out, only now wondering why I've come. Ruthie is still at work, I'm sure, and the likelihood of any of the rest having braved this downpour is very remote. I kill the engine and roll down the window, taking in huge draughts of the thick air, which hints of a hundred smells in this wilderness, the gamut from germination to decay. I hear a series of clicks and bumps from the house and then see the side door into Madame Marie's chamber swing slowly open, an invitation of a kind.

I understand now that she is why I've come. I knew she would be here; she's always here, and who better to consult on what is to come? I press the towel to my head and rub lightly, then finger comb my hair as best I can. I step from the car to a high spot on the gravel and wring out the bottom of my shirt, which changes the overall effect not a bit. I hopscotch the rutted surface and move to the stairs, pausing at the open door to wedge off my shoes, which have announced my sopping, squishing arrival.

I enter, stopping just inside the door, and instantly create a small lake on the entryway tile. "Hi," I say timidly, suddenly aware that I am cold and pitiful and not wearing a bra. I hug my arms across my chest as she approaches, sloughing a dark woolen shawl reeking of lilac from her layers, which she sweeps matador-like across my shoulders and draws tight beneath my chin so that it envelopes me in a warm and fragrant hug. "I'm soaked," I protest, though she must have discerned this for herself.

She directs me to a chair that is already draped with towels, and pours tea into a second cup, as if she has been expecting me all along, and in just this condition. To my right the orange coils of an ancient space heater glow near my feet, which I extend to take in the warmth. Madame Marie returns to the chair across from me and stares with a benign intensity. She picks up her tea, nods toward the other cup, and continues to study me through the steam.

My tremulous reserve crumbles, no more substantial than the vapor curling up from our cups. In one monsoonal torrent I unload everything: facts, feelings, fears; all my desires and doubts; my guilt and gratitude; anger and alienation. It comes in an unbroken rush that I doubt she can even understand, let alone absorb, but I barrel on headlong through tears, coughs, a hiccup. By the time I finish she must feel as I did on the steps at my house, soaked and slightly battered, though she appears no worse for this deluge. "I can't even think," I tell her. "When I look inside myself, there's nothing. It's all been ripped out." I am leaning fully forward now, almost pleading, chest pressed to my knees, as if the weight of all I've said has bent me double. "I don't know what to do."

She waits until she is sure I've finished, then sets down her cup. She has listened without comment to this point, and now she says, "Forgive the other one."

"I can't," I answer immediately. "I won't. Ever." She gazes steadily upon me, silent, Sphinx-like. When I can stand it no longer, I demand, "Why should I?"

Her hand peeks out from beneath her many layers, the palm upturned as if to present the quavering mess that I am as evidence of my spurious judgment, as if to say: *You see.*

We stare across the low table. How can she, too, ask this? Doesn't she, of all people, understand my rage? "But it's her fault," I insist. "All of it."

"It is an indulgence to cast blame," she suggests. "And what is it she is guilty of? Recklessness, perhaps? Being too self-centered? Do you truly believe she intended for this to happen?"

"But it did," I counter harshly. "And reckless or intentional, the fact is without her none of this would have happened. And nothing you, or my mother, or anyone else, says can change that."

She pauses, her lips puckered slightly, as if weighing this, or her next thought. "Cannot the same be said of you?" she asks finally, in the same, indifferent tone.

This simple, reluctant addendum hits me like a freight train. My eyes fill, the first salty tears brushing my lips before I can speak. "Is that what you think?"

"I only use your logic."

"Is that what you all think?" I demand, my words halting and shrill.

"Shouldn't we?"

"No!" I fall back in the chair, drawing my knees up to my chest and hugging tightly, feeling as if I am about to implode. "I loved him."

"And is that not also reckless and self-centered?"

"But they're nothing alike." I am almost screaming. I am screaming, in fact, though my defiance is shattered. She has somehow conjoined Kayla and I, and though she has managed to forgive us both, my righteousness demands a distinction. "What she did was evil and hateful."

"Yet the result is the same," she notes with breathtaking equanimity. "You asked me once if things happen for a reason. If so, I leave it for you to determine the logic in this." She stops to gaze placidly upon me, her lips pressed together as she waits, though no response is forthcoming. "What she did was self-centered and careless," she continues presently. "But she could never have suspected it would turn out like this. Nor could you." Her hands fold together in her lap. "Nor my son."

My resolve has abandoned me entirely in these few moments, though I am by no means sold on her logic. There is a difference, of that I am certain, but at least she has seen fit to include Nother, too, as complicit in this sad drama, and I suppose I will have to content myself with that for now. "So, you have forgiven her? Us?"

"There was no need," she replies. "But if it will help you to hear it, yes."

"It does help," I say, gratified. "And thank you." I resettle myself in the chair, sigh deeply. "Still, you must blame me a little," I point out, "or you wouldn't have said that."

"You forced me to say it," she explains. "Perhaps you should not be so demanding." She is speaking of my mother now, I'm sure of it. "It is not always so important to be proven right."

I wipe my eyes, sniff loudly, rub my hands dry. "Then I guess I go see her."

She nods ever so slightly as I frown. "It will be easier than you think," she promises. When she smiles I feel healed, pulling the shawl tight and inhaling the pungent aroma.

I stand to go, conscious, suddenly, of overstaying my welcome, and needing to be alone to sort all of this out. As I unfurl the shawl from around me I feel my necklace come loose, but manage to catch it tumbling down my front. I turn it over in my hand to see if it has broken, but it has only come unlatched. I move to her chair and drape the shawl across the back, then kneel beside her and draw the chain around her neck. "I want you to have this," I say. "From us."

She takes the pendant in her hand and regards it for a long moment, then releases it, so the chain hangs freely. "Thank you," she says thickly.

I hug her awkwardly over the arm of the chair. "And you."

She escorts me to the door, frowns at my still damp clothes when I sneeze, gently sweeps a lock of wet hair behind my ear. "How can parents so smart have failed to tell you to come in out of the rain?"

"There's a lot they never told me." I give her a final hug and step outside, where the rain has finally stopped.

I am in the bathtub when Gail gets home, steaming out the chill that has settled into my bones. The residual scent of lilac has followed me home, and now permeates the vaporous room, so that I can think only of Madame Marie, and replay our interview in my head. I have given up any attempt to understand that family; they will always be inscrutable, and wondrous, to me.

It is my intention, when I am again sufficiently warmed, dried and powdered, to sit down with my mother and convince her to go back, for everyone's sake, and to free her to do this with her conscience clear. My designs toward Kayla are less clear; I've told myself I will do it, and I know it is right, but I am as yet unable to form that picture in my mind. I doze heavily in the perfumed cloud and wake to knocking on the bathroom door. I turn sideways and groggily make out Gail's head peering in from the hall. "I'm going back out," she says. "Are you all right in here?"

"Fine," I say dully. "I must have fallen asleep." I sit up, sloshing the now tepid water against the sides of the tub. "You're leaving?"

"I have a dinner engagement," she says. "I just came home to pack."

"We have to talk."

She stares down at me. "When I get back," she says. "I won't be late." She glances at the mirror and wipes something from the side of her mouth with her thumb. "Can it wait?"

"Sure," I say. It's waited this long. "But before you go to Baltimore."

"Tonight, then," she repeats, pulling the door closed behind her.

I fall asleep around ten waiting for her. I read the next chapter in Chemistry, then do some French, and finally settle onto the couch with the remote, which is where I am when she and Pops walk in at eleven-thirty. "You'd be more comfortable in bed," he says as I drag myself upright.

"I was waiting for Mom."

"Oh, Teri, I'm sorry. I forgot all about that." She goes to a pile of books by the table and digs one out, then carries it to my father. "This one," she says.

Pops studies the cover, nods. "I'll take a look," he says. He pauses at the door. "What time did we decide?"

"Seven."

"I'll take her," I say abruptly. "Are you talking about the airport?"

"You have school," my mother says.

"I can miss first period," I say. "We have to talk before you go."

She looks at my father, who shrugs. "All right, then," she says. "I'm too tired to listen now, anyway."

Friday dawns bright and clear, the first rays of sunshine as we cross the yard to the car hinting of the oppressive heat to come. The trees are budding a luscious green as we head out of town, two coffees from the Circle K steaming between us. Gail is fidgeting in her purse; she unfolds a printout that confirms her flight, then checks her phone for the third time. "Look how green," I say, motioning along the side of the road so she doesn't miss it entirely. "It's almost May."

"Too almost May," she says without glancing out. She shoves the phone in the bag and sets the bag on the floor. "O.K., now," she says with forced brightness, smoothing her skirt and half-turning toward me. "What is it that dragged you out of bed so early?"

I exhale mightily and launch into it. "Mom, I think it's a huge mistake for you to stay here. Your position at Hopkins is too good and too important to throw away like this, especially for me. You belong there. I've been mean and very selfish the last few weeks and I'm sorry. But please don't tell them you're leaving. You can't."

She arches her eyebrows and tilts her head to stare down her nose incredulously. "And what, might I ask, brought this on?"

I explain about yesterday: the rain, my encounter with Madame Marie, the stuffed nose I have this morning. "I gave her my necklace," I say, though I don't know why, but lift my chin as proof nonetheless.

"I see," she says, sipping from her steaming cup. "So then, just to be sure I've got this straight, as evidence of your newfound maturity and independence, you are now taking instruction from a card reader, correct?"

"I'm listening to the only person who's lost more than I have," I say, biting back hard on my annoyance at her tone.

Gail purses her lips and stares ahead.

"Mom, she's not how you think, but there's no way to convince you of that now. It's you and me and Dad that we have to think about. Dad has to be here, that's obvious. I need to be here, I have unfinished business. You, on the other hand, have every good reason *not* to be here. Nothing is served by you staying."

We ride for a while in silence, past the first signs for the airport; my account of yesterday's events has been overly-comprehensive, I see now, cutting into what still needs to be said. "Just like that?" she asks finally. "I'm good to go." She frowns skeptically. "That might be enough to convince your father, but I've always been a bit more dubious, I guess."

"Well, could you at least hold off telling them for now?"

"Teri, it's very late as it is; they're already going to be angry—"

"Exactly, so don't."

"And then, if I tell them next month? What do you think they'll do then?"

"Mom, look, this is a really bad decision. You and I have been very silly. You know it, I know it, even Dad knows it. But we can still fix it." I look across the seat at her. "So, *what* would I have to do to convince you it was O.K. to go? Name it." We have left the highway and are already approaching the terminal, so I pull to the curb out of the circling traffic, but well short of the loading zone. I shift into PARK and stare at her. "Really, name it."

She stares back, slightly amused, it seems. "Did your father put you up to this?"

"Quit stalling."

"No, seriously. He was bargaining all last night."

"Now think about that," I say. "He came all the way here in the first place just for us to be together. If even he's encouraging you to go back now, it really must be a bad idea. Staying, I mean."

"That's kind of a twisted argument," she notes.

I continue to stare. "Well?"

She looks out the side window and drums her hands on the dash. She knows I'm right. It's just her own stubbornness she has to get past now. She glances at the clock, but we're early. "I want to believe you," she says, following a clammy silence. She cracks her window, letting in dense fumes. "I'm thinking I can, and that you'll be O.K. here with just him. And I'm moved by what you've said. I know it wasn't easy for you."

"Mom—"

"O.K.," she says, "you want to know what would really

convince me you've turned the corner? That you could really look past yourself? I mean, I know you want me to go back to Hopkins for me, and I appreciate that, but even you have to admit your life gets a lot smoother day-to-day with me up there, so even that's not entirely selfless."

"What, then?"

"I think you know," she says, inviting me to finish it.

"Go see Kayla."

"I'm impressed." A Fed Ex truck rumbles past as she eyes me levelly. "Well?"

"I'm going this afternoon," I tell her, which is news to both of us, actually.

Her eyebrows shoot up. "Really?"

I nod.

"Why the change?"

"Well, when the two smartest women I know tell me the exact same thing, I've got to figure there's something to it."

"And what do *you* think?"

"I think they're probably right."

She smiles slightly, then presses her lips together. "But just hearing it from me wasn't enough, of course."

"It's always good to confirm."

"That's very true," she says. "So how do I know you'll actually go?"

"Call Annie."

"I'm just kidding," she says. "If I can't even trust you that much, I *really* shouldn't go."

"We have a deal, then?"

She stares at me, her face earnest. "You'd do that for me?"

"I would," I tell her. "But I think I'm really doing it for me. And hopefully Kayla."

"Ooh, good answer," she coos, her head bobbing appreciatively. She waves toward the terminal, indicating we should go. "O.K., deal."

I take my time driving back. It's not even eight, and I could probably even make it to school on time, but I don't. It's a beautiful morning, and as I cruise the empty road home I crank down the window and feel no hurry to be inside. I feel good, like much has been put to rest. We are balanced now like never before, each with the other two, and the three of us together. A sturdy construction, at least for the time being. In the back of my mind I know there is a lot left to be worked out. I've thought of Nother half a dozen times already, so that seems destined to haunt me for a while yet, probably til I leave here for good, though I've determined not to let it chase me away. I picture telling Pops that Gail will be leaving after all, if she hasn't phoned him already. He will be pleased, of course, but it throws their marriage into even greater disarray. But that's their issue, I realize now, and all I need do is love them both. I will remain part of the equation, no doubt, but no longer the fulcrum, which is as it should be, and suits me precisely. I suspect I'll be going east too, before long, though where is still anyone's guess. Pops could end up back there, too, it suddenly occurs to me; if his book hits big, which I have this strange, strong premonition it will, the doors should swing open for him as well. If anything, I'm sure Towson could find a spot for him again, so who knows? We could all end up back there. I shake my head at the very idea; I mean, wouldn't that be a pisser.

I grow weary of sorting. *Let it come to you*, I tell myself; why even play at the notion of control? I push in the CD and straighten my arm out the window, catching the wind in my palm while Crosscut cries for a sad-eyed girl.

Sandy and I bail by mid-afternoon, it is too nice to be inside. We take a sidewalk table at The Chickory and soak up rays. "So then, will you guys move?" I hear her ask. "Or is your dad moving into your half?"

I keep my head turned up, feeling the sun on my face, eyes closed. "I think I'm going to try to get them to keep both sides," I answer.

Sandy snorts. "Good luck."

"I don't know," I say. "We'll still need room for when Gail visits, and it's not that much. Maybe if I help pay."

"With what?" she asks. "We were scrounging nickels just to get coffee."

"Well, there's the book, so he'll have money."

"Dream on," she says. We stay til our faces start to get tight, then she offers to accompany me to Kayla's, which I'm sure I wouldn't do for her, and so decline out of fairness. I have no idea what to expect—no one has confirmed that she wants to see me, after all—so it really isn't right to drag Sandy along just because she's foolish enough to offer. "Call me, then," she says when I let her out. "Don't forget."

"Relax," I tell her, but then have trouble taking my own advice. I realize on the way over that I haven't given this encounter any thought at all, have forced it from my mind, in fact, each time it has attempted to slip in. As I pull to the curb I decide to just play it by ear, it's too late for elaborate strategies now, so I'm just going to go with what feels right.

My heart is pounding as I move up the walk and mount the stairs to the porch. I can feel my pulse near my ear, and my neck and chest are clammy. Annie opens the door silently before I can knock and beckons me inside. We hug and I ask if Kayla is home.

"Through there," she says, nodding down the short hall toward the partially open door to Kayla's room.

My mind is racing. I think of that first night, the smuggled beers, the wisecracks, the genesis of the plot to paint the bridge. It seems like forever ago, and it might as well be. We'll be starting over, I understand now, if she'll allow it. It's the only way.

I want to run, to just turn and flee back to the car and drive off. How can I go in there knowing what I know? But then Annie rests a hand on my shoulder and smiles with infinite hope, and I know I must. I step softly down the hall, stopping at the door to gaze in at her. She is seated, staring blankly out the window, much thinner than I remember, with pale sunken cheeks and hollowed eyes. She looks ancient. Lifeless. I take a deep breath and she turns, a flicker of recognition in the vacuum of her eyes. There is a twitch at the corner of her mouth, like she wants to smile but has forgotten how.

"Hey," I say.